THE *Girl's* GUIDE TO (*Man*)HUNTING

THE *Girl's* GUIDE TO (*Man*)HUNTING

JESSICA CLARE

HEAT
New York

THE BERKLEY PUBLISHING GROUP
Published by the Penguin Group
Penguin Group (USA) Inc.
375 Hudson Street, New York, New York 10014, USA

Penguin Group (Canada), 90 Eglinton Avenue East, Suite 700, Toronto, Ontario M4P 2Y3, Canada (a division of Pearson Penguin Canada Inc.) • Penguin Books Ltd., 80 Strand, London WC2R 0RL, England • Penguin Group Ireland, 25 St. Stephen's Green, Dublin 2, Ireland (a division of Penguin Books Ltd.) • Penguin Group (Australia), 250 Camberwell Road, Camberwell, Victoria 3124, Australia (a division of Pearson Australia Group Pty. Ltd.) • Penguin Books India Pvt. Ltd., 11 Community Centre, Panchsheel Park, New Delhi—110 017, India • Penguin Group (NZ), 67 Apollo Drive, Rosedale, Auckland 0632, New Zealand (a division of Pearson New Zealand Ltd.) • Penguin Books (South Africa) (Pty.) Ltd., 24 Sturdee Avenue, Rosebank, Johannesburg 2196, South Africa

Penguin Books Ltd., Registered Offices: 80 Strand, London WC2R 0RL, England

This book is an original publication of The Berkley Publishing Group.

Cover photograph by Kostudio.
Cover design by Lesley Worrell.

PUBLISHING HISTORY
Heat trade paperback edition / May 2012

Library of Congress Cataloging-in-Publication Data

Clare, Jessica.
The girl's guide to (man)hunting / Jessica Clare.—Heat trade paperback ed.
p. cm.
ISBN 978-0-425-24735-8 (pbk.)
I. Title.
PS3603.L353G57 2012
813'.6—dc23
2011037775

PRINTED IN THE UNITED STATES OF AMERICA

10 9 8 7 6 5 4 3 2 1

For Cindy and Jane.
This book is entirely your fault,
and I mean that in a good way.

THE *Girl's* GUIDE TO (*Man*)HUNTING

ONE

Like everything else bad that happened in Miranda Hill's life, rear-ending old Mrs. Doolittle was purely the fault of Dane Croft.

She could have sworn that she'd recognized the broad shoulders, tight ass, and familiar swagger of her nemesis walking into the local coffeehouse. Her most hated enemy. The man who had ruined her life. In fact, she'd been so busy craning her neck to see if it really was Dane Croft that she hadn't paid attention to the stoplight . . . and had plowed right into the car in front of her.

Yet another thing she could add to the list of reasons why she hated him.

Miranda put her pickup in park and slid out of the cab to look at the damage she'd caused to the other car. Mrs. Doolittle drove a Buick that was older than Miranda herself, and the thing was built like a tank—a big, powder blue tank. The bumper wasn't even dinged, not that Mrs. D cared. The old woman crawled from the belly of the tank and scowled at her.

"You hit my car, Miranda." If Mrs. Doolittle had a cane, she probably would have shaken it in Miranda's face. "What on earth were you thinking, girl?"

Miranda gave Mrs. D an apologetic look and self-consciously tugged at the high collar of her pink sweater set. "I'm so sorry, Mrs. Doolittle. I was just . . . distracted." She was still distracted, actually. Her gaze strayed to the Kurt's Koffee on the far side of the street, but the windows were tinted and impossible to see into.

The elderly woman peered at her. "Young lady, were you using the Twitters while you were driving? You know—"

"No Internet," Miranda blurted, tugging on her collar again. "I just wasn't paying attention. I thought I saw . . . something."

Someone.

A car pulled up behind them. No surprise, given that most of the streets in downtown Bluebonnet were single lanes, with just enough room in the city square to park in front of one of the two restaurants. She waved for the driver to go around them, and then continued apologizing to Mrs. D, even as they exchanged insurance information. Anything to get out of the street and appease her curiosity. She kept glancing at the coffeehouse as she scribbled down her contact numbers.

Finally, Mrs. D was on her way, satisfied. Miranda pulled her truck into a parking space across the street and sprinted toward the coffee shop, but didn't go inside. Instead, she pressed her hands to the glass and peered in. A few people were seated, but she didn't see the man she was looking for.

No Dane Croft. Was she crazy? Had she imagined that she

saw him? Chewing on her lip, Miranda straightened the front of her sweater set in the reflection and then went inside.

"Well, well, well, if it isn't the Boobs of Bluebonnet," said Jimmy Langan from behind the counter. Jimmy was the town rebel, with purple, red, and black Rasta braids, a face that had never seen a tan, and enormous ear gauges that he'd probably regret when he was seventy. He grinned at her, giving Miranda the up-and-down look that she'd become far too accustomed to in the past nine years. "What can I do for you?"

"Shut up, Jimmy," she said. Three weeks. She could deal with the jokes and the sneaking glances at her breasts for three more weeks. Moving past the counter, she peered down the hallway at the restrooms. No Dane Croft. She resisted the urge to open the door, and instead wandered back to the counter. "Is anyone in there?"

"You want me to go and check under the stalls for feet?" Jimmy said dryly.

"Well, no," she stammered, her hand going to the collar of her sweater. "Maybe." She hesitated, reluctant to say the name of the man she was looking for. If she even so much as uttered Dane's name, the rumors would start flying all over town again.

You know that nice Miranda Hill? She never quite got over Dane Croft. She was asking about him in Kurt's Koffee. Poor thing.

Remember that man in the photos with Miranda Hill? She's still sweet on him. I heard she's still got the hots for him and that's why she hasn't married.

The town librarian? She's a slut. Want to see the pictures? She spent seven minutes in heaven with Casanova Croft back when they were both in high school. They even took photos of it. Just search for "Boobs of Bluebonnet" on the Internet and you'll see them.

Miranda clutched the collar of her demure sweater even harder. "So what kind of customers have you had today?"

Jimmy shrugged lazily, adjusting the thick black-frame glasses on his pasty, scruffy face. He'd been a stoner back when they'd graduated from high school together, and he was a stoner still. Asking him to remember the customers he'd had that morning might be beyond his pot-riddled memory. "Couple soy lattes, couple double espressos, a venti mocha frap with double Splenda . . ."

Great, just what she needed: a rundown of coffee orders. She feigned interest, her eyes skimming the restaurant as Jimmy rattled off a litany of special requests.

"And a certain someone you might recall," Jimmy added slowly, his gaze dropping to her breasts. "We went to high school with him."

She crossed her arms over her chest, doing her best to hide what the underwire minimizer wouldn't. Her heart was thudding hard in her chest, but she forced herself to be nonchalant about the information. "Oh? Someone from high school? Who's that?"

To her surprise, he reached behind the counter and pulled out a brown and green pamphlet. "You remember Dane Croft? Casanova Croft? Star of the Las Vegas Flush?"

The guy she'd been making out with in the closet? The one with his hand on her boobs and the other down her pants for all eternity thanks to a few ill-timed photos and the magic of the Internet? Who'd left the next day to be drafted into the NHL and become a star while she'd been stuck in town as her mother had a nervous breakdown? The Casanova Croft who'd been booted out of the NHL six years later for sleeping with the coach's wife? Life-ruiner and all-around jerk?

Yeah, she knew who he was. "I'm familiar with the guy."

"He's moved back to town," Jimmy said, offering her the pamphlet. "Him and two other guys we went to high school with are starting a business here. Something about survival training classes. They bought the Daughtry Ranch on the outskirts of town."

"The Daughtry Ranch?" Miranda echoed, taking the pamphlet from him and forcing her shaking fingers to open it. The Daughtry Ranch was ten thousand acres of private property, and when old Mr. Daughtry had died without an heir, the ranch had gone up for auction. No one in town knew who'd ended up buying it. Sure enough, there in the picture on the pamphlet were three men she recognized: Grant Markham, Colt Waggoner, and her nemesis—Dane Croft. The three of them were dressed in black T-shirts and camouflage pants, and the top of the brochure proudly proclaimed, "Wilderness Survival Expeditions: Bushcraft Training for Corporate and Military Groups."

Survival training? The Dane Croft she remembered was a hard-partying playboy who refused to do anything that didn't involve beer or girls—or both. She remembered Grant and Colt—one was a jock and one had been the richest guy in her class. Both had moved away when they'd graduated, just like Dane. And now they were back . . . just like Dane.

Could today possibly get any worse?

She tucked the brochure into her pocket, feeling faint. "Thanks, Jimmy. Can I get a green tea latte, please?"

"Sure," Jimmy said lazily, his gaze sliding to her breasts again.

"Venti, grande, or tall? Iced or hot? Two percent, whole, skim, or soy?"

Miranda had her phone out, dialing, and ignored Jimmy. Her other hand fluttered back to her pocket repeatedly, touching the brochure again and again.

"Right. I'll just make something up," he drawled, then turned away to make her drink.

Beth Ann picked up the office phone on the second ring. "California Dreamin'," she answered in a chirpy voice. "We do waxes, haircuts, highlights, and perms. Can I make you an appointment?"

"It's me," Miranda hissed into the receiver, covering the phone and turning away in case Jimmy planned on listening in. "You're never going to believe who's back in town."

"Who?"

"Dane Croft," Miranda gritted.

There was a long pause on the other end of the line. "*The* Dane Croft? The Vegas Flush player? The one we went to high school with?"

"That's him—"

"The one who put his hand down your pants—"

"Beth Ann!"

"I'm clearing my lunch appointments," Beth Ann declared. "Be here in twenty minutes and we'll talk."

For Beth Ann, a "talk" usually involved waxing Miranda's eyebrows, a trim for Miranda's split ends, and a manicure. They'd been friends ever since the fifth grade, and if there was one thing that Miranda knew about Beth Ann, it was that she liked her hands busy while she chatted. Her small salon was nearly empty at noon on a Wednesday, and Miranda waited patiently as Beth Ann unlocked the back room that housed a tanning bed and let in a teenage blonde.

"I keep telling Candy that she's going to look like a handbag by the time she's thirty, but she won't listen to me," Beth Ann said with a shrug, returning to the barber chair Miranda sat in. "And the tanning bed brings in almost as much money as manicures do." She spun the chair around, turning Miranda toward the mirror, and flung the pink satin styling cape over her clothes. "Now, honey, tell me your problems."

"My problem is Dane Croft," Miranda said, digging under the cape and pulling the brochure out. She held it toward Beth Ann. "He's moved back to town—permanently. And he's started a survival business with Grant Markham and Colt Waggoner."

"Survival business?" Beth Ann tucked a lock of perfectly highlighted blond hair behind her ear and gave Miranda an odd look in the mirror. "That doesn't sound like the Dane Croft we went to high school with."

"It's him—look at the picture." Miranda slumped in the salon chair, wishing this day would start over again.

Beth Ann's eyebrows rose as she stared at the pamphlet. "Professional survival services? That's kind of strange."

"I know," said Miranda flatly.

"Mmm. Just look at them. They've all filled out rather . . . nicely, don't you think?"

Miranda scowled and snatched the pamphlet back, glancing at the photo again. All three men were tall and fit, she supposed.

Dane's arms were especially toned with muscle. He had a dark tan and his black hair was cut incredibly short. The white smile on his face was as familiar as her own. He actually looked like a hunky, Hollywood version of a survival instructor. That made her feel worse. "This is just awful."

"Why is it awful?" She began to comb out Miranda's long, dark brown hair and trim the ends. "This is the perfect time for him to come back. You're leaving for that big job in the city in three weeks, remember? You only have to avoid him until then." And she sighed.

Miranda ignored Beth Ann's sigh. She'd heard enough of them to feel permanently guilty about the fact that she wanted to leave Bluebonnet behind for a job in Houston. A job with real benefits and a chance to move up the corporate ladder. A job that could lead anywhere, maybe even chief information officer. Or higher. Miranda Hill, the Boobs of Bluebonnet, would have a fancy title and an even fancier job. She could actually do something with her master's in Library Science instead of just recataloging books and taking complaints from old ladies who wanted the "dirty vampire books" removed from the shelves. "This is my chance to do something, Bethy. To get out of town. To be something other than the Boobs of Bluebonnet."

"It's what you've always wanted," agreed Beth Ann. "It doesn't mean that it won't make me sad to see you go."

Miranda regarded her friend through the mirror, watching as Beth Ann clipped her ends with careful, precise fingers. "I know. I'll come back and visit you all the time."

In the mirror, Beth Ann gave her a wry smile. "Sure you will."

Miranda glared down at the pamphlet and the three tanned,

attractive men on the cover. "You know, I was hoping for three quiet weeks to relax and get things settled. My last day at the library was yesterday. My apartment in Houston is leased. The house is almost packed. I've got nothing to do for the next three weeks except stare at this picture and stew. Except every time I look at this, I see them."

"Three sexy beasts?"

"Not them. The *pictures*."

The images were ingrained into her memory. If she lived to be eighty, she'd never forget one single detail of those grainy, horrible photos—her torso facing the camera, an expression of complete and utter abandon on her face. Her T-shirt pushed up around her neck, her breasts facing the camera. Dane's mouth on her neck and his hand down the front of her panties. Then the picture of her kneeling in front of him, as if she was about to give him a blow job.

She'd never known that there'd been a camera in the closet. Or that he'd pack up and leave town practically the next day to join the NHL, without a single word to her. Miranda had been forced to pretend that she wasn't hurt by his abandonment, but abandonment had soon given way to horror as soon as the pictures surfaced.

And with a town as small as Bluebonnet . . . everyone talked. She hadn't slept with Dane, but that didn't matter. She'd tried going to the police when the pictures first went up, but her mother had been so upset and sheriff had looked at her like she was trash, and she'd dropped the entire thing rather than acknowledge that the pictures were of her and Dane. At the time, she'd hoped it would all just go away. No such luck. Everyone in town assumed she had slept with Dane, blown him in the closet at a party, and they looked at her like she was dirt. In their eyes, she *was* dirt. The town slut. It had taken patience, a stiff upper lip, and years of a quiet existence as the town's librarian before she'd managed to grasp a semblance of her reputation again.

Beth Ann put down the scissors and leaned over the back of the chair, smiling into the mirror at Miranda's frown. "Well, you've got three weeks to burn, and your infamous ex is back in town. You can pretty much do what you want and you won't be here to suffer the repercussions. So what do you want to do? TP his house? Key his car? I'm sure we can think up something totally juvenile and completely satisfying."

Miranda stared down at the pamphlet, at Dane's confident smile. But what she saw? Pictures of herself on a webpage, in e-mails forwarded to thousands of people, tossed up on the Internet and forever linked to her name. Pictures of his hand down her pants, her breasts angled at the camera like twin beacons.

And she stared at Dane's casual, confident brochure smile again. *Professional survival training*, the pamphlet read.

Casanova Croft, kicked off of the Las Vegas Flush for sleeping with the owner's wife.

Professional survival training. *Professional.*

"I think I want revenge," Miranda blurted, then turned to stare up at her friend. "I know it's not rational, and I don't even care. Is that crazy?"

"Not at all," soothed Beth Ann. "What did you have in mind?"

Miranda held up the brochure, an idea forming. "I want to ruin his career like he did mine."

"I'm listening, honey."

Miranda flipped open the pamphlet. "They're just starting a business, right? What if pictures of Dane Croft surfaced on the Internet? Naked pictures of him? Naked, compromising pictures of him?" The idea began to grow in her mind, and she jumped out of the chair, almost trembling with excitement. "Naked, compromising pictures of him in a *survival situation*?"

Her best friend's blond brows furrowed together. "And where would you get such pictures?"

"I'd take them myself."

Beth Ann raised an eyebrow. "And just how are you going to do that?"

Miranda held up the brochure triumphantly. "I'm going to sign up for a survival course and use the legendary Boobs of Bluebonnet against him. Casanova Croft won't stand a chance."

"Are you sure that's wise?"

"I've never been wise around Dane Croft," Miranda said, thinking of the last time she'd seen him.

"Seven minutes in heaven," Chad announced, shoving Miranda and Dane toward his bedroom closet. Giggling teenagers surrounded them, and Miranda felt her cheeks heat with embarrassment, but she didn't let go of Dane's hand.

Dane nudged Chad and grinned. "Do me a favor, bro, and skip the timer."

Chad smirked.

She could have protested, said she wasn't that kind of girl, but she said nothing, not even when the door shut behind them. She wanted to be that kind of girl with Dane.

Chad's closet smelled like sweaty football gear and dirty clothes. It was crammed full of boxes and clothing on hangers, the single flickering lightbulb overhead not offering much in the way of light. She wrinkled her nose at the musty smell of the closet and waited, her breath catching. Would Dane make a move on her tonight? They'd flirted for weeks, held hands for the last one, and kissed under the bleachers. Given time, she knew she wanted him to be the one to take her overdue virginity.

But time was the one thing they didn't have. They'd graduated earlier that evening and after the cap and gown ceremony, they'd headed to Chad's for the last senior fling.

It was now or never.

She gestured at the light overhead as it flickered again. "Should we turn that off?"

"Leave it on. I like looking at you." Dane's hand gave hers a squeeze and he smiled at her. "You okay?"

Yes, *she wanted to say.* I'm fine. Did you have a nice time at graduation? *But it came out as a whimper, the words lodged in her throat.*

Dane chuckled at that. "I guess I should be telling you 'Happy eighteenth birthday,'" he said. "You're as old as me now."

Eighteen, and they'd be going off to college soon. The thought ran through her mind, urgent curls of heat rushing through her. Instead of responding, she pulled him close and began to kiss him instead, her mouth seeking his.

"Whoa," Dane whispered, but his hands went to her ass and he

pulled her against him, grinding his hips against her own. His tongue slid into her mouth, delving deep and tasting her in the sweetest kiss she'd ever had. His mouth pulled away from hers after a long moment and he breathed hard in her ear. "Damn, Miranda."

Her own breath thrilled at that, and she slid her leg between his . . . and stumbled, landing on him.

He cursed, trying to shift his weight, pinned between a row of jackets and a stack of boxes.

"Sorry," she whispered meekly, shaking her high-heeled boot. "I think my shoe got caught in his helmet."

They fumbled in the cramped quarters, and Miranda grabbed hold of a shelf and pulled herself up, then turned to remove the football helmet from her boot.

Dane shifted behind her, his hands sliding around her waist. "That's better," he whispered against her neck. Something tickled at her waist, where her shirt rode up—his fingers.

Her hand covered his, and she moved it farther up under her shirt, quivering with pleasure. "Touch me, Dane. Please."

"Love to," he whispered in her ear, and pressed a kiss against her neck, making her squirm. "You are the hottest damn thing in this town, Miranda Hill."

"You know it, Dane Croft," she whispered, craning her neck so his tongue could glide along her throat. Heat pulsed through her body. She didn't protest when his hands slid to her shirt and pulled it over her head in the near darkness. She even unhooked her own bra, since his fingers fumbled at her back for a long moment. But then his hands were cupping her breasts, his fingers warm against her skin. Fingers teased her nipples and she gasped, lifting her arms and twining them around his bent head.

From behind her, he pressed a kiss against her bare shoulder and she could feel his erection against her jeans. His fingers tweaked her nipples again, and her breath caught in response. "Dane," she whispered. "God, do that again."

"I'll do even better," he said against her neck. One hand grasping her full breast, his other slid down her belly and undid the button on her jeans. Her entire body tensed, tingles of excitement running through her. Was he going to touch her . . . there?

His fingertips slid into her panties, brushed the curls of her sex, and she let out a whimper of delight. Two seconds later, his fingertips slipped into her panties. One finger swept past the lips of her sex, grazed her clit. Oh yes. His hand squeezed her breast at the same time that he stroked her there, and her entire body stiffened, the anticipation of being in the closet with him rushing her toward an orgasm—

Click.

Miranda froze in place. Dane continued to finger her, biting at her shoulder, and she pulled away from him, sliding his hand out of her panties. "Did you hear that?"

His hands reached for her, brushed against her breasts again. "Didn't hear anything."

"I thought I heard a noise," she said softly, staring at the closet door. It was still shut, and the doorknob didn't move. Overhead, the light flickered again. Nothing. Maybe she was imagining things. Paranoid at being caught. If she listened hard, she could hear her classmates giggling in the other room, waiting for them to emerge.

She started to protest, but he bit her shoulder and pleasure crashed over her, and she didn't protest when his hand slid back into her panties once more.

• • •

Looking back, she had been so very, very dumb. She should have guessed that Dane would have hidden a camera in that damn closet. Should have guessed that he'd want all his buddies to see that he'd gotten into curvy Miranda Hill's panties and made her writhe against his hand in a closet. She hadn't blown him, either, but no one would believe that from looking at the photos.

And she should have guessed that he'd disappear as soon as the NHL came calling. Who was she to him? No one, it seemed, but a quickie in the closet.

TWO

After leaving Beth Ann's salon, she headed over to her mother's store, Hill Country Antiques. The store looked as ramshackle as ever, the wooden sign listing a bit too much on one side, windows dusty and full of clutter. Antiques stores came in different flavors—from austere and highbrow to cluttered and junky. Her mother's store was definitely on the junky side. More thrift and yard sale than actual antiques, it was a cornucopia of bizarre odds and ends that nevertheless managed to bring in a decent income for her mother.

"Hi, hon," her mother called when Miranda entered, the cowbell on the door clanging against the glass. "You're just in time."

"Oh? In time for what?"

"They had a storage unit sale over in Livingston, and Marilou picked up someone's old unit for fifty bucks!" Her mother said, moving to the front of the store and sashaying past Miranda.

She flipped the store sign to CLOSED. "I get to split everything in there with her, but we've got to clean it out before the end of the day. I could use an extra set of hands, too."

"I can't," Miranda said with a grimace, gesturing at her car. "I need to stop by the library and pick up my last check. Sorry." It was a bit of a white lie, but she really didn't want to go and spend the day picking through someone else's junk. The last time her mother had bought a storage unit, they'd found nothing but endless rows of comic-book boxes, their contents eaten by mice. "I'm about to head out of town for a week or so."

"Out of town?" Her mother looked surprised. "Where are you going?"

"Oh, just checking some stuff out in Houston," Miranda lied. "But I wanted to let you know that I'm not going to be answering my phone for a few days. I'll swing by when I'm back, okay?"

"But—"

She froze, waiting. In the past, any small thing that interrupted her mother's daily routine would be met with crying, anxiety, and comments about Miranda's reputation about town. She'd had a nervous breakdown when the pictures had hit the Internet nine years ago, and it had taken a lot of time and patience and support to get her mother steady again. Now that things were going well, Miranda was getting out of Bluebonnet once and for all. She knew Tanya was having a hard time adjusting to the fact that her daughter was finally leaving the nest, and things had been fragile for the past few weeks.

"—who's going to help me clean out the storage unit?"

Thank goodness. Miranda leaned in and kissed her mother on the cheek. "I'll see if Beth Ann can send her little sister Lucy over. I'm sure she'll help for a few bucks. Now, I've got to go, Mom. I'll talk to you next week."

"'Bye, hon," her mother said absently as they went out to their separate cars.

Miranda got into her truck, waved at her mother, and backed out, heading toward the library. Well. That had gone better than she'd expected. She turned down Main Street and waited at the town's only stoplight. Absently playing with her collar, she thought about her plans for this week. She'd need some camping clothing, should toss out the stuff in the fridge, maybe see if—

A car honked next to her.

Miranda glanced over, and immediately wished she hadn't. Two men sat in the car, both a few years younger than her. She knew their families. Had seen them around town. Both were grinning at her in that way that told her they'd seen her half naked. Seen the photos.

"Hey, Boobs," one called with a leer. "I've got an overdue library book. Wanna come to my house and get it?"

Next to him, the passenger began to pump his fist in front of his open mouth, mimicking a blow job.

Cheeks flaring with heat, she turned away, just in time to hear both men erupt in laughter. The light turned green and she floored the pedal, surging forward and down the street.

She couldn't *wait* to be done with this town.

"Remember, Dane. Hands off the clientele." Colt said the words with a grin and gave the game controller in his hands a twist, staring at the TV screen. "This is our make-or-break moment, and I need you to have your head in the game."

"Thanks, coach," Dane said sarcastically to his friend, stuffing a pair of spare socks into his bag. "Glad to have you riding my tail."

Colt glanced over at Dane, looking away from the TV screen for a brief moment. "I'd better be the *only* thing riding your tail this next week."

Ah, friends. If he didn't like the guy so much, he'd be tempted to deck him. Dane ignored Colt's gibes and double-checked his survival pack one more time as they waited in the Daughtry Ranch's rec room before meeting the clients that would be gathering shortly. They were taking a few moments to unwind before being "on" for the rest of the week. And while Colt chose to play a video game to get in the right mind-set for the trip, Dane felt better looking over their gear one more time.

The sounds of a cheering audience erupted from the television, and Dane's head snapped up. Sure enough, Colt was playing a hockey video game. It set his nerves on edge, watching the pixelated players skate around the ice. It reminded him of his old life, which he didn't appreciate as he was trying to start the new one. "Do you have to do that shit right now?"

Colt didn't look up from the screen. "Yes."

Dane snorted and moved to check his bag again, turning away from the screen. He didn't need distractions right now; he needed to be ready. This inaugural training needed to go perfectly.

First he double-checked the survival supplies he'd be bringing for the group: matches, flint, needles and thread, fish hooks and line, a compass, snare wire, a flexible saw, a medical kit, flares, and a utility knife. At Grant's request, he'd also packed six military MREs and a satellite phone in case the corporate guys couldn't hack it out in the wild. As the "wild" went, the Daughtry Ranch was pretty tame in comparison to where Dane and Colt had spent their survival missions, or the times that they'd roughed it off the grid, but it was perfect for the business. He checked his pack one more time. Dane felt comfortable viewing the small amount of survival gear, the familiar anticipation edging through his body and drowning out any lingering irritation from Colt's joking.

He lived for this. He loved it—pitting himself against the wilderness and using his skills to survive. It centered him. When he was out there in the wild, Dane could find peace in himself, no matter what was bothering him. No one but him, nature, the land . . . and six neophytes looking to him for direction, he added wryly. Still, he doubted they'd be able to take the enjoyment of the experience away from him. This was part of who he was now.

And it was why he'd lived off the grid ever since he'd left hockey behind. He was a new man, with a new life, and he liked himself now. The challenge of living off the land appealed to him. The simplicity of a survival situation couldn't be beat. Just you and nature. You didn't need electricity or television or telephones to survive. All you needed was skill and perseverance. He liked that much better than modern society.

He slung the light pack over his shoulder and gave Colt a friendly clap on the shoulder. "I assure you, man. The last thing I want to do is touch a woman right now." Not when their business was just about to take off. "Some things are more important."

"I'm just making sure," Colt drawled. "Everyone already thinks that your dick rules your business decisions. We need to prove them wrong if this has a hope of succeeding."

It irritated him that Colt was right. That everyone thought that his cock was in charge of his brain. Dane rubbed his jaw, grimacing at the thought. Back in his hockey days, he'd been a different person. Headstrong and reckless beyond belief, he'd played so hard and carelessly that he'd managed to score two serious concussions in a row, and when another man would have paid attention to the doctors and been more cautious, he'd gone back on the ice as soon as he'd had the okay . . . and walked right into concussion number three in a play-off game.

Tensions had already been high at that point, and that particular concussion was a career-ender. He was just injured far too often, and he was a good player, but not a great one. The coaches didn't want to take a risk on him. And then Samantha Kingston—the wife of the team's owner—had approached him. She liked younger players. He'd turned her down, but she'd turned to the tabloids to salvage her wounded pride, and "Casanova Croft" was born. She'd used him and made him look like a jackass, and it didn't matter how good a player he'd been. He'd turned into "that creep who nailed the boss's wife." His contract wasn't renewed, and a free agent with too many injuries was too big a risk for most teams to take on. Combine that with his tabloid notoriety, and no one would touch him.

It hadn't helped that his past was full of a string of C-list actresses who were interested in dating a professional athlete—the latest trendy fashion accessory. The tabloid notoriety—on top of his world crashing down on him—became too much. When he'd started getting offers for sex tapes, he realized just how fucked-up his life had become. He'd fled, with nowhere to turn. Colt had contacted him, invited him to take a monthlong survival course with him to clear his head. He'd gone reluctantly, expecting nothing but a month of no phone calls from anyone.

Going on the survival trip had been the best thing to ever happen to him. Forced to use his wits and skills to survive . . . it had been life changing. Nothing had been easy—no shelter, no supplies, no showers. At first he'd hated it—and Colt—for dragging him out into the Alaskan wilderness. But then things had changed. He'd learned to like making things with his hands, trapping his own food. It gave him a feeling of intense satisfaction. Dane had discovered a new passion, one that surpassed the adrenaline of even the most exciting play-off game. When they'd finished the trip, Colt had suggested that Dane join him at his lodge in Alaska, completely off the grid. They'd lived there for a year—no electricity, no running water, no food storage—nothing except what they could catch and take care of on their own. It had been rough and incredibly difficult.

It had been bliss.

He would have kept living off the grid indefinitely—not exactly hiding inasmuch as keeping a low profile—if Grant hadn't visited him and Colt in their cabin in Alaska to get away for a few weeks. Colt had invited him—the marine wasn't much for chit-chat, but he knew Grant was struggling, even years after the death of his wife. Once in Alaska, the three friends had quickly fallen into an old, easy camaraderie. Though Grant didn't share quite the same enthusiasm as Dane and Colt for wood smoke fires and catching game for dinner, the time spent roughing it at the cabin had given Grant an interesting idea. A survival business—run by the three of them. Colt and Dane could handle the trainings, and Grant would handle the business. They'd work for themselves and answer to no one. Neither Dane nor Grant needed the money, but the challenge of the business intrigued all three of them.

Now Dane found himself back in his hometown, and avoiding everyone there. If there was anyone who hadn't forgotten Casanova Croft, it was the people of Bluebonnet. He'd been leery to return to town, expecting the worst. As far as he knew, he was the only person from town who had ever had fifteen minutes of fame, and he expected harassment. So far, though, so good. He kept a low profile, and for the most part, the usually nosy citizens of Bluebonnet had left him alone. Just as he liked it.

Well, he wasn't being totally honest about not wanting to look up anyone. One particular person did spring to mind, but he was pretty sure Miranda Hill wanted nothing to do with him. The last time he'd spoken to her had been in person, and when he'd tried calling her from NHL training camp, she'd ignored his calls—or worse, made her crazy mother answer them.

After getting chewed out by Mrs. Hill three times in a row, he got the picture. He'd stopped calling, and stopped caring. There were always more girls willing to throw themselves at a hockey player, especially a hotshot up-and-comer.

He'd eventually forgotten about Miranda Hill, the one that

had gotten away. Well, sort of. And if he'd had a thing for long brown hair and girls with a soft Southern drawl, that was just how it went. Miranda Hill had probably moved away long ago. Maybe she'd gotten married and shot out five kids in five years like his cousin Tara had, and now spent her time chain-smoking and watching daytime TV. Either way, it was best if Miranda Hill remained a memory.

So, no, he wasn't going to look her up.

The business's only other employee—their coordination assistant, Brenna James—showed up a moment later with her clipboard and a beaming smile on her face. "Guess whose clients are here? Are you two ready?"

Colt kicked up out of his chair, putting down his game controller. "Soon."

Always so chatty, that Colt. "I'm ready," Dane said, grabbing the two packs. Colt had packed his hours ago in preparation for the trip, but Dane had delayed, waiting until the last moment. Almost as if he was delaying the inevitable.

Colt gave him a serious look. "Hope so."

Irritation surged in Dane and he ignored his friend's well-meaning look. The guys either trusted him or they didn't. He could keep his dick in his pants. It wasn't like he was some oversexed nutjob waiting to jump out of the bushes at the first pretty girl that passed by.

Not anymore.

Grant appeared in the room, grinning. He carried a champagne bottle and three glasses. "This is it, boys. Our big inaugural class. You ready?"

Dane was starting to wish that everyone would quit asking him if he was ready. "Gonna be a good one," he said, and rubbed his hands together. "You ready to sit on your ass and soak up the profits from Colt's and my hard work?"

Grant rolled his eyes and removed the foil from the top of the champagne bottle. "More like, you two get to have a weeklong vacation in the woods and I have to hold down the fort and do all the busywork. There are a million things to be done between now and when you guys get back, and Brenna's not going to be much help."

"You like busywork," Colt said. "You make more for yourself just so you have shit to do."

Grant popped the cork on the champagne. "Time to celebrate."

Colt looked at the champagne with distaste. "You shoulda brought beer."

"Beer isn't for celebrating," Grant said, ignoring Colt's sour mood. He poured a glass for Dane and handed it over.

Dane took it, but he only half paid attention until the other two men raised their drinks.

"To success," Grant said.

"Success," Colt echoed.

To a week of proving to his buddies that his dick didn't run his life. "To success," Dane said, and then downed the champagne.

The two men emerged from the lodge and Dane squinted up at the sun. It was perfect weather for their first excursion—sixty-five degrees with no rain. The rain could come later in the week, but today? Today was perfect. This was a good omen, Dane decided, his mood light. Piece of cake.

Brenna steered him toward one of two lines of waiting clients—men in camo clothes who had probably never been more "outdoors" than a corporate gym. He put on his camera-ready smile and began the meet and greet—okay, some things weren't all that different from hockey. The first guy was a small business owner, the next a lawyer looking to send his team of attorneys through the training if they liked the class. Dane hadn't believed Grant when he said that corporations would pay big bucks for this sort of thing, but sure enough, every single man he shook hands with was testing out the class for a corporate club or toastmasters or a professionals group.

No pressure.

Dane shook the hands of five men before coming to the end of the line and his sixth and final "student" for the week. To his surprise, the person that came out from behind the parked jeep was none other than Miranda Hill, the girl he'd left behind nine years ago. The one that had gotten away. The one he'd fantasized about for years.

He stared at her in surprise. "Miranda?"

She tilted her head, shiny brown hair sliding over her shoulder. "Don't I get a handshake, too?"

"What are you doing here?" She looked exactly the same as she had nine years ago—same great hair, same dark doe eyes, same amazing figure with an even better rack. This had to be a test from Colt and Grant. "I'm, uh." He glanced back at Colt, openly skeptical that his fantasy girl had somehow shown up on the first day of the new business, but Colt was busy greeting his own students and wasn't looking in his direction. "I'm a little busy right now."

She pulled a baseball cap over her hair and smiled at him. Well . . . damn. Miranda wasn't anything like his cousin Tara. If anything, she looked better than she had when he'd left nine years ago. Her slim figure was lush with curves, and she had a healthy tan. She wore a high-necked maroon top with a pair of scruffy jean shorts and beat-up sneakers. A bag was tossed over her shoulder and she was looking at him expectantly.

He didn't know what to say.

"Dane," Brenna said between gritted teeth. She poked him in the arm with her oversized pen. "Miranda has signed up for the survival training. You'll be her instructor this week."

Damn. He looked at the welcoming smile gracing her mouth, the casual hand on her hip, and a rush of memories flooded through him. Her soft mouth on his, the feel of her skin underneath his hands. The eager teenager had turned into an amazingly sexy woman. He looked into her smiling eyes and the curve of her mouth and felt his cock stir.

Hell. The week had just gotten a lot longer.

THREE

This was starting to feel like a mistake.

Miranda kept her nervousness hidden, though she shifted on her feet repeatedly as the survival class gathered and the two instructors talked in low voices in the distance. This had seemed like a great idea a few days ago. It hadn't been easy to get into the class at the last minute, but she'd made up some sort of excuse that her new job wanted some team-building work on her resume, forked over the ridiculous amount of money for the weeklong training, and passed the preliminary physical with flying colors. Easy enough.

Her goal was simple. Find Dane Croft, flirt up a storm, and use her feminine wiles to hook him. If it were any other man, she'd have concerns about playing the seductress, but Casanova Croft was legendary for his exploits. The man was a poon hound, and she intended to use that against him. She'd get him dancing to her tune, get him a little compromised, and then let the camera in her backpack do the damage.

This week, she was going to let her evil side rule things. Good Miranda was definitely going to be shoved to a back burner. Center stage? Evil Miranda.

Now, looking at the people surrounding her, this didn't seem like the brightest idea she'd ever had. The class was small—six people to an instructor. Five men lined up next to her, and all seemed ready to go and eager to spend the next week in the wild. Four of the five were dressed in camouflage, and one had even painted his face with black stripes under each eye, as if he were expecting to run a few downs of football after hiking. They'd also gone overboard on the gear. Since they'd been instructed to pack extremely light, she'd decided to wear comfortable clothing over her sexiest underwear. After all, she didn't want to seem too obvious. Her hiking boots were just beat-up jogging shoes, for example. But the others seemed like they had cleaned out the local sporting goods store, and their shoes were clean and crisp and had probably been taken out of the box minutes before they arrived here.

All of the men in her group—in both groups, really—were relatively fit and lean and likely in their late thirties or forties. In addition to being the youngest one here, Miranda was also the only female other than the assistant, who took everyone's waivers and wrote up their information on a clipboard.

It was an acute, disturbing feeling. A week alone in the wilderness with six guys and just her? It had all the makings of a bad porno.

Out of the corner of her eye, Miranda saw the second instructor approach the group of waiting clients. He was wearing a black T-shirt that had the survival school's logo on the back. When he turned at someone's question, Miranda recognized him, and not just from the photo. Colt Waggoner hadn't changed much since high school. He'd gotten taller, but he was still lean and muscled. Instead of wearing the sloppy, oversized T-shirts she remembered him in, he was dressed sharply, his T-shirt tucked into camouflage pants and shiny boots on his feet. As the client addressed him, Colt stood with his hands clasped behind his back.

"No, sir," Colt replied in a crisp voice to the man's low question. "No outside electronics."

The man looked at everyone else nervously. "Oh, well. I just thought I'd ask."

Colt gave him a crisp nod and then began to walk past the group. He stopped and paused in front of Miranda, recognition dawning on his face. "Miranda. What are you doing here?"

She pulled out a crumpled brochure and waved it in front of her, feeling like an idiot under Colt's piercing stare. "Thought I'd take the class. How are you doing, Colt? It's good to see you."

"Fine," he said stiffly, then tilted his head. "You're still in Bluebonnet?"

"Haven't left," she said awkwardly. Ever. Oh God. *Please don't ask me why I stayed. Please don't ask me why I stayed.*

"I'm sorry," he said in a short, clipped voice. His hands clasped behind his back, and his "relaxed" pose was still stiffer than most. Military, maybe?

"Sorry?"

"Sorry that you haven't left. This town is a joke."

A surprised laugh erupted from her throat. "So it is. What brings you back, then?"

"Business," he said. "Grant's here, too. We—"

"Colt," Dane yelled from behind him. "Hey, Colt. C'mere."

Colt tilted his head again, a little, and he didn't turn to look at Dane. "If you'll excuse me, Miranda. Nice to see you again."

"You, too," she said faintly. "Welcome back."

Colt turned and trotted off to Dane's side up the hill. Dane leaned in close, saying something in a rapid-fire, angry tone. Miranda couldn't make it out, though. Dane said something, and both men turned and looked back at her. Then they spoke again. To her surprise, Colt patted the front of Dane's pants and said something. Dane swung a punch, but Colt ducked out of the way, smirking. Dane didn't look amused—he looked pissed. When Dane gestured sharply in her direction, a bit of a smile curved Miranda's mouth. Well, at least that was something. Anger was better than nothing. When she'd first extended her hand for Dane to shake, there had been a blank look on his face, as if he didn't quite know what to make of seeing her here.

She had to admit, she didn't know what to make of him either. A smirk she'd have expected. A lecherous grin she'd have expected. The baffled look he'd given her? Not so much.

Brenna paused in front of Miranda, peering down at her clipboard. "Do you have your registration packet with you?"

She handed the paperwork to Brenna and was given a red bandana in return.

"You're going to be on the red team," Brenna announced. "The red instructor will be your leader for the next week. Wear your bandana at all times, as we're going to have a few team-versus-team challenges later in the week."

"Got it," Miranda said in a meek voice. "And my instructor is Dane?"

The assistant glanced up and gave her a searching look, a hint of a frown on her face.

"I'm a hockey fan," Miranda hastily explained, lying through her teeth. "Plus, he and I go way back. High school and all that."

She didn't point out that she'd gone to high school with Colt Waggoner, too.

"You're not here for hockey or class reunions. You're here for survival training," Brenna said. "If that's going to be a problem, I can switch instructors—"

"No!" Miranda squeaked, hiding the red bandana behind her back. "Not a problem at all. I just happened to notice it."

"Well, *un*notice it if you can. Mr. Croft doesn't care to discuss hockey," Brenna said, and peeked around, then leaned in to whisper. "You cause any trouble, and I'll move you to the other team." She gave Miranda a wide smile. "Okeydoke?"

Jeez. Miranda nodded. "No hockey. Got it."

"I'm glad we had this little talk." Brenna beamed at her and then moved down the line to the first person on the blue team. "Got your paperwork?"

"She's a bit much, don't you think?" The man next to Miranda chuckled. "Glad she's not going to be our instructor, or this would really be a long week."

Miranda gave a sheepish smile to the man. He was a tall, bordering-on-skinny guy who wore black-framed square glasses that hid his pale face. He seemed nice enough—strong jaw, thick sandy blond hair, and a friendly smile. Kind of cute, if you were into nerds.

Shame she'd always had a thing for jocks.

"I'm Pete. And you are . . ." He switched his bandana to his left hand and extended his right for a handshake.

"Miranda," she said, shaking his hand and trying to do her best not to peer around him. He was blocking her view of Dane.

"So what do you do, Miranda?" Pete asked with an easy smile. "Public relations? Pharmaceutical sales?"

She gave him an odd look. "I'm a librarian."

He laughed at that, as if anything she said was hysterically funny. "Really? Pretty young woman like you moldering in a library? I wouldn't have figured it."

Okay, that was definitely flirting. Miranda stared at Pete for a moment, unsure how to answer. Flirt back? Ignore the flirting? She settled for polite small talk. "I take it back—I used to be a librarian. I'm taking a new job down in Houston in a few weeks as Chief Information Officer at a start-up electronics company. What is it you do, Pete?"

"I own Hazardous Waste Games in Austin," he said, his smile widening with pride.

"Oh, wow," she said, her attention drawn back to him. "You own a company?"

"A billion-dollar company," he agreed proudly. "We make the biggest first-person shooter MMO in PC gaming."

Like she knew what that was. Miranda gave him a hesitant smile. "Wow. Biggest first, uh, shooter. That's great."

He nodded, glancing around the clearing in front of the lodge. "Our next project involves survival skills. I thought I'd check out the scene and see what it's like. Get a little first-person experience of my own."

"Good idea," she enthused, but her interest was rapidly waning despite his friendliness. Dane was marching back toward the group, a resigned look on his face and a red bandana wrapped around his hand. Her breath expelled from her chest in a whoosh of relief—she hadn't realized how tense she'd been.

If she'd been moved to the blue team . . . she'd have been screwed. And not in a pleasant way.

Now that Dane was approaching, she could look her fill at him again. Her memories of him from high school had been vague and steamy—she'd recalled a tall, lanky boy with dark, messy hair, shoulders that seemed too wide for his lean body, and an easy smile. The man who paused in front of the team seemed to be the same, but different. The Dane she'd had her hands on nine years ago had been lean—this man was nothing but solid muscle. His biceps bulged from underneath the sleeves of his black T-shirt and were tanned a delicious shade of bronze. Back in high school, Dane had almost been too pretty—with a beautiful mouth, perfect nose, lean face, and piercing green eyes.

The Dane before her still had the beautiful mouth and piercing green eyes, but his face had filled out, and his nose had been broken several times and had a large ridge in the middle proclaiming that he'd been in fights while on the ice. He had a scar just above it, and another one on his chin. She'd have thought the scars would make him less attractive, but for some reason they broke up the delicacy of his face and made him dangerous. There was even a third whisper-thin white scar running through his left eyebrow that gave him a rakish look. The rumpled black hair she remembered had been cut short and clung to his head in a thick cap that made her fingers itch to stroke it. And as he stood in front of them, she admired his shoulders. Still broad and blatant with muscles, but the rest of his body seemed to have caught up, and the entire picture was mouthwatering indeed.

She felt a bit dismayed at the sight of him. Why couldn't he have been more torn-up looking? Why couldn't his face be covered with hockey injuries, his nose broken beyond all hope, and his cheekbones crushed like a boxer's? Why did he have to have those scars that made him look so damn . . . delicious?

All the better to seduce him, Evil Miranda whispered in her ear.

Hm. Evil Miranda definitely had a point. This was all about seduction, and it'd be a lot easier to seduce a man when he was easy on the eyes. Heck, if he was easy on the eyes, it'd make it a pleasure for her to seduce him, rather than a chore. She could be down with that.

Dane turned to say something to Brenna, and Miranda's gaze slid to his tight ass, outlined in his camo shorts. Definitely easy on the eyes, all right. She felt a little hot and breathless just looking at the way his hips narrowed.

He turned and his gaze flicked to Miranda, catching her staring at his ass. A blush crossed her face and then she winked at him. To her vast delight, that seemed to fluster him even more, as if he hadn't expected that kind of reaction from her. Evil Miranda was delighted with that response.

Right then, she decided to let Evil Miranda take the reins this week.

"Welcome, everyone, to your week of survival training," Dane said in a low voice that made her thighs quiver. Heat flared, settling low in her hips. "For the next week, you're going to learn how to live out in the wild on your own. It's not going to be easy. You'll be sleeping on the ground, catching your own food, and learning the best ways to move about in the bush. We're going to have a team challenge against the blue team, and at the end of the week, you're going to have to survive on your own for a day using the training I give you. Understand?"

Survive on her own for a day? Did that mean she wouldn't be spending the full week with Dane? She hid her frown. Okay, then, *six* days to seduce the man and get naked photos of him. She could handle six days.

Evil Miranda would just have to work a little faster.

"The land we're going to be surviving on is the private property of the Daughtry Ranch. You're surrounded by ten thousand acres of nothing but trees and wildlife. We own this ranch, so anything you can bring down to serve as food, do so. No sport killing—this is to teach you how to survive, understand?"

He cast a stern glare over the group, arms crossed over his chest.

No one moved.

"Now," he declared, "we're all going to empty our packs and I'm going to make sure you're not smuggling in anything to make this easier on you. Our instructions said to bring a utility knife"—he ticked the words off on his fingers—"a change of clothes, extra socks, and three Ziploc bags. Nothing else."

Miranda stiffened, her hands tightening on the straps of her backpack. She was going to have to show the contents of her bag? Oh crap. This could be awkward. Or embarrassing. Or both.

As she hesitated, Dane smiled at the first person in their small line, took his backpack, and upended it on the ground. She groaned inwardly as the man's gear came spilling out and Dane began to pick through it. "Not allowed," he said, pushing aside the first item. "Not allowed, not allowed."

Oh yes. This was definitely going to be bad. She watched as the man—Will, she thought his name was—stiffened and looked as if he were about to mutiny before the class even started.

Assistant Brenna was right at Dane's side, taking the beef jerky, cell phone, and travel thermal blanket pouch that were handed to her. "You'll get this stuff back when the class is done," she said in a take-no-arguments kind of voice. "Not a moment sooner."

"I need that phone. My company is securing a deal this week—"

"I'm sorry, did you want to remove yourself from the class?" Brenna said with a cheerful, innocent smile, waving the phone in front of his face. "Because if so, I'd be happy to refund you the tuition—minus your deposit, of course."

"No, ma'am," Will said in a resigned voice. He gave the phone a last longing look and then sighed, stepping back into line.

Dane smiled and clapped the man on the back, leaning in and murmuring a few words of encouragement that Miranda couldn't make out. Whatever it was, it had the desired effect—Will perked up again and gave Dane a rueful smile.

He'd always been good at charming people. The prick. Even so, she squirmed a little, imagining him leaning in and telling her that she'd been a naughty girl. Even just standing in line, she was getting turned on by Dane's presence.

Evil Miranda was going to have a field day this week.

Miranda's nerves grew taut, her grip on her backpack tight as Dane went down the line. A few people grimaced and gave up their contraband—emergency flashlights, granola bars, another cell phone—and Pete had seemed extremely put out to relinquish bug spray. Still, he did so, falling prey to Dane's easy charm even as Brenna snatched the contraband from him.

And then Dane was standing in front of her. She swallowed hard as he put his hand out. "Well, uh," she said, stalling. "How about I promise you that I don't have any contraband and we'll call it even?"

He raised an eyebrow at her, his friendly smile curving into a frown. "Is there a particular reason why you don't want me to check your bag, Ms. . . ."

Miranda gave him a smile. "You know who I am."

"Nine years ago I did," he admitted. "A lot happens in nine years."

"It's still Hill. No marriage, no divorce." She wondered if he would think that was a good thing or a bad thing. And before he could respond, she offered, "And I'll show you my bag, but it has to be in private. You know. Because of girl stuff."

That scarred eyebrow went sky-high. He looked down at her for a long moment, and Miranda kept a casual smile on her face, though her skin was prickling from nervousness. If he dumped her bag out on the grass in front of everyone . . . well, it was going to be a *really* long week.

"All right," he agreed after a long, tense moment. "Let's go behind that tree and you can show me."

She nodded and headed in that direction, feeling a wild sense of relief. No public humiliation. That was good.

They moved behind a large juniper tree, the bushy spread of branches allowing for privacy. Dane gave her a speculative look as they paused, and he crossed his arms over his chest. "Now, what's this about?"

"What makes you think this is about something?" She opened her eyes wide, feigning innocence.

He arched an eyebrow. "Because this all seems a little coincidental, don't you think? My ex-girlfriend from high school shows up for my first survival class, and she's just as beautiful as I remembered?"

Her nipples hardened at the husky, almost teasing tone of his voice, and she placed a hand on the tree behind her, steadying herself. *Down, girl.* She felt conflicted, staring up into his rugged face. Was it possible to still be insanely attracted to the man even if she hated him? She'd only been around him for five minutes and already her body was perking up in response. So he thought she was beautiful? "This isn't a setup. I assure you."

At least, it wasn't in the way he thought it was.

He gave her an "I'm waiting" look and didn't budge from his spot in front of her. "It doesn't explain why you won't let me see what's inside your bag."

Ah yes. That answered it. She *could* be physically attracted to a man and still want to kick him in the balls.

Mentally steeling herself to put her plan into action, she shrugged the bag off her shoulder and then held it out to him. "Here you go."

Like the others, Dane took her pack, unzipped the top, and then dumped the contents onto the ground.

Lingerie fluttered to the grass: red silk bras, black lace thongs, and a pair of pink silk panties—her favorite—with a ruffle across the derriere. On top of it all lay her camera.

He stared down at the mix for a long moment, and then looked back at her, astonished. "What's all this?"

"Survival gear," Miranda said, her voice slightly husky with nervousness. She forced herself to step forward, her body trembling with nervousness, and laid a hand on his chest. Oh my. A really, really defined pectoral. That was new, and very welcome. Her mouth went dry and she glanced up at him, where he stood stock-still, looming over her. Her voice lowered to a whisper. "All those panties are terribly essential to my survival this week."

His body tensed under her hand, and she waited. Waited for him to push her away and scowl in her direction, all business . . . or for him to respond to her touch.

Dane looked down at her hand, small on his chest. Then he looked back at her, his expression inscrutable. His voice was low. "What's going on, Miranda?"

This was her moment. She knotted her fingers in his shirt and tugged him forward, and was gratified to see that he let himself be pulled forward. Her breasts bounced against his rock-hard chest and she felt a thrill of excitement, a spurt of adrenaline, and a heady rush of desire. She tilted her head back and looked up at him, her gaze sliding to his mouth. "We never slept together nine years ago, Dane Croft. Do you remember? You were supposed to take my virginity and you were a no-show."

"I remember lots of things about you, Miranda Hill," he said in a low, husky voice. "Miranda Hill," he said, repeating her name. "No marriage, no divorce. Just Miranda Hill."

Her toes curled and she pulled him a little closer. His mouth was now so close to hers that his breath fanned against her cheek, warm and sweet. "I heard you were back in town," she whispered, and she could smell the wonderful, crisp scent of him—all man and musk and just a hint of sweat and fresh outdoors. "And I wanted to see if maybe we could pick up where we left off, and see how that works out."

Then she deliberately licked her lips, her mouth so close to his that her tongue grazed his lips.

He groaned and moved forward—just an inch or two, but enough that his mouth brushed hers, and she felt his tongue brush against her own. Her lips parted and she welcomed the caress. When his tongue dipped into her mouth and thrust, she felt it all the way to her core, and her sex began to pulse with desire. Her lips parted wider, and her tongue met his next thrust, tangling with his.

He still kissed as well as she remembered. Better, she thought as he stroked against her tongue in a move that made her nerves thrill and her pussy clench.

Someone in the distance coughed, and Dane froze against her. She stroked her tongue along his lips, determined to win the contest of wills, and was rewarded when he pulled away from her grasp, dazed. "What's the matter, Dane?" Her voice was soft, playful. "Or is it time for the strip search?"

He pulled her hand off his chest and glanced over back through the trees, where the others still waited for them. Dane swore lightly under his breath and raked a hand over his crisp skullcap of hair. Then he knelt and pocketed her camera and began to stuff panties back into her bag, scowling. "This week isn't about hooking up, Miranda."

Says you, she thought, but said nothing. That merest brush of a kiss had inspired her. Nine years ago, she'd never gotten to hook up with Dane, and she thought she'd use this week to torment him, drive him mad with lust, and then get the pictures she wanted. But now that he'd pocketed her camera, she had a new idea . . . one that involved a side benefit for her.

She'd always wanted to sleep with Dane. At least, when she was younger, she'd wanted it. He'd been the only man who had ever been able to bring her to an orgasm—and they hadn't even slept together. After he hadn't shown up to take her virginity and the photos went online, she'd grown a bit of a hang-up about sex. She'd lost her virginity to the first nonlocal boy she'd dated, just because it wouldn't get around town. That had been an awkward, embarrassing situation for them both. Her relationships after that hadn't gotten much better. She'd bed-hopped between several men during her college years, all equally unable to get her to the point at which her brain would turn off and she could relax and orgasm. She *couldn't* relax, couldn't come, couldn't enjoy the moment, and every relationship of hers usually ended a night or two after sex was introduced.

After a while, she'd given up on dating, sure that her issues with Dane and her mother's issues with men had permanently ruined any chance of a normal relationship. She'd stopped dating . . . and had bought a vibrator instead.

But just being in Dane's presence already had her turned on more than any man she'd been near in years. And she remembered that the time she and Dane had been petting in the closet, she'd come hard and come fast.

She wondered if she could do it again—have an orgasm with

a man. It shouldn't be hard, but it seemed that every woman on earth could manage one but her. Maybe she just needed the right man to experiment on, even if it was Dane Croft, her most hated enemy. This week was the perfect time to find out, she thought as she gave him another predatory look.

He finished stuffing the last of the clothing back into her bag and patted his pocket with her camera. All right, her plans would have to change a little. Seduce and fuck the man this week. Have fun. Use him for sex—and, hopefully, orgasms. Then, when the week was over, she'd invite him back to her place and take the pictures then.

That still worked. She smiled wickedly. Evil Miranda approved of using men.

Dane scowled and shoved the bag back into her hands. "The memo said for clothing you can live in for the next few days. That means hike, eat, sleep, and possibly swim in your clothing."

Evil Miranda came out to play again. She leaned forward and trailed a finger down the front of Dane's chest. "I can hike, sleep, and swim in my lacy panties," she said, her voice a low purr. "But eating in my lacy panties? That's going to have to be left to you."

Then she licked her lips and smiled seductively at him.

Dane swore under his breath again, and then bolted back for the others, adjusting himself as he did.

Evil Miranda, one; Dane, zero.

FOUR

Well, damn.

Dane checked the equipment in his backpack one more time, determined not to stare at Miranda as she sauntered back to the small group, her rounded hips swaying in a completely seductive motion that had his cock erect. Hell. Five minutes into their inaugural class and he was already in trouble. Of all the women in the entire world, Miranda had to be here in his class.

Approaching him. Kissing him, her intentions clear. *I wanted to see if maybe we could pick up where we left off.* The woman had packed herself an entire bag full of lingerie for a weeklong survival trip in the woods, an obvious signal of her intent. And . . . damn. He pictured Miranda's curvy figure in a particular pair of ruffled panties, sitting in his lap at the campfire . . .

Then he promptly put it out of his mind, thinking of other things. Unsexy things, cold showers, anything to get his mind back in the game. He couldn't let a pretty flame from his past distract him from his job.

His eyes narrowed. Unless . . . that was why she was here. Maybe Miranda had volunteered to tempt him, bait for a very sexy trap.

She didn't seem like the type to sign up for a weeklong outdoor excursion, he thought, looking over at her smiling, too-cheerful face. Maybe Colt and Grant had set her up to be in his group. Colt had been awfully chummy with her back during the introductions. He remembered seeing the two of them in a conversation, and Miranda had laughed. The sound had scraped on his already ragged nerves, and he'd barked Colt's name to drag him away from her. When Colt had come back, he'd teased Dane. *Now it's gonna be extra-hard for you to keep this soldier at ease*, he'd said, and patted the front of Dane's pants. He'd tried to deck the guy in response. Still regretted missing.

Maybe she was in on this with Colt. Grant, too. Maybe they'd pulled out the sexiest girl in Bluebonnet and had hired her to come to the training class to test his willpower. Maybe they didn't trust him to keep his dick in his pants like they said they did. That certainly made more sense than anything else he could think up.

And it pissed him off.

Dane watched Miranda smile at the other men, her hand playing with the high neckline of her T-shirt. He frowned. She wasn't exactly dressed like a seductress. For one, her shirt was modest to the point of puritanical. For two, she didn't wear a bit of makeup, and her hair was simple—long, straight, and smooth. Not that she needed makeup to look good—her fresh skin and pretty brown eyes had smiled at him in a way that reminded him he hadn't had sex with a woman in a very long time.

Well then, if Miranda was a plant to test his willpower, it was one test that Dane intended to ace. They'd kissed, but that had been a mistake. He wouldn't let it happen again. Time to get down to business.

Miranda toyed with the collar of her shirt, a nervous habit from years past. At her side, Pete smiled at her in a way that seemed a little too friendly. He kept looking over at her and grinning, and she gave him a faint smile back because what else was she supposed to do? Ignore him? She wondered, briefly, if he had seen the waterfall of lingerie that had cascaded out of her pack when Dane turned it over, and she cringed. It'd be even worse if he'd seen her come on to their instructor and kissed him.

That would make this week really, really awkward.

"So have you ever been camping before?" Pete asked her as Dane moved back toward the group. "I have to admit, I didn't expect to see a pretty girl here on the team, but it's a welcome surprise."

Keeping the polite smile on her face, Miranda turned back to Dane, trying not to show her irritation. "I don't see why it's so unbelievable that a woman wants to go on a survival trip. I was in Girl Scouts. They do camping, though not quite like this."

He chuckled at her in a condescending way. "Well, get ready for the ride of your life."

She glanced over at Pete. "Why? Have you done one of these trips before?"

Pete flushed a little. "Oh. Uh, no. I've just heard that it's going to be a crazy week, that's all."

He seemed so very uncomfortable at being put on the spot that she gave him another smile to make him feel better. So far Pete seemed to be a lot worse with people than she was.

In the distance, the blue team began to hike into the woods, angling away from the enormous wooden cabin that served as the lodge and headquarters. Dane turned back to his team, clapped his hands together once, and rocked on his heels. "Are we ready to begin?"

She noticed he didn't look over at her. Instead, he made eye contact with every man on their small team and then swung away before his gaze could reach hers. Miranda bristled at that, twisting the red bandana around her wrist. Plenty of time to win him over. Lots and lots of time to seduce him. She just needed to be patient.

"I have a few rules before we move into the woods," Dane began. His hands moved to his hips and he stood before them, legs apart and arms akimbo, larger than life. "For starters, this is not going to be an easy trip. We're going to be doing a lot of hiking. Some swimming. We're going to learn how to make traps and tie knots. We're going to fish for our dinner and forage what we can't find in the streams. We're going to learn to build shelters and how to start and maintain a fire. It's going to be very cold at night and very warm in the daytime. You're going to sweat. You're going to get dirty. And if you're a little too fancy-pants for this sort of thing, it's best that you leave now."

Miranda watched Dane curiously. Did he . . . did he just blush when he said the word *fancy-pants*? His gaze slid over to her, and then back away again, and she felt a surge of triumph.

He was thinking about *her panties.* She let a smile curve her mouth. Well, now.

"Most of all, we're going to learn what it's like to work as a team." He turned to them and started to pass out PowerBars.

Three were handed to Miranda, and she stared down at them, then at the canteen that was handed to her. It didn't look like much water.

"Those are all of the supplies you're going to have this week," Dane announced. "The first day's meal and drinks are on me. The rest is up to you."

One person groaned. It might have been Pete.

To Dane's credit, he ignored it and continued speaking. "We're going to assign partners for this week, and sometimes you and your buddy will pair up for challenges. Are you with me?" At their nods, he gestured. "Now, each of you pick a buddy and let's get going."

Pete turned and gave Miranda a hopeful look.

Well, why not. Miranda gave him a thumbs-up and an awkward smile in return. He looked the least woods-capable, and she could always hope he would bail early, leaving her with no choice but to buddy up with Dane.

"All right," Dane said when they were standing next to their partners. He pointed at the two older men that had teamed up. "George and Jamie will walk at the front of the line. We're going to do this single file, since it makes things easiest. Next will be Steve and Will." He gestured at the other male-male team, and then finally at her and Pete. "Pete and Miranda can take up the rear. Miranda, you in front of Pete, since that's safest. Call out if you two start to get left behind."

"I know how to walk," she said in a bristling tone, offended.

God, the man really was a jerk. "Just because I'm a girl doesn't mean that I'm incompetent."

"No, of course not," Dane said. "You're right. You take up the rear. Pete, you walk in front of Miranda."

Well, that wasn't exactly better. She suspected that she was getting stuck with end-of-the-line duty so Dane wouldn't have to look at her. Figured.

"All right, let's go." Dane waved them forward and then turned, beginning to march through the trees. He pulled out a satellite phone, murmured something into it, and then shut it off.

One by one, they fell into place behind him. Miranda picked up the rear, her light pack bouncing against her shoulders as they walked. The ground was uneven and a bit rocky in places, and pebbles scattered under their feet.

"Now, one thing I should warn you guys about this ranch," Dane said, glancing back at them as they walked. "Five years ago, this ranch was the biggest emu farm in the South before the owner died and the assets were sold off. The emu were moved to different breeders, but there're one or two still trotting around on the property. Just warning you in case you run across one this week."

One of the businessmen—Miranda thought his name was Steve—stopped. "What the heck is an emu?"

"Big, giant bird," Dane said casually. "About five feet tall. Kind of like an ostrich, but with a nasty temper. Just be on the lookout."

"You mean to tell me that you've got overgrown birds out here?" Steve sputtered. "Are you even sure that's safe?"

"Not sure if it's safe," Dane drawled. "But there's not a lot that's 'safe' in the wild, if you catch my drift. You're here to learn how to take care of yourself in the wilderness, and maybe that includes a lesson on emu-avoiding, maybe not." His big shoulders braced and then he began to jog up an incline. "Come on, let's pick up the pace. We've got a long way to go tonight before we hit the area I've designated for our camp."

They had no choice but to follow their leader. One by one, they followed Dane up the incline, Miranda's sneakers sliding on the gravel a little.

"You all right back there?" Dane called.

"I'm fine," Miranda called back, her tone a little strained. This was already getting tiresome—she could walk just as well as any of the men. "Don't you worry about me."

"Oh, I won't," Dane called back. "Let's go, men. And woman."

And with that, he began to jog into the woods.

That day, Miranda began to have a reluctant appreciation for Dane's athleticism. They jogged for a bit—mostly to get away from the headquarters cabin and into the wild. Once the lodge had been out of sight for about fifteen minutes, Dane slowed the group to a brisk hike. He led the way, climbing over rocks and brush like he was born to the wild.

The rest of the team followed behind him, much slower and far clumsier. Two of the older businessmen were panting and frowning, but all kept up with their instructor as he skirted them up a dry creek bed, grasping tree roots for handholds. The others followed close behind, and when it came to Miranda's turn, Pete offered a hand down to her.

She ignored it and clambered up the side of the embankment

on her own. "I'm fine, thanks." Her voice was crisper than it needed to be, but she was getting irritated at him and it was only day one.

And what a long day one it was. She was covered in sweat—they all were—and tendrils of her hair were sticking to her face, but she was keeping up with the men and that was just fine. Pete seemed to be struggling, his steps slowing as they hiked.

As they walked, Dane began to chat with the students in his group, his voice casual. It had always been easy for Dane to make friends, Miranda remembered, and he seemed right in his element. The men told him about their jobs, their families, and previous hunting trips they'd been on.

When it came to Pete's turn, he immediately began to brag about his company. "I run Hazardous Waste Games. It's a billion-dollar company—"

Miranda rolled her eyes and tuned him out as he rattled on about shooters and gaming.

"—but that's me," Pete eventually concluded with a grin. "Married to the job unless I can find the right woman to make a new man out of me."

He grinned back at Miranda, obviously thinking that his business assets made up for his lack of other assets.

She made a face and hoped he couldn't see it. His chalk-pale face was flushed a florid red, and his hair was stuck to his forehead. Big circular sweat stains had bloomed under his arms, and he was beginning to smell.

He needed a woman to make a new man out of him? It sure as shit wasn't going to be her.

As if sensing her thoughts, Dane spoke. "What about you, Miss Hill?"

She jerked, startled. "Oh, I'm not interested in finding a husband, thank you. I'm here to learn survival skills."

The men snickered.

"I meant," Dane said in a patient voice. "What about you? Tell us about your family."

"You know my family, Dane Croft," Miranda said. "My mother, Tanya, runs the local antiques store, and my daddy was a no-good trucker who only showed up every few years. I'm surprised you forgot." Before he could reply to her jab, she hurried on. "But other than that, it's just me. No husband, no kids."

Two and a half weeks and she'd be working at a massive corporation, doing what she was always meant to do.

Everything between now and then wasn't important. It was just finishing off the story of Old Miranda, the Boobs of Bluebonnet. Soon she'd just be a local legend.

Her eyes narrowed at Dane's back. A local legend with a really good ending, she decided.

When the sun was high in the sky, the group made it to the area Dane had designated as the first campsite. The men grumbled and joked about how tired they were. Dane had half expected Miranda to complain, but she was the only one on his small team that took the rigorous exercise in stride. Her face was flushed and sweaty, but she remained strong and calm, and he was reassessing his initial thoughts about her. With those bright red bras and silky panties, Dane had thought she'd be a girly girl. Maybe not.

He was sweating, too, his body aching in a good way at the exercise. The weather was perfect. Just cool enough to make the day pleasant, and warm enough to take the edge off of the night. He inhaled the fresh air and grinned to himself. He was enjoying the time in the woods, even if his team was not.

But then again, it was his job to make them believers, and he had a week to do so. He pulled a piece of paper out of his pocket as they rested, mentally going over his notes. This week was more than just survival skills—it was about building teamwork.

Dane was not exactly an expert on teamwork. He'd sucked at it in a jersey, and just because he had survival skills didn't mean he could make people work together.

Colt and Grant had insisted, though—corporate sponsors wanted practical applications for survival skills, and couching fire-making and shelter-building as team exercises was the way to do it. He'd have to go by their rules. On his crib sheet, he read Brenna's flowery, bubbly handwriting, the *I*'s dotted with hearts. *Blindfolds for team-building. Make them do tasks together. Rope challenges. Team challenge on day 3.*

Right.

He turned to address his team. "We're going to make camp here tonight. And as we set up the camp, I'm going to show you how to do the basics. I'll build you a basic shelter and show you how to make fire and we'll boil drinking water. Then I'm going to set snares and show you how to fish, and we'll forage for what we can eat tonight." All eyes were on him, their faces expectant. He continued. "And you'll need to pay attention to these lessons, because tomorrow? It's going to be on you guys to do it all yourselves. Understand?"

They nodded.

"This doesn't seem like much of a team exercise," the nerd

with glasses complained. "It sounds like you're just showing us stuff. How are we supposed to apply that to our lives in the corporate world?"

His first nonbeliever. Grant had told him to prepare for this sort of thing. Didn't make him have to like the guy, though. Dane put on his most charming smile and tried to recall the man's name. He stared at him for a long moment.

"We just got here, Pete," Miranda murmured, shooting Dane a meaningful look. "I'm sure this all has a purpose."

Pete. He'd remember that now. "It does have a purpose," Dane agreed. "Which I was just about to get to, if you'd give me a moment." Though his words were harsh, he kept the smile on his face.

"Sorry," Pete said, but he wasn't looking at Dane when he said it. His gaze was on sweaty, too-cute-for-this-trip Miranda, with her high-necked shirt that was sticking to her rather admirable cleavage and outlining it in a way that was far more blatant than a low neckline would have been.

Concentrate, Dane. You've seen plenty of breasts in your life, and that particular pair is here specifically to distract you.

Dane cleared his throat. "Like I was saying . . . this afternoon I will show you how to do six different skills. Each of you should pay attention, of course, but each of these skills will be the sole responsibility of one of you on the team. It will be your job to handle that particular chore for the group all week, and it will also be your job to show the others how to do your job. As you learn each other's skills, you'll see that all hands are needed to have a fully integrated campsite, just like a team. Understand?"

"Yes," they chorused back to him.

"But first . . . we're going to do a different kind of exercise," Dane said.

"Can we get something to drink first?" Pete piped up, an edge of a whine in his voice. "I'm freaking parched and I drank everything in my canteen already."

This was going to be a very long week with Pete around. "There's a stream nearby," he explained. "However, that stream is filled with bacteria. Any water you drink is going to have to be boiled first, unless you'd like to be on the receiving end of a nasty strain of giardia. And to boil water, what do we need first?"

"A cooking pot?" Miranda said helpfully. It was the first statement she'd directed to him since they'd left the lodge area.

"This week, you'll be stringing your canteen on a tripod and boiling the water over the fire," he said.

Miranda gave him a slow smile, as if they were sharing a secret. "Fire, then. We need a fire first."

That husky, playful timbre in her voice jogged his memory, and he caught himself grinning at her despite himself. When she smiled, he couldn't resist her. But he guessed that Grant and Colt knew that, too, and that was why they'd sent her on this trip.

His friends needed to butt the hell out. His mood taking a sour turn once more, Dane gestured at the woods. "That's right. First we need a fire, and to make a fire, we need wood. Since we are going to have a fire going all night, we're going to need a lot of wood. And here's how we're going to get it." He clasped his hands together again, and then gestured at each of the mini-teams. "The three pairs will split up and go in different directions. One of the partners will be blindfolded, using the team bandanas that we've provided for you. The other partner will be instructing you on where the wood is and guiding you without touching you. When your arms are full, you'll return to camp, drop off your load, and then the blindfolded partners will switch. You'll have equal time under the blindfold, and equal time to be the guide. Understand?"

"How do we know we won't get lost?" George said. "We don't know our way around these woods."

Dane had been prepared for this, and he pulled out a package of wristbands from his backpack. "These are GPS trackers that emit an electronic signal. If you get lost, I can find you. No worries."

He passed them out to the teams and one by one, they strapped the GPS trackers on their wrists. As he handed Miranda hers, he noticed there was a tiny crease in her smooth brow, as if she were unhappy with this turn of events.

"There a problem?" he said in a low voice to her.

She looked up, startled. "Oh. No, no problem." She quickly strapped her tracker to her wrist and turned to Pete. "You can be blindfolded first, though, okay?"

Pete shrugged. "Fine with me."

The teams blindfolded their partners and began to set off in the woods. One of the businessmen—Steve—barked orders to his partner in a booming voice that echoed in the woods. Dane made a mental note to have a chat with Steve later and discuss why it was bad to talk at supersonic levels in the forest, especially when some of the tasks coming up would require stealth and avoiding the other team.

His ears strained, and he could pick up Miranda's soft, husky voice. "Left, Pete, left," she was saying as she guided him past one tree and then another. "Two steps forward—I, no, two, Pete. Pete. Pete! Look out—"

He watched her cringe as her partner ran into a low-hanging branch. They seemed to be having a bit of trouble, so Dane planted the team flag in the center of camp, and then jogged over to trail behind Miranda and Pete.

"You've got to give me better directions than that," Pete was complaining to Miranda, stretching his hands out.

"My directions are perfectly fine," she argued with him. "Or they would be if you'd actually listen to them. When I tell you two steps, I mean two steps, okay?"

"Two steps," Pete agreed. He leaned forward, his hands searching as he moved. "Is there any wood nearby at least?

Miranda thought for a moment as Pete's hands flailed. "There's a fallen limb about three paces to your left," she began.

Pete immediately did a complete about face and plunged toward her. His hands landed squarely on Miranda's breasts.

Shit. Dane strode forward, ready to break the two of them apart. It was day one and already it was looking like he'd have a sexual harassment suit on his hands. This was bad. This was very, very bad. And judging from the startled—yet pleased—look on Pete's face, it wasn't entirely unintentional. That did not surprise Dane. The nerd had been gunning for sexy Miranda since she'd showed up.

He was, however, completely surprised when Miranda shoved Pete away and decked him square across the jaw.

FIVE

This was not shaping up as she'd planned.

Miranda trembled with anger as Dane stepped between her and Pete. He stretched an arm out to keep Miranda off of the fallen man, not that he needed to. She'd flattened him with one well-placed punch. Her hand throbbed like mad but that was all right—it could swell like a balloon and she wouldn't take back the hit.

Pete had totally deserved it. He pulled off his blindfold and stared up at the two of them, his glasses askew over his eyes and his expression shocked. His hand moved up to rub his jaw. "You hit me!"

She resisted the urge to clutch her collar closed, to make sure that there was not an ounce of cleavage exposed. Instead, she forced her hands down to her sides, and they clenched there like fists. "You grabbed me," she hissed back at him. "Don't you *ever* do that again."

"It was a mistake," Dane said, turning to face her. He put a hand on her shoulder and shifted, blocking her sight of Pete sprawled on the ground. "Let's calm down about this, all right?" There was a thread of concern in his voice, and his brow was furrowed as he looked down at her, as if he hadn't quite anticipated having a woman on his team and didn't know what to do with her. "You okay?"

She nodded, biting off any angry words. Instead, she crossed her arms over her chest protectively and stalked back to the camp flag, where they'd left their packs.

"Pete," Dane said in that easy voice. "Why don't you go and gather firewood on your own? I'll talk with Miranda and make sure there's no problem."

"Why should there be any problems?" Pete said defensively, his long fingers swiping at the grass stuck to his shirt. "She's the one that hit me."

"Go on," Dane said equally pleasantly, though Miranda doubted his tone was sincere. It sounded a little forced.

She glanced over out of the corner of her eye and watched Dane help the other man up, brushing off his clothes. They glanced over at her before Pete shrugged and headed off into the woods, leaning over to pick up a fallen branch. At that, Dane turned and began to walk back toward her.

Miranda worried at the tense set of his shoulders and the frown on his face. Shit. This wasn't working the way she planned. Her temper had gotten away from her when that creep had touched her boobs.

This wouldn't work. She needed to clear her head and concentrate. She wouldn't be able to seduce Dane if she got sent home for fighting with her partner. When Dane returned, she tilted her head and offered him a half smile, her hand fluttering back to her collar protectively. "Sorry. Knee-jerk reaction."

"You sure you're okay?" He said, not moving from in front of her. He scratched his head, rubbing at the closely cropped hair in a gesture she remembered from high school. "Do you want to go back? I can take you to the lodge if it's going to bother you being out here with six men. I don't want any problems this week."

"I'll be fine. He just took me by surprise and I reacted."

Dane looked skeptical.

"Look," she said and took a step forward. The smile curved her mouth, and she forced her voice to be teasing again. "If anyone gives me any trouble, I'll let them apologize before I hit them. I've only got one good hand left." She tried to put her hand on his chest, bridge the space between them.

He stopped her, catching her hand in his, and examined her knuckles. His fingertips brushed over them and he pulled her hand close to his face. "Did you hurt yourself?"

She watched him curiously, her gaze focused on her hand in his. She could feel the rough callus of his hands against hers, and she had to admit that it sent a tingle through her. "I'm all right. I took a self-defense class in college. I know how to punch a creep without hurting myself."

Dane glanced up at her and gave her a wry smile, rubbing her knuckles with his thumb. "Can you refrain unless it's absolutely necessary? That creep paid the same two grand you did for the survival trip. And if he needs to be hit again, I might have to be the one to do it."

She laughed, and then was horrified at the giggle that escaped her throat. Evil Miranda *never* giggled. She should have given a sultry chuckle instead. But it made Dane smile, and so she moved forward to lay her hand on his chest again, giving him a very interested look. "Want to kiss my boo-boos and make them better?"

He released her hand as if he'd been burned, turning to the campsite. "We need to start building the fire. Bring over some of that wood, will you?"

Miranda resisted the urge to put her hands on her hips, frustrated at his skittishness. "Fine," she said, careful to hide the annoyance she felt. She had Dane alone for a few precious minutes, and she needed to capitalize on it. She glanced over at him as he crouched near the spot he'd selected for the fire, tossing a few rocks out of the area. Her gaze slid to his ass, tight in his shorts.

And she got an idea. Moving to the firewood, Miranda bent at the knees and crouched in a way that would make her shorts ride low and expose her black lace thong and the pale expanse of skin it drew across. She glanced over her shoulder, but Dane was facing the other direction. Dammit. She turned and looked at the biggest log—no more than the size of her arm around. She could pick that up no problem, but doing so wouldn't serve her purposes. So she feigned a deep sigh. "I think this one is too heavy. What do you think?"

She glanced over her shoulder again to see if he was looking at her.

This time, he was. He turned and she saw his expression change from exasperation at her weakness to . . . something else. His gaze slid down to her skimpy black thong, evident over the low waist of her shorts, and she resisted the urge to stand up and cover her backside and then clutch at her neckline.

Evil Miranda would *not* approve of covering up.

He seemed to swallow hard. "Are you wearing a thong?"

"What, this old thing?" she drawled, and gave her hips a little wiggle that caused her to wobble slightly on her feet. "Of course." As if she never left her house in anything but Victoria's Secret's tawdriest.

He moved closer to her, his gaze still on the expanse of flesh she was exposing. "You do realize that's not exactly camping appropriate?"

She shrugged and tossed her long hair over her shoulder, watching as his gaze flicked to it, then back down to her thong. "It's a little tight against my skin," she admitted in a coy, secretive voice. "I don't suppose you could . . . help me with it?"

Even that was a little forward. Very Evil Miranda. Good Miranda would have been totally mortified.

But Dane moved down next to her, his voice low and husky in her ear as he spoke. "Sure thing."

She arched her back and closed her eyes, anticipating his touch.

His hand grasped the back of her panties roughly, and her eyes flew open at the uncomfortable wedgie. Before she could protest, he pulled the thong away from her skin. She heard the click of his knife, and then the chopping hiss as he sliced through the fabric.

Dane let go of her and she fell forward, the fabric loose between her legs. Her hand flew to her bottom and sure enough, he'd cut the thong square up the backside. The crotch of it dangled against her leg. She gasped. "What did you just do?"

"We're on a survival trip, Miranda." The look in his cool green eyes was no-nonsense. "First rule of survival is to be as comfortable as you can, and you should remember that." He stood and turned away, then extended a hand toward her. "Or wasn't that what you had in mind when you asked me to help you with them?"

His eyes were knowing as they looked at her, glimmering with amusement. Dane knew her game and he wasn't going to make it easy for her.

She glared at him.

He gestured at the wood behind her. "Hand me one of the lighter logs, would you?"

"I can't believe you just cut my panties!"

"Probably a good thing you packed a whole bag of them, then, eh?"

Forget revenge and ruining his life. She was going to kill him before the week was out. Forcing a tight smile to her face, she slapped a piece of wood into his hand. "Good thing," she echoed sourly. "I'd hate to have to go without."

His laugh strangled off and he gave her an intense look, and then stomped away.

Evil Miranda two; Dane Croft zero.

Miranda was going to be the death of him this week.

Dane couldn't get the sight of her thong out of his mind. He tried not to think about her panties when the others returned with enough wood for the evening. He tried not to think about it when he cut a few longer branches and began to show Steve (who had been designated as the shelter expert) how to build a shelter. He tried not to think about the pretty thong or the sweet curves of skin it laced over as he showed Will how to strain water using a waterproof hat. He tried not to think about it when he showed Miranda how to build a fire using the bow method and her long, glossy hair swung over her shoulder as her arms worked. And he really, really tried not to think about the fact that he hadn't had sex in more than three years.

But he thought about it anyhow.

It was like the image was burned into his memory and no matter what he tried to focus on, the vision of it kept rising in his head. Of the soft globes of her ass, pale against the thong, making him think of how she'd look riding his cock, that delicious ass bouncing as he pumped into her. He'd been hot for the teenage Miranda, but the Miranda nine years later was burning a hole in his mind and making his dick primed for sex 24/7.

Correction, he thought, his mind going back to that damned thong. Nothing but sex with *her*. No one else. *You've been waiting nine years for this. And she wants it—wants you.*

They banked the fire and prepared for sleep. It was early in the evening but the team was drooping and the sun was down. They looked exhausted and tired, and even water and their PowerBars couldn't perk them up.

"We'll call it an early night," he announced, throwing a heavy log over the fire's coals, steering his gaze away from Miranda, where she looked slightly sweaty and disheveled and completely and utterly delicious. "Be ready to get going first thing in the morning, as we're going to change campsites and the real survival will begin."

One of the men groaned, but the others got up and stretched, heading to the larger of the two shelters. It was a lean-to with a thick amount of deadfall tossed on the wind-facing side and crosshatched with leaves and branches. The ground had been smoothed and the packs lay underneath.

"How's this going to work?" Steve had said earlier. "We have one shelter, six guys, and a woman."

They had ended up building Miranda a separate small lean-to a few feet away so she didn't have to huddle with the men. She went and sat under it, adjusting her pack before lying down on the hard ground and using it as a pillow. As Dane watched, she crossed her arms over her chest and seemed to huddle in, bracing against the cold. She looked small and alone as the other men piled into the larger shelter, and Dane couldn't help himself—he went over to check on her.

"You going to be okay over here?"

"No problem." She gave him a tired thumbs-up, then hugged her arms close again.

He hesitated. "If you get too cold, just crawl in with us. We'll be fine thanks to body heat."

"I'd rather not, but thanks for the offer," she said, closing her eyes to end the conversation. "I'm good here."

Dane nodded and went back to join the others. He glanced over at Miranda one last time, but she had her back to him.

Dane's offer was the perfect opportunity, Miranda thought as she shivered in her shelter. Sleep wasn't happening—not with the chill bite on the ground and the fact that she really didn't have anything much warmer to wear. This camping trip was an exercise in survival, but the next time she opted to "survive" she'd pack some thermal underwear first. As it was, her light jacket wasn't helping much.

The men didn't seem to have the same problem—she could hear them snoring quietly. Occasionally one would move around, shifting to try and get comfortable. The fire popped, but other than that, the camp was silent.

It gave her a lot of time to think. And the main thing she thought about? Her battle plan to seduce Dane. The fact that he'd sliced her thong off had thrown her for a loop. He'd seemed interested—really interested—but he'd given her the worst kind of brush-off with that insulting move.

Did he not find her attractive? Was that it? In high school, he'd been a flirt and had teased all the girls—including her. When he played hockey for the Vegas Flush, she'd heard all kinds of rumors about whom he was dating—London Harris, the sexy socialite who loved to be in the tabloids. Molly Sun, the starlet with the yellow curls and huge breasts. Susie Lynn Jacobs, the ingénue country singer. The list read like an issue of *People*'s Most Beautiful. And he was totally ignoring her.

Miranda's hand went to her collar and she grasped it, making sure that it didn't gape open. Men flirted with her occasionally—at the library, at the county fair, when she'd gone for her job interview. Even Pete had shown interest. Why was Dane not interested? She was practically throwing herself at him.

Well, she amended, "throwing herself at him" was relative. As she was not the best flirter in the world, she acknowledged that maybe she wasn't doing enough to show her interest. Maybe he thought she was just being a tease? It was time to be totally straight with Dane and show him exactly what she wanted.

Sucking in a deep breath, she got up from her lean-to and approached the men's.

They were bundled together like puppies—all neat and lined up, their feet hanging out of the shelter. She studied them for a minute, looking for a familiar form. Dane was on the far edge of the shelter, lying on his side. She approached and knelt beside him.

All was silent in the camp, and Miranda inched closer to Dane, studying him as he slept. His shoulders seemed broader than ever from this angle, his hips narrow and tapered. She moved in and gave him a slight shake. Nothing. She frowned and slid her hand onto Dane's pant leg, just above the knee.

He didn't stir.

She grew bolder. Her hand moved to his groin. She cupped his cock in her hand and sighed at the warmth—and weight—there. Very nice.

Dane stirred, and she felt him jerk awake. Felt him wake up below, too, just as she slid her hand away. *Count on a little late-night fondling to wake a man up,* she thought wryly.

"Miranda?" he whispered in a strangled voice.

"Dane," she said, kneeling close and leaning low toward him. "Can I talk to you?"

"Everything okay?"

She waved for him to keep his voice down. "Yes. I just . . . want to talk. Away from camp."

He squinted up at her, then at the campsite. "We can talk in the morning," he said, rubbing his eyes. "Go back to sleep."

God, the man was obtuse. She was tempted to reach over and

grab his cock again, because that seemed to be the only thing he was listening to. "Dane, I need . . ." she paused for a minute, thinking. Then she lied, "I need your help. Something bit me."

His eyes flew open at that, and he stared up at her, then got to his feet. "Something bit you?" he whispered again. "Where?"

Might as well go all in, she thought. "In a personal spot."

Dane swore under his breath and then raked a hand over his closely trimmed hair. He reached into his backpack and grabbed one of the emergency flashlights and the first-aid kit, then gestured for her to follow him out of camp.

When they got into the edge of the woods, out of the clearing and away from the camp, he clicked the flashlight on. "Now, show me where—"

She rushed forward and put her hands over the flashlight, hiding the beam. Miranda glanced over where the others slept. No one had stirred—good. "Can you turn that off? I don't want the others finding us."

He gave her an exasperated look. "How am I supposed to tell where you've been bitten if I can't see it?"

"I'll show you," she said. "You can feel it on my skin. Just, please. Don't wake up the others." If he did, her window of opportunity tonight was going to end up a big fat failure.

A long moment ticked past, and then Dane sighed, clicked off the flashlight, and turned to her. "All right."

She could see the silhouette of him in the moonlight, highlighting the wide sweep of his shoulders, and she felt another excited thrill pass through her. When was the last time she'd been this hyped up to touch a guy?

Answer: nine years.

"Show me, then," he said in a low voice.

She took his hand and instead of placing it on her skin, she began to walk farther into the woods, to put as much distance between camp and the two of them as possible.

She expected Dane to protest, but he only followed her lead, his large, warm hand loose in hers. When they'd walked a good distance away and made it deeper into the woods, she stopped under a tree. "Here's good."

"You said something bit you?" Dane's voice was skeptical, as if he wasn't sure what she was up to anymore. Was that amusement in his voice? Oh, she hoped so—if he was furious, she'd never get to put her hands all over him.

And I'll never get my revenge, she added at the last moment, a bit ashamed that it hadn't been the first thought to spring to mind.

"It did," she lied, pulling his hand against her stomach under her shirt. She hid the shiver of desire she felt at his fingers against her bare skin. "Let me show you."

His chuckle rumbled low. "I'm guessing it's not a snake, then, if we're trekking all over the woods."

"Not a snake," she quickly agreed, looking up at him. God, his cheekbones looked amazing in the moonlight. She'd forgotten how incredibly sexy Dane was, how much looking at him made her wet with excitement.

"Does the skin burn?"

Oh, *absolutely.* Her hand pressed over his where it rested on her flat stomach, just above her belly button.

His fingers brushed against her stomach, sending a pulse of heat through her body. His whisper grew intimate, as if the fact that he was touching her and they were very, very alone had suddenly occurred to him. "I don't feel anything, Miranda."

"It's lower," she lied, her eyes watching his moonlit face, waiting to see if he'd take the bait. They stood so close together that she could feel his warm breath on her neck.

Dane paused for a long, long moment, and then gave her a knowing look. "Lower?"

She nodded, not trusting her voice. *Touch me*, she wanted to whisper. *Please. Everything hinges on you touching me.*

His fingers brushed at her waistband. "Lower?"

"Yes," she said. Her hand clutched at his shirt as she waited.

He looked up at her and his hand moved boldly down her belly. His hand slid into her shorts. "Where are your panties?"

"Some guy cut them off of me earlier," she said, her voice husky.

His hand skimmed past the curls of her sex and slipped between the folds of her pussy in a sudden move that had her gasping.

"Down here?" he asked in a husky voice. "Is this where you're burning? Because you're certainly wet." His fingers brushed against her clit and her body stiffened in a hot rush of desire. He rubbed the slick bud with his fingertips. "I'm starting to think you haven't been bitten at all."

She clung to his shoulders, her fingernails digging into his skin as his hand flexed in her shorts, small gasps erupting from her throat. "You—you have me all figured out, it seems," she managed to whisper, the whisper turning into a whimper as his clever fingers gave her clit another stroke. Her head tilted back and she leaned against the tree, her hips bucking against his hand. Oh my God. That was so good. If he could just keep touching her there—

His hand started to pull away and she gave a small cry, her hand moving down to rest over his.

"What are you playing at, Miranda?" he said low in her ear, his face pressing against her neck. He didn't move his hand from her hot, wet sex, but his fingers had stopped their rubbing of that most delicious of spots.

She could have wept in disappointment.

He stared down at her, his gaze intense. "Is this some sort of trick?"

"Trick? No," she said, tilting her face toward his. "I'm just . . . I . . ."

What could she tell him that he would possibly believe? The words froze in her mouth. His lips were inches away from hers and she longed to move her face closer to his, kiss him, feel that tongue stroke into her mouth in each conquering sweep. But his lips were firm and hard with anger. He wouldn't kiss her back.

"Then why don't you tell me what's going on? You've been after me ever since we laid eyes on each other, Miranda. And while I'm flattered, I have to wonder what your game is."

Shit. Well, okay, maybe she was being obvious—too obvious.

She stared up at him, acutely aware of his hand still down her shorts. One nice squirm and she bet she could get his fingers to brush against her clit again—but how humiliating would that be? To try and get off against a man who wasn't responding?

So she took a deep breath and pulled her hand off of his, placing it on his T-shirt. That wasn't much better—she could feel the finely corded ropes of muscle in his arms, and that made her think of his hand down her shorts all over again. She was getting wetter just thinking about it. "I . . ."

His fingers twitched against her clit, a little prompting motion, and he leaned in toward her, pinning her between his hard body and the tree. "Well?"

"I . . . um . . ." She stalled, thinking hard. Then she bit her lip and confessed the truth—or at least part of it. "I can't have an orgasm."

That was clearly not the answer he'd been expecting. He frowned down at her, and then his fingers gave a little swirling motion against her clit, eliciting another shuddering gasp from her. "Really? Because you seem to be responding to my touch pretty well."

His voice has dipped husky again, and she could have celebrated. He was listening to what she had to say. She fought a surge of excitement.

Her fingers dug into his shoulders again and she gave a little trembling gasp when he slid a finger farther down, away from her clit. One thick digit brushed against the opening of her sex. Her knees threatened to collapse. "I can't have an orgasm. With a man. In bed."

She was finding it hard to concentrate, his finger making small little circles against the opening of her sex, where she was wettest, tickling her in the most erotic fashion.

He leaned even closer to her, her breasts pressing against his chest, and she lifted her face to his, startled to see his face looming so close that she could practically see beard stubble. His lips were close to her own. "Women, then?"

"What? No." Her hips rocked against his hand and she whimpered. It was so hard to concentrate.

"What do you mean?"

"I mean . . . I can't shut my brain off during sex. And when I heard you were back in town, I remembered . . ."

"That night in the closet?" he said huskily. "Back at graduation?"

She flinched, thinking of the camera.

"I remember that," he said in a low rumble, and his mouth dipped against her neck, pressing a light kiss there. "How my hand had been on you, just like this, and you came all over my fingers."

She shuddered at that, pleasure washing over her. "I remember that," she murmured.

"You didn't have a problem coming apart in my arms then," he said, and his finger slipped deep inside her, giving a gentle thrust.

"I know," she said, her breathing coming hard and fast. She wanted to lift her leg around his hips, to grind her hips against his hand, to do . . . something. But she was pinned between him and the tree. "But that was a long time ago. I've had—trouble—since then."

Trouble was putting it mildly. More like counting tiles on the ceiling while her boyfriend of the moment tried unsuccessfully to elicit a reaction from her.

His mouth brushed against her throat again, and she could feel the hint of beard stubble scrape her skin. "So you want to try again? With me?"

She nodded. "See if it's me, or if it's them."

Dane's face lifted away from her neck and hovered an inch from her lips. "Miranda Hill," he said in a low, husky voice. "You should definitely know that it's them."

"Is that a yes?"

"It's a definite yes."

And he kissed her again, his lips descending on her own parted ones, his tongue sliding into her mouth with a powerful thrust that his finger deep inside her mimicked. Her hips rocked with that, and she made a sound of need low in her throat.

His tongue thrust again, in time with his finger, and she began to feel that slow, wonderful build that only seemed to come with her vibrator. Her mouth parted wider under his, and when his tongue stroked into her mouth again, her tongue caressed it, submitting to him, telling him how much she wanted him.

He gave one last thrust of his finger into her sex and then broke off the kiss, staring down at her. His finger slid from her pussy and brushed her clit again, sending electric currents of desire racing through her. "I suppose heavy petting isn't going to cut it?"

"It might," she admitted, clinging to him. She didn't want his hands to move away from where they were, setting all her nerve endings aflame. "We can keep trying. I don't mind."

Dane pressed another long, searing kiss to her mouth, and then his hand slid from her skin. She could have wept with disappointment at that.

He chuckled at her reaction. "I'm not going anywhere just

yet. Take your top off. I want to see those pretty breasts. I've been thinking about them nonstop all day."

The words sent a shiver of delight racing through her, and a dash of fear. *There won't be a camera here*, she told herself, fighting the urge to check her surroundings. Dane wouldn't have known that she was trying to seduce him, wouldn't know to wire this area. It was all in her imagination.

But her moves were mechanical and jerky as she gripped the hem of her shirt and pulled it over her head, then tossed it on the ground. Her black bra cups stood out in stark contrast against her pale skin in the moonlight, and he groaned at the sight. His fingers brushed against the curve of her breast and she shuddered.

"Are you sure you want to do this, Miranda? We barely know each other anymore."

She gave a small, nervous laugh and slid her hands under his shirt, feeling the warmth of his rippled, taut muscles under her fingertips. "You should have thought of that before you had your hand in my shorts."

There was a flash of white in the darkness—his grin, she realized—and he pulled his shirt off, tossing it next to hers on the ground. Her mouth went dry at the sight of him. She remembered Dane from high school—tall and rangy with a wide triangle of too-lean shoulders, and a boyish chest. Nine years had changed that; he rippled with muscle now, his body thick with it. His chest was still almost hairless, and she saw a tattoo of a twisting playing card on one shoulder—the logo for the Las Vegas Flush, his old team. Her fingers brushed against it, then down his chest, exploring his body. Not an inch of fat anywhere. She supposed if she had to use a man for revenge, this was the best sort of specimen.

"Do you approve?" he said, one palm moving to cup one of her breasts. "Been nine years since we saw each other with our tops off."

"It's . . . acceptable," she teased, her fingertips scraping over one taut nipple, and then she gasped when he used the same motion on her. "And what about me? Do I pass muster?"

His fingers slid to her bra strap, easing it down her shoulder, and he kissed the bared flesh of her shoulder. "You are the sexiest thing I have seen in a long time."

That made the liquid heat surge back through her body again and she trembled a little, leaning in and sliding her hands to his waist when his kiss on her shoulder turned into his tongue dancing along her collarbone. Heat built and began to throb between her legs again, her sex getting wet with need once more.

His hand reached behind her back and Dane unhooked her bra. Before she could squeak her surprise, his mouth captured her own again, and he kissed away any sound she might have made, the delicious stroke of his tongue hypnotizing her once more. This time, when she moved to lift a leg against his, he encouraged it, letting her slide over his braced thigh and straddle it. Her dark hair fell forward over her shoulders and she watched him, breathless, waiting to see what he thought of her breasts.

He curled his fingers around one heavy globe and brushed his thumb against the nipple. "When we were in high school, I thought you had the most amazing breasts I had ever seen." He stared down, seemingly fascinated as a nipple puckered against his touch, and then palmed the other one. "Hasn't changed. Damn, Miranda. You are beautiful."

That sent a quiver of pleasure through her body and she rocked her hips against his thigh, lifting her arms to wrap around his neck and pull him in for a kiss again. She wanted to press her breasts against his chest, to feel her nipples against that hot wall of muscle.

He didn't release her breasts from his grasp, just continued to brush the peaks with his thumbs, turning them into twin points of heat as he kissed her, his tongue sweeping and stroking against her mouth. She had thought she'd be the aggressor in the encounter, but as soon as he'd realized what she wanted sexually, he'd become the dominant one . . . and she found it incredibly arousing.

He leaned back a little, letting his mouth trail down her collarbone and working his way downward, pressing kisses against her skin, sliding down until he reached her breasts and his mouth flicked against one nipple. That brought a gasp of pleasure to her lips, and she arched against his thigh again, rubbing her sex against the hard angle of it.

"Damn," Dane swore against her skin, then pressed a kiss there. "You have the most amazing breasts. I could spend hours here." But before she could tell him that was fine with her, he moved up and captured her mouth in another hot, short kiss. "Take your shorts off, Miranda. Now."

He took a step backward and she complied, undoing the laces that held her cargo shorts up and shimmying them down her thighs. She dropped them to the ground and stepped out of them, her hands going back to his clothing. Miranda slid her fingers to his fly.

Dane groaned at that, letting her fingers dance along the zipper of his shorts, undoing it and helping him slide them down his legs. They were quickly followed by his boxers, and his cock was exposed. It was a nice specimen, she had to admit—no wonder Dane had been so popular with women. His cock was long and thick and utterly beautiful, with a large crown and just a hint of a curve to it where it jutted from his body.

Definitely a lot larger than her last boyfriend's, she realized with pleasure. She glanced down at his naked legs and noticed he still wore his hiking boots, just like she still wore her sneakers. "Should I take off my shoes?"

"No," he said, and when she reached for his cock, he wrapped her fingers in his and turned her around, until her back was resting against his chest. "Not tonight. The ground is wet."

"But—"

His arms wrapped around her from behind and he nuzzled her neck again. "You're thinking too much." His hand trapped one breast, his other sliding to her sex as he pressed more kisses on her neck and shoulder.

She forgot all about shoes.

Then his fingers touched her clit again. She clung to his hands, riding his motions as he thrust against her bare backside, his fingers mimicking the rocking of his hips. His fingers slipped into her sex and thrust again. "You ready for this, Miranda? Ready for me?"

"More than ready," she breathed.

"I can tell you are," he said against her neck, his fingers thrusting into her pussy one last time. "You're so wet you're soaking."

She shivered at that, and didn't protest when he moved away from her and bent to retrieve the first-aid kit. He pulled a box of condoms out and stared at it in surprise. "Fucking Brenna packed an entire box of condoms," he rasped. "Don't know if that's just fucked-up or brilliant." He ripped the box of condoms open and pulled one from the rest. He glanced back to her. "Put your hands on the tree."

Her hands rested on the bark of the tree and she glanced over her shoulder, watching him. He rolled on the condom and put his hands on her hips, pulling her backward a little. He nudged her knees apart until she was spread wide, her outstretched arms bracing against the tree for balance, her legs cocked open, her body bent over slightly.

Miranda's entire body tensed, waiting.

Dane's hips brushed against hers and she felt the head of his cock nudge against her sex, seeking entrance. She sucked in a breath, anticipating the hard slide of him into her body. Nothing happened for a long moment, and she was about to protest when she felt him sink in.

She whimpered in response. She hadn't had sex in a while and he felt . . . big.

"So fucking tight," he said in a low voice; his teeth gritted. "Feels so good."

Her fingers dug into the bark of the tree and she bit her lip, willing her body to relax. She flexed her hips, encouraging him to move, but Dane wouldn't be rushed. He anchored her hips against his and gave a slight pump before withdrawing.

She gave a whimper of distress at this, not liking the fact that he drew away. Her body was on fire with need, her blood throbbing in her veins, and she was so tempted to just reach down and start to play with her own clit so she could go over the edge that he'd been teasing away from her—

With a swift motion, Dane thrust again, and she forgot what she was thinking. A deep push, and he rotated his hips slightly as he pressed deeper into her, this time not stopping until she'd taken all of him.

She gave a low moan at the sensation of being filled—desire began to move through her faster, and she gave a little squirm, flexing her hips and encouraging him to fuck her.

"Tell me what you want, Miranda," he said in a low voice, leaning over her until he covered her, his stomach pressing against her back. "Tell me what you want and I'll give it to you."

Her breath rasped in her throat, and she swallowed hard, her thighs quivering when he gave another small thrust, more of a tease than what she wanted. "I want you to fuck me," she breathed.

She was rewarded with a hard thrust, but then he stopped again.

"Please, Dane," she said, flexing her hips so she could slide along his cock. "I want you to fuck me harder. Faster."

Dane thrust again, and again, two sharp bolts that made her toes curl with pleasure. Then he slowed, pumping in and out, slow and methodical and so very good. The constant, steady motion of his body rocking into her own drove her utterly insane with need. He'd thrust, then pull back, then thrust again, all slow and unhurried, and she raised her hips roughly against him, a wordless request. He seemed to realize that she needed something more. "Is this how you like it, Miranda? Or do you want it rougher?"

"Rougher," she breathed. "I need you to drive me crazy. Make me think of nothing but sex."

The next thrust was so hard she nearly bounced off her feet, and she gave a small cry and clung to the tree. "Oh God," she said. "Like that. *Yes.*"

He gave her another wild thrust, and then began to pound into her as hard as he could, ignoring all their playful games, and she could have cried out with delight. This was what she wanted and expected from her first encounter with Dane. For him to make love to her, rough and wild, forcing her to concentrate on the slam of his body against her own, the slap of his balls against her pussy as he thrust over and over again.

She felt the familiar elusive heat building, and began to cry out softly with each successive thrust, until her cries came together so quickly that she was doing little more than keening her need into the forest, despite Dane's halfhearted attempts to shush her.

And still it wasn't enough. She felt the build but couldn't quite seem to find the edge. Couldn't quite get there, even as he pumped harder and harder. Frustration began to make her building orgasm ebb, and she fought even harder to bring it back, but it was no good. "Dane," she said, her voice sobbing the word. "I need . . . I can't . . ."

"I've got you," he said against her ear, and she felt his hand slide between her legs, felt him stroke her clit. "Come for me."

He'd wait for her to come. The thought exploded in her mind

at the same time as the orgasm did. She immediately shattered, an involuntary cry escaping her throat, her muscles locking in the onset of the most intense orgasm she'd ever had. He said something but she didn't hear it, the blood roaring through her ears as he drove into her a few more times and came himself, his body stiffening behind hers.

Miranda panted, still clutching the tree. She should turn around, give him a flirty look. Toss him an airy smile and thank him for proving a point for her. But she was so stunned in the aftermath of the orgasm that she was . . . well, she was just a little lost for words.

She remembered their make-out session in the closet all those years ago. She remembered her previous boyfriends, unable to bring her to orgasm, who'd eventually given up on satisfying her in bed when she remained cold and unable to respond. She remembered buying a vibrator just because she'd been so frustrated, and it had helped, but it was nothing like . . . this.

Holy shit.

One thing was clear—she *totally* had to do this again.

SIX

Well, fuck.

Dane hitched his pants around his hips again, trying not to look over at Miranda. It hadn't even been twenty-four hours and he'd broken his word. The first piece of tail that had come swinging at him, and he'd gone after her with grabby hands.

Colt and Grant were going to kill him. Murder him dead and bury him in the woods. And he'd deserve it. He scrubbed a hand over his face, thinking hard. It just wasn't fair. Of all the women they'd decided to rope in for their little scheme, did it have to be Miranda? And did she have to look as good as—no, better than—she had in high school?

He glanced over at her, where she remained propped up against the tree. She hadn't moved. Waiting to gloat at him? He pulled his shirt down over his pants and studied her face.

Miranda wore the most blissed-out expression he'd ever seen. Her mouth hung open slightly, her lips curved into a smile, and she stared dreamily out into the forest. Her clothes were still on the ground, her naked breasts bare in the moonlight. She'd propped her arms up over her head and simply leaned against the tree, as if she needed time to contemplate everything.

That was unexpected. The sight of her languid smile made his body surge with lust again, and he felt the urge to reach over and pull her away from that tree and against him, and see if he could make that contented look change to one of desire again.

But he couldn't. She was off-limits. Clenching one fist to rein himself in, Dane waited for Miranda to say something. And when she didn't move, he took the initiative. "Well?"

Those blissful, sleepy eyes turned to him, and she gave him a satisfied look. "Well, what?"

"What now?" He scowled at her. Was she going to run to Colt and Grant and tell them that he hadn't been able to keep it in his pants after all?

She blinked, then looked at him, really looked at him for the first time. "Right. We're done here, aren't we?" She tugged her long hair over her breasts and bent over to pick her shorts back up.

"We need to talk—" he began.

"No, we don't," she said cheerfully.

"What about your bite?" he said.

Her gaze moved back to his mouth and she looked confused—and turned on—for a moment. Hell. His body hardened in response.

"You said you were bitten . . . ?"

"Oh!" Her expression changed, and he could have sworn she was blushing in the dark. "That's right." She looked up at him, sheepish. "I lied."

He'd guessed that. "So it was all a plot to drag me out here into the woods and have sex with me?"

She tied the laces on her shorts and gave a throaty giggle as she put her shirt back on. "Sort of. Yeah. I guess it was, wasn't it?"

"And that's why we need to talk about this. I need to know what you plan on saying to the others—"

She yawned, patting her mouth delicately. "I'm not going to tell them anything. That would ruin any fun we plan on having this week."

Fun? This week? Did she intend for them to do this again? He stared at her in surprise. So this wasn't some sort of trap after all? Or was it, and he just couldn't seem to figure it out?

Miranda moved away from him and gestured to the camp. "I'm going to head back now. You hang back a few minutes, and then follow me in so it doesn't look like we were together."

He said nothing.

"Oh, for heaven's sake," she said, then moved back to him, grabbed the front of his shirt, and pulled his mouth down against hers for a quick, hot kiss. Her tongue flicked against his, and then before he could react, she pulled away again. "Like I said, we're not telling anyone about this. All right?"

And then she walked away, leaving Dane behind her in the woods, dumbfounded and staring.

What the hell had just happened? Had she just used *him*? For sex?

That . . . was unexpected.

• • •

Always a light sleeper, Miranda stirred awake before the others. The sun was just beginning to purple the edges of the sky. After she'd returned to her solitary shelter, Dane had paced around camp. She saw that he'd bunked down with the rest of the men in the shelter, his body slightly apart from theirs. The others still snored.

She stretched in her bunk, feeling incredible physically . . . and incredibly torn emotionally. She was a bit sore between her legs and her palms were scratched up from how hard she'd gripped the tree last night, but . . . her body felt alive and the blood sang in her veins.

And it was all due to that bastard Dane, which was why she was a little torn at the moment.

She'd slept with her worst enemy. Told him her biggest secret—that she couldn't have an orgasm with a man. Just blabbed it and left herself completely vulnerable to him. It was an uneasy feeling. Part of her hadn't expected to get so caught up in the moment. She'd suspected it would end up like every other sexual encounter she'd ever had: She'd come on to the man, they'd kiss, and when it progressed past kissing, her body would turn off like a switch and she'd spend the next ten minutes waiting for him to be done and faking an orgasm. But last night? She hadn't had to fake anything. He'd caught her off guard and had knocked down all her defenses.

And she'd come. So incredibly hard that it had nearly made her see stars. Miranda wasn't sure if she should be happy that she'd had such intense sex, or devastated that she'd responded like a wanton to a man she professed to hate. She shouldn't be upset about that, though, right? She was on this trip to be strong and aggressive and take charge of her life . . . and to ruin his.

So she'd used him a little last night. It was payback, in a sense, for the way he'd destroyed her reputation. And so she got an utterly amazing orgasm out of it—the first one that hadn't involved her vibrator in nine years. So what?

She didn't regret it. In fact . . . she wanted to do it again.

Using a man for her needs had been so very gratifying. There'd been no emotion involved, just animal attraction. Even this morning, she knew that any rational woman would be riddled with guilt, but, she admitted to herself, her guilt was not nearly as great as that pleased part of her that had enjoyed herself, enjoyed using Dane, and wanted to do it all over again.

After all, she had an entire week left in this class. Why *not* enjoy herself? Explore what Dane's body had to offer, and then discard him like yesterday's trash once she'd gotten her revenge?

It sounded good to her. A little mercenary, but she didn't care. After all, it was her life. She was going to take something for herself, damn it. So she didn't have her camera with her. She'd have a week of naughty, illicit fucking, and top it off when she got back home and exacted her revenge. Sounded good to her.

Feeling a bit wicked this morning, she moved to Dane's side and lay down next to him, a mere few inches away from his face. Miranda stared at his sleeping features. His mouth was parted slightly and the lines of his face were eased, making him look younger than his twenty-seven years. Her gaze skimmed the scars on his face—one on his nose just above the break, the small one through his eyebrow, and a longer one slashing across his chin and up to his lip. She was so close she could see the stubble on his face. It wouldn't take much for her to lean over and kiss him awake.

So she did, because she was all about taking what she wanted this week.

His mouth was relaxed against hers, and she felt the stubble of his cheek graze against her smooth skin. She kept the kiss gentle at first, pressing her mouth against his lightly, sucking on his lower lip and tasting its softness. His lower lip was full and it gave him a slightly pouty look that she'd gone wild over as a teenager. She'd loved tugging on that sultry lower lip with her teeth, and she remembered that he'd liked it, too. She did it now, heat curling through her body when she felt his tongue brush against her mouth as he awoke and responded to her kiss. He was kissing her back.

Encouraged, she let her tongue stroke into his mouth, at first coaxing and then bolder. His mouth relaxed against hers, and her tongue swept inside, tangling against his. When his tongue touched hers in return, the stroke hard and sure, her nipples tightened with pleasure at the sensation.

His hand tangled in her hair, and instead of kissing her back, he pulled her away. His expression was dismayed. "Miranda?"

"Hush," she said, tracing a finger along his jaw and leaning in for another kiss. Kissing Dane had been a delicious experience. She hadn't wanted to enjoy it, but . . . she had. Quite a bit. It was further proof that no matter how awful a person Dane was, she was attracted to him. The moment she'd placed her lips on his, her body had immediately flared with need. It had been a long time since she'd been in a relationship with a man—since college. And she was suddenly keenly aware of the lack and seemed to want to make up for lost time.

If revenge had to involve kissing Dane a lot, then she'd gladly turn herself over to the task. She slid a little closer, trying to take his mouth with her own again.

His hand remained firmly anchored in her hair, trying to hold her in place. She was trapped an inch away from his face. "Miranda, what are you doing?"

"Trying to kiss you," she whispered, her gaze focused on his mouth. It had thinned out into a hard line that she was very tempted to kiss into softness. His confusion just turned her on more. "Let go of my hair and I can get back to it."

Instead of doing as she asked, Dane sat up and rolled away. She gave him a frown as he stood up, but it smoothed away when he reached for her hand.

Miranda placed it in his and allowed him to help pull her off the ground. Immediately he began to tug her away from the camp, into the woods. An excited flutter started low in her belly, her pulse throbbing in all the right places. Were they going to go hide in the woods and have sex again? Could she handle a morning orgasm? She suddenly liked the thought of that very much, and licked her lips in anticipation. Oh boy, could she ever.

Who knew that her revenge would be so much *fun*?

There was a large tree with low-hanging branches at the edge of camp, and Dane pulled her toward it, his hand tight on her own. When they were behind the branches, she reached for him again, tilting her face up to his, a slight smile on her mouth. "Good morning, sunshine," she said and slid a hand along the front of his chest. Oh yum. She could feel washboard muscles and well-defined pectorals through the fabric of his shirt. Miranda resisted the urge to rub her hand all over his chest and explore his physique.

He pulled her hand off his chest and frowned down at her. "I think we need to talk."

She stiffened. That had not been the response she was expecting. Didn't most men like a sexually aggressive woman? "What's there to talk about?"

"This!" He gestured at her and then at his mouth. "The kissing and the . . . you know. Last night in the forest." He dropped his voice and looked over at the campsite to make sure the others weren't awake. "You and me. What the hell is going on here, Miranda?"

She rolled her eyes. "Do we really have to analyze it? I wanted to have sex with you to see what it'd be like, and so I did. Satisfied?"

Dane shook his head, frowning. "Whatever it is Colt and Grant set you up to do, you won, all right? No sense rubbing salt in the wound."

That made her flinch. She released his hand as if he were diseased and took a quick step away. "*Excuse* me?"

He crossed his arms over his chest, his mouth firming in disapproval. "I know Colt and Grant are behind this. I mean, it's pretty obvious. Our first week on the job and who happens to show up? My high school crush, looking just as amazing as the last time I saw her, and wanting nothing more than to jump my bones. Convenient, isn't it?" Dane glared down at her, as if he was cursing the fact that he was attracted to her. His hot gaze raked over her body. "They're obviously paying you to test my willpower. And it's obvious that I failed."

Her jaw dropped. Her hand went to her collar and she nervously tugged it up closer to her neck. "Well," Miranda said nervously. "That's a first."

"What is?"

"I've never been called a whore in one sentence, and flattered in the next. I'm not quite sure whether I should be insulted or amused, though I have to admit that I'm leaning toward insulted."

He rubbed a hand over his mouth, and it curved in a slow smile that irritated the shit out of her. "If it makes you feel any better, if I weren't on the job, I'd take you back into the woods again and fuck a few more orgasms out of you." His eyes smoldered down at her. "Since that's clearly what you're here for."

The arrogant piece of shit! Did he think she was all over him because someone had paid her money? Her hand clenched even harder. So much for enjoying kissing Dane—all she wanted right now was to kick him in the groin. Hard.

"That's sweet," she said in a dry voice. Her arms crossed over her chest and she gave him an angry, mulish look. "But if you call me a whore again, Pete's not going to be the only one nursing a bruised jaw. Understand me?"

"Are you mad at me? I was trying to flatter you. I haven't seen you in nine years and I have to admit that you look amazing." Dane's smile tilted. "Sorry if that offends you."

"That's not the part that offends me," she bit out. "It's the part where you keep saying someone paid me to sleep with you."

His easy grin disappeared entirely. "You mean Colt and Grant didn't approach you to . . . come to me?"

A sour taste built in her mouth. "I said all of three words to Colt yesterday. I haven't talked to Grant since high school. Why would they pay me to come out on a survival trip?"

Dane remained silent for a long moment. "That . . . wasn't what I meant. Did they ask you to hit on me?"

"No!" Her voice raised an outraged octave. "Why would I sleep with you for money?"

A hand covered her mouth. Dane pressed his hand over her lips, his palm warm. He glanced back at the camp to see if the others had awakened from the sound of their argument, but they slept on. Dane reached over and touched her arm, pulling her closer so they could talk quietly, his hand falling from her mouth. "Miranda . . ." he began, then stopped, studying her face for a long moment.

She felt the insane urge to tug at her collar.

"If you're not doing this because Colt or Grant put you up to it, then why did you sleep with me?"

"Jeez, I didn't realize I was that bad of a lay."

His gaze dropped to her mouth. "Not in the slightest," he said, his voice dipping to a husky tone. His thumb brushed against her lower lip. "But you can't think I wouldn't be suspicious of your motives. You packed an entire bag of lingerie for a survival trip."

"I told you why," she said defensively, pulling away. "I wanted to see if I could have a . . . you know"—she waved a hand—"with you, or if I was totally broken. And now that I know that I can . . . come"—she still blushed at saying the word—"with a man and not just a battery-powered toy, I'm satisfied. I don't need you any longer."

She was lying through her teeth, of course, to see if he would take the bait.

"Were you?" he said in a low, husky voice. His gaze remained on her mouth and he brushed his thumb over her lip again, tugging her mouth open a little. "Satisfied with that? Because it was just a quick meeting in the woods, Miranda. If you think that's the best I've got to offer, you're sorely mistaken."

Her knees trembled a little at the thought. "Oh?"

A slow smile curved his mouth, and he pulled her closer to him. His hand caressed her cheek and stroked down her neck, playing with the neckline of her shirt. Touching her as if he owned her—possessed her. The thought made her weak. "That was just one tiny little orgasm," he said. "I bet if you give me the chance, I could make you come two, maybe three times in a row."

"Three times?" Her breath caught a little at the thought. She'd read romance novels where the heroine screamed the entire time they had sex, and movies made it look like an hours-long marathon, of course, but her experiences had been sadly underwhelming in that respect. Even her rendezvous with Dane—while mind-blowing in itself—had been a brief excursion. "Is that normal?"

"It is when you're in bed with me," he said softly, and his hand slid down her back, fingers tickling her spine before resting on the small of her back. "Don't tell me you've never had a man lick that sweet pussy of yours for hours, making you come so often that your legs won't support you any longer?"

Her legs were having difficulty supporting her body right now. She felt weak, boneless like he described, and the urge to lean against him and sink into his warmth was nearly overwhelming. She realized he was watching her, waiting for her answer, and she shook her head. "It's none of your business, Dane, but I've had plenty of oral sex." That was a lie. She'd had some, but when it became obvious that she was just uncomfortable instead of enjoying herself, it was quickly taken off the table.

After a while, she'd given up on oral altogether. "Lots. So don't you worry about me."

"And no orgasms? I'm heartbroken at the thought. Those must have been some shitty boyfriends."

A laugh escaped her throat, and she quickly muffled it again, then gave him a skeptical look. "What makes you think I'm interested in another round, Dane? Maybe I sampled the goods and found them lacking."

"You didn't," he said confidently. His hand slid back up her spine and he cupped the base of her neck, pulling her close and tilting her head back. "Did you? I bet if I dropped to the ground and kissed that pussy of yours, you'd let me do whatever I wanted to you."

Dear God, it was true. Her fingers wrapped in his shirt and she clung to him. Dane was taller than her by a few inches, but he'd bent near and their faces were so close together that she could smell the musk of his skin and see the shadow of a beard on his chin. He licked his lips as if he were still thinking about putting his mouth on her pussy, and her entire body tingled in response, a throb starting low in her sex. His other hand slid to her ass, pulling her body against him. Her nipples grazed his chest and she gasped.

His mouth brushed against her own, giving her the most fleeting of kisses. "How about," he said softly, "I drop to my knees right now and give you a taste?"

"Do it," she breathed, her heart pounding in her breast.

He grinned at her and slid his hands to her waist. As she watched him, he dropped to his knees, his face going to the cradle of her thighs and—

"Hey," called a voice back at the camp. "Anyone seen Dane?"

Dane jerked upright, nearly knocking her over in his haste to get to his feet. The look in his eyes had gone from sexy to wildly paranoid in a flash.

With a sigh, she realized that she wasn't going to get what he'd promised after all. "Guess we'll never find out if you're full of hot air, will we? Shame."

The look he gave her was hot, and he pulled her in for a quick, fierce kiss. "Tonight. You don't say a thing, I don't say a thing, and we meet again tonight." Then he disappeared into the bushes, trudging his way back to camp.

Tonight? She curled her toes in anticipation at the thought, then sighed. The blood still throbbed in her veins and tonight was a very, very long day away. She waited a few minutes, then sauntered back to camp herself, tying the strings on her shorts as if to make it look like she'd been in the woods for a different reason.

Dane looked up as she reentered the camp and gave her a light wave, as if just now seeing her. What a faker. "Morning, Miranda. Sleep well?"

"Like a baby." She said the lie with a grin, and moved to the far side of the camp to get her pack. As she walked, she let her hips roll, and swung her long, tangled hair over her shoulder, knowing that he was watching. Dane wanted to see her tonight. That thrilled her just a little too much to fit in with her plans, and she frowned to herself. If this revenge idea was going to work, she needed to keep control of the situation. And Dane had just taken control a few minutes ago. Worse, she'd been ready and willing to give it to him.

She was going to need to be tougher if she wanted to get revenge on Casanova Croft, rather than just be one of his conquests.

SEVEN

Once the entire team was awake, they ate a small breakfast of the last of their carefully saved PowerBars, boiled water to refill their canteens, and then broke camp. The shelter was disassembled, the fire put out, and their bags repacked. Then they shouldered their packs to move on to the next location.

Dane showed them how to make a fire bundle that would keep an ember smoldering while they walked, and he handed it to Miranda to carry. "It's very important that you keep this going at all times," he said to her, his face utterly serious. "If you keep it smoldering, you can rekindle a fire with just a touch."

She stared at him, then at the fire bundle, her thoughts on things other than fire. Was his meaning what she thought it was . . . ? She decided to test that theory. "I think I can manage to keep a spark burning," she said in a low, husky voice, and licked her lips. "Even if it requires working it a little to fan the flame. It'll be worth it, don't you think?"

The look in his eyes grew hot, and she knew they were thinking the same thing. "See that you do. I'd hate to have to start all over, though . . . I'd be happy to show you how to tend it again, if need be."

Her pulse fluttered and she tried not to blush. Show her how to tend her fires, indeed.

As the team hiked, Dane pointed out flora and fauna to them. He showed them a poisonous spider, demonstrated which nuts were edible, and gave them a nature lesson as they walked. Occasionally he'd pick up a bit of tinder or a particular leaf, his eyes constantly scanning the environment.

It was actually really interesting information, and Miranda would have appreciated it if she hadn't been quite so distracted all the time. The vision of Dane's tight ass muddied her thoughts of revenge, as did the incredible sex they'd had last night. And the conversation this morning. She couldn't stop thinking about three orgasms. Three. It seemed like a sinful concept to her, when she struggled so hard to have just one in bed. Here he was offering her three. Her pussy clenched at the thought of him between her legs, languidly licking her to orgasm, and she felt the slick wetness of arousal.

Her spark was definitely going to keep going all day. By the time they were able to sneak away tonight, she'd probably come as soon as he said hello to her. And then he'd give her a smug smile, showing her that he was the shit and she was just another dumb girl who had fallen for his prowess in the sack . . .

But even as she said it to herself, the puzzle pieces didn't fit. Last night, when she'd come on to him, he hadn't acted like it was his due, or that he'd expected it. He'd seem shocked—and then flattered. And then, he was just as turned on as she was. That didn't match the womanizing flirt she remembered and the tabloids had loved to harass. The man in her mind was far more self-centered and smug than this one seemed. Had Dane learned humility at some point? Had Casanova Croft had all the womanizing arrogance beaten out of him?

She doubted it.

They hiked over a ridge and Dane suddenly staked the flag in the ground. "This will be our next campsite."

Miranda glanced around, but there didn't seem to be anything particularly special about this spot. They'd passed the stream again about five minutes ago, so maybe that was why—nearby water in easy access.

The team dumped their packs on the ground and began to stretch, Pete wiping his brow. The gamer CEO was in worse shape than the rest of them; he began sweating as soon as they started hiking and didn't stop until he went to sleep.

"What do we do now?" George said, looking expectantly at Dane.

Dane grinned and clapped the man on the back. "Now you're going to get a chance to show me the survival skills that you've picked up. I showed you some things last night and this morning, and I want to see what you've learned."

With that simple command, the team set to work. George left to go into the woods and begin setting up traps, and Pete headed off with the fishing line to do his task. He looked uncomfortable at the thought, but no one offered to help him with it. After the disastrous incident involving her boobs, Pete had been reassigned from water and firewood to fishing (to get him away from her, she suspected). She couldn't say she was sorry for it.

So now it was Will who was assigned to help her with the firewood, and while she waited for him to bring back the first bundle, she examined their new campsite. There was a small, scorched area that told her someone had built a fire here in the past, and she ran her shoe over it, looking for small rocks that would pop when heated. Nothing. Holding her fire bundle in her hands, she glanced around.

Dane stood nearby, arms crossed, leaning against a tree. He'd been muttering something into his satellite phone. Even though he was concentrating on something else, his gaze was on her, watching her as she worked around the campsite. For some reason that made her blush. *Dane Croft,* she thought. So very, very arrogant and self-assured. So certain that she'd take him up on the three orgasms he'd offered her that evening, now that he was assured she wouldn't run and tell his partners that he was sleeping with the clientele.

She wanted to put him in his place . . . or kiss him. Right now she couldn't decide which, and loathed herself for it. She was supposed to hate the man, not think about his mouth on her body all day. Not blush when he looked in her direction. Where was her righteous indignation? Or was she starting to lose her edge?

Scowling at the thought, she turned back to the fire. She needed to focus on work, not on sex. Starting a fire would distract her.

There was a scatter of larger rocks nearby and she spent some time gathering them and forming a circle to ring the fire and keep it from spreading. Once that was done, she dug out the small area inside the rocks and then began to place the wood on it, stacking it the way she had been shown as Will came back with armful after armful. Poor Will had a thankless task—yesterday they'd realized just how much wood was needed to keep a fire going all night, and she suspected he'd gotten the raw end of the deal . . . and she'd gotten the easy job that kept her at camp and close at hand.

Miranda's mouth soured at that. Protecting the girl? Or keeping her close for other reasons? Frowning to herself, she stacked the wood and then sat back to examine her fire pit. Not bad. She'd gathered some fallen leaves and dried grasses to use as tinder as they'd hiked. Her pockets had bulged with the material and now she pulled it out and began to set it at the base of the fire. Her fire bundle had been carefully tended all day, and every time she'd coaxed a bit of smoke out of the coals, she'd grown aroused all over again, thinking of Dane and his promises to her.

I've had plenty of oral sex.

And no orgasms? I'm heartbroken at the thought. Those must have been some shitty boyfriends.

She pictured Dane between her legs, her hands rubbing on his too-short hair as he kissed the lips of her sex. Her nipples went erect just thinking about it and she squirmed, clenching the fire bundle tightly.

"Miranda, before you begin," Dane said, interrupting her thoughts.

She looked up and jerked backward when she realized that Dane was standing over her, his crotch at eye level.

Damn. Was he thinking what she was thinking? She looked up at him and licked her lips, confused.

A bolt of desire crossed his face and he glanced around to make sure the others weren't watching, and then he crouched next to her. "Stop that, Miranda," he whispered.

"Stop what?"

"Stop looking at me like you want me to throw you on the ground and fuck that dazed expression off of your face." His voice was husky, as if he'd been thinking about the same thing. "Hours to go before sunset and it's not a good idea to let the others know what we're planning."

"Oh," she said, and frowned at him, resisting the urge to give him a shove. "If you don't want me thinking about later, then don't shove your junk in my face, all right?"

Sure, she'd gotten a glimpse of the package last night, but when he practically pushed it into her face? She couldn't help but think of other things. And to make it worse, he was definitely . . . well equipped. *Of course he was*, she thought sourly to herself. Dane Croft had been built like an Adonis and she was being swayed by his good looks and godlike smiles. She hated herself for being so very shallow.

He chuckled and patted her on the shoulder, standing up again. "That's better. Now, can I see your fire bundle?"

She slapped the bundle into his hand, then winced at his surprised expression. It wasn't like it could hurt him anyhow. The fire bundle was nothing more than a long piece of rubber pulled from the inside of a shoe that had been wrapped tightly around an ember buried in packed tinder. The bundle had been tied tightly with a shoelace. He'd shown them how to make it—to carry fire from campsite to campsite without having to make it all over again.

It was extremely important to survival, Dane had said, and Miranda had treated it so. She'd kept a careful eye on it, blowing on it from time to time to stoke the embers again. It had smoked and smoldered all day long.

Just like the desire that still burned through her body. And it irritated Miranda that Dane had decided to just waltz over and put his hands all over her bundle. "It's still lit," she pointed out. "Give it back."

"Can't do that," he said with a smile. As she watched, he carefully unwrapped the fire bundle and exposed the ember, then poured water over it.

She sputtered in shock and tried to snatch it back from Dane. "What are you doing? That's our fire!"

"It is," he agreed with a grin. "Or I should say, it was."

"I worked hard on that," she blurted. "I kept it going all day long." Was this some sort of message he was trying to send to her? If so, she was not amused. "Or does this mean you're no longer interested in nurturing my spark, Dane Croft?"

Her voice had risen to a rather loud level, and he winced and gestured for her to lower her voice. When he'd glanced around and had determined that no one was listening to them, Dane looked back at her. "Doesn't mean that at all, Miranda, and you know it."

Actually, she *didn't* know it.

"This course is about survival," he said a little louder, and handed her the wet fire bundle. "And I need to know that you can make a fire on your own. So no bundle today."

"You are a horrible man."

Dane only laughed and smiled down at her with a satisfied expression. "You won't be saying that tonight, I promise."

Flustered, she knelt next to the fire pit. Her hands searched through the wood, trying to recall what he'd taught her. Focus on work, she told herself. Not Dane. Think about fire, not about his mouth on her body. So she sat back and concentrated, gathering her thoughts. She needed to make a bow. After a few moments of searching, she found a long piece for a bow and a second piece of soft pine that would be suitable for a baseboard. She examined the wood for a moment more, and then glanced over at Dane.

He crouched near the fire pit, looking like he had nothing better to do than to sit and harass her.

"You can quit hovering," she pointed out. "Don't you have someone else on this team to bug?"

He grinned, seemingly unbothered by her prickly attitude. "Fire's important. Once I've established that you can get a spark going all on your own, I'll check on the others."

She wasn't going to touch that double entendre with a ten-foot pole. "You're going to be waiting a while if you think I'm going to spark anything with you sitting there staring at me."

He didn't move.

Miranda rolled her eyes in exasperation. "If you're going to stay here, hand me your knife, then."

He did. "I should make you get your own knife."

She rolled her eyes again and used his knife to make a notch in the baseboard, like he'd showed her. Once that was done, Miranda handed his knife back and began to pull the laces off of her shoe to use to string the bow. He was watching her, and it made her nervous. Made her think about sex again, and that wouldn't do. She needed a distraction. "So, Dane," she began as she tied one end of the laces to her chosen stick. "What made you decide to run a survival school? I have to admit it's not what I pictured for you."

His easy grin began to fade a little, and he hesitated for a moment, as if choosing his words carefully. When he answered, it was simple and direct. "I enjoy it. I spent the last year living off the grid."

"Living off the grid?" she asked, finishing her bow and testing the cord. It was tight, with just enough slack to wrap around a stick. Hopefully that would do. "What does that mean?"

"No electricity, no running water, no power," Dane explained, his gaze on her hands as she began to set up the fire-making implements. "Just you and the wild. Colt and I had a cabin in Alaska that we built. It was . . ." He paused, thinking. "It was nice."

"Not a lot of girls up in the wilds of Alaska," she teased. "Were you pinch-hitting for the other team or just doing a lot of masturbating?"

He laughed at that. "You have a filthy mind."

"What? Admit it—that's the first thing you thought about, too."

Dane grinned. "I was there to camp. As for masturbating, nah. It wasn't on my mind at all. By the time I got to Alaska, I was pretty much done with dating. It was nice to have a vacation from everything in my life."

"You, done with women?" She laughed. She looped a stick through the bow and aimed it over the notch she'd carved in the baseboard. "That doesn't sound like Casanova Croft at all."

His look became shuttered immediately. "Yeah, well, sometimes what you get isn't always what you want."

Before she could comment on that, he reached over and corrected her hands. "Hold it like this. And don't forget to put your tinder under the notch so your ember has something to fall on."

She looked at him in wary surprise. His voice had been cold, efficient. Gone was the warm, teasing note. What had she said that was so wrong? Miranda put a bit of tinder under the baseboard and swallowed down the defensive feeling. She was here to fuck—and fuck with—Dane Croft this week, and if she pissed him off, she could kiss her revenge good-bye. Irritated at herself, she began to saw the bow, turning the spindle and creating friction against the baseboard. It was harder than Dane had made it look, and she gave it another rough tug, causing the spindle to twist again.

An uncomfortable silence fell, the only sound the sawing of her spindle against the wood. After a few minutes of watching her work, Dane glanced over at her again. "So, what about you?"

She glanced up, still sawing at the bow and turning the spindle. It was hard to concentrate on the conversation, especially when she was trying so hard to get enough friction to create a spark in the small notch she'd carved in the baseboard. Crap—why did she get the fire-making task? This was hard. Concentrating on her task, she didn't look up. "What about me?"

"You wanted to be an editor or something, right? How come you never left town? Bluebonnet's not exactly a hotbed of activity." His voice was wry. "I couldn't wait to get away from here."

She didn't like where this was heading. So she remained silent, hoping he'd continue talking until he moved long past what she had or hadn't done with her life.

But he paused, waiting for her to respond.

"Journalist," she finally offered, her arms beginning to ache from sawing at the fire-making bow. How long did she have to keep doing this before she got a spark? She didn't even have smoke yet. Frustrated, she sawed it harder. "And you weren't the only one who wanted to leave."

"So why didn't you?"

She was going to start throwing a temper tantrum if she didn't get a wisp of smoke, she really was. So she just sawed harder, her teeth gritted. "Couldn't."

"How come?"

She didn't answer.

He wouldn't let it go. "Did you have to help your mother with her store? She still runs that antiques shop, right?"

That was a little too close to the ugly truth. What sort of game was he playing? Did he want her to come out and admit that the pictures he'd taken had ruined her life? Was this some sort of nasty revenge for somehow offending him? Reminding her who she was? Putting the slut of Bluebonnet back in her place? She threw the fire-making implements down and stood up. "I need to take a walk."

"Miranda, what—"

She whirled around to face him, glaring. "Leave me alone. Understand? I need to take a walk, and not with you." With that, she turned and stomped out of the camp.

Christ, but that woman was prickly. Dane stared after Miranda, wondering at her explosion and subsequent exit from camp. What exactly was she hiding that made her so upset? He was tempted to ask one of the other men, but they wouldn't know anything about her either, being out of towners. Anyone in Bluebonnet could have told him the truth, he suspected. Everyone in town knew everyone else's business.

And Miranda's was apparently unpleasant business, at least in her mind. He stared down at the tools she'd dropped on the ground. Then he moved to go after her.

"Dane! Look! I got dinner!" Pete held a fish aloft, trotting back through the woods. "I caught something!"

Dane glanced at Pete, then back at the woods, then sighed and turned back to him. The man's forehead was beaded with sweat and his pants were splotchy with water. He held aloft a fish, about a foot in length.

"Good job," Dane said absently, glancing at where Miranda had disappeared one last time before turning back to Pete. "Get a flat rock and I'll show you how to scale it."

Pete gave him a funny look. "I have to scale it?"

He chuckled at the other man's expression. "Only if you plan on eating it. You're going to have to gut it, too."

The gamer looked a bit green at the thought, and Dane wondered how he'd managed to catch the fish if the thought of touching it was so revolting. He nodded at the fish. "Here, give it to me and I'll show you how to do it this one time, but after this, it's on you. Understand?"

Pete seemed reluctant to hand the fish over, but did so after a moment, and Dane immediately saw the problem.

"This fish is dead," he pointed out, angling his face away from the smell. "Very, very dead. Several days dead."

Pete crossed his arms over his chest. "Is that a problem?"

Dane held it toward Pete's face, watching as the other man flinched away. "Do you want to eat it?"

"Well, no."

He held it back out to Pete. "Take this out there and bury it somewhere. You're supposed to be catching live fish, not scavenging dead ones. Leave that for the coyotes."

The other man suddenly looked panicked. "There are coyotes?"

"Don't worry about the coyotes," Dane told him. "They're terrified of people. You're more likely to see a unicorn than a coyote out here. Now head back out and actually fish. *In* the water. *With* line and bait. I'm going to go find Miranda."

"Speaking of Miranda," Pete said, his voice low and thoughtful. "You guys know each other?"

The hair on the back of Dane's neck prickled at Pete's question. "We went to high school together. Why?"

"She single?"

Hot jealousy speared through him. He resisted the urge to bite off that no one was going to be touching Miranda but him. They were supposed to be keeping things a secret. Clenching his hands, he reached for a piece of kindling and began to snap it into smaller pieces. "I didn't ask her. Why?"

Pete gave him a smug look. "She was checking me out the other day. I thought I might see if she's interested in going out when we get out of this little hellhole called nature."

For some reason, that really irked Dane. Nature wasn't hell. And to think that Miranda had been checking the skinny creep out . . . he didn't buy it.

"Unless you're planning on tapping that ass?" Pete said, interrupting his thoughts. "I've noticed the way you've been looking at her."

His jaw tightened. The urge to suddenly pound Pete's face in washed over him, and he clenched his fists. "No, I'm not," he lied. In that moment, he missed hockey and the ability to punch the hell out of your opponent. "She's just an old friend."

He couldn't say yes—*Sure, I slept with Miranda last night and she was wild. It was hot as hell, and I plan on doing it again. I want to see the expression on her face when I show her how to come again. I want to see the expression on her face when I put my mouth on her sweet pussy, and her expression when I feed my cock into her body.*

He couldn't say any of that. And even if he thought about Miranda's sassy little thong or her curving smile or the way she'd made those soft, surprised little cries of pleasure when he'd pounded into her, as if she hadn't been expecting to enjoy it so much. He couldn't say a damn thing. This was business, and Miranda was business, and no matter how much he might like for it to be otherwise, it couldn't be.

Pete adjusted his glasses and smiled. "Excellent. Then you don't mind if I go after her?"

If his jaw gritted any harder, his teeth were going to snap. "Not during survival week."

"Oh, after, of course." Pete stared off into the woods where Miranda had disappeared. "I wouldn't want to see her before she could take a nice, long shower."

Fucking asshole. As if Miranda smelled bad. Just the opposite, in fact. She'd smelled like the woods—wood smoke and the wind and just a hint of sweat—and he'd found it incredibly appealing. This little creep wouldn't know what was appealing if it decked him in the face. Hiding his anger, Dane pointed at the dead fish. "You need to get rid of that and catch a real fish. Got me?"

The other man gave him a reluctant nod and then headed back away from camp, muttering under his breath. He swiped at the branches as he walked, the actions of a petulant child and not a grown man.

Dane gave it two days before Pete bailed out on the class entirely. *Good.* The man was acting like a brat and the class would only get harder. That was one of the things he appreciated about Miranda, he thought as he turned in the opposite direction and began walking. She didn't complain about the class, about being unable to shower or sweating in the dirt and sleeping on the ground. When he'd seen that bag full of lingerie, he'd been worried that she would be a huge pain in the ass this week. But . . . she wasn't. She actually seemed to be enjoying herself in the outdoors, and he was enjoying her presence as well.

Then again, he hadn't expected to have sex with her. It made him a little uncomfortable to think that he'd automatically assumed that she'd been a plant from Colt and Grant—she had been so offended at the thought that he knew she was sincere. He shouldn't have slept with her. Shouldn't have, and yet . . . he couldn't resist. When her gaze went soft, he wanted to bury himself deep inside her and make love until morning.

Still, he wasn't entirely sure Miranda's motives were innocent. Why would a woman who liked lingerie and sexy things want to spend a week in the wilderness? Things didn't add up, he decided. Either Miranda had a really killer dual personality—girly-girl of the backwoods—or he was missing some vital element.

For the life of him, he couldn't figure out what.

As he contemplated the Miranda situation, he walked through the woods, idly noticing the play of footprints in the dirt. Though he wasn't the best tracker, it wasn't hard to see that someone had come this way. He touched a broken twig and knelt by the ground. The hard dirt hadn't seen rain for a few days and showed the wavy lines of a boot sole perfectly. Judging by the size of the shoe, it wasn't a man unless the guy was packing some seriously dainty feet. He followed the footprints, thinking about his small class. With one glaring exception, they'd been interested and willing to learn. The others were corporate hounds—it was easy to spot the type, as they were aggressive and driven. The desire to succeed was clear.

Tracking wasn't on the week's menu, but he thought of Miranda's face and the way it lit up when things clicked and she learned something new. Maybe he'd show her a few things when he found her. After she'd cooled down, that is. She'd almost had her fire—a few more minutes of sawing and she'd have had a spark for sure. Her quick mind had picked up on the implements and had followed his instructions almost to the letter. She'd been so close . . . until they'd started talking about town. About Bluebonnet.

Then she'd bailed on him.

He ducked under a tree branch and scanned the woods as he thought about their conversation. Dane had immediately steered it once they'd gotten to his personal life. He liked Miranda but he didn't feel like sharing why he'd left the NHL—no matter what she'd heard. No one believed him anyhow. They liked the tabloid version of things far too much. That he was a pussy hound who couldn't turn down a woman. That he was a user. He had been, once upon a time . . . until someone had used him. Then he'd changed. He wasn't the old Dane anymore, and he got tired of trying to prove it to everyone he met.

Of course, Miranda had been equally prickly. She'd bristled as soon as he started asking her why she hadn't left town. Was there a boyfriend still in Bluebonnet? Someone she'd stuck around for? A surge of jealousy tore at his thoughts. Was that the reason she'd packed all the sexy panties? Had her hands on his cock as soon as they were alone together? To make someone jealous?

Dane frowned as he spotted another set of footprints near the stream. He approached on the far bank, his movements quiet and stealthy with years of practice.

And there she was.

Miranda stood in the creek, hip deep, her back to him. She wasn't totally naked. Under the thick, spill of dark brown hair that cascaded down her back, a thin black bra strap stretched over her shoulder. From his viewpoint on the bank, he could see the creamy small of her back, perfect in its symmetry and the way it dipped inward just above her bottom. He groaned at the sight of her rounded ass as she leaned forward, exposing the heart-shaped flesh. Definitely a thong. He barely caught it peeking between the cleft of her full, firm buttocks. Damn. Dane stared. Miranda had the most singularly perfect ass he'd ever seen.

He closed his eyes and leaned against the tree he was gripping for support. Hell. She was bathing. And here he was, standing on the bank and peeking at her like some sort of creepy pervert. His hand slid over the hard rise of his cock in his shorts, and he swore. He was a creepy, *turned on* pervert watching her bathe.

She might enjoy flirting with him and their midnight trysts, but he was pretty sure she'd hate the thought of him spying on her like some hormonal teenager. Yet he couldn't stop staring at that perfect ass, and he thought of how she'd felt last night with her sweet pussy wrapped around his cock, clenching him deeper every time he thrust. Of the cries she'd made—so turned on and so very surprised that she'd been so lost in the moment. Of the look on her face when she'd finally come, as if he'd just handed her a million dollars.

Fuck. If he got any harder, he was going to charge into the water after her and forget all about the "tonight" part of their next meeting. He'd take her on the creek bank, in broad daylight, and wouldn't care who saw them. The heel of his hand rubbed down the front of his cock again, need surging through him.

Before last night it had been two long years since he'd been with a woman. He hadn't missed one in all that time. There was always something to distract him—chopping wood, hunting, a ten-mile hike through the snow back when they'd lived in the cabin . . . and when all else failed, there was his hand. Last night should have gotten her out of his system. Quenched the urge so he could stop thinking with his dick and get back to his job. But as he watched Miranda raise her pale arms to her back and toy with the clasp of her bra, he knew that it was going to be close to impossible to think about anything but taking Miranda again.

And he palmed his cock once more.

EIGHT

She couldn't do it.

Miranda's fingers trembled on her bra clasp, ruining the sensual movement she was going for. She tried again, squeezing her eyes closed and focusing on undoing that one stupid strap, but every time she came close, her fingers locked. The pictures on the Internet flashed through her mind over and over again. Her kneeling before Dane. Her breasts thrust against the camera in another shot. That triangle-shaped mole under her left breast had identified her even if her face hadn't been in the picture . . . and it had been. Her expression in the photos had been contorted in rapture, and she remembered Dane's big hand toying with her nipples. She'd loved his touch.

Nine years later, she still loved his touch, though she hated herself a little for it now. She'd recovered from her tantrum walking through the woods, realizing that she wouldn't be able to keep Dane trotting after her if he was mad at her. So she'd calmed down and sat on the banks of the stream, staring at it as she tried to think up her next battle plan.

After a moment, the solution had become glaringly obvious, of course. Strip naked in the stream until Dane ran across her, then seduce him again. Keep the control firmly on her side. Never let him get the upper hand in their relationship. Keep him guessing, above all else.

Except . . . her hands weren't cooperating. Her subconscious had a strict sense of modesty even if Evil Miranda was trying to shed it. Last night she'd been able to provoke and flirt with Dane, and hadn't thought twice about shedding her clothes. In the daylight? It was different—more exposed. And knowing that Dane was on the bank watching her? Made her even more nervous. Last night it had been dark and he'd only been able to get quick glimpses of her body in the moonlight. They'd kept some of their clothes on even as they'd had sex. Standing here in the stream in nothing but a thong and lacy bra in broad daylight felt . . . naked. Was he looking at how much her body had changed in the past nine years? Comparing her breasts to that old photo?

Her fingers twitched and she opened her eyes, blowing her long bangs off of her forehead in frustration. Why was this hard? She'd hit on him last night and he'd given her the screwing she'd asked for. He'd made her come so hard that her eyes had nearly crossed. This was just a stupid bra and striptease. Why was it such an issue for her? *You're being a baby*, she told herself, even as her fingers clamped down on the front of her bra, clutching it to her chest protectively. Anyone could be watching her, not just Dane. What if someone else had stumbled upon her bathing and it wasn't Dane at all? What if he had a camera, too? Oh God. What if—

A noise to her left got her attention—had Dane moved to the other side of the bank? Or was there truly another watcher here at the stream? Miranda's hand slid forward over her the cups of her bra, protecting her breasts from prying eyes, and she turned.

A gigantic bird stood on the bank, about two feet away from her. It looked like a giant ostrich with enormous, round black eyes and a nasty beak. It ruffled its feathers in alarm at the sight of her, the long neck rearing back as if it were about to peck her eyes out.

It squawked at her, the sound angry and strident.

Miranda yelped.

She stumbled backward. She lost her footing and skidded into the water up to her neck. Gasping, she struggled to regain her balance and then continued to slide away as the bird squawked again and ruffled its massive black wings. The thing paced on the bank, storklike legs twitching nervously.

Shit! Could birds swim? Did emus attack people?

"Miranda," Dane said in a low voice behind her. "Careful."

Screw careful. She turned and vaulted for the opposite bank, toward Dane. Forgetting about her state of undress or the fact that she was in danger of losing her wet bra, she plowed toward him. When he extended a hand to help her out of the water, she grasped it and hauled herself onto the bank.

The thing across from them trumpeted in alarm, and Miranda yelped again. She didn't stop at climbing out of the water, and began to climb up Dane himself.

She leapt onto him, her legs locking around his waist and her arms around his shoulders. Her only thought was to get away from that damn bird, and Dane was safe. Dane wouldn't let it eat her.

Once she'd climbed on top of him, she squeezed her eyes shut, breathing hard and waiting for the stupid thing to attack. A long moment passed in which she could only hear her own rapid panting, and then she heard a disgruntled cluck from the bird, a ruffle of feathers, and then nothing else.

Daring greatly, she peeked across the bank, and sure enough, the bird was leaving. She exhaled loudly in relief.

"Miranda?" Dane said in a weird voice. "Are you all right?"

She looked down at him.

Dane's face was pressed between her breasts. Her bra straps had fallen low on her shoulders, the entire garment slipping down several inches. Her nipples were barely covered by the damp cups and were clearly outlined. Worse than that, she was clutching his head to her breasts in an effort to anchor her body on the high point that she'd climbed in her distress . . . aka, him.

As she took stock of her body parts, she realized that her legs were still wrapped around him. She was pretty sure those were his hands all over her ass, too. "Hi there," she said brightly, trying not to blush. "Guess what? I found an emu."

"Looks like it," he said in a husky voice, his hot gaze on her face.

Her bra strap slipped farther down her shoulder, and she shrugged a little, trying to get it to move back up.

His gaze focused on the strap. As she watched, Dane moved

forward and his mouth brushed against her arm. She shivered as he caught the bra strap in his teeth and began to slide it slowly up one pale shoulder.

The breath escaped her lungs. She watched him gently use his teeth to slide her bra strap into place, scarcely daring to breathe. His hands still clutched at her ass, his fingers digging into her flesh in a way that turned her on.

"Dane," she said softly, the word a breathy plea. While she'd hoped to tease him a little—okay, a lot—with her bathing, the reality was almost overwhelming to her senses.

And it made her hungry for more. After her bra strap was back in place, his mouth remained on her shoulder, and he very softly pressed a kiss to her collarbone. Miranda shivered, her hands clasping his neck harder. She wanted to be the one in charge—to tell him where and how to kiss her. But at the feathery kisses he was pressing to her skin, she shuddered and let him lead. It felt so good. With a small sigh of pleasure, she tilted her head to the opposite side, moving her wet hair and exposing her neck to him.

He took the suggestion. His mouth moved to the base of her neck, and he pressed a light kiss against the hollow next to her collarbone, then teased the spot with his tongue.

That gentle lick caused her pussy to flare with need, and she gasped, pulling him closer. "Dane," she murmured again, her voice softer than before.

He unhooked her legs from around his waist and slid her to the ground, and the lovely skin contact was broken.

Miranda gave a disappointed sigh as her first foot touched down. Her sigh was swallowed up when he continued to hold her other leg behind the knee. It forced her to hang on to his neck, pressing her sex against his body in a blatant fashion. Pressing her right up against his cock, which, even through his pants, was clearly hard and ready.

She gasped at the sensation, her gaze flicking up to his. Dane's eyes were hooded and sleepy with desire, mere slits of green in his tanned face. There was a hint of a smile tugging at the line of his mouth, and she watched that mouth as he turned and leaned forward. Her ass rested on a low-hanging tree branch, and she was trapped between the tree and Dane's massive form. Not that she wanted to escape. She wanted him to lean closer, to put those lips on her skin again.

She got her wish. Dane's mouth swooped onto her own, capturing her gasp before she could release it. His tongue dove into her mouth, giving her a hard, possessive flick. It danced along her own tongue, twining briefly before darting to graze against her parted lips. He pulled away just long enough for her to catch her breath, and then he was sucking on her lower lip, as if he could devour her whole.

His fingers gripped behind her knee and pulled her closer, and she felt his hips rotate ever so slightly. The subtle gesture pressed his erection against the core of her sex, sending liquid heat flooding through her body. She felt her pussy grow slick with desire, the thin scrap of her panties not leaving her much protection against the abrasive fabric of his jeans—something that turned her on as well.

Gasping her pleasure, Miranda dug her fingernails into his shoulders, leaning in to take his mouth in her own again. As their tongues locked, his hips pressed against her own, and she felt the hard length of him pushing, pushing against her core. Her mouth devouring his, her hand slid between them and rubbed along the hard ridge of his cock in the jeans, and she heard him groan with need.

The sound, raw and full of hunger, made her toes curl with utter pleasure.

His mouth pulled away from hers again, as if it were a fight between the two of them to take control and a kiss was a surrender. Instead, his mouth slid to her chin, tasting her skin there and then sinking lower, to her throat, her collarbone, and her breastbone, teasing the sensitive flesh there where the curve of her breast began.

Miranda suddenly wished her bra had fallen off entirely. She wanted his mouth on her nipples; tugging at them with his teeth was driving her crazy.

His mouth slid over her bra and his teeth nibbled at her sensitive skin, then he stopped with an odd expression on his face. "Tastes like stream water," he said. That was all the warning she got before he tugged at the cup and exposed her breast, and then his mouth was on her nipple. His tongue rasped against the aching tip, eliciting a gasp and a writhing arch from her. "Much better," he said huskily, the words blowing across her nipple before he dove at it again.

A strangled sound of delight escaped her throat and Miranda bucked her hips against his jeans-clad cock, throwing her head back at the sensations. God, he knew just how to touch her.

Her arm locked around his neck, and she thrust her breast against his mouth, her breath coming in harsh little gasps. Taking his cue from her, his lips brushed against her nipple, grazing it. She watched him as he nuzzled her breast, as if he simply enjoyed the feeling of her skin, then watched as his mouth closed over the tip, and she felt the delicious scrape of his teeth against her nipple as he took it between them and bit down gently.

A cry broke from her throat.

"You like that? Miss sweet, innocent Miranda likes it a bit rougher? You have no idea how incredibly sexy that is." His eyes were slits of desire, and he plumped her breast with one hand, making her nipple poke out, a beacon for his mouth. But instead of biting down like she wanted, he glanced back at her. "Or do I remember wrong? What do you want, Miranda?"

"Oh," she breathed, pushing her nipple back into his mouth when he pulled away. "Please, Dane."

"Please what?" His lips brushed against her nipple as he spoke, and his mouth grazed the creamy white flesh around it. "Please . . . lick you gently?" As if to prove a point, he licked the tip of her breast and then blew on it, his hot gaze moving back to her face.

She whimpered in distress. That had felt good, but it wasn't what she wanted. "Dane, please."

"Please . . . bite you?" He leaned in and his teeth flicked against her nipple, more suggestion than action.

"Yes," she breathed, a shiver of excitement lancing down her body. "Bite. Please." In response, she strained against him, trying to offer him her breast in suggestion. God, she needed him inside her. Right now. Right fucking now. Her legs locked around him tighter, pulling her wet pussy against his cock even harder. "Oh God, bite me everywhere. Make me come like you promised."

He gave a low growl in his throat. "I promised I'd make you come tonight, Miranda. Or were you just too impatient to wait?"

He pushed her harder against the tree, and she felt one of his hands slide away from her ass and brush against her sex, pinned between them.

The flutters of excitement turned to pulses of need, and her fingernails dug into his back. Oh lord, that felt amazing. Her eyes closed as he moved back toward her breast, anticipation surging. “Touch me. Don’t make me wait.”

His fingertip grazed past her panties, one thick digit sliding against the silky heat of her pussy, and he groaned against her breast. “You are fucking soaked.”

She could feel it—feel how totally slick her pussy was, how his rough finger slid along the heated flesh. Her hips twisted, and she desperately needed him to touch her right—

Her eyes flew open just as he sank one thick finger into her pussy, the gasping cry threatening to escape her throat suddenly swallowed by Dane’s mouth on hers.

“Hello?” A voice called in the distance. “Miranda? Dane?”

Miranda’s orgasm built, so very, very close to the edge, and she bucked her hips—to find that she was suddenly the only one participating. Dane had frozen against her, and though he hadn’t moved, his eyes had gone wide, and his mouth was on hers only to keep her cries from escaping. When she pushed her hips against his hand, he didn’t move.

Her orgasm fizzled at the look on his face: chagrined and a bit ashamed. Ashamed of the thought of being caught with her by one of his clients. For some reason, that made her feel . . . dirty. Her memory filled with mental images of the photos in the closet, and she winced, shame slamming into her like a brick to the head. Her hand pushed at his, trying to break free.

"That's Pete," he whispered into her ear, disentangling his hands from her body and lowering her so her feet rested on the ground. His gaze focused on the woods, not her face. "We can't be seen together. I'll meet him and distract him away while you get dressed."

She said nothing.

He leaned over and gave her a rough, brisk kiss. "I'll see you after dark." With that, he adjusted the crotch of his jeans with his hand, shook himself as if to clear his mind, and headed off into the woods, leaving her here alone.

So he *did* want to have sex with her. He just didn't want to have sex with her and have others know about it. Fair enough. If they found out about the two of them before the week was out, her chances at getting her revenge would be slim. After all, what was the point of ruining someone's reputation with dirty photos if she'd already been caught making out with him? He was right—they had to remain a secret from the others on the survival trip.

So why did she feel so freaking dirty all of a sudden?

To Miranda's surprise, Dane had turned out to be an excellent teacher. Once she returned to camp, she was able to get a roaring fire going. They ate fish that night and a few berries that Jamie had foraged in the woods for them. And the shelter was a bit lackluster but the evening was warm, and they had spent their time in front of the fire, sharing stories and listening to Dane's camping tales.

He had stories of when he and Colt had run into a black bear in Alaska, of being stuck in the woods and completely lost and following train tracks for a week before finding civilization again, of fishing and foraging odd things. Of making stew out of squirrel or whatever else they could find when times were lean. Of hiking across the wild with nothing but a multi-tool. Dane's stories were told with a zealous enthusiasm that she found easy to like. He seemed to honestly enjoy the survival thing, she realized. The sparkle in his eyes wasn't only due to the firelight. He seemed . . . happy.

It was weird. The Dane she remembered had been a smug teenage boy who'd always been rushing to his next hockey practice. She'd loved that sulkiness as a teenager, found it irresistibly sexy. The adult Miranda was drawn to the enthusiastic Dane, though. The man who went after what he wanted with both hands and approached the wilderness with an obvious pleasure that turned her on just to see. The new Dane was incredibly sexy. The reasonable, confident man who tended the fire and showed Steve where the shelter had a weakness. The man who took everything in stride, complimented his team when they did a good job, and encouraged them when they did not. He was like a big, grown-up Boy Scout with a wicked, naughty side, she thought, remembering the way he'd slid a finger deep inside her mere hours ago.

Just thinking about it made her want to stick her hand down her panties and play with her clit. She was really, really turned on and she'd gotten no payoff. And every time Dane looked over at her, she couldn't help but think of their conversation earlier.

Three orgasms tonight. He'd promised her three.

She watched him across the fire, saying nothing. Her gaze

went to his hands, watching them move as he retied a hunting knot. Her mind dwelled on how those hands had stroked her wet flesh, and how they had felt against her body. How they had gripped her hips so tightly as he'd pounded into her.

God, this day was taking *forever* to be over.

This day was going to last forever.

Dane glanced at the sun—still too high in the sky for his liking—as he showed George a deadfall snare for the seventh time that day. The older man meant well, but he wasn't quick to pick up on the basics, and Dane regretted not assigning the trap-making to Steve instead, who had shown a lot of competence in all the tasks he'd been given. Not that he was thinking about much of anything. His mind kept going to Miranda. How she'd looked with her sexy body wet and glistening from the water. How she'd crawled all over him, and how hot and tight she'd been when he'd slid a finger deep inside her.

He'd gone into this thinking that he could be strong against the lure of an old girlfriend, but at the first opportunity to touch her, he'd caved. Like a weak, starving man offered food, he'd abandoned his obligations and had sex with her, if only to get her out of his mind once and for all. But he'd underestimated how scorchingly hot she'd be after all this time, and how naughty and wicked she'd been in his arms.

And he couldn't quite get it out of his head, which was why he kept messing up the trap as he tried to show George. She was distracting him. Though she sat completely across from him in the camp, the blazing fire separating the two of them, he could feel her gaze on him. Every time he looked up, she was watching him with those big brown eyes. Her eyes would watch his hands, and he could almost guess what she was thinking. And damn if it wasn't going to make him hard, right in the middle of camp.

Dane cleared his throat and shifted, making excuses about going to get more firewood. He returned a few minutes later, his desire under control once more, and dropped the armful of logs in camp. While he was gone, Pete had sat down next to Miranda, and the young CEO was talking her ear off. She seemed uninterested, though she was smiling politely, her legs drawn up to her chest as she sat. It was clear that Pete was totally smitten with her.

Dane picked up a piece of wood and began to break off the smaller branches, rounding off the wood so it would burn evenly. He moved toward the fire, listening to their conversation.

"So like I was saying," Pete said, his body turned toward Miranda. "There's a huge awards show next month. E3 convention. It's a big thing in gaming. I haven't designated a date yet, though there are tons of women who would kill to go."

Miranda's smile was polite but distracted. "Sounds like a nice time," she said absently.

"I was wondering if you'd want to check it out," he said in a lower voice. "I could get you in as long as you were with me."

Dane's hands tightened on the log and it threatened to snap. *As long as she slept with him,* Pete meant. He was just pussyfooting around the concept.

Either Miranda didn't hate the idea or it was too subtle for her. She gave Pete an absent smile. "We'll see." And her gaze stole back to Dane's hands, and she clutched her knees a little tighter to her chest, the look in her eyes going soft again.

Fuck. She was thinking about their interlude by the stream earlier. He recognized that soft, melting look in her eyes. She'd had the same expression on her face right before they'd been interrupted. Fuck, fuck.

The memory of that seared through his mind again. "We need more wood," he barked at the group and walked away again before they could catch his returning erection.

Eventually, the camp turned in and went to bed. Dane didn't sleep, his body tense and aware of the others. In the middle of the night, when the other men were snoring, Dane got up from the shelter and began to poke at the fire. He was intensely aware of his surroundings, of the quiet hum of the forest, the snores of the men piled into the makeshift shelter, and of Miranda's small lean-to on the far side of the fire.

He was especially attuned to her actions, and when her eyes opened and she sat up, giving him an expectant look, he put a finger to his lips. A glance backward showed that the others were still asleep, which was perfect.

She yawned and gestured that she was going to go out to the woods first, and for him to follow.

He nodded, and watched her pick her way across the campsite and toward a large landmark tree. It gave him a small bit of pleasure to notice that she'd been utterly silent as she'd crossed the campsite—Miranda was smart and clever, and she knew that the snap of a twig could potentially blow their cover. He liked that about her—that she used her brain. That she knew this required stealth and silence. They were on the same page.

Dane adjusted the fire for a bit longer, then moved to the woodpile, pretending to be unsatisfied with the size of it. No one was awake, but he felt better acting out the ruse just in case. He placed another log on the fire, and then left camp in the opposite direction from Miranda. Anyone who woke up might think he was heading out in search of more wood. Miranda would know better.

Once the campfire was out of sight, he tracked back and headed in Miranda's direction. He saw her waiting ahead in a clearing, her arms hugging warmth close to her body. She had her back to him, and he silently brushed a hand along her spine, alerting her to his presence. To his gratification, she didn't yelp in alarm. She simply turned and gave him a shadowy smile in the darkness, and slipped her hand in his. "Lead on," she whispered.

He did. He knew these woods well; even in the darkness, the paths were familiar to him. Her hand gripped his tightly and she let him lead the way. When they were in deep enough that he knew the others wouldn't be able to find them, he paused and cupped her chin, tilting her face up to his for a brief kiss. His lips grazed her mouth, and he could feel his cock harden just thinking about what they were about to do.

"Give me a moment to set up, all right?" he said.

Her expression grew puzzled. "Set up?"

He pulled out a small plastic packet and ripped it open. "Grant insisted that we pack some basic survival supplies just in case someone on the team couldn't hack it. I brought an insulated blanket so you won't have to lie on the ground."

"Oh," she said softly. "Thank you."

Dane unwrapped it, wincing at the wrinkling noise in the quiet woods. He spread out the blanket—made of a silver, crinkly sort of cellophane, it was the loudest sort of blanket, but it was the only one he had available. It'd have to do. He got down on his knees to spread it on the ground, and then when it was flat, he turned to Miranda and offered her his hand.

She placed her hand in his, trembling a little. He could feel the shivers working through her body. The evening was cool, but he suspected nervousness on her part. "You okay?" he asked softly.

"Of course," she said quickly, pulling her hand back out of his and sitting on the blanket promptly. "But . . ." She hesitated, and he watched her bite her lip in the moonlight. "I'm warning you, this might be more difficult than you think with the whole three-times thing."

So that was it? She was worried that she wouldn't be able to perform? That was a bit of role reversal. He swallowed the laugh that threatened to rise in his throat, guessing that she wouldn't appreciate that. "Miranda, you're thinking too much about this. If it takes all night to get you to relax, then it takes all night. All right?"

"Sure," she said lamely, and he knew she didn't believe him.

He nodded at her shoes. "Why don't you take those off? Get comfortable?" She did so, kicking them off and wiggling her feet in her socks. He moved onto the blanket with her and she stiffened, so he pulled back again. This was . . . different. When Miranda had come on to him, she'd been confident, sexy, and wild. But he'd told her his plans and she'd stewed all day on what he wanted to do to her. Now he could see it was a mistake that he'd let her anticipate their meeting tonight. Gone was the confident woman from earlier—in her place was a skittish girl who seemed to be terrified that she was going to somehow prove one of them wrong and disappoint them both. He knew her mind would be working hard on the fact that she needed to have an orgasm—more than one—to please him.

In other words, his sexy promise had completely stressed her out. Not exactly the desired reaction.

He sat next to her and took her hand in his. "Hey."

She looked at him, wary. "What is it?"

"I promise to come all over your face if you take too long on your end. Deal?" He said it purely to ease the tension from her shoulders, the strange worry that he'd somehow put there by promising her pleasure.

Miranda giggled, and the sound washed over him like an electric current, lighting up his nerve endings. That soft, sultry little giggle made his cock instantly hard. But he ignored that, studying her face.

"Gosh, thanks," she said sarcastically, but her face was lit up in a smile.

He liked seeing that smile. Dane leaned forward and put a hand at the base of her head, pulling her forward. His mouth captured hers in a kiss—hot, wet, and open. She gasped and stiffened against him, her mind clearly starting up. He didn't want that. Apparently when she thought too much, she worried about her own responses and whether they were right or not. He just wanted her to *respond*, not to think about responding. So he stroked his tongue into her mouth, a wicked, hard thrust designed to take her off guard and remind her what they were here for.

She stiffened for a moment, and then he felt her melt against him. Her hands moved to his chest and shoulders, fingers curling into his shirt as she held on. His tongue thrust into her mouth again, then he rubbed it against hers, teasing her, coaxing with every slow, deep plunge of his tongue. Each thrust was a reminder of what he was going to do to her very shortly, and he wanted her to know it. Make her feel every deep lick into her mouth straight to her pussy.

With each breath, she gasped, making soft little noises in the back of her throat. He liked that—he liked that a lot, but he continued to kiss her, not rushing a thing. Instead of the deep, searing kisses, he changed tactics on her. With one last lick into her mouth, he started nibbling at her lips, tasting the plump softness, appreciating the way that she responded to his kisses. And he slowly, slowly pulled her forward with each kiss, until he hauled her into his lap and forced her to straddle him.

He expected her to stiffen again, but she didn't—she eagerly straddled him and her hips rocked against his, her hands going to his neck as she began to kiss him back with eager intensity. And when he pressed another light kiss to her mouth, she made a noise of frustration and took the initiative, moving away from the soft kisses and back to a deep, searing one, her tongue seeking out his.

Fuck yes. He pressed down on her hips, letting her feel the hard length of him against her, and was rewarded with a low moan in her throat. "Feel that? I've been walking around hard all day, thinking about you and your sweet little mouth, that long hair, your tight pussy. I can't wait to taste you."

She stiffened against him, and he felt the uncertainty wash over her. Damn. Back to square one.

He gave her another deep kiss, but he could tell she was pulling back again. The only way he was going to get her over this ridiculous fear was to show her she had nothing to be afraid of.

"Miranda," he whispered, leaning in to kiss her mouth lightly again. "I'm going to show you that you can come as often as you want to. Just because you dated a bunch of fools in the past with sausages for fingers doesn't mean that you're the problem. Understand?"

She shook her head, and that sexy fall of dark hair brushed over her shoulders. "What if it was a fluke?" she whispered. "What if we try tonight and we can't make it happen?"

She sounded so brokenhearted at the thought that his chest ached. In that instant, he decided that he was going to make her come if it killed him, just to prove to her that she wasn't the problem. And if it took until dawn, then he was going to enjoy every last minute of it. "You're focusing on the wrong things," he told her, using every ounce of willpower he had not to thrust up against her hips. Tonight was going to be about her, not him. "It's not about how fast you can come. It's about how much you enjoy yourself until you do. Understand me?"

She gave a small snort in the darkness. "I'm not stupid, Dane. I know what sex is about."

"Of course you do. And that's why you're going to let me show you how to enjoy yourself, aren't you?" He grinned at her and rocked forward, tipping them both onto the crinkling blanket until Miranda was pinned beneath him and he lay on top of her.

Her eyes widened as his weight settled over her and she stared up at him. "You don't have to worry about me. I'm going to enjoy myself."

Dane grinned down at her. "Good. Now, can I take your top off?"

She hesitated a moment, then nodded. When he reached for

the hem of her shirt, she wiggled and helped him pull it off. Her bra was another lacy confection, this one so sheer that he could see her dusky nipples in the moonlight through the fabric. He leaned down and brushed his mouth over one, feeling the fabric abrade against the sensitive peak.

Miranda's breath sucked in and her hands went to his shoulders, her body tensing slightly under him. She'd liked that.

Just that small reaction made him feel like the fucking king of the world.

"Tonight you're going to let me take control, Miranda. I'm going to decide what you like, and I'm going to take that and use it to pleasure you, understand?"

She rolled her eyes at him and attempted to get up, but he took her arm and pinned it above her head, his grip gentle but firm. "Understand?" he said softly. "This is about letting me have control over you. About me giving you pleasure."

Her body trembled under his, and her hips flexed in an automatic gesture of need. She widened her eyes, staring up at him, and slowly nodded. "All yours," she said. "For tonight."

"Very good," he murmured, and slid a hand over her shoulders, feeling the warmth of her creamy skin, enjoying the way the moonlight played over her body. He could feel her heart pounding under his hand, and he glanced up at her face. She had the same melting, soft expression in her eyes that he'd recognized from before—the one where she was lost in desire. Good, that was exactly what he wanted to see from her.

His fingers hooked to the front of the pretty bra. There was a tiny bow at the front, and he tugged at the fabric beneath it. "You've got another one of these, right?"

A frown creased her brow. "Why?"

He'd take that as a yes. Dane snagged his finger under the fabric and ripped it straight down the center. The flimsy fabric split in half, exposing her breasts to the moonlight. "Because it's in my way."

"You Neanderthal," she said, but a laugh bubbled up in her throat and she halfheartedly tried to slap his hand away.

He kept her other arm pinned and just grinned at her, his hand moving quickly to cup one of the breasts. It was perfectly rounded, and he felt the hard little nipple scrape against his palm as he touched her.

Her laugh died in her throat, her eyes widening just a little at the caress, her expression going soft.

Dane cupped her breast, feeling the weight of it against his palm, and put his other hand on her opposite breast, watching her reaction. She didn't move, her arm still above her head as if he yet pinned it. Her cheeks were flushed with desire and her breathing had sped up slightly. That was good. That was very good.

He brushed a thumb across one nipple, finding it hard and peaked. Her breath sucked in at the small touch, so he repeated it, rubbing the tip back and forth with his thumb. She arched underneath him, her lips parting, her eyes closing in ecstasy. He continued to rub at the nipple with one hand, enjoying the small whimpers that poured forth from her, and bent over the other peak. He brushed his lips against it, then nibbled at the tip.

It hardened underneath his lips and he lapped at it, then he swirled his tongue while she moaned in response. Her back arched under him, pressing her breasts harder against his hands, and he felt her hips give a tiny instinctive buck.

How had Miranda thought she was unresponsive in bed? How had her boyfriends of the past not been able to wring orgasms from her? Were they idiots who hadn't cared if she came or not? Or had they always let her have control of the situation, never realizing that what she truly craved was to be the one out of control? The one off guard? He'd discovered that when she was thinking, she worried. His goal had been to stop that thinking, and all it had taken was kisses on the soft skin and attention to her breasts. And her responses were delicious—already she writhed under him, needing more.

And damn if it wasn't making him as hard as a rock. His cock was thick and heavy in his shorts, straining against his clothing, but he ignored it. He wanted to bring her to where she needed to be before he even thought about himself. And right now, she needed him touching her.

He pressed another kiss on the tip of her nipple, enjoying the way her skin prickled in a thousand tiny goose bumps in reaction. So responsive. He bit lightly at the pale flesh, then kissed the nip away, replacing his mouth with his hand and cupping her breast once more, his thumbs grazing the nipples to keep her fevered. And as he touched her, he lowered his mouth to the cleft between her breasts, kissing the soft skin there.

Her response was a small sigh of pleasure, her fingers tightening in his shirt. She liked to be kissed. He decided in that moment that Miranda Hill needed a lot more kissing. He pressed a kiss lower, on her ribs and belly, then another, and another, enjoying the silky feeling of her skin. Her body was perfect in the moonlight, softly rounded but sleek, all curves and delicate skin.

He nibbled at her stomach, enjoying the flutter of her laughter.

"That tickles," she whispered.

"Good." He kissed her sweet belly because he could, and because he liked tickling her. His thumbs brushed over her nipples again, and he felt her chuckle turn into a rasping inhalation of pleasure. He could sit here and play with her gorgeous breasts for hours, he mused to himself, moving back to her breasts and replacing one hand with his mouth again. The nipple looked sadly neglected and he leaned in to bite at it.

She jumped and shivered again.

"Such pretty skin," he told her, plumping both breasts together so he could switch back and forth between the nipples. Even as he ran his tongue over one tip, she faltered underneath him, and he noticed her hands sliding off of his shirt. When he bit her nipple again, she gasped, but it wasn't the sexy, excited little gasp that she'd given before.

Miranda was thinking again. What on earth was she thinking about?

He lifted his head and moved forward to press a kiss to her mouth. "Miranda?"

She gave him a hesitant smile, but said nothing.

His hands moved over her breasts and he pinched both nipples at once, causing her body to jolt. The blurry, dazed look returned to her eyes, and then quickly faded again.

"What are you thinking, Mir?"

She bit her lip—fuck, that did amazing things to his cock when she did that—and then glanced away.

He pinched both her nipples again, harder—and she yelped.

"Miranda," he said in a husky voice. "Don't make me bite you into a confession."

She shivered at that, but he couldn't tell if it was a good shiver or a bad one.

"I was just . . . I'm enjoying myself," she said after a moment. "Really."

But what? He watched her face, then watched her expression as his thumbs gently brushed over the tips. That flutter of excitement passed over her face again, then quickly disappeared, followed by the faintest line between her eyebrows, as if she were concentrating very hard and somehow failing. Did she think she needed to come already? Because hell, they were just getting started.

He slid back down over her, pressing kisses to her neck and collarbone before returning to her breasts. Damn, he liked her breasts. He plumped one breast in his hand and then licked the nipple like he would an ice cream. "So," he said casually. "I knew a girl once who could get off on nipple play."

Her expression became bewildered, then flustered. Her hands pushed at him. "Why are you telling me this right now, you creep?"

Dane pinned her arm over her head again, his face leaning in close to hers. Her arm over her head left her breast high and arching, and he reached out to casually play with the nipple, toying with the tip, enjoying the goose bumps his touch left behind on her skin. "I said that I knew one girl, Miranda. *One.* She was one of the locker room bunnies that would show up and hope to bang a player. My buddies passed her around for a while. She'd show up at every home game, looking to score, and she'd come over the smallest touch. And she came a *lot.* She was noisy as hell, too. She really liked having her breasts touched, and she'd come as soon as someone touched her there."

Miranda's glare could have melted steel. She'd gone completely stiff in his arms.

"One time I went in to the locker room and noticed that she was in there, waiting for one of the guys to pay attention to her, and in the meantime, she was rubbing herself up against a doorknob, and getting off."

Her glare turned into a smothered laugh. His own smile returned, and he leaned in to give her a gentle kiss. "She was the only girl I'd ever known who could get off on some guy touching her nipples. Most girls require a lot more work and a lot more foreplay, and I don't want you thinking there's something wrong with you because you can't get off on doorknobs."

She laughed, that sultry little giggle that she always tried to smother but leaked out anyhow. His cock went even harder at the sound. He was going to lose control if he didn't start thinking about something unsexy. Like hockey. That always made his dick want to shrivel.

"Understand what I'm saying?" he said huskily, teasing that perky nipple. Fuck, he loved touching her breasts. He could caress them all night, and he told her so. Her eyes widened at that, and the soft, melting look returned to her eyes. "When I touch you, Miranda," he said softly, "I don't expect you to shatter instantly. I expect you to enjoy it and tell me what you like. Understand?"

She bit her lip again, and nodded. "I wasn't a virgin the other night, you know. I realize that I seem like a big nervous idiot, but I just want you to know—"

"You don't have to explain to me," he said huskily. "Just let me touch you. I enjoy touching you."

Miranda hesitated, then relaxed underneath him.

Clearly Miranda wasn't used to men moving slowly in bed. That was a shame. Maybe she rushed them, trying to speed along the inevitable. Not him. He could spend all night playing with her breasts, teasing her body just to watch her reactions. But if he was losing her, that wasn't good. He sat up, and moved his hands to her belt.

Her body tensed underneath him, her eyes wide as she watched him undo the button on her shorts and lower the zipper.

Her stomach moved up and down with her excited breathing, but when he looked up at her face, she showed anticipation . . . and a hint of nervousness. If she'd had oral sex, she hadn't had it often, he decided. And he determined right then and there that she was going to enjoy it with him.

He lifted her hips off the ground and pulled the shorts down off her legs, tossing them aside. All that was left was a tiny pair of panties low on her hips, a charming pink ruffle on the waistband.

As if sensing his thoughts, her hands flew to the panties protectively. "You can't rip these. They're my favorites."

Dane grinned down at her. "Better take them off fast, then."

She lifted her hips and slid them down with a quick shimmy, then pushed them aside.

He moved between her legs, forcing them to part, and pulled his shirt off, throwing it on the blanket next to her clothing. He wanted to take his shorts off, but right now that was the only thing keeping him from sliding between her legs and fucking her right away, so he left them on. He groaned when her fingertips slid over his stomach, tracing his muscles.

"You have an amazing chest," she said in a soft, low voice filled with wonder. "It looks so perfectly formed—like a sculpture." Her fingertips trailed to his belly button and brushed the line of dark hair on his stomach, moving to the waistband of his pants.

"Not yet," he said, his voice husky. He slid down on the crinkling blanket, kissing her belly again. The quiver returned to her body, her skin reacting with shivering goose bumps every time he kissed it. He kissed her belly button, then moved lower, and she began to tense underneath him. He reached up and took her hand in his, twining her fingers with his own even as he kissed the soft skin lower. "You just tell me if you want me to stop, all right?"

She laughed, the sound a little nervous. "Why would I ever tell you to stop?"

Ah, bravado. He recognized it well. He said nothing, simply continued to kiss the soft crease between thigh and pelvis, running his tongue along it in a way that made her body tremble. Then he placed one hand over the warmth of her mound, and she jumped slightly.

Her fingers clenched in his. "Sorry," she whispered. "I'm jumpy tonight."

"No worries," he said, then brushed his fingers over the trim brown curls hiding her sex. He ran a finger over the edge of the lips, from the front all the way down to where it led into the deep well of her body, then ran his finger back up again. She was soaked, her sex slick and wet, and his fingertip was damp just from her wetness. The body shivers hadn't stopped, and her fingers clenched his tightly—but when he looked up, she still had the soft look in her eyes. Good. "You have a lovely pussy, Miranda," he said. "So soft and shy. Been waiting all day to kiss it."

Her back arched slightly, as if anticipating the kiss, but he simply continued to run his finger over the seam of her sex, before dipping in a little farther and sliding through the slick wetness there. Her breath hissed out of her lungs, and when, again and again, he'd raise that skimming finger up to her clit, her hips would lift in need. He didn't give her what she wanted, though—he'd flick over her skin and then sweep down to the warmth of her core, brushing his fingertip there as well.

She moaned. Her fingers twisted in his, clenching hard. "Please," she breathed.

He slid a finger closer, rubbing in the slick wetness of the hood of her sex, circling close to her clit—close enough to torment but too far for her to get satisfaction from it. "Please what, Miranda?"

"Please touch me," she breathed. "There."

"Where?" he teased, his voice husky. "Tell me where you want me to put my fingers."

Miranda arched, her mouth working silently. He watched her, his cock jumping in response every time she gasped. He continued to run his finger along the wetness, teasing and coaxing the words out of her. "On my clit, please."

He slid a wet fingertip around her clit, circling it once, enjoying the gasping cry that it wrung out of Miranda. "Like that?"

"Oh God," she moaned, her fingers clutching his hard. "Again."

He decided to do one better. Taking one of her legs, he let go of her hand and pulled her leg over his shoulder. Then he did the same for the other leg, until he knelt with his face inches from that hot, wet pussy, and her legs were over his shoulders. "Want me to touch you again?" he murmured against that hot, damp flesh. His mouth watered, waiting to taste her.

She moaned a response, her fingers digging into the thin plastic blanket.

He'd take that as a yes. Leaning down, he nuzzled against her sex and then swept his tongue over her clit.

Her entire body tensed and she shuddered hard, her thighs clenching against his face. He could hear the blanket crinkling madly from her hands fisting in it.

He lifted his head to watch her. "Did you like that, Miranda?"

She gave a jerky nod, her hips quivering so close to his mouth.

"Tell me if you want more."

Again, a jerky nod.

"Well?"

"Just fucking lick me, Dane," she snarled at him.

"Absolutely," he said in a low, pleased voice, and gave her another slow, sensual taste from the heated well of her sex all the way back up to her clit. Her legs trembled again, and her breath was coming in short, sharp pants. Excellent. His own cock was rock hard, his shorts painful against the hard length of him. Soon, he told himself. She was close. Not there yet, but closer. It was time to think about hockey again. He started to mentally run down penalties in his head. Icing. Boarding. High sticking.

She flexed underneath him, impatient.

He gave her another sweeping lick and then settled against her clit, slowly circling it with the tip of his tongue, coaxing it with teasing flicks before circling it again. Miranda's entire body was tense with desire, and every time he licked, her entire body shivered and a small, breathy little cry erupted from her throat that drove him wild. He wanted to stop and ask her if she was enjoying herself, but making her think was off-limits. Dane swirled his tongue around her clit and sucked lightly, and he was rewarded with her sharp inhale. He increased his efforts, swirling his tongue around her clit faster and faster, brushing against the small button repeatedly as her cries increased.

Her hands fisted against his short hair and her hips bucked against his tongue. "Oh . . . like that," she cried.

Hell yeah. He increased the attention, licking and sucking at her clit rapidly. She continued to whimper, her fingers desperately digging against his hair, scratching at his scalp as she tried to find purchase. After a few minutes, she began to push his head down and raise her hips against his tongue, her cries turning into short, sexy little pants that had no words, just whimpers. He increased the pressure, his next lick stroking hard against her clit, and then sucked hard, and then sucked again.

A startled cry erupted from her throat and she came, wetness on his lips and tongue as her entire body trembled and undulated underneath him, her legs clamped tightly around his shoulders, her breath whistling out of her lungs in a low, slow, deep cry that seemed to go on forever.

Holy fuck, that was sexy. She'd come so hard. How had she ever thought herself unable to come with a man? He gave her clit one last slow lick, and was rewarded with a long, shivering aftershock that quivered through her body. She was still up the mountaintop, still lost in pleasure. God. He started to think about penalties again. High sticking. Slashing. Spearing. Fuck, no, spearing made him think of how badly he needed his cock deep inside her—

"I . . ." She panted, her hands falling back to her breasts and she struggled to think of something to say. Her eyes were wide. "I . . . oh wow."

He kissed the inside of her thigh, his own body tense with need. "Like that, did you?"

"That was incredible." She stared up at him in surprise. "I mean, last night was really good but that one . . . wow."

Her knee was close to his mouth and so pretty he reached out and kissed it, too. "That," he told her, "was one. I promised you three."

She licked her lips, the glazed expression returning to her face. "I . . . but . . ."

Dane slid a finger through her drenched sex again, enjoying her latest shudder of response. He slid the digit into the hot well of her pussy, noticing how she spasmed against his finger when he thrust. The low moan began to build back up in her throat again, a moan that he felt all the way down to his cock. Damn. He was so close to coming in his pants. He pressed his forehead against her belly, trying hard to get his body back under control again.

High sticking, he reminded himself. Icing. Hooking. Holding. Hand pass. Fuck it, why did all the penalties sound totally fucking dirty when he needed them to keep his mind off of sex?

He forced himself to concentrate on teams, instead. Montreal Habs. Los Angeles Kings. Vancouver Canucks . . .

When he was safe from going over the edge again, he grasped her breast and teased the nipple, thrusting his other finger deeper into her wet pussy. She was hot and slick with need, and her moans turned quickly to gasps. He moved his mouth back down to her pussy, flicking his tongue against her clit in time with the thrust of his finger, and when she began to quiver hard, he added a second finger, twisting them and repeatedly thrusting them into her wet sex, mimicking the fucking he was dying to give her.

It didn't take long for her to go over again. She started to tense under him, her muscles clenching as if she were preparing for the next orgasm, when suddenly her entire body stiffened and she sucked in a long, deep breath. Her pussy contracted—hard—against his fingers, and he smiled against her clit. He gave it one last, long lick.

"That's two."

She looked up at him, dazed, the look on her face utterly blissful. "Holy . . . shit."

Damn. He loved her expression, the way she hid nothing. Dane let her legs slide down to his sides, and he leaned forward and kissed her deeply, liking that her mouth was so soft and giving under his own. She was boneless with her orgasms, soft and sated and warm. He'd give her one more so she'd know he wasn't full of shit . . . and because he wanted to hear that soft, throaty cry when she came a third time. He could listen to that sound forever.

He quickly divested himself of his shorts and underwear, releasing his cock, aching hard under the need to come deep inside her. Pre-cum covered the head, and it throbbed with need. His entire *body* throbbed with need.

Miranda's gaze went to his cock and she reached for it, her fingertips brushing against the damp crown. "Can I—"

He hissed, dangerously close to spilling himself, and pulled her hand away. Icing. Icing. Had to think about icing. "Give me two seconds, Miranda, and you can have all of me that you want." He pulled a condom out of his pocket and rolled it down his shaft quickly, then took a deep breath. He needed to pace himself if he was going to make her come again, and not bust as soon as he sank deep into her. Normally he had no trouble with control, but Miranda did something to his insides, where he lost all his macho swagger and became this addicted fool who lived to see her smile, to see that expression when she came . . .

Slow was the key here. Slow and steady.

He spread her legs wide, his hands caressing her soft, pale thighs and pushing them forward so that her feet were up in the air, her hips tilted at the perfect angle. With one hand on her thigh, the other guiding his cock, he fed the head of his cock into her tight, wet heat.

Miranda let out a cry, her hips bucking, trying to pull him in deeper. "Oh God."

"Just hold still," he told her, teeth gritting. She was clamping around him so tight. So hot and wet and so very tight. Sweat beaded on his brow, and he sank another inch into her, slowly. Carefully. One massive thrust and he'd lose it. Spill inside her and never give her that third orgasm.

With gritted teeth, he ignored Miranda's breathless response and fed her several more inches, moving excruciatingly slowly.

Icing. Icing. New Jersey Devils. Atlanta Thrashers. Wait, Atlanta was sold—

"So full," she said, interrupting his wild internal monologue. "God, it feels—"

"Shh," he told her, a hair trigger away from losing control. "Miranda, just hold on."

She moaned underneath him and he felt her pussy flutter tight around his cock again.

His control snapped. He rocked forward and impaled himself in her to the hilt.

Her gasp as she arched underneath him was fucking beautiful. She gave a soft little whimper, lifting her knees and tucking her hands tight behind them to pull her legs close to her chest. Her posture pulled him deeper, her pussy tight and wet around him. He held still, on the verge of losing it, doing his damnedest to maintain control. After a moment, he pulled out, slowly, then buried himself to the hilt inside her again, the long sweeping stroke of his cock plunging deep inside her. Her gasp turned into a throaty moan, and her fingers clenched on his shoulders, nails digging in. Fuck, where had the Atlanta team moved to . . .

"Oh God," she whispered, her eyes closed with the intensity of sensation. "So deep . . ."

Oh, fuck Atlanta. He pulled out and drove into her again, noticing that this time, she raised her hips to meet his thrust, and gave another trilling moan as he sank into the hot, tight depths. He drove into her again, and then again.

Each time, she rose to meet him. Her hips slammed against his, intense and powerful, as if he couldn't get deep enough to satisfy her. He moved hard against her, pounding deep into her core, his hands moving to pin her hips to just the right place. He thrust hard, then circled his hips in a long, languid motion, hoping to hit the right spot.

Her eyes flew open and she gave a stuttering gasp, staring up at him. He felt her calves tense on his shoulders.

Bingo. G-spot.

He thrust again, repeating the motion, rolling his hips until he hit just the right spot and she clenched up against him again, trying desperately to raise her hips. His hands kept them firmly pinned in place, and he gave another sweeping, circling thrust. "Do you like that?"

Miranda's lip quivered, and she began to say something, but at his next thrust, her words dissolved into a choked scream.

"What was that?" he teased between gritted teeth, about to come just from her reaction. So intense on her beautiful face. "I couldn't hear you."

Her hands suddenly clenched on his, her ankles digging into his shoulders. "Harder," she gritted. "Please, Dane."

He didn't need to be asked twice. He thrust again, rocking her backward on the crinkling blanket, and was rewarded with another stuttering gasp of delight. Again, and again, and then he was pumping into her repeatedly, her hips pinned against his thrusts, her choked cries echoing in the forest as he thrust into her over and over again.

A full-body tremble started and as he drove deep, he watched her arch again, her shoulders rising as she tensed, her mouth working in a silent scream of pleasure. Her pussy clenched and fluttered around him, hard. Miranda was coming again, and she was fucking beautiful in her abandon. He watched her, thrusting again—once, twice—her pussy spasming around him, milking him—until he couldn't stand it any longer.

And then he went over the edge behind her, his own orgasm coming over him so hard and fierce that he growled, digging his fingers into her hips, his entire body tightening as if one single motion would shatter him. He came with a shout.

She gasped for breath repeatedly, as if there was not enough air in the forest to fill her lungs, her legs still in the air, ankles on his shoulders. He leaned heavily on her, still sunk deep into her body, and stared down at her with a panting grin of his own.

"That's three," he said smugly, and didn't care how pleased his voice sounded.

Miranda laughed, soft and breathy. "You win."

NINE

They folded the crinkling plastic blanket, but it was obvious that it had been used roughly and wasn't going back into the tiny pouch it had come from. "Maybe we could bury it," Miranda suggested.

They did at the base of a tree, and put a stone over it to mark the spot. Dane made a mental note to come back and get rid of the evidence once the trip was done. After it was buried and hidden, they walked back to the campsite, fingers linked as if they were both reluctant to lose the intimacy they'd formed. Dane knew he wasn't ready for it to go away just yet.

When they could see the coals of the fire in the distance, Miranda tugged at his hand and gave him a wicked, satisfied smile. "We going to do this again tomorrow night?"

Sounded like a good idea to him. He was just about to respond when he heard the sound of a heavy log being dropped on the fire. It crackled in the distance and he froze. Someone was awake? Panic swept over him. They'd see him with Miranda and figure out that they'd been on a rendezvous in the woods. And if the clients found out, it'd get back to Colt and Grant.

He'd fuck up the business, and then his friends would hate him for dicking over the team. All over again. Just because he couldn't keep his cock in his pants.

He dropped her hand, regret washing over him. "Miranda, we can't do this again. Ever."

She gave him an offended look. "What the f—"

He clapped a hand over her mouth and stared down at her, face grim. "There's someone awake back at camp. I want you to wait ten minutes and then come back like you've just gone to the bathroom. Understand?"

She glared from under his hand, but nodded.

His own heart was thudding madly as he tucked in his shirt, pretending he'd just been on a bio break of his own, and reapproached camp.

Steve was up, the older man giving him a proud look. He pointed at the fire. "Got it going again."

"So you did," Dane said, his voice forced with casualness. "Thanks, man."

"You seen Miranda anywhere?" Steve asked, his expression puzzled as he scanned the woods.

"She was here when I left," Dane lied. "Dinner did a number on me, though. Maybe it made her sick, too."

As if that were her cue, Miranda came to the edge of camp, holding her stomach. She looked the part—her hair was disheveled, her face flushed, her clothing askew, breasts loose under her

T-shirt. Of course, he knew the real reason why she looked so rough, but it suited his needs.

She glared at the two of them. "Good night."

"Night," Dane said softly and moved back to the bunk. His heart was still hammering. Would Steve suspect something?

But no, the older man puttered at the fire for a moment longer, then returned to the shelter. After a few tense moments, he began to snore.

They'd been so close to being found out. His entire life, fucked up in one glorious, well . . . fuck. That couldn't happen.

He couldn't touch Miranda again. Not until the class was over and done and no one thought of her as his student anymore. Playing around with her this week was just too dangerous.

But there was always after.

Next time she planned on a survival trip, she'd bring a comb, she thought grumpily as she dragged her long, tangled hair into a ponytail. And shampoo, she decided, and thought longingly of her shower back home. Maybe she'd invite Dane to come shower with her. She wouldn't have minded soaping him up and exploring his body with her hands . . . great. She was still horny, even hours after the best night of her life, ever. It seemed that the more she had sex with Dane, the more she wanted to have sex with him. Not exactly conducive to a revenge plot.

She was the one who was supposed to hook him and make him dance to *her* tune, not the other way around.

"Let's break camp," Dane said, looking alert and utterly scrumptious this morning. There were no circles under *his* eyes, she noted sourly. "Miranda, put out the fire. Will, go refill the canteens. Pete, you help Steve take apart the shelters."

Miranda knelt next to the fire and began to put together her fire bundle for the day—a task that she'd shown George how to do last night as part of their cross-training.

"Are we going to switch camps every day until we leave?" asked Steve.

"Not every day," Dane said. "But today, we have our first team-against-team challenge. The winners get a special treat and a special camp."

"And the losers?" Pete said, always the pessimist. She hated to admit it, but she was really starting to dislike Pete.

"The losers get to find their own camp. I'll leave that up to you guys, if you lose." His voice sounded cheerfully confident. "But we're not going to."

"What sort of challenge?" Miranda asked, using a twig to roll one of the coals out onto the tinder bundle.

"You'll see," was all Dane said to them. "And you're all competitive people, so I think you'll enjoy it."

Miranda didn't say anything. Was she competitive? She didn't really fit the mold of the average camper on this trip—she wasn't looking to learn skills that would bring her ahead in the corporate world, or learn about teamwork. She was here . . . well, she was here to bag the trainer. She gave Dane a thoughtful look. He was ignoring her this morning. It seemed a little off, given the mind-blowing interlude from last night. Hell, she couldn't stop thinking about it . . . or the fact that he'd turned her down flat afterward.

She'd known he was skittish but his rejection had still come as a surprise. More than that, it made her determined. She was not going to go home with her tail tucked between her legs, wondering what might have been. Taking his rejection as the final word on things. Dane hadn't been trying to hurt her last night. She knew that; she wasn't being silly or emotional about this week. He was protecting his ass. She just needed to convince him that a week with her was far more enticing than a week without her.

It was time to change up her game. Perhaps she wasn't being competitive enough. She began to think, devising a new game plan.

The team hiked for a short time once camp was broken—Miranda falling to the rear again. She didn't mind. Not being in the midst of things gave her time to think, and she had a lot of thinking to do. Pete was chatty but she wasn't all that interested, and her responses to him were short and noncommittal. After a while, he got the picture and stopped talking.

They entered a particularly rocky area, with a shale cliff off to one side. On the other side, atop the cliff, she could see an ATV trail, and she heard the sound of an engine in the distance. A flash of blue caught her eye as they ascended the ridge and as she watched, the blue team emerged from the woods a short distance away, led by Colt Waggoner.

For some reason, she wasn't enthused to see them. Seeing Colt reminded her of what Dane had thought—that they'd set her up to flirt with him. That she'd been some sort of grand test that he'd failed. She frowned in his direction. If they didn't trust that Dane was on the straight and narrow, they were going to ruin her plans to ruin him. If anyone was going to destroy his life, she wanted to be the one to do it. Dane was going to be hers to make or break.

Strange how that thought left a bit of a sour taste in her mouth this morning.

She blamed it on the camping.

A purring engine revved and a bright red four-wheel ATV sped up the trail, dragging a wheeled cart behind it. A woman was perched on the ATV, her sunglasses masking her expression and her shoulder-length curls sprouting from underneath a cheerful, decal-covered helmet. Brenna the assistant, Miranda remembered, and disliked it even more when both Colt and Dane's faces lit up at the sight of her. "Got your gear, boys," Brenna called out. "One gun for each person on your team and a hundred rounds apiece."

Guns? Rounds? This did not sound like a good idea.

Forgetting their team lineups, the groups splintered and gathered around the ATV as Dane and Colt began to dig through the equipment cart that Brenna had lugged up the trail. Sure enough, there was a stack of what looked like paint-splattered rifles in the back, along with some boxes.

"What's all this?" one man asked before Miranda could.

"Paintball competition," Colt said, his expression cold and unfriendly.

Brenna chimed in for Colt, casting beaming smiles at everyone. "That's right. Today is paintball day. Doesn't have much to do with survival, but everything to do with teamwork. And it sure is fun."

"Greaaat," Miranda said unenthusiastically. A bunch of men running around in the woods shooting at one another did not sound like her idea of a good time. She eyed the others on her team—clearly she was the only one with reservations. The others looked positively giddy at the thought. She took the helmet handed to her and gave it a wary look—it was a full face mask with goggles built into the faceplate. "Are we playing paintball or heading to a *Star Wars* convention? Because I call dibs on the Boba Fett costume."

Pete laughed uproariously at her joke, but the others just stared at her. Well, so much for that. Miranda put the mask on to hide the blush on her cheeks, took the dark red jumpsuit they handed to her, and zipped it over her clothes. This was apparently so she wouldn't get paint on her own clothing. Thoughtful. There were enough jumpsuits for both the red team and the blue team. Brenna also passed out protective cups for the men.

"Can I have two of those?" Miranda asked, and Brenna's eyebrows shot up. Miranda patted her breasts, and the other woman laughed, but didn't hand her a pair. Oh well. She finished dressing as Colt read off the rules of the game. It was a capture the flag game. Each time a team's flag was captured, they would score a point. The team with the most points at the end of the day would win the special campsite. The others would just have to go to whatever campsite was the reject campsite.

Clearly the reward was the game just as much as it was the campsite. At least, it was for everyone but her. Alone time with Dane was the true reward, as far as she was concerned.

As Brenna distributed gear and counted out bullets to the teams, Colt gestured that Dane should join him off to the side. Dane swore under his breath. Great. Colt wanted to have a chat, and Dane didn't feel like talking. He knew what this chat was going to be about. *How are you handling your team? Miranda giving you trouble?*

At least, he hoped that was how the conversation would go.

He jogged over to the tree line and nodded at Colt. "How's your team doing?"

Colt shrugged, his tall frame relaxed as he leaned up against a tree. "It's doing." He looked at Dane expectantly. "You?"

Dane shrugged and glanced back at his small group. They were crowded around the ATV, laughing and teasing one another as they were handed equipment. Miranda seemed to be in high spirits like the rest of them, but she kept glancing over at him, as if curious as to what he was doing. Damn. He hoped Colt didn't notice her watching him. He turned back to Colt. "They're all right. They're learning. It's not quite what I expected, but it's not bad either."

Colt crossed his arms over his chest, the muscles on his forearms flexing. With his lean build, ever-present dog tags, and high-and-tight haircut, he wore his U.S. Marine background like a badge of honor. It always made Dane slightly uneasy. He'd had a very different path than Colt to get where they were today. And while he tried very hard to rid his life of everything hockey, Colt still lived his life as if he were in the marines every day. He grunted now. "They're soft."

"They are civilians," Dane said dryly. "If they were efficient killing machines, I doubt they'd need our class."

Colt grunted again, scowling as he stared out at the team. The friendliest of instructors, he was not. He wondered how Colt's team was faring with the monosyllabic trainer. He knew Colt well—he'd take a bullet for his brother—and the man knew survival like the back of his hand. Teaching and conversation, however, were not two of his strong points. Colt nodded at the teams gathered. "Yours are worse than mine."

"I don't doubt that," he said with a half laugh. "I had one try to pass off a dead fish as his catch."

Colt's glare swiveled and turned to Dane.

He scowled at the ex-marine. "What?"

Colt's eyes narrowed. "Why are you *happy*?"

Oh, here we go. The interrogation begins. "I'm not. Fuck off."

"You just giggled."

"Fuck you, bro. I did *not* giggle."

Colt snorted. "Like a schoolgirl."

Dane elbowed Colt, hard, and was rewarded with his grunt. "Not fucking giggling. I'm just enjoying myself." When Colt still looked skeptical, he added, "I like being out here in the wild again. Reminds me of Alaska. Sometimes I miss Alaska. We didn't have a care in the world up there, you know?"

It was a half lie. While he enjoyed being out in the wild, the reason he felt so relaxed and calm lately was largely due to Miranda. He liked being around her, liked seeing her smile. Liked feeling her hips rising under his. Liked that flushed, startled-with-pleasure look she got on her face when he licked her. But if Colt knew that, he'd kick Dane's ass for fucking up their new business. Colt liked a rigid adherence to rules. He wouldn't understand a deviation. So Dane watched and waited, hoping that Colt would shut up and go back to his team so he could go back to his.

But Colt only grunted. "Alaska was cold. Hated that. Made my dick shrivel."

Dane grinned and clapped his friend on the back, then leaned in. "I don't give a shit about your dick."

Colt punched him, and Dane punched back, back to being friends and ribbing each other like nothing had ever changed.

The bullhorn clicked on and Brenna's chirpy voice screeched over the trees. "If you two are done beating the crap out of each other, can we please play some paintball?"

Bags full of paintball ammo, bottled water, and PowerBars, as well as other miscellany she didn't recognize, were handed out, and the teams shouldered their packs and readied to go into the woods. Through her lashes, she watched as Dane stripped his shirt off before putting on his jumpsuit. Watching his naked back gave her all kinds of ideas, and she smiled to herself as he zipped up and then turned to his team.

Oh, she had lots and *lots* of ideas suddenly.

The blue team set off into the woods as Brenna called instructions after them. "Stay on this side of the stream," she warned. "Don't rove out too far. You all have a fifteen-minute start before I sound the air horn that tells you to begin. No stealing ammo . . . and no nut shots!"

With that command ringing in their ears, the red team set off as well. George was elected the leader—despite his gray hair and a MFA in business administration, George was also a passionate paintball player in his spare time, so he'd been elected the team captain. Miranda had thought Dane would assume the position of leader, but he was happy enough to let the others take charge. Perhaps this was part of his training plan as well—letting others take the initiative.

Clever *and* subtle. She had to admit, she liked that in a man. Too bad it was Dane Croft who housed those qualities.

George led them over a few hills and through the trees. They ran across a hill—heavily treed and with a sandy ridge that was sloughing away due to erosion—that George declared to be the perfect spot to plant their flag. They did so, and then he began to direct orders. "All right—we need one person to stay at camp at all times to guard the flag. Miranda, that's you."

She snapped out of her musings and glared at George. "Why is it me?"

He looked as if he was going to comment that it was because she was female, and then thought better of it. "All right, Pete, you can stay at base this round. We'll take turns. Plenty of time to score points. All we need to do is get to ten first."

That seemed fair enough. Mollified, she listened as George laid out a battle plan—but she was only half paying attention. Evil Miranda needed to make a play today to win back Dane's attention, she had decided. She had tried walking next to him as they'd marched out to plant the flag, but he'd slowed down, acting as if he were re-lacing his boots. Painfully obvious.

Was he afraid that just being seen with her meant that someone was onto their little midnight trysts? Or was he regretting their rendezvous? Or simply done with her?

He didn't get to be done with *her*, she thought with a scowl. She got to decide who was done with whom, not him. And today, she'd just have to up the game a little. No problem.

And if her plans failed, well, she could always resort to one of the nut shots they'd been warned about. That stirred a thought in her mind. A dirty, naughty little thought that made her a bit scandalized . . . and a lot excited. She shouldn't . . .

But she really, really wanted to.

She peeked over at Dane, his paintball gun resting on his shoulder. He slouched, leaning one shoulder against a nearby tree, and avoided looking in her direction. That decided her. Dane Croft wouldn't stand a chance against Evil Miranda.

After a few minutes, the team split up to take positions for the game. Some of the team would be sniping from secluded positions, and others would attempt to take out the camp. Miranda had volunteered to snipe from a vantage point. She grasped her gun, put on her helmet, and began to stalk through the woods. Once she was out of sight, she cut through the trees. She was supposed to guard a lookout point a good quarter mile away from the flag, but screw that.

Instead, she cut across the forest back to the trail that she'd passed on her way out of camp and headed down it, and after Dane.

He was a decent clip ahead of her, and she lagged behind to make sure that he didn't see her. If he did, he might warn her away. She trailed him for a bit, and when he arrived at his location, she ducked behind the nearest bush and unzipped her paintball jumpsuit. She stripped off her clothes—all of them—and then put the jumpsuit back on again. The air was definitely crisper without that second layer of clothing, and she felt her breasts bob and jiggle with every step she took. She put a gloved hand on her breasts and held them still against her chest. She hadn't thought about the bouncing. Hopefully the others wouldn't notice if they should run across her.

She buried her clothes in a pile of leaves and arranged a branch over it so it would be easily recognizable when she came back. Then she went to find Dane. She found him a short distance away, crouched behind one of the taller trees in the area and scanning the distance. His helmet was on, but she remembered that he had the only one that was a solid black. Plus, nobody else out here had those broad shoulders or that ridiculously tight ass. She moved toward him from behind. He hadn't noticed her yet, which was good. She liked the element of surprise.

Smiling to herself, she crept quietly behind him and pulled off her helmet, carefully placing it on the grass nearby. Her gaze dropped to the ground and she noticed a nearby berry bush. A mental image filled her mind of nibbling berries off of his naked body, and she pulled a few of the berries off of the bush. What would be sexier than slowly licking and eating the berry in front of Dane? Just another gun in Evil Miranda's holster, she decided. She slid up behind Dane and when he was close enough to tap, she reached out to run her hand along his nape.

He turned so violently that she stumbled backward in surprise. With a lightning-fast motion, he raised his paintball gun, then lowered it almost as quickly. "Miranda! What are you doing here?" Dane checked behind her. "Are you being followed by someone on the other team?"

"Nope," she said in a sultry voice. She pulled out one of the berries and began to toy with it, playing with the small red fruit along her lips. "Guess what?"

His gaze became glued to that berry, just as she anticipated. Nice. "Uh, Miranda," he began.

"I couldn't wait to see you," she purred in her best Evil Miranda voice, then tapped the berry against her lip playfully. "You've been very naughty, Dane Croft. Why are you being so cruel and ignoring me?"

"You know why." He swallowed hard. "Can I tell you something?"

Her smile curved and she leaned forward to flick the berry against his mouth. "Of course."

He caught her hand and forced her to drop the berry. "That's poisonous."

"Oh." She stared at him blankly for a second, and then added, "I knew that."

He raised an eyebrow.

She furtively scrubbed her mouth. "Poisonous . . . by contact?"

"Digestion," he told her, his look very serious. "How many did you eat?"

"None." Thank God.

He nodded at her and then turned back to his paintball gun. "You'd better go back to your post, then."

She frowned. This was not how she'd envisioned their rendezvous going. Now he thought she was stupid. Rubbing her lip one last time, she slid over next to him and tossed her gun aside. "Was that all you wanted to tell me?"

He glanced over at her briefly, then went back to scanning the woods. "That was it. What else did you have in mind?"

She shrugged. "I don't know. I guess we could talk about

what happened last night." She kept her voice light and sultry. "You've been avoiding me all morning."

"That's because the others are going to find out about us." His gaze flicked back to her. "You know I can't let that happen. I made a vow to my partners that I'd be on my best behavior and I lied. I'm not proud of myself right now, Miranda."

That didn't sound like it would fit her plans at all. If he was going to be this cold with her for the rest of the week, she doubted he could turn it back on like a switch as soon as they were out of here. Her window of opportunity had to remain open, and she had to keep Dane hooked and insatiable.

So she bit her lip and thought for a moment more, then scuffed her hiking boot on the ground. "Hey, Dane."

He didn't turn back around, his voice short. "What?"

She unzipped the top of her jumpsuit an inch or two—not enough to expose skin, but just enough for him to notice the sound. "Guess who's not wearing anything under their jump-suit?"

Crouching at her feet, Dane froze. Slowly, he turned back toward her. "Miranda, what . . ."

And she pulled the zipper down the rest of the way.

TEN

Dane stared at Miranda as she slowly unzipped the jumpsuit. Sure enough, she exposed inch by sultry inch of her perfect skin until the zipper paused below her navel, and she looked up and gave him a naughty look. "What do you think?"

I think you're trying to kill me. "I think we need to talk, Miranda—"

She reached up and placed a finger over his mouth to shush him. "You've talked enough, and I'm not liking what you're saying."

"Miranda—"

She shook her head at him. "I like you, okay?" Her eyes were big and wide as she said that, as if she were trying to convince herself of that as much as him. "And I can't stop thinking about what happened last night. And you know, I liked the three-peat."

She blushed at the words, trailing her finger down his front, as if fascinated by him. "And I thought you liked it, too."

He had. He'd liked it too much. That was exactly the problem. He was losing his head where Miranda was concerned, because all he could think about was bending her over and sinking into the wet, slick satin of her pussy again. Just at the thought, his cock started to rise in his jeans. His mouth tightened and he glanced down at Miranda's body, the tantalizing narrow strip of flesh made visible by the gaping zipper. "I like you, too, Miranda, but—"

Again, she put her finger over his mouth. "So many buts," she said softly. She took a step forward and then she was pressing those amazing, soft breasts against his chest and his cock grew hard as a rock. "You're not going chicken on me, are you?" she said in a soft voice, and trailed a finger up the zipper of his jumpsuit. "Because I thought a big man like you wouldn't be afraid of anything."

She'd deliberately sighed over the word *big*, and that made him all the harder. It was getting difficult to think straight. All he kept seeing was that curve of her breast exposed by the zipper, that sexy dip of her belly button. "We don't have any privacy here in the woods."

But that was the wrong thing to say. Her smile grew brilliant. "We have privacy right now," she said, and her hand tugged the jumpsuit over to one side, revealing the perfect globe of one pretty breast, the tip taut and rosy. Underneath her breast, he saw that small triangular-shaped mole that seemed to almost mock him. "And I really want you to touch me again," she said, her voice almost a sigh. "I keep thinking about your hands all over me, and your mouth, and your cock deep inside me . . ."

Her fingers skimmed over the tip of her breast, as if just the memory made her want to touch herself right in front of him. "And I keep thinking about how much I enjoy touching you, too."

He was having a hard time swallowing. His throat was so fucking dry all of a sudden. Dane's Adam's apple bobbed as he fought to swallow hard, but it was useless. He couldn't see anything but that perfect breast. "Oh? So you've been thinking about touching me?"

"I have," she agreed, and when she reached for the zipper of his jumpsuit, he didn't stop her. She was a sultry enchantress, so sexy and confident and utterly sensual. Her gaze followed the zipper and it exposed his bare chest underneath. He let his hand brush over her covered breast, pushing the fabric back and exposing the other to the air.

He loved Miranda the seductress in that moment.

"Fuck," he said in a ragged voice. Despite his resolve, here he was giving in to her demands. All it took was for her to show him one lovely breast, a pink nipple, and a teasing mole and he was a goner.

"Would love to," she said with a sultry smile. "But right now I'm interested in a little something else."

His hand went to cover her breast and he laid his palm over the peak, his tanned, callused hand looking foreign against her smooth skin. "And you want me to touch you?"

"Oh yes," she breathed, then almost looked embarrassed at how it had come out. A hint of a flush touched her face and crept down to her breasts. "I lose my mind whenever you touch me. I like it. It allows me to . . . lose myself in the moment."

"And lets you come?" He whispered in a husky voice, leaning

in close to her. Even after several days in the woods, Miranda still smelled good. Clean and fresh and warm. She bathed in the stream every morning, and he had to admit that he had picked campsites by streams for that very reason.

"Every time," she admitted, biting her lip as if she felt scandalized bringing this up.

He let his hand slide to her belly button, then slid it into the V of the zipper and felt the curls of her sex. They were completely soaked and he hissed at that. "You are so wet."

Her hands gripped him, her body locking as if it was too much to process, and she gave a shuddering gasp. Her hips flexed against his hand. "Oh, Dane. Touch me, please."

As if he could resist when she begged so very sweetly. With one hand gripping her around her waist, he pulled her closer and dug one blunt finger between the damp curls. She gasped as he grazed her clit, then sank the finger into her hot, silky warmth.

"Mmm, I like that," she said, and her arms wrapped around his neck, dragging his face down so she could kiss it. Naked and panting, he twisted so her breasts pushed against his chest, and her hips worked over his hand.

He slid the finger in and out slowly, enjoying the way she moaned and twisted with each small motion.

Her mouth frantically searched along his jaw as he pressed the heel of his palm against her clit and sank his finger in again. Miranda gave a muffled gasp that echoed in his ear right before she bit down on his earlobe, and he thrust his finger into her hot core again. Once, twice, and then she shivered all over, released his ear and buried her face in his neck to muffle her low moan.

Warmth spilled over his palm as she gave a deep gasp and

came against his hand, unable to hold out longer. It was incredibly erotic. He continued rubbing her pussy, enjoying the little quivers and involuntary jerking pulses she made as she came down from her orgasm. Her eyes were closed and the flush had returned to her cheeks and breasts, and she looked gorgeous in the dappled sunlight.

He didn't care if this was a mistake. Seeing that open, raw look on Miranda's face and feeling her come all over his hand? He'd do it again in a heartbeat.

Her brown eyes opened slowly. She smiled up at him, the expression languid and satisfied, as if she'd never felt so good. "We're getting better and better at that, aren't we? Soon I'm going to come just from you looking at me."

Hearing that made him even harder. If he was any harder, he'd start losing blood to his brain. "Where's the fun in that?"

She gave a throaty, sexy little laugh and slipped out of his arms. "It's fun for *me*."

His hands slid from her body and he watched her move away with a bit of regret. She had the most beautiful breasts. "But you've made me all distracted. That isn't what I came here for," she said in a coy voice.

He raised an eyebrow. "Oh, no? What are you here for, then?"

The tiny, sly smile remained on her mouth and she reached for his zipper. She pulled it down below his waist, and then her hands went to the top button of his jeans, causing his straining cock to jump. "Want to guess?"

Dane swallowed hard. Without even a second of hesitation, he reached out and brushed her long brown hair back over her shoulder, where it had fallen over her breast. "Sure."

"How about I just show you?" She wiggled her eyebrows at him in a look that managed to be playful and sexy all at the same time. And then she dropped to her knees in front of him.

He groaned under his breath as her hands slid to the hard bulge in his jeans where his cock rose, desperate to be free. "Miranda," he said softly. "What are you doing?"

She gave him a playful look and undid the buttons of his fly. "I'm touching you."

His hand went to her hair, tangling in the silky locks. "You are driving me crazy. Are you usually this naughty?"

Her hands slid to the front of his boxers. "Actually, I'm normally just a buttoned-up librarian," she said and winked up at him. She tugged at the sleeves of his jumpsuit, and he helped her, pulling his arms out. She pushed his clothes down until they bunched at his knees, then followed suit with his jeans and boxers, until all his clothes were pooling at his knees and his cock was free. The breath of surprise that Miranda sucked in was immensely gratifying. "Oh my," she breathed, her hands going to cup his balls. Her other hand slid to the base of his cock. "I never get tired of seeing this." She gave him a pleased look and wrapped her fingers around the base, as if testing the girth.

The squeeze was almost enough to send him over the edge, and he leaned his head back, his hands moving to grip the bark of the tree. He dug in with his fingers. Miranda was amazingly sexy, kneeling before him and handling his cock, and he did not want to blow his wad before he had a chance to thoroughly enjoy himself with what she was offering. "You don't have to do this," he mentioned, because he felt like he had to. Just because he'd touched her didn't mean she had to go down on him.

She rolled her eyes at him. "Like I'm doing this for you." She leaned in and her breath touched the head of his cock, hot and silky. "I'm doing this for me. Understand?"

He did. "In that case," he said, digging his fingers into the bark harder so he wouldn't reach out and touch her and somehow ruin this moment, "be my guest."

From below his waist, Miranda grinned. She leaned in and gave his cock another squeeze, then slid forward and swiped at the head of it with her tongue. Her tongue flicked against the crown, tasting the drop of liquid beaded there. He groaned. Goddamn. He held his breath, unwilling to do anything to spoil the moment. His entire body tensed, waiting for her to lean forward again and take more of him into her mouth.

And she did. She moved in and the head slid past her lips, into the wet, sucking cavern of her mouth. He could feel her tongue tickle the vein on the underside of his cock, and she pumped the base as she pulled him farther into her mouth.

Dane panted, his gaze glued to her intent face. She looked as if she was concentrating hard, as if she wanted to get it just right. For him. The expression on her face was driving him almost as crazy as the feel of her tongue against his cock. He felt her suck him all the way into her mouth, felt the head of his cock butt against the back of her throat, and then she released him, pulling away before pumping the base and sliding him deep into her mouth again in one long, sinuous motion.

She was amazing. That playful look was back on her face again as she let his cock fall from her mouth, then rubbed the head of it on her lips. He wanted to fuck her mouth, to fuck the playfulness off of her face and have her return to that intense look that he liked better than anything. The intense look that told him she was concentrating so hard because she was so very distracted.

When her lips curved around the tip of his cock again, he put a hand to her hair and tangled it there, guiding her head. Would she like this? Some women didn't.

She gave a little moan of pleasure around his cock and let him lead as he fucked her mouth, stroking into it over and over again. He noticed that as she worked his cock, she pushed her breasts against his thighs, making sure that her nipples scraped against his skin repeatedly.

He reached down to help her with that, his other hand moving to tease the curve of one breast, rubbing against a nipple. She arched her back and leaned in to his touch, and he felt the low groan in the back of her throat against his cock, still buried deep in her mouth. He loved touching her. The way she felt, the way she responded—there was something about Miranda that just drove him crazy with lust. He wanted to see her come again, to see her eyes flutter as she rocked into another orgasm.

"Touch yourself, Miranda," he murmured, his hand tangling in her hair again, guiding her back and forth as her mouth stroked his cock. "I want to see you touch yourself." Her hand had been teasing his balls and it fluttered on his thigh.

She looked up at him with those brown eyes, and then her hand slid into her jumpsuit. She rolled her hips and gave another whimper, and he tweaked a nipple as he drove into her mouth again. "You are just about the hottest thing I have ever seen," he murmured, unable to stop touching her. One hand anchored in her hair, guiding her head, and the other skimmed along her breast again, then her arm, her cheek, anywhere he could touch her, to let her know how much he liked her mouth on his cock.

Her hand began to work frantically between her legs, her hips giving that delicious shiver he was starting to recognize as Miranda being close to an orgasm, and it made his entire body surge. She was about to come again, just from taking him in her mouth, pleasuring him.

The thought drove him wild, and he began to go over the edge. His balls tightened and he nearly lost it, but froze, breathing hard. "Miranda . . . I'm about to come. Do you want me to . . ."

In response, her hand stole out from between her legs and she cupped his balls, toying with them with her fingers. Her mouth sucked down on his cock and she pulled him deeper into her throat.

That was enough for him. Hand tangled hard in her hair, he pumped into her mouth and came, groaning her name as he did so. Cum shot down her throat but she didn't tear away from him, and he finished with a heavy breath, his cock sliding away from her lips as she closed her mouth and swallowed all that he'd given her. Her hand fluttered between her legs again, working her sex as she tried to come again.

He pulled her up to her feet and she stopped, but he guided her hand back between her legs. Her eyes met his and he leaned in and kissed her neck as she stroked her flesh. When he bit her, hard, on the neck, she came in a soft little scream.

She collapsed in his arms, as if the orgasm had made her totally boneless, and he cradled her and helped her slip to the ground. He expected her to sit up, brush off, something. Instead, she lay back in the grass and the leaves and gave the most sultry, satisfied giggle he had ever heard.

He moved to sit next to her, a hint of a smile touching his mouth at her satisfied expression. "What was that laugh for?"

The look on Miranda's face was dreamy. "I was just thinking I should have done that days ago."

That had not been what he expected to hear from her. He watched her, her breasts pointed up to the skies, her hair pooled back behind her, and in that moment, Dane was truly and utterly caught.

Hell. When he got back to the base camp, he was going to have to tell Colt and Grant that he'd been messing around with one of their new clients.

Because there was no way he was letting Miranda Hill get away from him again. He grinned at the thought. He'd tell them when he got back. They'd understand . . . eventually.

The little minx glanced over at him, and smiled. "Your pants are still down around your ankles."

"You're still naked under your jumpsuit," he rebutted.

"Mmm, true." She looked as if she didn't care. She didn't move to cover her breasts. "You know, I've decided I like the woods," she said softly.

"And why is that?" Dane hitched his boxers back up around his waist, and then his pants.

"No prying eyes," she said with a light sigh, as if it were the most blissful thing in the world. "It's just you and nature. No nosy townspeople." Her fingers played with a leaf near her head.

He chuckled at the thought. Now she sounded like him. It was the very reason he'd gone off the grid in the wilds of Alaska—

he just wanted to get away from everyone. To never see another city again. People hadn't understood his decision at the time—they'd assumed he'd go to Hollywood and cash in on his notoriety. It was just another part of Miranda's appeal that she felt the same way he did. Though it was odd that she had a reason to. "Someone in town giving you a hard time?"

She glanced over at him and the smile slid off of her face, as if she had realized what she just said. Her hands stole to the zipper of her jumpsuit and she quickly zipped it shut, then stood. Her hands pulled leaves out of her tangled hair and she shrugged. "Nah. Just thinking aloud." With that, she glanced at the trees in the distance. "I think I'm going to go find my clothes. See you later, Dane."

With a casual wave, she turned and left him, stopping only to swoop over and pick up her paintball gun from where she'd dropped it.

He was oddly tempted to follow her. But instead, he turned and picked up his paintball gun, put on his helmet, and hoped it covered the satisfied smile on his face.

Miranda flopped to the ground once she found her clothes and just breathed for a few minutes, determined not to let panic sink in.

Dear lord, what the hell was she doing?

It had all seemed like such a brilliant plan. Find Dane, flirt with him. Flash him a little cleavage. Taste that big cock—to please herself—and then leave him wanting more. But she'd been an idiot and started yapping about town and privacy of all things, and hell, why didn't she just confess her entire plan to him right then and there?

She put a hand to her forehead and rubbed. Stupid. Stupid, stupid. She'd let things get carried away, and then she'd been so hot and bothered and content afterward that she'd just started spouting all kinds of crap.

Good Miranda needed to back the hell off and let Evil Miranda stay in charge. Evil Miranda would have just sucked his dick, winked at him, and left. Good Miranda had to have her cuddle time and let him see the vulnerable side of her.

Good Miranda was an idiot.

She didn't regret pleasuring Dane—it had been far too enjoyable. What she regretted now was that she was losing control of herself. This was supposed to be *her* revenge. And while she was twisting Dane around her finger . . . she found herself enjoying his kisses and his touch far too much. She could still taste him in her mouth, still feel his hands on her body.

When had she started to like spending time with him? When did the revenge lose its focus in exchange for the next orgasm?

Shit. Shit, shit, shit. Good Miranda kept going on about her *feeeeelings*. Feelings only got in the way of things. Frowning to herself, Miranda pulled out her panties and resolved that from now on, she was going to stay in control. Emotionless flirting and a teasing fuck or two in the woods. She needed to keep him off guard. Most of all, she needed to keep in control. She wouldn't let herself lose control of the situation again.

Because apparently she couldn't be trusted around the man. He touched her and she just lost all sense of reality.

And that couldn't keep happening.

• • •

The afternoon of paintball did a lot to distract Miranda from her worries. There was something incredibly cathartic about shooting a man, which probably said a lot about more about her mindset than it should have. To her surprise, their team won the afternoon—despite the fact that both she and Dane had been distracted for a good while. George had been a superb leader and a terrific paintball player, and his skills and enthusiasm had pushed them over the top, though it had been close.

The special prize had indeed been a nice campsite. There was a tiny cabin in the woods with two sets of bunk beds and extra blankets. It was situated next to a well, and the only roughing that was required was cooking and eating the steaks that had been left for them. The team was in high spirits, and no one even pointed out that this wasn't much of a survival skill. No one cared.

They had a nice, quiet evening—it was Steve's turn to set up the fire and she helped the others collect wood while George and Pete went to set up a new trapline.

Dane had gone back to treating her like one of the guys, but it was Miranda who put a little distance between them. She'd been opening up to him too much. He didn't want to know what she was thinking or how she felt—he just wanted his next roll in the hay. It was time to take a breather on the chatty stuff and just seduce the man when she needed to. So she stayed on the far side of camp and kept to herself. Dane didn't seem too thrilled at that, but it was nice to have the tables turned at least.

That evening, they drew straws for cots, and Will, Jamie, and Dane ended up sleeping on the ground. Miranda got a top bunk and slept warm and cozy for the first time that week. So the bunk smelled a little stale—didn't matter. She was happy to have her own bed, even though she was unable to sleep. In the middle of the night, she leaned over the edge and glanced below. Sure enough, Dane was down there, looking at her. He grinned and pointed for the door, a wordless question.

Her body quivered with need at the thought, but she forced herself to shake her head and roll back on the mattress and go back to sleep.

She was going to call the shots around here, even if she wanted to give in.

And right now, she really, *really* wanted to give in.

Morning dawned, and that day was Miranda's turn to learn foraging from the designated subject matter expert. Jamie was their forager for the week, and that suited her just fine. She wanted nothing more than to get away from camp for a few hours and clear her head. But Jamie had left early that morning to learn traplines, and now she sat at camp drumming her fingers.

Nearby, Dane sat making more knots in some rope for Pete. He'd shown the poor gamer CEO the same knots every day that week, and every day, Pete needed to be shown again. Dane didn't lose his temper, but she was pretty sure he was getting sick of Pete. The man was lazy around camp, whined, and took every opportunity available to tell them how much money he was making at his company. No one liked him.

"You know, Miranda, I can show you how to forage," Dane offered with a casual sideways glance. "I'd be more than happy to take you out and show you if the others aren't going to be back for a while."

She could just bet how that would go. As soon as Dane left the campsite, she'd become entranced by the flex of his muscles as he bent over to pick up something and then she'd throw him down on the ground and hump him with abandon. Flushing at the thought, she shook her head. "That's okay, thanks."

Pete seemed to wake up at that. He stood up and brushed off his shorts, drawing attention to his pale, bony legs. "Miranda, if you want, I can show you fishing. You still need to learn that, right?"

This made Dane frown, and he gave Miranda an imperceptible shake of his head.

Well, she loved driving the man crazy by doing the unexpected. She stood. "That sounds lovely, Pete. Thank you. Let me just change into some shorts."

She did, and they set off into the woods, Dane giving her an odd look as they left. He looked as if he wanted to talk to her. She decided she'd let him stew for a bit instead.

After all, she'd been stewing all night and she was horny. Angry and horny—it was a terrible combination. She would be strong, though, and not give in to his sexy smile and tight ass. Damn Dane for thinking he could snap his fingers and she'd be on all fours, ready and willing. Of course, that mental image didn't help her libido, and she gave a sigh.

The stream wasn't too far away—thanks to the better campsite—and she took the line that Pete offered her. He showed her how to set up the hook he'd created from crudely carved wood and how to string a dead grasshopper on it. There wasn't much more to it than tossing the line in and watching the piece of wood (tied to the string to form a makeshift float) bob on the surface.

It was a soothing sort of task, with nothing more to do than occasionally tug on her line to see how things were coming. Pete was chatty but she wasn't all that interested.

It was a pleasant way to spend an afternoon—peaceful and quiet after living in close quarters with six men for the past few days. Best of all, it allowed her to get away from Dane for a few hours and clear her mind. It definitely could use some clearing. Right now she was feeling so lost about him that she didn't know what to think.

"How's the fishing coming?" Pete said a while later, wading over in the water to get closer to her.

His question broke her nice quiet reverie. So much for relaxing. "It's fine. No bites just yet." And there wouldn't be if he kept wading around close to where her bobber floated. "Let's just give it some time."

He moved to stand next to her and threw his line out again, crossing over hers.

She flashed him an irritated look, but said nothing, simply moved out of the way and dragged her line over a few feet. Was the man not even good at fishing? Wasn't fishing hard to screw up?

"So . . . Miranda," Pete said when she'd gotten her line resettled. "How are you enjoying being out here in the wild with nothing but a bunch of big, sweaty men?"

Her hackles went up. It could have been a perfectly innocent question, but the way he phrased it made her think otherwise. "Trip's going just fine," she said tersely.

He nodded. "Good, good." There was a moment of silence, and then he looked over at her again, the smarmy grin on his face. "Any particular man you have your eye on?"

She immediately rounded on him in irritation. "Where is this going, Pete?"

The look he gave her was innocent. "I'm not sure what you mean, Miranda. I was just asking if you had a favorite guy you liked hanging out with this week. That's all."

What did he think he knew about her and Dane? Miranda's eyes narrowed at the gamer CEO. "What makes you think I have a favorite out here?"

"Oh, I don't know." He said casually, trailing his fingers through the water and making little circles that were certain to scare away any remaining fish. "You seem like the type who wouldn't mind a strong, attractive man at your side to make you feel beautiful and shower you with attention. To see to your every need . . ."

She stiffened. Had he seen her and Dane in the woods?

". . . and I think you're the type that might appreciate the perks that come with dating a CEO." He paused and gave her an expectant look.

Blank, Miranda stared at him, trying to piece together his thoughts. Was Dane a CEO of something? The only CEO this week was . . . Oh. She began to laugh with relief as she realized just who he was referring to.

At her laugh, Pete scowled. "What's so funny about this?"

She tried to smother the laugh behind her hand, but a bubble still escaped her. "Nothing. Sorry. It's not funny. It just wasn't what I expected, that's all."

His look became cunning. "Maybe you expected me to mention Dane? I see the way you're slobbering after him."

That quieted her laughter. "I'm not slobbering after anyone, you jackass."

"Oh, come on. Don't think I haven't seen you snuggling up to Dane every chance you get. You follow him around like a puppy and hang on his every word. It's pretty obvious that you have a thing for him."

That was sobering. Did everyone think she had a thing for him? And here she thought she'd been so very sly and clever this week, so very careful to only let Dane see what she was offering. Her hand went to her collar anxiously.

Now that Pete had his feelings hurt, he seemed to be on a bit of a rampage. "If you think you have any hope of scoring time with our instructor just because he's some big shot hockey player, I'm here to disabuse you of that notion," he said, curling his lip at her. "I asked Dane flat out if he was interested in you. If he was going to pursue you. And do you know what he said?"

Her entire body froze. Somehow, it had become very important for her to hear the words. "What did he say?" Her voice sounded incredibly calm despite the hammering of her heart.

"He said that I was welcome to you. That he wasn't interested in you. So there."

Miranda turned her gaze back to her fishing line, watching the stick bob back and forth, and not really caring if anything was biting on the other end. Of course Dane had said that, if confronted. Why wouldn't he? And yet . . . had he really said that Pete was welcome to her? Seriously? That stung.

As if realizing that he'd gone too far over the line, Pete moved forward and put his hand on her shoulder in an effort to comfort her. "Hey, Miranda, I'm not trying to hurt you. I'm just trying to make you realize that you could do better than that cocky dickhead."

She swallowed the knot in her throat and gave him a skeptical smile. "Like you?"

"Yeah, like me," he said, offended that he had to point out the fact. "I'm a multimillionaire, you know. I—"

"You're the CEO of Hazardous Waste Games. Yes, I know," she interrupted, then turned and held her fishing pole in his direction. "And while the offer is very sweet, Pete, I'm really not looking to hook up with anyone on this trip. I'm starting a new life in two weeks, and I don't plan on leaving any baggage behind."

"That's fine," Pete was quick to offer. "I'm totally game for a one-night stand."

She rolled her eyes and turned to leave. "Take my fishing pole, please. I need some time alone." She shoved it into his hand. "I think it has a bite." Ignoring his yelps of surprise, Miranda ducked past a tree and moved deeper into the woods. She needed time to breathe. Time to think.

Was Dane just using *her*? She'd thought she'd seen real interest in his eyes, but was she being blind? Was this just round two of Dane's twisted games, nine years after he'd ruined her life the first time?

The thought made her sick to her stomach, because she couldn't tell what Dane was up to.

ELEVEN

Something was amiss. Dane scowled at Pete as he returned to camp, a fat fish strung through the gills on a large stick. The man looked utterly proud of himself for finally catching a fish, but he also looked . . . guilty. He wouldn't meet Dane's eyes as he returned to camp.

So he approached Pete. "Caught something, I see?"

"I did," Pete agreed, and before Dane could even ask him to, he sat down and began to dress the fish.

Well, that was an improvement. Pete never did anything voluntarily. Dane glanced at the woods, looking for Miranda. It was getting dark and she should have been with Pete, but there was no sign of her. "Where's your partner?"

Pete's skinny shoulders raised in a shrug. "She went for a walk." When Dane continued to loom over Pete with a frown, Pete added, "She was in a bad mood. I didn't ask. You know how women get."

Not only was that sexist, but that was unfair to Miranda. She'd had good reason for getting mad at Pete the times that she had. He crossed his arms over his chest, deciding to wait it out. It could have been that something had upset her stomach and she was ill, and she wanted to be sick in the woods away from nosy Pete. That he could understand.

As he fed another branch to the cozy fire, he turned and looked at the others in the camp. Steve was showing Jamie how to lash the shelter properly, but it was finished for the evening, with even a cozy side shelter for Miranda. George and Will had caught a squirrel in one of the traplines and Will was busy cleaning the kill. Their little camp was busy and productive. Except for Miranda, who had run off into the woods.

He decided to wait a few more minutes, to see if she would come back. So he gathered wood and answered Steve's questions—Steve always had more questions—and loitered around camp as they cooked dinner. Pete whistled an annoying, off-key tune as he finished scaling the fish and trussed it up through a stick to roast over the fire next to the squirrel. They had some pecans and dandelion greens to go with the small meal, and spirits were high.

When the food was ready and dark had set on the camp, the men looked at him expectantly. "Should we wait for Miranda before eating?"

"The portions are awfully small for seven people," Pete helpfully pointed out. "Maybe she's already eaten something and we should go ahead without her?"

That little shit. Part of him wanted to tell Pete to fuck off, and that if he touched Miranda's share of the food, he'd skewer him over the fire next. But that wouldn't make him a great teacher, would it?

He frowned and moved to his backpack, pulling out the GPS tracker. He turned it on and punched in the code for Miranda's bracelet, and she began to beep on his radar. "You guys eat without us. I'm going to go check on Miranda and make sure everything is all right."

Gray-haired George immediately stood and moved to Dane's side. "I'll come with you, just in case she's hurt herself and you need help."

"No," Dane said quickly, thinking of his last few rendezvous with Miranda. She'd surprised him from out of nowhere repeatedly and pounced on him. Maybe this was another one of her sexy little games. The last thing he wanted was for George to come upon Miranda trying to seduce him in the woods again. "I'm sure I can find her. Don't worry about us. If I need help, I'll radio back to the base. You guys go ahead and eat. Don't worry about Miranda."

George nodded and moved back to the fire, and Dane set off in the woods, tracking Miranda.

He found her a short while later, a mile or so from camp, sitting alone in the woods on a fallen log. Though the sky was darkening and the stars were out, there was plenty of light to see by thanks to the rising moon that leaked in through the trees and the flashlight in his hand. He could have found her without the flashlight, but it would give her a chance to see him coming and to not be scared.

Miranda was anything but scared, though. Instead, when he came up to her, she looked pissed. "Miranda, are you all right?"

"Fine," she said in an oddly flat voice. She didn't sound fine.

"Did you hurt something? Did you get bitten?" He gestured with the flashlight back the way he came. "The others were waiting for you at camp."

"I needed to clear my head," she said, and didn't offer more. Dane frowned and clicked off the flashlight.

"Clear your head? Why?" He watched her tilt her head to the side, as if considering his answer and how she would respond.

After a moment, she gave a long, weary sigh. "It's complicated, Dane. Very, very complicated." She sounded so dejected that he felt a ridiculous urge to go and comfort her. Miranda didn't need comforting, did she?

"So complicated that you can't talk to me about it?" For some reason, he didn't like that. Miranda didn't need protecting, but while she was on this trip, she was his responsibility, and he didn't like seeing her troubled. He liked seeing that playful smile on her face. It wasn't there right now, and he hadn't realized how much he'd enjoyed seeing it. So he moved toward her and tilted a finger under her chin, forcing her to lift her face. "Hey," he said softly. "You can talk to me."

She gave a small, brittle laugh at that. "Can I really, Dane?"

"Of course," he said, a little stung. "You can trust me."

Another mirthless laugh escaped her with that.

"What's so funny?"

"Nothing," she said with a sigh, standing up and brushing off her shorts. "Just laughing at myself, really."

He moved forward and put a hand on her arm. "Miranda," he said, brushing his thumb across the bare skin of her upper arm. "No one is . . . approaching you incorrectly, are they?

They're not harassing you?" He remembered Pete's "accidental" grab of her breasts and his jaw clenched, hard. Client or no client, if that little shit had tried anything . . .

"No," she said in a soft voice. "It's nothing. I'm just mentally not all here today." Her arm patted his. "Really. It's nothing."

He decided to make her smile, instead. "It's because you missed me, right?" His hand reached up and touched her chin. "Couldn't stand the thought of being away from me for a few hours, and spending it with Pete was enough to make you sad?"

She laughed at that, and he felt her mouth pull into a genuine smile. His thumb grazed over her lip, and a long, quiet moment passed between the two of them. "See? It's not so bad being with me," he teased.

That seemed to sober her again. He frowned. Was she mad at him for some strange reason? The last time they'd had a moment alone together, she'd flopped back on the grass after giving him the best blow job of his life. She'd looked content and just a little pleased with herself. Miranda had him turned inside out lately. What had brought around this newest change of heart?

Before he could question her further, she reached up, grasped his ears, and pulled him down. Her mouth devoured his in a wild kiss, her tongue thrusting into his mouth.

Was Miranda fired up, then? Practically every time she saw him alone, she attacked him. The woman had a killer libido.

Still, he wasn't looking this gift horse in the mouth. His arms wrapped around her and his hands settled on her waist, then he grasped her ass and pulled her in closer. His tongue thrust back against hers, a willing partner.

Her kiss broke off with a low growl, and she stared up at him in the moonlight for a long moment. Then she said, "I started this, Dane. And I'm going to be the one to finish it. Understand me?"

What the hell was she talking about? "Not really," he said with a half grin. "Care to explain?"

"No," she said. "We're going to do this by my rules." And she pulled him in for another searing kiss. Her hands went to the front of his shorts.

His cock jumped. "You want to do this right now?"

She gave him another wicked smile. "Are you chicken?"

"Hell no," he said, and pulled her in for another searing kiss. He wanted to kiss that smirky little smile off her face, get her expression to change from the almost-angry intensity to softness. To watch her mouth part and hear those soft little noises she made in her throat when he touched her. So Dane continued to kiss her, his tongue licking into her mouth.

Her hand slid over his cock in his shorts, rubbing the length of him in a way that made his entire body flare with need. He groaned against her mouth, trapping her hand just as she brushed her fingertips over his sac. "You're a little wild today, aren't you?"

She grinned against his mouth, and then ran her tongue over his lower lip. "I've heard you have a thing for wild, Mr. Croft."

Did he ever. Miranda's flirty freight train of lust was driving him insane. When her fingers squeezed his sac again, he groaned and pulled her against him, turning so her back was cradled against his stomach. His hands pinned her hips against his, and he leaned in and whispered against her ear. "How would you like it if I turned the tables on you, Miss Wild?"

"Why, I thought you'd never ask," she purred.

Dane's hand skimmed over her breasts. Her nipples were hard little pricks under her T-shirt, and he coaxed each one with a gentle brush of his fingers. She inhaled sharply, and he leaned in and kissed the side of her neck, which was slightly damp with sweat. He loved it when she was sweaty, her skin slightly dewy with exertion. When she arched into his hand, he teased her nipple a moment more before skimming lower. His hand went to the waistband of her shorts, and then he skimmed his fingers along the edge of the fabric, teasing her.

Miranda wriggled in his arms, as if anxious for his touch. Her hand curved backward, stroking the short burr of his hair. "Are you going to touch me or not?"

He nipped at the side of her neck. "Depends on how badly you need it."

Her other hand slid between them and he felt it brush against the hard length of his cock again. "Seems like I'm not the only one who needs it bad," she teased. "You're as hard as iron back here."

Dane groaned at her touch. "I am."

She slithered out of his arms and turned toward him with a mischievous look on her face. "I can help you with that."

"Can you, now?"

She dropped to her knees, tugging down his pants and freeing his cock from his boxers. A second later, she was taking him in her mouth and her hot, wet tongue stroked the underside of his cock, along the thick vein there. He shuddered hard, his hand going to her hair. He should tell her to stop, should take control again, pull her back in his arms, and tease the ever-loving hell out of those pretty nipples. But then Miranda's hand stroked his sac as she lapped at the head of his cock, looking up at him with a teasing glint in her eyes.

And he pretty much forgot everything.

When she took him deep in her throat and began to hum, he groaned and began to thrust into her mouth. He was building fast and hard, and he wasn't going to last long. Miranda seemed to know this, encouraging it with her fingers dancing across his sac.

"Miranda," he gritted out. "Might want to pull away if—"

She bore down on him, pulling him deep into her throat and humming louder. The vibration of her vocal cords made his entire cock feel like it was bathed in sensation.

He came, shooting hot cum down the back of her throat. She continued to stroke his sac, fondling him as he came down from the short, violent orgasm. When he finished, she looked up at him with a very naughty expression and wiped the corners of her mouth. "Not much staying power, I'm afraid."

Minx. He hitched his shorts back up and, when she stood, snagged her in his arms. "Not so fast. Turnabout is fair play." His hands went to her shorts and he began to unbutton them.

She stiffened in his arms for a moment, then relaxed and helped him slide them down her legs. Her panties quickly followed after them, he tugged her against him and slid to his knees, burying his mouth in her wet pussy. She gasped in shock and then her fingers curled in his hair, her body shuddering as his tongue darted into the slit of her pussy and stroked her clit.

He wanted to make her come as fast and as hard as he had. One hand stole between her buttocks and he ran his fingers along the seam of her sex, then plunged a finger into her wet core. His tongue continued to flick and suck against her clit, relentless and determined.

Miranda shivered against him, and then he heard her breath choke in her throat, and her fingernails dug into his scalp, rough, and she came in a wet, salty rush against his tongue.

He gave her clit one last, satisfying lick, savoring the taste, and then looked up at her and grinned. "Not much staying power?"

She gave him a dazed laugh, the tension in her face gone. "Guess not."

For the next two days, they didn't have a chance to sneak in any alone time. It was starting to make Miranda antsy—each time they'd sneak off into the woods, someone would follow them. They hadn't been able to do more than steal a kiss or two, and Miranda was starting to feel anxious. It was going to be tricky to keep Dane interested if they couldn't have sex, after all. So she did her best to cast him longing glances and let her fingers linger on him when she had the chance. Not that she had to try hard to look at him longingly—she couldn't wait to have sex again.

Day six was designated as team-building and team exercises. Brenna showed up again on her ATV and brought more props, and they had obstacle races and puzzles that couldn't be solved without the help of all team members. There were challenges and the prize of the reward camp again.

Their team lost. By the time they got back to their last designated camp and restarted their fire, they were exhausted and curled up in their respective shelters. Miranda didn't approach

Dane that night at all, remembering what Pete had said about her snuggling up to Dane over and over again. Yet another night of enforced celibacy. Miranda went to bed hoping that Dane was starting to feel just as sexually frustrated as she was.

The final day dawned rainy and wet, and with it came an odd sense of anxiousness on Miranda's part. This was the last chance—her chance to "hook" Dane Croft. She wasn't ready, she thought as they broke down the camp as the rain trickled over them, the skies gray and the ground underneath their feet slushy and wet.

Once the campsite was pristine once more, Dane gathered them all together. "You've all learned a lot this week, and I'm proud of you. You have one more task to go—I'm going to send you out in the wilderness on your own until tomorrow, and we'll see how you do."

Miranda crossed her arms, watching Dane as he gave them a pep talk about the final day. She knew what it would be about—they'd go out, make a shelter, build a fire, catch some dinner, show off their skills, and then go home with a blue ribbon. She'd had different plans for this day earlier in the week—seduce Dane at her little campsite and take pictures of him, naked. But her camera had been confiscated and she'd been sleeping with the object of her revenge all week.

And she liked it. And him. And she didn't know what to think about that. She could still implement the revenge plot, of course. Tease him, invite him to her camp, and then she'd find out if she'd hooked Dane enough for her to put the next phase of her revenge into action. Otherwise, this was all for nothing.

Not nothing, she amended with a flush, thinking of all the

times she'd gone boneless with ecstasy in his arms this week. If anything, this crazy little revenge-slash-experiment had proven something very important to her: that she was sexual after all, and the problem wasn't on her end. That made her feel immense relief. If she could have an orgasm with her nemesis, she could surely have one with a regular boyfriend.

Strangely, the thought of archenemies and revenge was making her uncomfortable. She shifted on her feet and hugged her arms close, only half paying attention to the lecture Dane was giving them. The others were eating it up, but she didn't plan on showing off her skills. She planned on getting Dane alone and seducing him. He'd shown her knots two days ago and as he'd demonstrated the appropriate knots to use for trapping, her nipples had gone hard for reasons that had nothing to do with trapping. Something about the way he'd pulled the rope taut and held it out to her had made her instantly wet.

He'd noticed it, too, the heated look returning to his own eyes. But all he'd done was pass her the rope and say nothing more.

She knew he was conflicted—that Colt and Grant would eat him alive if they'd found out what the two of them were up to. The thought left her with uneasy guilt, and she pushed it aside. Guilt was for the weak, and she was finally going to take what she wanted even if she had to step all over the man she was sleeping with to do so. Too bad he was so distracting. She thought of his naked body, gleaming in the moonlight, all hard muscles and that amazing little dip at his hip that she always wanted to run her tongue along—

"Here you go, Miranda," Dane said, appearing before her.

She blinked up and automatically took the items he handed to her. It was a tiny bundle with a tightly wrapped piece of plastic-covered paper and what looked like a wristband of some kind.

She raised an eyebrow at him.

"Were you listening to what I was saying?" he said patiently.

"Um, sort of," she said with a half smile. "Refresher?"

He chuckled and took the wristband from her, pulling her arm out and snapping it around her wrist. "That's so I can find you if you get lost." He handed her the plastic-covered piece of paper. "That's your map. You're going to be at camp six tonight. You need to find it and set up. I'll swing by later to check on you."

"Oh, of course," she said hastily. "Sorry. I thought you were talking about something else. Camp six. Yep. Got it." God, she was babbling. "Thanks."

They stared at each other for a moment, and then he gestured at the forest with a lazy smile. "You going to go or stick around here all day?"

Oh! She looked around but sure enough, almost everyone else had shouldered their packs and was heading into the woods. She looked back at Dane, then the woods. "Are you going to, um . . . find me?"

He looked at her very calmly, then seemed to scan the woods, as if she'd asked him about directions instead of a rendezvous. A quick glance showed that Pete was hanging around camp, obviously waiting to talk to her. Sigh. Steve immediately broke off from the others and began to jog into the forest, eager to start out on his own. The others were just as eager. Not Pete. He wanted to wait for his new BFF Miranda, it seemed.

So much for inviting Dane to her campsite tonight. She

glanced over at him. "You know where I'll be," she said in a soft voice that she hoped was inviting. "I'll skip the panties."

And with that, she turned and walked out of camp, heading for the trees, armed with her tiny map. Camp six was across two creeks and over a hill—quite a hike for her. That was okay; in the last week she'd found she enjoyed hiking quite a bit.

Pete hung behind for a minute, and when Miranda moved forward, he showed her his map. "I'm at camp three, Miranda. Where are you at?"

God, he was annoying. In the last week of spending every day with the man, she'd learned to appreciate not having him in her life. He was bothersome as hell and didn't seem to realize it. He was also clingy and tried to go with her everywhere.

"I'm at six," she replied after a moment, thanking the powers that be for the extra campsites between theirs. She didn't want to be his neighbor.

He looked crestfallen at the thought. "Camp six is all the way on the far edge of the map."

"That sucks," she lied. It really didn't suck much at all. Had Dane given her the most private campsite on purpose? Was he going to meet her tonight?

Pete gestured at the woods. "You want to walk the same way until we hit the creek?"

This would be the last time she'd have to deal with his aggravating self, at least. So she plastered a cheerful smile on her face and didn't even look back at Dane. "Sure thing, Pete."

TWELVE

She ditched Pete on the far side of the stream. He'd offered to follow her to her campsite and help her with setting up, but she'd been a little affronted that he thought she needed his unasked-for help and had chased him off with a few cheerful encouragements that he should set up his own camp. She was glad he was gone, though. Pete was just underfoot too much, was too eager, too chatty, too everything. He was a nice guy—cute in a geeky sort of way and well off, but her mind was laser-focused on Dane.

The silence left behind by Pete's departure was pleasing. Without him in her ear making small talk, she was able to relax and enjoy the day. She'd given up on stressing over Dane. If he showed up tonight, great. If he didn't, well. If she couldn't keep him interested long enough for phase two of her revenge plan, then it wasn't meant to be.

Picking up a piece of firewood, she frowned to herself at the thought.

Jeez, where had the laissez-faire attitude come from? She'd come out here to destroy a man in the most cutthroat manner. She was blatantly using him for her own ends. When had she gone from "Destroy Dane and everything he touches" to "Oh well, it is what it is"? That wouldn't do at all.

She stopped for a minute, picturing the photos on that horrible cheap website with "Casanova" flashing in some poorly animated gif. The looks she got in town. The snickers. The awkward conversations at the town get-togethers. Her mother's total mental breakdown. The old familiar pain began to burn in her belly, filling her with an angry reminder of what she was doing here.

She was here to destroy a man. So she'd ended up sleeping with him. It didn't mean that she had to change course. And it didn't mean that she had to have feelings for the man. She didn't.

She wouldn't.

She couldn't.

Scowling to herself at the traitorous thoughts, she scooped up a few likely branches as she walked. Her camp was easy to find—there was a nice clear spot with a small red flag stuck into the ground. The creek was a short distance away, the trees were tall, and the area was secluded. Nice. She set down her wood, her pack, and set to work. The first task for the day would be a fire. Once she had it going, she could begin the next task—a shelter. That would be a bigger project, as she needed to make it big enough for two. Just in case. Food was last on the priority list, since it would probably involve leaving camp, and she wanted to stick around, just in case Dane showed up.

When he showed up, she amended. He'd said he'd come by to check how her "survival day" was coming along. No sign of him yet, she thought as she laid the wood in a pile for her fire, but it was early.

After an hour's hard work she'd produced a fire with a spindle and bow and was oddly pleased she was able to do so. You couldn't make a fire every time with rubbing sticks, but she'd been able to do it today, and that was a nice feat. Wouldn't Dane be impressed? She fed it more kindling to build the flame, and when it was nice and healthy, she added a few small logs to the fire. Then she set to work on her lean-to. She took her time, the task requiring a lot of work, a lot of trekking back and forth, and tending the fire.

First she had to build the A-frame and lash it together. When it was solid, she made a lattice of small branches on one side to form the windbreak, and then continued to stack tree branches on it, shoving dirt high against the bottom edge to ensure that nothing could crawl under. Then she worked on laying some soft pine branches as a bed, and spread her spare hooded sweatshirt down over the branches. After that was done, she stood up and wiped her brow, exhausted and surprised at how much the tasks had taken out of her.

There was still so much to do—she had to catch dinner or go foraging, boil water for her canteen, gather more wood for the fire . . . She eyed the creek, then eyed the sun, low in the sky. She'd do that stuff after she had a nice rinse off. If Dane showed up—*when*, she corrected herself—she didn't want to be sweaty and exhausted. She wanted to be fresh and sexy.

She stripped and took a quick dip in the stream, letting the water refresh her spirits and ease her aching muscles. She quickly dressed in her last pair of cute, clean panties and her last bra—a delicate pink set edged with black lace, just enough to make it girlish with a naughty side. A quick glance around camp told her that food wasn't going to magically spring forth, so she sighed and grabbed a stick that would make a likely fishing pole. The creek had had a few deeper, slower-moving areas with overhanging branches, which were the perfect spots for fish to hide. She would have the best luck there.

She fished for two hours (with frequent trips back to her campsite to check on her banked fire) but by the time the sun was going down, she'd caught nothing. Well, she'd eat tomorrow.

It didn't matter, really. She could survive on her own—she had fire, a shelter, and she could eat some grasses and nuts. She had water to drink, and a fire to boil it over. She was set. She wondered if the other students had had as much success as she had.

After a moment, she gave a rueful smile and decided they probably had. Dane was a good teacher.

When she returned to her campsite, she knelt next to the fire and adjusted the logs. The bushes behind her rustled. Miranda whirled, startled. Was Dane finally—

But no. To her surprise, Pete emerged from the woods, sweaty and unkempt. A smear of dirt bisected one cheek, and he held a fish strung through a small branch, carrying it toward her camp.

Well, hell. She glanced around uneasily—was Dane not coming? Was she going to be stuck entertaining Pete all night?

"Hey, Miranda," Pete said cheerfully. "I brought you a fish."

"Pete, what are you doing here?"

He looked confused that she wasn't greeting him more happily. "I brought you a fish." And he raised it in the air, as if it weren't obvious. "Just in case you weren't able to catch your own."

Irritation flashed through Miranda, but she quickly tamped it down again. He meant well, even if he managed to insult her with everything he did. "Thanks, Pete, but I'm good. I don't want your fish. We're supposed to be surviving on our own, remember? No help from the others."

He looked surprised at her rebuke, as if it had never occurred to him that he'd need to do stuff on his own—or that she'd be capable of handling herself. "Oh. I see. Well, I just thought I would help." He gave her a wounded-puppy look. "Sorry, Miranda."

She sighed and forced a smile to her mouth. "It's a sweet thought, Pete, but don't you think you should get back to your own campsite with that fish before Dane drops by? You want to pass the course."

"Oh, he's already dropped by," said Pete casually. "I'm guessing he's already stopped by the others, too."

"Oh?"

He gave her a knowing look. "Miranda, I'm not stupid. I know what's going on between you two. I think we both know where Dane's last stop is going to be tonight."

Her heart pounded hard in her chest, her breath disappearing. "What do you mean?"

He gave her a wry look. "Come on, Miranda. I've seen you and Dane sneaking off to be together this week, and I've seen the way you've been looking at him. I just want to tell you that you're going to get your heart broken. He's not interested in a relationship."

The constriction in her chest relaxed a little, and she felt absurdly like laughing. Was that what he was worried about? That she might be used by Dane and would need a bit of rescuing by a white knight? Generous of him, but totally incorrect.

She was being the user in this relationship.

"That's very nice of you, Pete, but I'm a big girl. I can handle myself."

"It's not right," Pete said, a hint of peevishness in his voice now. "He shouldn't be sleeping with clients. I've half a mind to go and tell his partners what he's been up to."

Alarm shot through her body. He couldn't do that. If anyone was going to ruin Dane's career, it was going to be her, dammit. And just the thought of Pete messing things up made her nerves fray. "Pete, please," she said softly. "I would prefer if no one knows but us."

He looked unconvinced.

"For my sake?" she said, turning on the charm and moving forward to touch his arm. She swung her hair a little, mentally wishing she could punch him in the face for even suggesting such a thing.

He looked at her and licked his lips, then sighed. "I won't say anything, Miranda. I just . . . I wish you were interested in me, not him."

She smiled and leaned forward, impulsively kissing him on the cheek. "I wish I was, too."

He turned his head into her kiss.

She recoiled. So much for her goodwill toward him. She pulled away and smiled tightly. "You should go back."

He had the grace to look embarrassed. "I'm going."

With arms crossed, she watched him leave her campsite, still carrying his fish. She wouldn't miss him when this week was over. The only one she'd miss was Dane.

The thought made her breath whoosh out of her lungs.

Miss Dane?

Ridiculous. She was here to destroy the man.

Really? Good Miranda said inside her mind. *Because you seem more interested in sleeping with him than actually getting revenge.*

Damn. She hated Good Miranda. Especially when that sounded closer to the truth than she liked. Confused by her own feelings, she moved toward the fire and tossed another log on.

Did she like Dane? Really? Or did she only like playing with him? Where had her hate gone? She had been brimming with it earlier this week, and yet now she couldn't seem to muster it.

There was no question that the two of them were compatible together—every time he touched her, her entire body exploded into feeling, every nerve ending singing with delight. No question that he knew how to touch her and what she wanted in bed. But relationships weren't built on that, and she didn't want a relationship with the man. She wanted to make his ass sorry for what he'd done to her nine years ago, and then shake the dust of this small, annoying town off her boots. She wanted to leave the Boobs of Bluebonnet behind. She wanted a life that didn't involve Dane Croft.

Didn't she?

And yet . . . she stared down at the camp around her. She'd worked hard this afternoon to make her camp perfect. Her fire was roaring, her shelter done, and he'd find no fault with it. She'd tried extra hard this week so he wouldn't think of her as lazy. She'd never complained, even when she was dripping with sweat. She wanted him to like her, too.

Not like, she corrected with a wince. *Respect, not like!* If he respected her, the revenge would ache all the more.

A warm arm wrapped around her from behind, and a hot mouth pressed a kiss to the side of her neck.

She yelped in fright.

"You're lost in thought," Dane said between nibbles.

A shiver of delight charged through her body at the affectionate touch, and she had to stop herself from leaning in to his embrace. "Just thinking of this week," she said lamely. "Sorry I wasn't paying attention."

"Here I thought you were thinking up new ways to ambush me again," he said, his eyes gleaming with the firelight. "But obviously not, since I scared you."

"I thought you were Pete," she admitted.

He stiffened against her and turned her to face him. Gone was the playful expression, replaced with a possessive, angry glare. "Miranda, has he been harassing you again? Say the word and I'll go over there and wring his little pencil neck—"

"What? No, I'm fine."

He growled low in his throat, his hand clenching possessively in her hair. "I've seen the way he's been looking at you. Say the word and I'll make him regret it."

Funny, Pete had been at her campsite a short while ago saying the same thing about Dane. She gave him a weak smile. "It's fine. I can handle myself."

She tried to ignore the thrill that his jealous protectiveness shot through her. She didn't care, remember? Didn't care. This was all part of the master plan. "Besides, you can't go beat him up. He's a client."

"I don't care," Dane gritted. "You need me to beat him up, and I will."

That was . . . sweet. She smiled and turned her face up to his for a short, hot kiss. "I'm fine," she repeated. "So, are you here to check out my stuff?"

His hand slipped to her ass, cupping it and drawing her body against his. "Exactly what stuff did you have in mind?"

Her arms twined around his neck and she gave him a flirty smile. "My fire, of course. I worked hard to give it just the right spark."

"Looks like it's burning hard to me," he murmured, not glancing away from her face. "Shall I check?"

"What?" she said, turning in his arms and giving him a playful look. "You're not going to pass me simply because we're sleeping together?"

He grinned. "Nope. Your campsite needs to make the grade. And that means you need to show me your stuff." He slapped her ass. "Hot stuff."

A girlish giggle escaped her throat and Miranda sidled away.

Now that she'd slipped out of his arms, he moved forward to her shelter, inspecting the frame of it. "Not bad, not bad."

"There are boughs on the bottom of the shelter to make it more comfortable," she blurted. "And I packed the earth around the bottom so there's no breeze going through the cracks." For some reason, she was anxious to please him—to show him that she'd been paying attention this week. That she wasn't like Pete. That she was someone he could respect.

"Very nice," he said.

"I have a nice fire going, too," she added. "No fish, though. A few nuts and some dandelions for greens." She gestured at the food that she'd set aside on a hastily made plate of a few long strips of bark that she'd washed clean. "Hungry?"

"Starving," he said, grinning, and his hands moved to her waist again, pulling her close.

"For some reason, I'm thinking we're both not talking about food," she said softly, her gaze going to the curve of his mouth, the scars that gave him that rakish look.

As if sensing her thoughts, he tugged her against him and pulled her in for a kiss, his tongue stroking deep between her parted lips. It made her think of sex, and she gasped at the pulsing response of her body. His tongue thrust into her mouth again and then stroked against her own tongue, the feather-light touches tickling and making her quiver with desire. No one kissed quite like Dane, as if he had all the time in the world to do nothing but kiss her and his entire goal was to devour her body. That was one of the things she liked the most about him—his devoted attention to her pleasure, and how he took charge, making sure that she would get her orgasm before he got his. She'd let other boyfriends take the lead in bed before, but they'd hesitated, asking what she wanted. She didn't know what she wanted most of the time, but Dane seemed to instinctively know, and he used that to play her body like a violin.

And she liked it. A lot.

His tongue stroked into her mouth again, and she brushed hers against it, returning his caress with one of her own. She could feel each stroke, and each one reminded her of his mouth on her pussy, his cock thrusting deep inside her, and she grew wetter and wetter with each thrust of his tongue, until her hips were squirming against his own. Her arms wrapped around his neck and she lifted one knee. He grasped it and pulled it tight against him, pulling the cradle of her hips against the thick ridge of his erection. Just the feel of it against her sex made her moan with desire. She needed it inside her. Deep, hard, plunging . . .

With one last teasing lick, Dane broke the kiss and gazed down at her, brushing a strand of hair away from her cheek with his free hand as she clung to him. "Miranda."

"Yes?" Her voice was breathless, soft.

"Show me your knot work."

She blinked for a moment. "My what?"

"Your knot work," he said in a husky voice, as if it were the sexiest thing imaginable. "I need to check your traplines and your knots to make sure you've passed that portion of the course."

Miranda frowned up at him. Who cared about knots at a time like this?

But he only gave her ass a friendly pat and released her leg, leaving her throbbing and wanting, her pulse pounding through her veins.

Confused and utterly turned on all at once, she stood there for a moment, watching him. When he didn't move, she gave him a bewildered look and gestured at her pack. "I have my rope over there."

"Good," he said. "Show me a square knot."

The man was odd. Couldn't they do this later if he did want her? Grumbling mentally to herself, she moved to her pack at the base of a nearby tree and pulled her assigned length of rope out.

Though Dane had showed them all how to create a rope from dried reeds and grasses, it was a task that would require more time than they had left in the training and they'd been parceled out a length of rope instead. There hadn't been time to practice her trap-making.

He moved to stand over her, looming and blocking out the rest of her fading light just as she began to tie the ropes in the knots that he'd shown them this week. His attention made her flustered, and she dropped one end of the rope, her knot falling to pieces.

"Tsk," Dane said in an oddly pleased voice above her. "Looks like someone needs a lesson on ropes after all. Stand up."

"I can do it if you're not looming over me," she grumbled, but stood and handed him the rope.

He quickly began to make a complex series of knots, the rope forming a loop on one side. Then he extended a hand to her and waited.

Miranda frowned down at that outstretched hand. "I don't have anything else."

Dane's look was utterly serious. "Give me your hand."

A small, naughty thrill shot through her, and she stared at him. Then, ever so slowly, she put her hand in his.

He grinned and kissed her mouth once—quickly, hard. Then he took her hand, slid it through the loop he'd created, and raised it over her head. The rope slithered over a branch just above her head and came down on the other side, and Dane extended his hand to her again.

"Do you trust me?" he asked.

Alarm bells shot through her body, and she immediately

thought of the camera in the closet, long ago. The pictures of her breasts. "I . . ."

He leaned in and kissed her forehead, an oddly tender gesture. It was a small caress, but a reassuring one. "If you don't want to, it's all right."

She thought quickly. Odds were that there weren't cameras in the woods. Even though Dane had picked out this campsite for her, she hadn't seen any evidence of equipment when she'd foraged and gathered nearby. And if she didn't trust him, their little games would come to a screeching halt.

And for some reason, she didn't want that. Not at all.

"I trust you," she said softly, a slight waver in her voice. She hoped she didn't regret that trust soon. Dane didn't know her plans. There was no way this could be a setup. "But if there's another emu lurking around here and I can't run away, I'm going to kick your ass."

"No emu. I promise." He pressed a kiss to her nose and then quickly fashioned a knotted loop in the rope to hold it in place, hiking her other arm above her head.

Now she stood, both arms pinned taut above her head, the rope looped over a high branch. She gave each arm a tug and realized that the ropes were knotted tighter than she'd imagined. She couldn't slide free. Miranda shivered, alarm and excitement pounding through her.

Dane grinned at the sight of her, his hands running slowly up and down her sides, stroking her body. "Someone should have learned her knots," he said in a husky voice.

"Someone didn't have the chance to show what she knew," she retorted, twisting one arm in protest. "You're cheating."

"I am," he agreed, his fingers sliding to the waistband of her shorts and tugging her shirt free. "I admit that I've been thinking about this all week."

A shiver crossed her skin as he slowly hiked her shirt up, past her breasts. The material bunched under her arms and he tugged it over her head, until it lay trapped behind her head. Her body was exposed, her bra stark against her skin.

His gaze was rapt as he stared down at her, eyes hot with need. Dane brushed the back of his hand over one lacy cup and her breath sucked in. "So lovely," he murmured. "Delicate and rosy. The only thing prettier than these breasts are your nipples," he said, and brushed the backs of his fingers against those very spots.

She gasped at the jolt of sensation that rocketed through her. Her hands clenched against the ropes. Her body was exposed, helpless to do anything against his touch. Not that she wanted to escape.

Dane's eyes gleamed and he pulled a length of fabric out of his pocket. "Let's raise the stakes a little, shall we?"

And then he blindfolded her. The bandana cut off her vision, and her tremors of excitement were mixed with apprehension. She couldn't see where he was.

His hand brushed along her arm and felt her quivers, and then his mouth brushed against hers. "I'm here, Miranda. Anytime you want to call this off, just tell me to stop and I'll take you down. All right? Let me know if it gets too intense for you."

She gave a jerky nod.

"That's my girl," he said in a pleased voice, and rewarded her with a kiss along her jaw. She hadn't expected his mouth there and trembled at the feeling. With her vision blocked and her hands unable to touch him, her senses were narrowed down to passively feeling, to smelling, to hearing. His lips were soft against her neck, and she felt the flick of his tongue against her pulse, the strum of it matching the spike of pleasure that shot to her pussy. The stubble of his beard rasping against her skin was an oddly pleasurable sensation, and she barely felt his fingertips gliding along her side in light, ticklish motions as he explored her body.

"And that, my sweet Miranda, is how you tie a square knot."

A nervous giggle escaped her throat. "Very funny."

"Now let me think," he said softly. "Since you're completely at my mercy, where shall I touch you first?"

She quivered at the thought, her body tingling with anticipation. "My breasts?" she offered.

"Hush," he said, and gave one outthrust breast a teasing slap that made her body jolt. "I get to decide, and it's much more fun if you're surprised."

"Then why'd you ask?"

"It was a rhetorical question," he said with a chuckle. "You're all laid out and delicious, and I need to concentrate."

"Fine, I'll be quiet." She liked this playful side of Dane. It gave her heart a funny little flip to hear his soft chuckle.

That's just desire, she told herself. Nothing more.

His hands—rough with callus—skimmed along the soft flesh of her outstretched arms. She shivered at the feather-light touch moving along the inside of her arm and grazing back down until his fingers skimmed her collarbones.

"So pretty," he said huskily. "Do you mind if I play with you tonight? Have all the control?"

Her nipples tightened at the thought. She swallowed hard. "I don't mind."

A hand fisted in her hair, tugging her head backward, and the breath caught in her throat. "Do you think I'm going to hurt you?"

Her breath coming in anxious little pants, she forced out a light, "I wouldn't let you tie me to a tree if I did."

Dane laughed at that, and his mouth brushed hers. Her tongue slid out to caress his, but he was gone an instant later. "I won't hurt you, I promise. If you tell me to stop, I'll stop. But I want to give you pleasure tonight. To drive you out of your mind with it."

Her entire body tightened in anticipation at the thought.

"I've noticed a little something about you, Miranda. Whenever that brain of yours gets going, that body of yours stops enjoying. And I noticed that mind of yours working overtime this morning." His finger brushed against a rock-hard nipple and she gasped in response, her entire body pulsing with need. "What were you thinking about?"

She knew immediately what she'd been thinking about all day—Pete's words to her about Dane and how he was using her. Of course, she couldn't confess that. "I . . . I was thinking about what I needed to do to make sure that I could get the camp set up properly."

"Liar," he whispered, and tweaked her nipple again.

Desire shot through her and she groaned, her pussy clenching with need. "Please," she panted.

"Not until you tell me what's going on in that head of yours." His knuckles slid to the curve of her breast, rubbed the fabric covering them.

A small cry of frustration escaped her throat and she twisted in the bonds, trying to angle her breast so his touch would graze her nipple. As soon as she did, though, he pulled away.

"Bad girl," he said in a husky voice that thrilled her to her core. "Tell me."

She licked her lips and was gratified by the sudden intake of his breath. "I was thinking about you," she admitted, since that was part of the truth. "Thinking about how you had touched me and how it's been three long days since we've been able to have sex. I was wondering if you'd come back to me tonight, or if I'd have to spend all night touching myself."

He gave a low groan of desire.

Feeling bold at his reaction, even though she couldn't see it, she licked her lips again and continued. "I was thinking about the hard, thick length of you deep inside me, pumping into me so hard that I can feel you slamming through my body—"

He groaned and the hands were in her hair again, his mouth angling over hers in a thrusting, hard kiss of possession. Greedily, she sucked at his tongue. His hands stroked up and down her back and her hands fisted in the bonds, her core so wet she could feel the slickness between her clenched thighs.

His mouth broke from hers and she gave a small whimper of distress, then felt his tongue graze along the column of her throat. She tilted her head back, enjoying the caress as his tongue trailed along the collarbones and back down to her bra. His hands plumped her breasts together, forming a valley that his tongue slid between, his thumbs grazing her nipples.

Miranda groaned, arching her back into his touch. "My bra," she panted. "Take it off. Please."

"You're not the one that gets to decide," he said, and his hands slid to the waistband of her shorts, tugging them down her legs. They fell to the ground, pooling around her ankles, and at his light touch, she lifted a foot, then the other, so he could remove them. She wiggled in place, longing for him to remove her thong next. She'd saved her sexiest one for that evening—lace with a saucy bow just above the cleft of her ass, the front a mere satin strip that covered nothing and teased everything.

She'd worn them for him, saved them for this night. Miranda gave her hips a little wiggle. Did he like?

His hands moved to her ass, clenching the rounded cheeks of her buttocks, and she quivered, waiting for him to spank her. Something.

Instead, she felt his teeth graze one of her pebbled nipples and then bite it through the bra. A shuddering bolt of desire blasted through her, and she whimpered. "More."

"Does sexy little Miranda like having her breasts bitten?" he teased in a husky voice, and she felt him rub his chin against her breast, his stubble catching on the fabric. Then his fingers pushed her bra away, exposing her nipple, and his mouth was on it again, sucking hard at the tip and then giving it another tiny bite. At her quiver of pleasure, he flicked the other nipple with his fingers. Dane tugged her bra down, exposing both breasts to the air—and his touch. He teased one with his tongue, then licked it, over and over, as if he were a cat lapping at cream. His other hand brushed against the other nipple, teasing it to a hard, aching point. Each lick sent an erotic thrill straight to her pussy, and her hips flexed involuntarily with each touch.

"Such pretty breasts," Dane told her, then gave one a harder nip. She could tell he enjoyed seeing her gasp, because his laugh was a low, husky rumble. "Your breasts bounce when I startle you. Fucking love that."

She arched against his touch, her breath coming in hard, quick bursts when his mouth moved away and his fingers slowed. "Then keep touching me, if you like it so much."

He plumped her breasts again, his fingers working them, then bit at the nipple of one breast, then the other. "Do you like being tied up, Miranda? Like giving all your control to me?"

She tugged at the ropes again, but he was right—she had no control. He could walk away and she'd be left here, topless, helpless—wet with need. The thought both excited her and terrified her. "I—I like it," she said when he nipped at the peak of her breast again. "It's just different. Scary. Exciting."

"You're thinking again," he said, and his mouth dipped to her belly button. "Time to put a stop to that."

And then she felt his hands slide to her hips and give a nudge that she should part her legs, and she got even wetter in anticipation.

Tension coiled through her body as she waited for him to put his hands on her, his mouth on her. Prickles of anticipation made her nipples harden.

Then she felt him. Fingers tugged her scrap of panties down her thighs and she wiggled to help them along. Then his hands—his thumbs—parted the slick heat of her pussy and she felt his tongue dip in and tease the wetness.

Her breath sucked in.

Again, the tiny insistent flick—no more than the tip of his tongue. But it drove her wild with need, every nerve on her body springing to life and crying out. His fingers gripped her hips and then dug into her buttocks as his tongue plunged between the damp folds of her pussy again, a long smooth stroke from her core all the way to her clit. When he reached that small hard button, he circled it with his tongue, hard and wet. Tiny gasps erupted from her throat. She needed . . . she needed . . .

One hand lifted from her ass and slid between her legs. She felt the brush of fingers between her thighs a mere moment before a hard, thick finger glided into her heat.

She whimpered. God, that felt so good. And God, it felt like not nearly enough. She bucked against his finger, crying out when he thrust it deep into her again, his tongue flicking against her clit in soft, teasing motions. Not fast or frantic, just slow and steady and making her pulse race with need and want. As if he had all the time in the world. As if he could sit there on the forest floor and lick her pussy for days on end, every stroke of his tongue slow and sensual as if the taste of her were a treat all its own. A fresh whimper rose in her throat at the mental image. "Oh, Dane," she moaned when he gave her a particularly long, sensuous lick. The words came out as a breathless sigh. "I need . . . I . . . I need . . ."

The words slipped from her brain with every stroke of his tongue, as if she couldn't think while he tasted her. Her hips circled, trying to move his head to just the right place. She needed something. She was so close.

The finger thrusting deep into her core suddenly felt thicker, harder, and she realized he'd slipped a second finger into her slick warmth. His tongue began to flick against her clit faster, the same tiny stroke of his tongue over and over again. It was maddening and she felt the hot spiral of her orgasm begin to slip over her again, and her cries became more urgent, her arms pulling hard at the bonds over her head. The tree branch rattled and shook, raining leaves. She didn't care. She was so close, her breath hot, panting gasps that ran into one another.

Suddenly Dane's mouth was gone, and his fingers slid from her pussy. A sound of dismay escaped her throat, and then she felt his mouth kiss a breast, her shoulder, and his fingers were on the rope knots. Her hands fell free, and she tugged the blindfold off, staring up at him in distress, her orgasm ebbing away as if it had never been. "I don't understand. Why did you—"

He leaned in and kissed her tenderly, then took her hand in his. "You were hurting yourself. I don't want that."

She stared down at the rope burns on her wrists. They were reddened and chafed. "Oh. I didn't even realize."

"I know," he said with chagrin. "That's one of the things I love about touching you, Miranda. It's that you lose yourself when you're in my arms. I just need to remember that. No more rope play for you." His thumb brushed her cheek in a soft caress. "My fault."

She stared at him, uncomprehending, then slid a hand to his cock, hard and thick. Her finger glided over the pre-cum coating the crown. "We're not stopping, are we?"

"God no," he groaned, and swept her up in his arms.

Dane carried her the short distance to the shelter she'd made, and he laid her down on the freshly cut boughs she'd placed on the ground as a makeshift bed. No sooner had he laid her on her back than he was over her, and she heard the rip of the condom package. Then Dane's weight was on her, pushing her thighs forward, and he was sinking hard and deep into her, a swift stroke that took her by surprise.

Her delight emerged in a muffled shriek as her body surged back to life, remembering the orgasm that had been so close. Her calves tensed as he pushed down on her, her knees pressing against her breasts as he pulled back and stroked deep again and again. "So tight and hot," he gritted, slamming deep into her again. "Dreamed of doing this to you for years." Thrust. "Taking you in my arms and fucking the living daylights out of you." Thrust. "Better than I ever thought it would be."

Her pussy clenched hard with every word, her moans turning into a soft, continuous cry. Every time he stroked, a hard pulse of pleasure washed through her, her entire body tightening until she felt as if she'd explode. It was like she was trapped in an endless orgasm—coming and coming—and yet with each hard thrust, he pushed her just a little higher.

Then something shattered in her, and a broken little cry escaped her throat as her entire body pulsed, hard, and he bit out a curse at the same time. "Fuck yeah," he growled. "Come for me, Miranda."

She did. Hard. And when her cries died down, he bit out another oath and got his own release. Then he collapsed on top of her, panting, his forehead damp with sweat. Her legs eased down to his sides and she wrapped them around him, easing her arms over his shoulders and clinging to him as her body quivered in aftershocks.

That had been . . . intense. What he'd made her feel . . . there were no words. Or if there were, she didn't know them. The way he'd been so intent on her pleasure made her blush just to think about. And she thought of the words he'd said as he'd fucked her deep and hard.

Dreamed of doing this to you for years. Better than I ever thought it would be.

He'd been thinking about her? Daydreaming about her? For years?

And all this time, she'd hated his guts so bad she'd fuck a man just to ruin his life.

Miranda didn't like herself very much in that moment.

Dane's hand cupped her head and he turned her face toward him, kissing her lips softly. "Thank you," he said in a husky voice.

A knot formed in her throat and she closed her eyes, pretending to yawn. "For what?"

He toyed with a lock of hair—damp with sweat—on her forehead. "For this. For this week. It was pretty much perfect. I . . . have to tell you something."

She stiffened under him. Oh God. What was he going to say? She couldn't open her eyes, couldn't bear the thought of looking at him and seeing the truth. "Dane—"

"Shh. I want to tell you." His fingertips tucked the strand of hair in place and then glided along her cheekbone. "I had a . . . rough time when I left the NHL. A woman . . . she was responsible for me being fired. I turned her down and she made up a bunch of stories about me to the press."

A knot formed in her throat. So he'd been used and publicly humiliated? She didn't know what to say. Did he want her to speak? Or was there more to tell? Hesitantly, she brushed her hand across his nape, stroking the soft skin there. It was a touch to comfort and encourage. To let him know she was there, and she was listening.

"I hated her," he said after a long moment, as if warring with himself. "I hated her so much, and felt so betrayed at the moment when I was the most vulnerable, and I thought . . . well. I thought I was going to give up women for a long, long time. Maybe forever. Because I couldn't look into a woman's face and not see that bitch glaring back at me."

She opened her eyes and continued to stroke his neck, waiting.

He turned back to her, his eyes hooded. She met his gaze, and he searched her face, as if looking for something there. "But that was before this week. Before you. I haven't touched a woman in over three years. Didn't want to . . . until I saw you again, and realized what I wanted. And I wanted to say thank you. Like I said, this week was perfect."

He kissed the side of her mouth.

She twitched under him, not saying anything. After a moment, he chuckled and rolled off her, then pulled her close, cuddling her. Miranda said nothing, simply closed her eyes and waited for more. He snuggled close, his breath in the curve of her neck, and his breathing grew deep and even. Sleeping.

She couldn't sleep. Her mind was freaking out.

Dane had just confessed why he'd been kicked out of hockey. Someone else had done it to him. Casanova Croft was a fraud. He wasn't a ladies' man or a poon hound. Underneath the sexy, ultraconfident exterior was a man who'd apparently been thinking about nailing her for nine years, and who had been so hurt by a woman that he'd not had sex since being betrayed.

The jerk had a soft side. A really big soft side. A vulnerable one that he'd launched straight in front of her bull's-eye.

And in that awful, wonderful, tender, horrific moment, Miranda realized two things.

One—that she wasn't going to be coldhearted enough to get her revenge on Dane Croft after all.

And two—that she was still terribly, horribly, head over heels in love with the man and likely had been since high school.

Well . . . fuck.

THIRTEEN

The next morning dawned crisp and cool, though Miranda had been warm curled up next to Dane all night. They'd made love several more times before she'd fallen into an exhausted slumber in his arms. Part of her hadn't expected him to stay at her side all night, but when she'd rolled over and yawned, he'd woken her up with a kiss.

"Hey, gorgeous," he'd said with a grin and a light smack to her ass.

She given him a flustered smile back, but her mind was racing a million miles a minute. He hadn't left her last night. They'd slept in each other's arms. That felt like relationship material.

Under no circumstances could she entertain a relationship with Dane. None. Zero.

Preoccupied, she hadn't minded when he'd kissed her forehead, dressed, and went about breaking down camp.

She dressed just as quickly. "So . . . shouldn't we be heading back?"

A grin broke across his handsome face, and she felt her breath catch. Lord, he was easy on the eyes. She'd grown too used to seeing that face when she woke up. That'd change soon enough.

"Right." He belted his shorts and pulled a piece of paper out of it and handed it to her. It was a small map with instructions. "When I met you yesterday, I was supposed to give you this." He gave her a look that was part chagrin, part pleased with himself. "Looks like we forgot. You can follow this back to the main camp. I need to swing by and check on the others to make sure they broke down their campsites."

"Great," she said with a bright smile. "I guess once I have things taken care of here, I'll see you back at base camp."

His look immediately became troubled. "Miranda . . ."

She moved toward him and couldn't stop herself from plucking a pine needle off of his shirt and brushing it clean. Her hands lingered on his chest, thinking of last night and how good it had felt to be in his arms.

"I'm not going to say anything to anyone," she said softly, knowing that was his unspoken question. "It's your job, and I know that if we exposed our secret, it could ruin you."

"Wrong," he said, and tugged her closer, pulling her hips against his as if he wanted to drag her back to the remnants of camp and lie in bed for a few hours longer. He smiled down at her. "I've been thinking . . ."

"Oh?" She forced a light smile to her face. Nothing good ever accompanied the words *I've been thinking.*

"When I get back, I'm going to talk to the guys. Let them

know about us. We shouldn't have to hide what we did. I'm not ashamed."

She stared up at him. "What?"

"I'm going to tell them about us," he repeated patiently, and tugged at her hips as if it could drag her attention back to the conversation. "You and me . . . I want them to know about us. I just need some time to talk to the guys. Ease them into it. Leave it to me. I want them to know you're mine, and we're together."

Miranda smiled up at him, the pit of her stomach sick. "If you're sure . . ."

"I'm sure. Just leave it to me." He reached down and touched the side of her neck, then pulled her in for a long, hard kiss. "See you back at camp."

Miranda broke down her campsite and headed back to the base camp. It took about half the morning, but along the way, she ran into Steve and they walked back together in cheerful companionship. Though she forced herself to answer his conversation with calm, happy responses, her mind was wild with uncertainty.

Dane wanted to continue their relationship. She was leaving for Houston far too soon, starting a new life. There was no room for him there. What could she do? Tell him the truth? That she'd been out for revenge due to a high school prank but he was so amazing in bed she'd changed her mind, and they should make a go for it until she had to bail out and move to Houston?

Say nothing and just disappear? Confess the truth? She was torn.

Following the coordinates on the tiny map, they were able to find a finish line tape set up between two stout trees. Brenna and

Grant waited there, excited to see the students trickle in from the woods. Nearby, a few other students had already returned. They still had their backpacks on, and stood chatting, clearly not ready to leave yet. In the distance, Miranda could see the ranch house that was the business headquarters.

Brenna wore a party hat. She blew a paper horn at the sight of them and whirled a noisemaker as Miranda and Steve stepped through the ribbon at the same time. "Congratulations!" she called. "You both passed with flying colors! Come over here so I can give you your certificates."

Miranda was suddenly surrounded by other well-wishers—people from her team, people from the other team, Grant, Brenna—everyone wanted to shake her hand and chat with her about how the week had gone. Brenna handed her a certificate. "Thank you for being a part of Wilderness Survival this past week."

Dazed, Miranda took the certificate and glanced around. No Dane, no Colt. No Pete, but that was a good thing. "Is . . . everyone here?"

"Not yet," explained Brenna. "I think we had one or two get lost in the woods. Dane went to track them down." She grinned at Miranda. "Still working the kinks out in everything with it being the first class. Glad you made it, though!"

Miranda gave her a weak smile.

Grant stepped in front of her, camera in hand. Oh. "Hey, Miranda," he said with a friendly smile. "Good to see you again. I heard you'd signed up. You're just in time for me to get your picture for our graduation board."

Miranda froze, her skin crawling at the sight of the camera.

Suddenly, she did not want her picture taken. She didn't want to stand here and awkwardly wait for Dane. She didn't want the others to smile and hug her and chat.

She wanted to run very far away. She wanted to leave this week behind and forget it had ever happened. She was sorry she'd ever gotten in the closet with Dane Croft nine years ago. She was sorry about the pictures, and about her revenge that had gone so very, very wrong.

Houston and her new job was her future. Bluebonnet was her past. And that past now included a very torrid week with Dane Croft.

She held up a hand in front of her face, blocking the camera. "Can I talk to you, Brenna?"

The assistant cocked her head and studied Miranda with piercing green eyes. "Sure."

She moved to the edge of the trees, away from the others, and waited for Brenna to follow. When the assistant did, Miranda pitched her story, careful to place a hand on her lower abdomen and look pained.

Her excuse? Girl problems.

Brenna looked sympathetic, and when Miranda said she wanted to leave early, even escorted her out to her car. She had to sign some paperwork certifying that she'd finished the class, but within a few minutes of arriving back, she pulled her car out of the gravel parking lot and was turning onto the highway, her mind whirling.

Okay, so she'd just run away from her problems. Cowardly, yes. But it was for the best. A nice, clean break with Dane would be easiest.

After all, it had been a nice clean break nine years ago, hadn't it?

Sort of?

"Here we go," Dane said, forcing a cheerful note to his voice as he clapped George on the back. Brenna had set up the finish line again and tooted her celebratory horn as he led the older man back to the finish line. Others stood around and clapped, laughing and smiling. They looked happy. Dane was glad.

Right now, he was just tired. It had been a long week and he wanted to crawl into a shower, and then crawl into bed.

Preferably both with Miranda at his side. She'd been quiet that morning, no doubt wondering how their relationship was going to last now that the class was over. She probably thought they were just fuck buddies, and he'd seen a hint of something in her eyes last night. Something had been bothering her.

And he knew, after seeing that unease and unhappiness in her eyes, that he wanted to take care of it for her. Wanted to be there for her. And it seemed he'd never really gotten Miranda out of his system, had he? Even now, they'd spent a few hours apart and he craved seeing her, scanned the crowd for her pretty, flushed face and that long sweep of silky brown hair that made him hard as a rock when it brushed against him.

Nine years and it had felt like it was just yesterday that he was holding hands with Miranda after graduation, lusting after her.

Being with her had reset something cold and hard in his system. Something that he hadn't liked in himself. The part of him that had withered when he'd quit hockey. It was back now.

Damned inconvenient timing, but you didn't get to choose when you felt yourself stirring back to life again.

Sometimes life just happened.

So Dane shook hands and smiled and posed for photos with his students for a time, but he didn't see Miranda. Bathroom break? Had she run off to freshen up? He kept glancing around, looking for her, waiting to hear her sultry laugh.

A big hand clapped him on the shoulder, and he turned to see Colt grinning at him. "Good week."

"Good enough," said Dane evasively. "How'd it go on your end?"

"Uneventfully," Colt said. He crossed his arms over his chest and nodded at the group milling around. "Everyone passed, though there were one or two that had no sense of direction and needed some help. Thought we were gonna starve on day two, but they figured it out after a while." He eyed Dane. "You?"

"One fool," he said, thinking of Pete. "Other than that, no complaints."

"So how was Miranda?" Colt asked. "She whine the whole time about getting her hands dirty or something?"

He forced himself not to stiffen or act evasive. Why was Colt asking about Miranda specifically? "She was a real trouper," he said. "No complaints."

"Huh," Colt shrugged. "I remember her being friends with Beth Ann, is all. That blonde is way high maintenance. Thought Miranda'd be a little more prissy and scared of the woods. So what made her sign up?"

"I didn't ask," he said. Was Colt fishing for information?

What did he think he knew? Dane wanted to talk to him privately—Grant, too—but with all the clients around, now was not the time to have a discussion about the client he'd been sleeping with. He knew Grant was not going to react to the news well. They needed quiet, and a bit of time to wind down from the class before he let them know about Miranda and him. And if they didn't like it, well, it wasn't any of their business.

Plus, he really just wanted to find Miranda at the moment. "Listen, I thought she'd be able to find it back on her own, but I might need to go rescue her."

"She's already come and gone," Colt said with a shrug.

His eyes narrowed and focused on the other man. "What?"

"Like I said, gone." Colt turned away, done with the conversation.

Frustrated, Dane scanned the small crowd and saw Grant's tall form in the distance. He plowed through the crowd and approached his friend, who was messing with a tripod. "Where'd Miranda Hill go?"

Grant shrugged, double-checking the settings on his camera. "Saw her chatting with Brenna and then she hightailed it out of here fast. Shame she's gonna miss the team photo."

Had to be a mistake. Miranda had come in his arms so sweetly last night. She'd liked him. Trusted him enough to let him tie her up. Hell, trusted him enough to fuck him like her life depended on it. Surely she wouldn't have left without giving him her phone number. Something.

He stalked off after Brenna.

"Good to see you, too," Grant said drily as he walked away.

Brenna was busy at her little table, filling out certificates and chatting with the clients. She gave him a cool sideways glance under her long lashes. "'Sup, Dane?"

"Where'd Miranda Hill go? I don't see her here with the rest."

She looked unconcerned, and returned to filling out the latest certificate. "She left already."

Disbelief flared. "What do you mean, she left already?"

"I mean she left already," Brenna said slowly, as if she were speaking to someone mentally incompetent. "She got in her car and left. Said she was done here anyhow."

What the fuck? Was she cutting and running? Why? "Un-fucking-believable."

"Oh, don't get your panties in a bunch," Brenna said, misunderstanding his reaction. "We can take the team picture without her. One person isn't going to make a difference." When he said nothing, she added, "It wasn't because she was unhappy with the class or anything. Said she was real pleased. I think she was sick."

Sick? He shot Brenna a look of disbelief. "She was sick and you let her go off on her own?"

Brenna gave him a look of disbelief, lifting her pen from the endless pile of paperwork. "Are you serious? What was I supposed to do? Cling to her leg as she tried to get into her car? You want me to do that to everyone that tries to leave? I hate to break it to you, Dane, but every single one of these people is going home today."

He ran a hand down his face and sighed. "Never mind. Just give me her contact information."

Brenna pulled one folder out from the stack on her folding table, grumbling about how she preferred it when he was out in the field. "Here," she said finally, flipping through the waivers and handing him one.

Miranda's curly handwriting stared up at him. He remembered it from high school, from the notes she'd passed him. Seeing it now brought back a surge of memories. Without asking, he grabbed Brenna's sat phone off the table and dialed the number Miranda had given.

It picked up on the second ring. "Bluebonnet Library," said a sour voice.

Okay, that was unexpected. "Miranda there?"

"Ms. Hill no longer works here."

So why'd she give a bogus number? He murmured his thanks and hung up, then stared at the paper to make sure he hadn't misread it. The address caught his eye.

1 Honeycomb Drive. He knew that address—it was the high school, named after the school mascot of the Bluebonnet Bees. "You don't go into the city much, do you, Brenna?"

"Should I?" she asked, wrinkling her freckled nose. "Do I need to be familiar with the city, too?"

Dane sighed and handed her back the paper and the phone. Brenna wasn't local. She didn't know what anyone in Bluebonnet would have immediately picked up on. "Never mind."

Why had Miranda given bad information at the beginning of the week? Why so secretive? It didn't make sense. She wasn't the type to come up with fake addresses just to be a jackass about it. She'd genuinely not wanted anyone to contact her when they were done.

Fuck that. He was heading into town as soon as they were

done here, because he wanted to know what the hell was going on and why she'd run off.

He was starting to think she'd lied. Maybe she was married after all. If she was . . . hell. He didn't know what he was going to do. The thought made him want to punch something.

Miranda should have headed home first. She was tired and hungry, and she needed a shower. Most of all, she needed to have a good cry and figure out her head.

Still, instead of heading home, she found herself turning down Main Street and parking in front of California Dreamin'. There were two cars already parked there, so Beth Ann was busy, but Miranda didn't care. Grabbing her keys, she headed inside.

Beth Ann's tiny salon had one chair in the waiting area, and it was occupied. In the waiting area, a teenager with orange-dyed hair and blue bangs flipped through a hairstyle magazine. Across the room in the barber chair, a white-haired elderly woman had her curls teased into a bouffant by Beth Ann.

Beth Ann glanced up and her eyes widened at the sight of Miranda. "You're back," she exclaimed, her lovely face breaking into a smile. "How'd it go?"

Miranda leaned against the wall and closed her eyes. "Not . . . well."

"Hold on just a sec," Beth Ann said, and finished brushing the last stiff curl into place in old Mrs. Porter's hair. "There you go, Janey. All good for this week."

The old woman put on her glasses and paid, departing in a cloud of hairspray and powdery perfume.

The teenager stood and Beth Ann turned to her. "Can I get you to reschedule, Laini?"

The girl rolled her eyes. "You serious?"

Beth Ann opened the front door and scooped up a piece of paper, holding it out. "I'll give you a free mani if you come back tomorrow."

"See you then," she drawled, grinning, and snatched the ticket from Beth Ann.

Beth Ann flipped her OUT TO LUNCH sign and then shut the door, turning to Miranda with wide eyes. "Tell me everything."

Miranda dropped into the barber chair Mrs. Porter had vacated. It still smelled of powder. "I don't even know where to begin," she said wearily.

Beth Ann automatically reached for her hair and then recoiled. "God, Miranda. I don't mean to be mean, but you stink like smoke and dirt."

"Do I?" She sniffed her shirt, but really couldn't tell. Dane hadn't seemed to mind her smell at all, but maybe he'd smelled the same and she'd been around it so long she couldn't tell. The scent of campfire would always remind her of Dane after this point. She sighed. "Oh, Beth Ann, I totally messed this one up."

Her friend's eyes widened and Beth Ann turned the chair to look Miranda in the eye. "What happened? Did you see him? Talk to him? Get the pictures?"

Miranda hung her head, unable to meet Beth Ann's gaze.

"What?" Beth Ann said, horrified. "What's so awful? Were you not able to get pictures of him after all? Did he find you out?"

Miranda sighed. "I saw him. And I slept with him."

Beth Ann blinked. "Okay. I didn't realize that was in the plan."

"A lot," Miranda added. "I slept with him a lot."

"Oh." She appeared to digest this for a moment, then asked, "So this was part of the revenge scheme? Lots of sex?"

"That's the worst part about it," Miranda said with a wail. "It was supposed to be a meaningless hookup. I was supposed to have sex with him and just toss him aside when I was done. Use him like men use women. Get my revenge pictures and then move on. Except . . . now I like him. And the sex."

Beth Ann pursed her perfectly made-up lips and then grabbed Miranda by the shoulders. "You're going to sit down over here so I can do your nails, and you're going to tell me everything."

Miranda sniffed, and nodded.

Beth Ann steered her friend to the manicure table and while Miranda explained what had happened in the past week, Beth Ann filed her nails and cleaned a week's worth of grime out of her nail beds. She listened without a word as Miranda spoke, not judging.

Miranda avoided the part about her inability to have an orgasm prior to Dane. That was a little too personal and open even for her best friend, who wouldn't understand. Beth Ann had always had a steady relationship up until this year, when she was taking time off from her relationship with Allan, her high school sweetheart and on-again, off-again fiancé.

"So that's what happened," Miranda said softly as Beth Ann put a glossy coat of clear polish over her short nails. "I went into the woods knowing I wouldn't be able to get the photos, and I did it anyhow. And I figured that okay, I'd just sleep with him and then get the pictures after the class was over. But last night, when we were sleeping together, I . . . I couldn't do it." She squeezed her eyes shut in anticipation of Beth Ann's response. "You think I'm an idiot, don't you?"

"Honey, no," Beth Ann soothed. "Not at all."

"But you don't approve."

Beth Ann's pink lips pursed. "No, I don't. He's always been the guy that dicked you over in high school and left you out to dry. I don't care if he has puppy dog eyes now and a particularly fine ass. He's always going to be that jerk who hurt my best friend, even if you don't want your revenge."

Miranda managed a miserable smile. "Thanks, Bethy."

She patted Miranda's hand. "I can't judge you for sleeping with the wrong guy. Heck, look at me. I've had a relationship with a man who can't keep it in his pants, and yet I somehow keep forgiving him, right?" She gave Miranda a sad smile. "So who am I to judge?"

"You guys have been split for a year now, Beth Ann. You stood up for yourself," Miranda said encouragingly.

Beth Ann gave her a weak smile and wiped away a stray smear on Miranda's cuticles. "At least you believe in me. Everyone else seems to be waiting for me to 'come to my senses.' "

Miranda snorted, and Beth Ann grinned.

"Well," Beth Ann said after a moment. "One thing's for certain."

"What's that?"

"Next time you go on a camping trip, I should probably give you a bikini wax."

Miranda smacked her best friend on the arm and laughed.

FOURTEEN

Dane pulled his jeep up on Main Street, looking for a familiar building. Several things had changed in Bluebonnet since he'd last lived here, and while he hadn't been into town much since he'd returned, he knew there were a few things that had stayed the same. One of them was Hill Country Antiques, the little shop window just as cluttered as ever, the wooden sign hanging crookedly. And Miranda had mentioned that her mother, Tanya, still ran the place.

He stepped inside the shop, a cowbell clanking against the glass door to signify his arrival.

"Just a minute," a warbling voice called from the back.

He didn't answer, just waited, looking around. The entire place needed a good dusting—it reminded him of something from the show *Hoarders*, always had. Like all kinds of a yard sale,

Hill Country Antiques was stuffed wall to floor with old junk. A massive glass case along the back wall locked up the really "valuable" stuff, and he could see a few Elvis plates on one shelf. An old rocking horse and some wooden furniture were scattered on the floor to his left. Shelves listed under the heavy weight of their items and needed obvious repair. There seemed to be a fine coat of dust on everything, and he brushed a finger under his nose, anticipating a sneeze. This place hadn't changed in nine years, he decided, remembering how embarrassed Miranda had been as a teenager that her mom was the crazy junk lady.

But if anyone knew where Miranda was, Tanya Hill would. He knew Tanya didn't like him—when he'd called Miranda's house, right after he'd joined the NHL, she'd screamed and screamed at him as if he'd gotten her daughter pregnant or some shit, and then had never let him talk to her. But he'd tried his other options already—no one at the library would say where she lived, and she was unlisted in the phone book.

Tanya Hill was his best option.

Two minutes later, he wasn't so sure. The woman popped out of the back room, clutching a stack of old LPs. She still wore her hair in a feathered fringe of bangs, but it had all gone gray and the ponytail down her back was shorter than he remembered. Her face was heavily lined, and her eyes widened behind a pair of glasses at the sight of him.

"You!" she screeched. "Get out of my store!"

Well, he'd known she'd hated him, but he hadn't realized how much. "Mrs. Hill," he began. "I just want—"

The woman picked up a cast-iron frying pan from behind the

counter and hefted it with both hands, as if she were going to swing at him. "Get out of my store, you bastard, or I'm calling the cops!"

He raised his hands, brows going up. "I just need to know where Miranda is."

"You need to get the hell outta my store, you two-bit trash!"

"Look, I'll buy something if—"

"Get out!" she screeched again, then raced for the phone. "I'm calling the cops!"

Great, just what he needed. He put his hands up higher in surrender. "Don't call, I'm leaving."

As soon as he left the store, he heard her feet clomp across the wooden floors, and the door locked behind him. The OPEN sign in the window winked out.

Well. Not the reception he was used to getting. Dane scratched his face ruefully. Damn. He probably smelled like ass and was all unshaven. Maybe her mother thought he was a wino or something? The woman had always been a little off. Frustrated, he glanced across the street. Kurt's Koffee was new, and had a few people in it. Maybe an Internet search . . .

As soon as he entered, the man behind the counter broke into a wide grin. "Well, shut my eyes and call me a blind man," the stoner drawled. "If it isn't the star of the Las Vegas Flush, Mr. Dane Croft, come to pay us another visit."

"Hey, Jimmy," he said casually, though his mind was racing. Damn. So much for keeping his presence quiet. "I'm looking for Miranda Hill."

"I'll just bet you are," the stoner said with a smirk and raised his hand in a high five.

Dane ignored it. "So you know where she lives?"

"Small town," Jimmy said, lowering his hand and nudging his sad tip jar down the coffee bar at him. "I know where everyone lives."

He scowled at the barista, but pulled a few bills out of his pocket and shoved them into the empty tip jar. "This is a coffeehouse, not a bar, Jimmy."

"Barista, bartender, it's all the same. We're just a couple of dudes slinging drinks for a few bucks, man. Tip's a tip." He leaned forward. "So. You remember where Old Johnson Lane is?"

Miranda's house was just as empty and small as she'd left it. Boxes were scattered through her living room, but she hadn't had a chance to pack much. She set down her backpack on the end of the couch and felt the overwhelming urge to collapse. She sat on the edge of the couch and then stood up. First, a shower.

Someone knocked at the door.

Miranda groaned. Not today. Not now. Her mother had called seven times in the past week and she'd been furious that Miranda hadn't answered. She'd soothed her mother with a cover story about scoping out her apartment in Houston, and she'd managed to deflect the worst of her anger. Miranda had avoided going over, but her mother still called. In fact, she'd called three times in a row just now, and Miranda had avoided all three calls. She didn't want to talk to her again. Not while she felt so utterly lousy and unhappy and lonely.

Miranda hesitated, staring at the door with frustration. Her mother wouldn't go away. She'd just keep knocking, even if

Miranda pretended not to be home. With a heavy sigh, she moved to the front door and pulled it open. "Mom, I'm just not—"

A big, male form stood in her doorway. Broad shoulders and a gorgeous body lounged just inside her screen door, and Dane gave her a slow, pleased smile. "Surprise."

The look of unhappy surprise on her face wasn't a pleasant welcome. Miranda stared up at Dane with her mouth hanging slightly open, her pretty brown eyes fuzzy, as if she wasn't quite able to piece together exactly how he'd managed to show up on her doorstep.

That just made his stomach sink all the way down to his work boots and confirmed his suspicions. Miranda was married and he'd been nothing but a cheap fling on the side. His mouth tightened and he shoved his hands into his pockets, doing his best not to crane his head and see who sat in the living room of the tiny house.

Still, he'd gone to all that trouble—he wanted confirmation at least. "Should I go? Is your husband home?"

Her astonished expression grew even more confused and she opened her mouth wider, then closed it, then tilted her head in a way that made her hair spill over her shoulder and drove him absolutely wild. "Husband? I—I'm not married."

"Good," he growled low in his throat, feeling pleased. "Can I come in, then? I think we should talk."

He half expected her to put up a fuss or make excuses, but she only pushed her hair back over her shoulder and then stepped aside, swinging the door wider so he could enter.

"Sorry, the place is a bit of a mess," she mumbled.

His gaze moved to the boxes scattering the room. "You just move in?"

She gave him an odd smile. "Yep. Still haven't unpacked." And then she darted past him, picking up shoes and the bra she'd apparently discarded as soon as she'd come in the door. She scooped up the items and tossed them into her bedroom, then shut the door. "Have a seat on the couch."

He didn't want to sit on the couch like some uninvited guest. Dane wanted to pull her into his arms and kiss her now that they didn't have to hide it from prying clients. He wanted to hold her body against his and feel every curve, soft and naked, and pull her down to the floor and make love to her. To kiss and tease and coax that vague, worried look out of her eyes that told him she was thinking entirely too much right now. "Miranda, come here."

"Oh, no," she protested with a half smile, retreating a step even as he advanced. "I smell like I've been living in the woods for a week."

"You smell good to me," he murmured, snaking one arm around her waist and drawing her close. "But then again, I've been living in the woods, too."

A girlish giggle escaped her throat and her gaze went to his face, and she smiled, her body melting against his. His cock grew instantly hard.

"You and I," he said slowly, "need to talk about why you ran away earlier today."

Her smile disappeared and she tried to slide out of his arms. "I wasn't feeling well. Girl troubles."

He didn't buy it. "So did you have girl troubles before or after you wrote down a fake address and phone number on your documentation?"

Her eyes flew open. "How did you—"

"Because I tried calling you, dammit. Once I found out you disappeared this morning, I wanted to know where you'd run away to." His voice dropped and his hand slid down her back; he sensed she was escaping him, trying to flee even if she stood stock-still in his arms. He needed to anchor her or cut loose for good. So he told her the truth. "I thought we'd had something. It wasn't just a fling in the woods for me."

Miranda had never been "just a fling" for him. She'd been the one that had gotten away. The one he'd dreamed about for years. The one that he was going to risk his job for when he told his friends they'd been sleeping together. But he didn't tell her that. He simply said, "I want to keep seeing you, if you want it."

She seemed to hesitate, then she slowly melted against him, as if all the things that had been bothering her had dissolved and left her boneless. One hand slid over his shoulders, touched the hair at the nape of his neck, and her gaze roamed over him in a gesture that was both shy and possessive. "You do?"

"Of course I do. Did you think I was just fucking you in the woods and jeopardizing our first class simply because I'd nail any hot piece of ass that walked past?"

"The thought occurred to me," she said meekly.

He winced.

"Sorry," she added. "You were just . . . flirty, back when we were teenagers."

"Flirty with you," he said.

"And half a dozen starlets afterward," she added in.

His jaw set, aching with tension. "So my past is going to be a problem?"

"If it was," she said in a low, trembling voice, "I wouldn't be in your arms right now. I just don't want to get hurt, Dane." Miranda's eyes met his and he saw stark terror in them. "I'm terrified of being used."

She seemed intensely vulnerable in that moment, and he didn't know what to make of it. Like she was offering him everything she was—and was completely terrified to do so. He brushed her cheek with his fingers and leaned in and gave her a featherlight kiss, sweeping his mouth over hers. "How about you just use me instead? I thought that was how our relationship worked, remember?"

A soft chuckle escaped her, the sound going straight to his cock. Damn. He loved to hear her happy. "Very well," she said in a playful voice. "You are mine to use and abuse."

"Sounds good," he agreed.

She reached for his shirt and then wrinkled her nose up at him. "I smell."

"I do, too," he said with a grin. "I came to find you before I showered. Hope that's okay."

She smiled, a wide, lovely smile that covered her entire face. "I had no idea I was such an urgent matter."

"To be honest, I was afraid you were going to waltz back out of my life again, and it scared the shit out of me."

She looked pleased. "Come on," she said, giving his shirt a tug. "You can scrub my back."

"Yes, ma'am," he drawled. "You wanna wash me, too?"

She gave him a sultry look over her shoulder. "Absolutely."

As she entered the bathroom and began to run the water, he moved into her small bedroom. Though it felt like an invasion of privacy, he hadn't brought any condoms with him, and he needed to find some. He wasn't leaving this house until he'd made love to Miranda again. Guessing, he pulled open the drawer of her nightstand. A magazine lay inside, a scatter of condoms, and a bright blue vibrator.

Now, that gave him ideas. Grinning, he grabbed a condom—close to expiration. It was pretty obvious Miranda didn't buy them often. He'd fix that. Tucking the condom into his pocket, he headed into the bathroom after her.

Like her bedroom, Miranda's bathroom was neat and clean, the counters shiny and white. A cheerful yellow shower curtain matched a plush bath rug, and she sat on the edge of the tub, peeling off her socks. "I can't wait to shower," she admitted with a tiny smile at him. "I'm not exactly feeling sexy at the moment."

"That's fine," he said, trying not to think too hard about the condom in his pocket. "We'll clean up first, and then have sex."

She laughed and finished stripping her clothes off. "All right."

This, Dane decided, was going to be the shortest shower ever. He quickly stripped out of his own clothes and tossed them on the rack while Miranda stepped into the streaming water. Just the thought of her naked body all wet and gleaming made him hard, and her moan of pleasure made his balls tighten. Damn. Get in, wash himself, wash her, then back into the bedroom. Five minutes, max. He could do this.

Steeling himself, he stepped into the shower. She stood in front of the spray, the water only grazing his body as she soaped up. Her long hair trailed rivulets of water down her back and he sighed, hard, thinking of how he'd like to take her in this shower, bend her over, and—

"You want the soap?"

He took the pink bath pouf she offered him, accepted the squirt of fruity shower gel, and began to rub it on himself with grim, quick intensity, concentrating on getting himself clean rather than on the warm, soapy woman who stood less than a foot away, her face blissful as she washed her hair.

"Do my back?" She turned and presented it to him.

Dane set his jaw. He began to methodically scrub her back, swiping the pouf over her in quick, rapid strokes. Miranda yelped in surprise and jerked away. "Are you trying to scrub my skin off?"

"Sorry," he said, averting his eyes. Damn, he'd looked over and her breasts were dripping water, the globes of them slick and inviting. He wanted to shove his cock between them and come all over those pretty tits.

Five minutes, he reminded himself. She'd asked him to wait five minutes. Surely he could do that.

"Your turn to rinse off," she said, and parted the curtain, stepping out. "I'm done."

Thank Christ. This was the longest shower in all eternity. He quickly rinsed his body off, staring through the small gap in the shower that showed pink buttocks being rubbed dry by a fluffy towel—

Fuck it, he was done with this shower. He turned the water off and shoved the curtain aside, reaching for Miranda as soon as he stepped out of the tub. She squealed in surprise as he pulled her into his wet embrace, and he kissed the surprise out of her voice. She was lovely and soft and smelled like fruit, and she was driving him utterly insane just by being here. His tongue slid into her mouth and he gave her a long, sensual lick that told her exactly what he wanted to do to her.

She shuddered in his embrace and wrapped her arms around his slick shoulders.

The hallway would do. His hands on her, he dragged her a few feet out of the bathroom onto the rag rug that ran down the length of the hall and dropped to his knees, pulling her down with him.

Her throaty giggle just made him harder. "Right here?"

"First time right here," he agreed, separating from her for just a brief moment, long enough to reach for the condom he'd stolen from her drawer. His other hand continued to roam over her body, his mouth kissing her pretty jaw and throat. "Next time, in the bed. Time after that, we'll wing it."

"Mmm," she said in response, and he knew she approved of his plan. Her fingertips slid over his abdomen, feeling the wet muscles and sliding lower to grasp his cock.

Goddamn. He closed his eyes and groaned, bracing himself. He'd nearly lost it then and there.

"Need a condom."

He tore the packet open with his teeth. "Got one."

Dane slid between her knees and she wiggled on the rug below him, her breasts jiggling with that small movement. Beautiful sight. He leaned down and kissed one tip as he quickly rolled the condom on.

Her breath caught in a sexy little gasp. Fuck, he wanted to hear that all over again. Condom in place, he hauled one of her legs up around his waist and slid a finger down through the heat of her pussy, seeking her entrance. Was she wet? Was he moving too fast?

Her gasps turned into soft cries and she pushed against his finger, raising her hips.

Not only was she wet, she was hot and slippery with need. Beautiful. He let his fingers graze her clit once before removing his hand, enjoying the little jump her body gave in response. Then he took his cock in hand, guided it to her opening, and slammed home.

Miranda gave a breathy little shriek, her eyes widening. Her hands found his shoulders and her nails dug in. "Oooh, that was good."

"You like that?" he gritted out, doing his best not to fuck her right across this floor and spend himself in two seconds flat. He needed to make sure she came, or else he'd be as bad as those other pricks she'd dated.

"I did," she said in a soft, breathy voice, lifting her other knee so her hips tilted up.

He circled his hips against her own, rocking deep inside her, and she moaned.

"Like that?" he murmured again, watching her head fall back with pleasure. "Want me to fuck you slow, baby, or fast and hard?"

"Fast and hard," she whispered, her nails digging like claws into his back, her hips twitching under him.

He didn't need any more encouragement. He drew back until he was almost out of her, then slammed home again, and was rewarded with her calves tensing against him, a slight flutter in her pussy in response. The only sound she made was another sharp gasp.

"Like that?"

She nodded.

He thrust again. And then again. And again, until he was pumping her hard, his fingers digging into her hips to keep her anchored in place. Each thrust slammed into her, and he knew he wasn't going to last long. She was covered in droplets falling from his skin, her body wet and slippery like his, and those breasts gleamed and bounced with each hard drive of his cock, and it just made him wilder with need. She gave a small moaning breath with each thrust, her eyes closed with pleasure, and she raised her hips to meet his thrusts almost violently, until he was afraid he was going to hurt her. She wasn't hurting, though; her moans grew louder with every lift of her hips.

He felt his balls tighten, knew he was close, but she hadn't come yet. Though it killed him, he slowed, circling his hips gently again, still embedded deep into her hot, tight passage. He needed to think about something else to pace himself. As always, when he needed to slow his orgasm, his thoughts went back to hockey. Drills. That was what he needed to think about. Think about passing. Better yet, passing in the offensive zone. That was what he needed to do. Pass to her—get her to come first. He slid a hand between them, searching for her clit.

When he found it, she nearly came off the floor. "Dane!"

That's right, baby. Now he was on the offense. He brushed her clit with his thumb, circling the wetness over it as she shuddered under him, crying out. Her nails were scratching the shit out of him, but he didn't care. He wanted her to come just as hard as he was about to. Patiently, he continued to circle it with the pad of his thumb, waiting for her to fall apart and then he'd finish claiming her. But first, she needed to score.

A tiny, keening whimper rose in her throat and she pushed against his thumb, harder and harder, and then froze. He felt her pussy flutter and clench around him, hard, as she began to come, and he continued rubbing, extending her orgasm. She continued to clench around him, her voice calling out his name in a broken, rasping half sob, and he lost his control. He shuddered, trying to think about hockey. His mind was full of visuals of sliding the puck home, like he was sliding his cock home inside her. With one final, hard thrust, he came, gritting his teeth against the yell of pleasure that threatened to erupt, emptying himself deep inside her even as she quivered and her pussy clenched around him in multiple aftershocks. He continued to move in her, slowly thrusting even as he came down from his orgasm, cock throbbing, blood pounding in his ears, and then he collapsed to the side of her, pulling her close in his arms.

They lay there for a long minute, neither one moving. Dane felt his heartbeat slowing, felt Miranda's breathing returning to normal.

Then she gave a low, throaty chuckle. "Are we going to cuddle in the hallway?"

He leaned in and kissed her shoulder. "Would you rather cuddle in the kitchen?"

She smiled, her eyes still closed, the blissfully dreamy expression on her face. "I was thinking more along the lines of the bedroom, but hey."

Dane grinned at that, thinking of the bright blue vibrator she'd had in there. "We can go to the bedroom."

She untangled herself from him and stood, moving back into the bathroom and grabbing fresh towels. "I should probably clean this water up first."

"Leave it," he said, then turned away and disposed of his condom. "Come on."

Taking her hand in his, he tugged her back into the bedroom and down onto the bed. They were still wet from the shower, but he didn't care and he suspected she didn't either. Her dark, glossy wet hair flew across the blankets and she grinned up at him. "You don't look like you're in a cuddling mood."

"No? How do I look?"

She ran a finger over one pectoral, outlining it. "Predatory," she said, the sound a sigh of delight. "Like you want to capture me and eat me."

"While that sounds delicious, I have other plans for you tonight," he said, and waggled his eyebrows at her.

She gave him a curious look, a smile curving her lips. "Oh?"

He loved looking down at her, soft and warm and curvy under him. Dane grinned. Was it possible to fall in love in a week? He wasn't a romantic, but there was something about being with Miranda that made him feel whole, centered.

He liked it. And he liked her. And while the timing wasn't ideal, he loved being with her, and he was going to keep being with her. Colt and Grant would just have to adjust.

He wouldn't tell her that just yet, though. Getting all sappy and yakking about feelings with a chick after a week would probably make any sensible woman run like the wind.

He teased her belly button with one finger, toying with the dip. "How much do you trust me?"

The look that Miranda gave him was immediately wary. "Why?"

Well, damn. His playful mood deflated in an instant. She looked almost frantic with worry, her body tensing under him. What was going through her head right now? "In bed," he clarified. "How much do you trust me in bed?"

"Oh." Her fear dissipated so abruptly that it stunned him. "Of course I trust you in bed."

Well, what the fuck was all that about? Why was she so terrified of trusting him? Had she been burned in the past and that was why she flinched every time trust came up? A fierce, possessive surge swept through him. Whatever bastard had hurt her, he was going to find the man and take him apart, piece by piece. Miranda was a funny, loving, sexual, incredible woman, even if she didn't think she was.

All he had to do was prove it to her. And if that took three weeks or three years, he was up to it.

"So you trust me?" he repeated. "Trust me to bring you pleasure?"

She nodded at him, her brown eyes soft and sexy. "Of course."

"Trust me to make you come so hard your toes will curl?"

She grinned and wiggled her toes at him in response. "Every time."

He reached over her and opened the nightstand drawer, then pulled out the bright blue vibrator. "Enough to let me use this on you?"

Her playful look froze on her face, and then she blushed—not the delicate, charming usual blush—fiery red. "Dane!" Her outraged expression was delightful to see. "You're not supposed to know about that."

"Not supposed to know about what?" he teased, pulling it out of the drawer and examining it with great thought. She reached for it, but he continued to hold it out of her reach. "I had to dig for condoms earlier, and I saw this. Hope that's all right."

"It's just embarrassing, that's all," she said in a hushed voice, and then reached for it again. "Give it back. I don't need it when I have you anyhow."

"My sweet, darlin' Miz Hill," he drawled, and winked down at her. "Now that's where you're wrong. I think there's plenty of room in this bed for the three of us."

Her blush gave way to confusion. "You want to use my vibrator?"

Dane grinned. "Maybe some other night you can use it on me. I'm more interested in using it on you and watching you come again."

The crimson returned to her cheeks.

He moved up on the bed and kissed her lips. She was pliant underneath him, and he detected a slight tremble of her body—in excitement or uncertainty?

"I won't do it if you don't want me to, Miranda," he murmured against her lips. "Not if you're embarrassed."

"A little," she said.

"What embarrasses you about it?"

She thought for a moment, then shrugged. "I guess when we have sex, we're in it together so I'm not thinking too much about you staring at me or watching my reactions. But with this . . ."

He chuckled and slid a knuckle over the soft swell of one breast, enjoying how her nipple tightened under his touch. "You think I'm not going to participate here? That it won't turn me on?"

"Kind of silly, huh?"

"Very silly," he agreed. "Hell, I got turned on just watching you make fire when we were on the trip."

"Must have been because I was handling all that wood," she teased, lightly skimming her fingers over his arms. Then she looked over at him and bit her lip. "It's okay," she said after a moment. "I want to do this. I trust you, remember?"

He felt like he'd been given a gift. Miranda trusted him to take her out of her comfort zone, and he wouldn't disappoint her. Dane kissed her again, nibbling and sucking at her lower lip. When she gave a low moan in her throat and her arms slid around his neck, he slipped from her grasp and began to move down her body, kissing a path. Her chin. Her collarbones. Her breastbone. He lingered at the twin mounds of her breasts, so lovely and full. He nuzzled each nipple and made them stand erect, leaving the tips wet and gleaming and Miranda squirming and panting under him. Farther down, he kissed her belly button and noticed that her body was beginning to quiver with tension. A good sort of tension, he hoped. When he got to her mound and pressed a kiss there, she didn't make a sound. He glanced up and saw her dark eyes watching him, biting her lip as if she were afraid to show him her reactions.

Well now, that wouldn't do at all. She was thinking too much again.

Dane sat up and slapped her thigh lightly. "Pull up your knees, baby."

She frowned at him, and slowly did as she was told, pulling her knees close to her breasts.

"Hug them to you," he said. "Lock your hands behind them and don't release until I tell you to."

He watched the blush return, and she pulled her knees in tighter, her head tilted to the side. Now she could no longer see what he was up to, and he'd have the freedom to work her over like he wanted to.

She was lovely like this, her legs pulled back, displaying long, lean thighs pressed together tightly. Between them, the dark strip of her pussy and the wet gleam of the folds there. She looked so delicious that he leaned in and brushed his tongue over the wetness, tasting the salty flavor of her.

She shuddered underneath him, her breath catching in her throat. Now, that was more like it.

With one finger, he parted her pussy lips and slid his finger back and forth, making sure she was juicy and wet. She was—her core was hot and slick, and he rubbed the slippery wetness up and down through her labia. She whimpered every time he touched her clit, but he didn't linger there.

"Soft and pretty. And so very wet. Are you excited about me using the vibrator on you?"

The tremble swept over her again, and her pussy clenched when he dipped a finger deep into her core. He teased it deep, then slid it back out again, and waited for her response.

"Y-yes," she finally allowed. "It feels . . . naughty."

"Well, I happen to love a naughty girl," he said, and rewarded her with another thrust of his finger. She jerked her hips in response, but she seemed tense, waiting for something. He knew what it was.

He clicked on the vibrator, and she seemed to almost vibrate with need herself. He didn't insert it—not just yet. He wanted her to anticipate it for a minute more. Instead, he continued to let his finger circle the heat of her core, then glided it through the wetness back up to her clit, as if he had all the time in the world. All the while, she made soft whimpering noises and her legs tightened and flexed, over and over again, her thigh muscles working repeatedly. It was beautiful to watch.

Miranda's vibrator was a long, smooth blue column, the head slightly flared and curved to brush against her G-spot. It shivered in his hand, and he spread her pussy lips and laid the vibrating head of it against her clit.

Miranda nearly came off the bed. A cry escaped her throat and she clenched, hard. "Keep your legs up," he reminded her, and placed his own arm over hers to keep her stationary.

"Oh God," she moaned. "Dane, please—"

"Please what?" he said in a husky voice. "Please tease it against your clit?" He rubbed the vibrating head against the hard, swollen little nub.

She jerked against his grasp but he held her pinned there, using the head of the vibrator with great precision, rubbing it back and forth against her clit. He was as hard as a rock watching her reaction. Her pleasure was so overwhelming that her eyes were closed, her mouth working in soft cry after cry.

And then she shattered, her legs clenching hard. He continued to rub the head of the vibrator against her clit, milking her reaction until her muscles loosened under him and she began to pant. "Oh, Dane," she said in a husky, wondering voice that made his balls tighten with need. "Oh God."

He rubbed the head of it through her labia, getting it good and slick, and then he sank the tip of it into her pussy.

He felt her tense under his arm, felt the shiver building through her legs. Her moan rose again. When he sank the vibrating length in to the hilt, she cried out his name again. "Dane!"

"Do you like it, baby?" He twisted the vibrator inside her, rotating it in a circle like he would his cock if he were deep inside her. "Like it when I make you come?"

"Yes!"

He pulled it out, then thrust the slick length of it deep again, enjoying the way her body jerked in response to the thrust. He repeated the motion, then began to piston it slowly, letting it glide in and out between her wet pussy lips, and leaned in to flick his tongue against her clit. She was so wet that she was soaking, and he lapped at the taste of her and was rewarded with another hard clench of her pussy. Then another.

"I'm coming again," she cried out, and her pussy clenched hard against the vibrator. He continued to work it and she cried out, over and over. He kept thrusting it into her, and her cries turned into a shriek of his name as she spasmed hard with her orgasm.

Dane turned the vibrator off, breathing hard. He'd made her come so freaking hard and his own breathing was shallow and panting, his dick hard as a rock. He wanted to be deep inside her, wanted to be the one fucking her and making her shriek. Wanted to be the one she clenched around. He slid the vibrator out of her still-clenching pussy and pulled his arm off of the backs of her thighs, trying to compose himself. He'd give her a moment, and then he'd finish what they'd started.

She was on him in a flash, rolling up on the bed and kissing him hard. Surprised, he kissed her back, and then hissed when she reached for his cock.

"Let me do you," she said against his mouth, then tugged at his lower lip with her teeth.

"With the vibrator?"

She shook her head and gave him a naughty look, her face gleaming with a sheen of sweat. "The old-fashioned way."

And she slid a hand down his chest and pushed him backward.

He went, his cock standing straight up in the air. As he watched, Miranda straddled him and went straight for his cock, her mouth suddenly sliding over the head and encasing it in warmth. Her warm hands grasped the shaft and then she sucked, hard, on the head.

Oh fuck, he was going to come if she did that again. "Miranda, baby," he groaned. She only wiggled her ass and continued to swipe her tongue against his cock, licking the head and tasting the pre-cum that beaded there, then taking him deep into her throat and pumping the base with her hands. His fingers were wrapped in her still-wet hair and he held her as she worked his cock, using her tongue in wicked little licks that made him want to come all over her face.

Then she got the naughtiest look of all on her face and pulled him deep into her throat, sucking hard. It was so fucking good he nearly saw stars. He almost missed when she switched on the vibrator and held it against his balls. A raw shock wave of pleasure coursed through his body.

Then he was exploding, shooting hot jets of cum down her throat and yelling, fucking her mouth even as he came, and she continued to rub the vibrator against his sac, working her mouth over his cock and getting every last ounce of cum from him.

When he collapsed back on the bed again, she sat up and licked her lips, giving him the most satisfied expression.

"Damn," he panted, grinning up at her. "I think I need another shower."

She smiled and moved up to kiss him. "In a minute," she said. "I just want to touch you for a while without my head exploding in another orgasm."

"Is that such a bad thing?"

"Hell no."

He grinned, pulled her into his arms, and tucked her close, trapping her leg in between his.

No way was he letting Miranda Hill get away again. She was amazing. She was wild in bed, and hot as hell.

And she was all fucking his.

FIFTEEN

One week later

Beth Ann dropped by Miranda's place after she closed her salon. Usually when Miranda had a day off, she'd stop in to chitchat, and Beth Ann would trim her ends, give her a manicure.

But the salon had been strangely quiet this week, and Beth Ann's suspicions were roused.

She'd called Miranda a few times, and her friend had seemed cheery but distracted. "You busy moving?" Beth Ann had asked her, and Miranda had said she was. But Miranda had the week off, and she hadn't stopped in to say hello or hang out. *Fine way to treat a friend when you were moving away for good.*

So she brought a roll of contact paper with her to work that day, and when Miranda didn't drop by the salon, she went to Miranda instead, toting her present as an excuse.

Miranda had a small, neat little cottage on a quiet street. Tall pecan trees littered the yard, and her tiny rental house was older, but charming. Beth Ann had half a mind to take the lease off of Miranda's hands when she left—anything would beat another month living at home with her parents until Allan got his act together . . .

She sighed. She needed to stop thinking that way. Allan wasn't getting his act together, and she wasn't getting together with him ever again. That was her mother planting ideas in her head.

She swung the screen door open and knocked on the wooden door. Silence. Beth Ann glanced in the window—lights were on. She leaned in close to the door. A murmur of voices, and then a scramble to get to the door.

Annoyed, Beth Ann hit the doorbell.

The door swung open quickly, and a flushed Miranda answered, pushing strands of her hair out of her face. "Hey, girl," she exclaimed in greeting. "What are you doing here?"

"Thought I'd help you pack," Beth Ann drawled, not fooled for a second. Miranda's shirt was untucked, the zipper on her jeans was down. Her feet were bare.

Yeah. Beth Ann wasn't dumb. She shoved the contact paper roll into Miranda's hands and pushed her way inside. "Since you're so busy packing, I thought I'd come and help you finish," she said. "Brought you some contact paper for the new place."

The house was just as she suspected—boxes lay scattered in the room but nothing seemed to be put in them. In fact, if she looked hard, it almost seemed as if there was less stuff in them than the last time she'd been over. Beth Ann whirled, tapping one pink fingernail on her chin.

"You didn't have to do this, Beth Ann," Miranda said awkwardly. "I'm almost done with the packing."

Beth Ann turned to look back at her friend, hurt. "You are a terrible liar."

There was a sound in the bedroom, and Miranda stiffened. A dreadful feeling began to rise in the pit of Beth Ann's stomach. Before Miranda could stop her, Beth Ann moved to the bedroom door and pushed it open.

A large man sat on the edge of the bed, sliding on his shoes. He wore no shirt over his bronzed, rippling muscles, and he looked up at the sight of her in the bedroom door.

"Hi," said her best friend's worst enemy. "Beth Ann, you haven't changed."

"Neither have you," she said through clenched teeth, and shut the door in his face. She turned and gave Miranda a look of disappointment, and then walked right back out of the house.

Miranda followed her out. "Beth Ann! It's not what you think—"

"Really?" she snapped, angry and afraid for her friend all at once. "Because I'm thinking he's moved in."

"Don't be silly," Miranda scoffed. "We've only been seeing each other for the last week."

Beth Ann crossed her arms over her chest. "And how many times has he slept at his place in the last week?"

Silence.

Beth Ann gave her friend an exasperated look. "Really?"

To her credit, Miranda blushed. "I know what you're thinking—"

Beth Ann whipped out her cell phone. "That I should just take the picture of your tits and post it on the Internet right now so we can get this over with?"

Miranda flinched, and immediately Beth Ann felt like a jerk. She sighed and moved to hug Miranda.

"I'm sorry, girl," Beth Ann said.

"You're just worried about me," Miranda said in a soft voice. "I know."

"He hurt you so badly," Beth Ann said, and hated the knot rising in her throat. "Humiliated you in front of everyone and broke your heart. I know what that feels like, too."

"Of course you do," Miranda said soothingly, and patted Beth Ann on the back. "But this is . . . this is different, Beth Ann." Her face flushed with pleasure, and her pretty brown eyes gleamed. "He's not the guy I thought he was. He's different. You just have to trust me."

"Oh, honey," Beth Ann said, and gave her best friend another squeeze on the arm. "Of course I trust you."

It was that low-life fink Dane Croft that she didn't trust.

She and Miranda chatted for a moment longer on the porch, and then Beth Ann made up an excuse about having to go back to the salon to make sure she'd unplugged everything.

Miranda looked uncomfortable. "You sure you don't want to stay for a few? I made some sweet tea."

She shook her head and managed a cheerful smile. "Gotta run, but thanks for asking. I'll stop by tomorrow and help you pack for real." She gave her friend a stern look. "No excuses."

"No excuses," Miranda said with a smile.

Beth Ann moved back out to her small, sea green Volkswagen Bug and started the car. But instead of turning back toward Main Street, she got on the highway and headed outside of town, toward the Daughtry Ranch.

She'd find out on her own if Dane Croft was playing games this time. If Miranda wasn't worried . . . Beth Ann would be worried for her. One of them needed to be ready, and Beth Ann wanted to be prepared for the worst.

Beth Ann parked her car in front of the Daughtry Ranch. There was a gravel parking lot and a scatter of cabins, but other than that, it really didn't look like much. In the distance, she could see a long barn, but it looked deserted. Beth Ann got out of the car, gripped her keys, and headed for the big ranch house. A sign hung above the door, proudly proclaiming WILDERNESS SURVIVAL EXPEDITIONS, and a plastic pamphlet case nailed to the porch wall was stuffed full of brochures.

She considered knocking, but it was a business, right? She'd treat it like one. No one had to knock before entering her salon. She opened the door and stepped in.

No one looked up as she entered. A woman she didn't recognize had a phone to her ear and was writing furiously in a steno pad. Grant Markham—a total blast from her high school past—didn't even look up from his computer. Gee. He'd gotten friendly in the last nine years.

One person stood and moved to the door. "Can I help you?" he said in a low, almost raspy voice.

She stared at him in surprise. Colt Waggoner—she remembered him from high school, too. She shouldn't have been surprised—she'd seen his picture in the brochure. He was . . . different. He'd been silent in high school, and she guessed that much hadn't changed, but there was something hard and lean about him now. Something slightly dangerous. He'd filled out from the rangy form she remembered, too—this man was all ropy muscles and coiled strength. And he was devouring her with his eyes. Taken aback, she stifled the surge of pleasure that his appreciation brought. It was nice to have someone make her feel pretty again, but that wasn't why she was here tonight.

"Thought I'd come by and ask you if you know where your friend Dane is," she said, keeping her voice mild.

Colt crossed his arms over his chest. "Ain't his keeper."

"No, you ain't," she said, emphasizing his slang. "But you are trying to run a business here, aren't you? How's that going to look if your instructor is having a relationship with one of his students while on one of your retreats? You'll never have another woman sign up ever again."

Colt's appreciative look turned to a scowl as he glared at her. When the woman put down her phone and Grant looked up from his computer, Colt took her by the elbow and dragged her back outside.

"Beth Ann Williamson? Is that you?" Grant said, getting up from his desk. "Wow, long time no see. Did you say something about students—"

"She doesn't have time to talk," Colt gritted, pushing outside and dragging Beth Ann with him.

She glared as he pulled her along, and when they were back

in the parking lot, she jerked away from him. "That's far enough, thank you."

"There a problem?" Colt's tone was abrupt.

"Darn right there's a problem," Beth Ann said, crossing her arms over her chest. She refused to be intimidated by his raw, physical power and that sexy rasp in his voice. Funny, but that wasn't how she remembered him at all. He'd been a silent, aloof jerk in high school, and nothing had changed, it seemed, except the package. "The issue is your friend. He's ruining the life of mine. Again."

Colt stared at her a long, long minute, his eyes piercing. When she thought he was ignoring her, he finally said, "Don't know what you're talking about."

"No?" She eyed his lean body, the casual set of his shoulders. "Where's your buddy Dane? Not at work, I see."

Colt was silent.

Ah yes, she remembered why he'd infuriated her so much in school. She'd always been lively and chatty, and he was anything but. "Well?"

"Heard you didn't marry Allan."

She stiffened. "That's none of your business, and I'll thank you to keep your nose out of it."

He grunted.

Flustered, she brushed her bangs behind her ear. "Look. All I'm saying is that Dane and Miranda are hooking up, and I think it's mighty unpleasant that one of your instructors is hooking up with one of his students."

Colt continued to watch her in that scrutinizing way she found so unnerving. "Not true," he said finally. "Dane's not seeing anyone."

The man was unreal. "Are you blind? Should I have taken a snapshot to savor the moment and show to all my friends? Oh wait, that's y'all's job, isn't it?"

He scowled.

"Look. I came up here to warn you."

"Oh, you did, did you?" His cool tone suddenly got thirty shades cooler. "Came to warn me that we're not welcome here?"

"I don't care if you pitch a tent in the middle of town," she declared. "But if Dane hurts Miranda one more time, I'm going to geld him with my haircutting scissors, understand me?"

"Miranda's a former student. No more. She's done with the class and he's done with her." Beth Ann could have sworn his mouth turned up in a hint of a smile.

"All I'm saying is that he needs to back off and leave her alone. All of you. Understand me?"

The interested glint in his eyes died and was replaced with ice. "Yes, ma'am," he drawled, then nodded at her car. "I'll see you out."

"We're already out."

"Then I guess I'll see you gone."

Jerk. The town jackass count was higher by one with him back. She turned on her heel, hair flaring over her shoulder as she stomped away.

Grant looked up as Colt reentered the office. "What was that about?"

"Town shit," Colt drawled, and picked up his Xbox controller. "Nothing worth repeating."

"She came all the way out here to talk to you about town shit?" Grant asked. "Sounds like bull to me."

Colt shrugged. "She's just imagining shit. Or making it up."

"Why would she drive out here over something she made up?"

"Maybe she's hot for me."

Grant snorted. "I must have mistaken that look of desire on her face for rage." He grabbed the stack of paperwork on his desk and began to pick through it, oblivious to Colt's silence. Then again, Grant always was preoccupied with one project or another. The man focused—okay, obsessed—so much that he lost track of reality. After a few minutes, Grant spoke again. "Is it about a girl?"

"Huh?" Colt looked up from the TV.

"A girl," Grant said, shoving a stack of ledgers aside to glance at his friend. "Dane hasn't been himself lately. Distracted. She mentioned a girl. Think he's seeing someone in town?"

"Nailing, maybe," Colt said with a shrug. "If he was really seeing someone, he'd bring her around."

"Because we're both so cuddly and lovable? We read him the riot act about keeping his dick in his pants. The guy probably won't bring a date within twenty miles of this place because he thinks we'll flip out on him."

Colt grunted. "She's just being hysterical and overreacting. Dane promised he'd keep his hands off the clients."

"True." Grant stared at the door, then looked back to Colt. "You keep your hands off all your clients?"

Colt scowled. "Fuck off. That's not even funny."

Grant just grinned, ignoring Colt's anger. "You never know, I think any woman would run screaming if she realized she'd have to spend time with you and your sunny personality."

"I'm all charm, no harm."

"That doesn't even make any sense."

"To you, maybe." Colt nodded at the enormous stack of paperwork on Grant's desk. "Anyhow, it ain't a girl. He hasn't said a thing about anyone and he would have said something to me. He never misses a class and he never shows up smelling like cheap perfume or with lipstick on his collar."

"I asked if he was dating a girl, not your mom," Grant said dryly.

Colt shot him the bird. "Funny. You done with that shit so we can go get a beer in town?"

Fingers drummed on the stack of paperwork as Grant weighed the options. Then he stood and shoved his chair out from the desk. "I guess those press releases can wait another day or two."

"Damn straight," Colt said, getting to his feet. He gestured for Brenna to take her headphones off. "We're going into town to get a beer," he yelled.

She brightened and pulled the headphones off, her freckled face lighting up. "Beer? Can I come?"

"No," Grant said sharply. "You still haven't finished the supplies inventory I gave you two days ago."

She scowled at him, slipped the headphones back on her head. "Haters."

Grant looked as if he wanted to take the headphones off the girl and choke her with them. Colt nudged his friend on the shoulder. "Come on. What's that place in town with the bar?"

"Maya Loco," Grant said, finally turning away from glaring at Brenna to move toward the door. "You sure it wasn't a girl?"

"If it was, he'd say something," Colt drawled.

"Huh. True."

Miranda played with Dane's fingers, locking her own with them as she rested her head on his chest. "Do you have work today?"

"Classes," he said. "School camping trip. After that, I'm free until the weekend. What about you?"

She stiffened in bed. She should be packing. Should call her job to confirm that everything was lined up. Instead, she'd spent the past week lazing in bed with Dane, and when they weren't in bed, they'd spent every waking moment together. Being with him made mundane trips—like going to the grocery store—a pleasant experience.

It was depressing how much she was enjoying his company, even more because she knew it couldn't last.

The thought made her unreasonably sad. "No work today."

He locked his fingers around hers and wiggled their linked hands. "You haven't been to work in more than two weeks. You on vacation?"

"Yeah." It was easier than telling him the truth. That she was leaving in less than a week, and that she didn't plan on seeing him ever again.

"My trip's an overnighter," he said, then tapped her arm with their linked hands. "You want to come with? I'm sure we could come up with a reasonable excuse."

"No, that's okay," she said, feigning a yawn. "I'll clean up around here."

"You should probably finish unpacking," he agreed, though

he didn't get up from the bed. His free hand played with her hair. "It's my fault you haven't had a chance. Want me to help when I get back?"

"Nah," she said, her heart thudding. "I can handle it. I've taken up enough of your time lately."

To her surprise, he lifted her hand and kissed it. "I don't mind," he said huskily. "I'll miss you when I'm gone."

Me, too, she thought, but said nothing.

His arms went around her and he rolled over in the bed, dragging her until she was pinned underneath him. Dane gave her a wicked grin. "Class won't be there for at least another hour or two."

She smiled back at him and wiggled her hips suggestively. "Plenty of time for you to make me breakfast, then."

He tugged at her clothing. She only wore a tank top and panties to bed, and Dane seemed to appreciate her clothes—or lack thereof. His hands slid under the hem of her tank top and his mouth descended on her belly button, licking and sucking at the indention. "I had something else in mind."

Miranda's laughter died in her throat, emerging as a low moan, her hips rising when his fingers brushed along the edge of her panties. Then he was sliding them down her thighs, and a moment later, he tossed them to the floor. His breath was warm on her stomach, and he leaned in to kiss her navel again, his tongue dipping in.

Her hands flexed over his shoulders, her nails digging into his skin. God, she loved the feel of him over her, all hard muscles and delicious masculine scent. She'd miss wrapping her legs around him and feeling him sink deep inside her, miss the taste of his skin when he was slick with sweat from fucking her for so long . . .

A needy sound escaped her throat, and she tugged at his shoulders. "I want you inside me, Dane. Please."

He moved up her body and loomed over her, leaning down to press a quick, hard kiss against her mouth. She pushed up against him, making the kiss urgent with need. She wanted to forget that this was all going to be over soon. That this might be one of her last moments with him. Her hands went to his cheeks and her tongue stroked deep in his mouth, her hips rising, and she felt the hard, hot length of him against her thigh.

He chuckled at her eagerness, moving to press hot kisses along her face, her nose, her chin. "I'm only going to be gone for a few days, Miranda. Then we can spend the next two in bed together."

She shook her head, still pulling him against her with need. She couldn't tell him why she felt this intense urge to have him deep inside her. He wouldn't understand. "It's going to be a long day," she said. "Can't I just miss you?"

Dane reached over her and grabbed a foil packet from the nightstand, then ripped open the package and rolled the condom on as she clung to him, kissing every inch of toned flesh that she could reach. A brief moment later, his hips settled between hers and she raised her legs, locking her ankles behind his back just as he surged deep into her.

Miranda cried out. Her hands tugged at him wildly. "God yes, like that."

He gave a low growl deep in his throat and began to fuck her hard, each thrust pumping deep. "Miss you, too," he breathed, leaning in for another hard, possessive kiss. He ended it with a slick thrust that seemed to almost reach her core. His tongue teased along the seam of her parted mouth, thrusting when he drove deep again. "Think about you the whole time. You in this bed, your dark hair all wild, in nothing but your tank top and panties, waiting for me to come home. Thinking about that vibrator and then thinking about you using it while thinking of me."

Her pussy clenched at his words.

"You like that?" He surged deep inside her again, then began to pump slowly, punctuating his harder thrusts with another searing kiss.

She clenched again, and was rewarded with a hiss of his breath—he'd felt the contraction of her muscles deep inside. "I love it when you touch me," she said softly, gazing up into his green eyes, cloudy with lust. "Love it when you're deep inside me, so hard."

He stroked deep inside her again, and his mouth descended on hers, swallowing her soft words into another intense kiss. Her hips rose to meet his and they began to move in rhythm, her hips rising to meet each thrust, rocking together. Miranda's nails dug into his skin and she began to whimper with each thrust, the intensity overtaking all rational thought. Her movements became jerky, jagged, and she lost the rhythm as her legs began to tense. He stroked deep and then circled his hips, and her breath choked as he grazed her G-spot deep within. Then he pushed deep, surging hard inside her, and held. His green eyes stared into her own, and she memorized his face in that moment, gleaming with sweat, the intense gaze framed with spiky, dark lashes. The stubble on his cheeks and chin, the curve of his mouth.

He was beautiful.

He rocked inside her again and she came, a low moan erupting from her throat. Her muscles quivered as the orgasm swept through her. She gasped with relief, curling her toes as he surged deep again. Then he was coming too, the cords in his neck standing out as his entire body shook with the force of his orgasm. Miranda watched him with fascination, memorizing the lines of his face in that vulnerable moment. She could watch him forever.

Dane leaned heavily over her, panting, and pulled her close for one last kiss. "Thank you."

She gave him a breathy laugh and wrapped her arms around his shoulders, pulling him on top of her fully. The heavy weight of him atop her was a delicious feeling. "Why are you thanking me?"

He leaned in and kissed her nose. "Morning sex always takes the edge off the day. Now I don't have to worry about those kids getting on my nerves. I can just go through the day in a daze of endorphins."

Miranda laughed. When he tried to roll off of her, she shook her head and tugged him close again. "Not yet," she said softly. "You have a few minutes before you have to leave, and I kind of want to hold on to you for a bit longer."

He grinned down at her. "You do realize I'm only going overnight, right?"

A day, true. But she didn't have many more days here. She avoided his gaze and ran a light finger over the muscles in his arms, tracing the veins. "Even that can seem like forever," she said lightly. "Is it such a crime to like the feel of you over me?"

Dane gave her an intense look, all teasing leaving his gaze. The grin slid from his mouth, and she recognized the flare of desire in his eyes. "Not in my book."

And with that, he rocked his hips, just a little. Enough to remind her that he was still seated deep inside her. And he was already hard again.

The breath caught in her throat and her gaze flew back to him.

"You said we had a few minutes yet, right?" He leaned in and kissed her, then tugged her lower lip into his mouth, sucking on it lightly for a moment before releasing it. "I think we should make the most of it."

"I'm game," she said lightly and pulled him closer. Sometimes, she thought she could stay in his arms forever.

After Dane left, she picked through some of the stuff in her house. She was restless, something vaguely nagging her. Guilt for her relationship with Dane? Beth Ann hadn't been happy when they'd talked last, and she hated the thought of disappointing her best friend.

She picked up her phone to call and noticed her mother had called again, twice. No messages. Probably just checking in. She should stop by and visit her anyhow. She had a box of stuff to drop off, and it'd give her a chance to swing by the salon and visit Beth Ann. Talk for a bit, maybe explain that things weren't the way they seemed.

Because really, they didn't seem like wise decisions at the moment.

Miranda drove into town, parking her truck in front of her mother's antiques store. The crooked sign wobbled in the breeze, and she sighed at the sight of it. Someday she'd have to pay to get that fixed. The inside of the store was quiet, and she found her mother sitting on a trunk, crying quietly in the back storage room.

"Mom?"

Her mother looked up as Miranda entered, and only cried harder.

Oh jeez. Her mother had always been a little fragile of spirit, and her crying jags could mean anything. Lately they had meant that she was sad Miranda was leaving for Houston, but they'd talked about this already. She tamped down the feeling of annoyance and sat next to her mom on the trunk, patting her back. "You okay, Mom? What's bothering you?"

"Oh, Miranda," her mom wept. "I don't know how to tell you this. It's just like before."

"What's like before?"

Her mother waved a dramatic hand in the air. "The rumors, the laughing. The staring. The people that come by to tell me what he's doing to you."

A cold pit started in Miranda's stomach. Her mother was overreacting again. "You mean my dating Dane, Mom?"

Tanya hissed, as if the thought caused her pain. "Not dating. He's using you," she accused. "Just like before. He's going to use you for sex and then post pictures of it all over the place to inflate his own sorry ego."

Miranda flinched. "It's not like that."

"It's not?" her mother said bitterly. "I looked. The pictures are still up. If he liked you so much, why are they still on the Internet for everyone to see?"

Miranda pursed her lips, hard, and continued to stroke her mother's back. She'd always had to be the adult in their relationship, the one who assured her mom that everything was okay. Even still . . . her question made twisted sense, and Miranda didn't like that. "It's not like that—"

"No?" Her mother turned tear-bright eyes to Miranda, and her chin wobbled as she mopped at her cheeks with wadded-up Kleenex. "Then tell me how it is, Miranda Jane Hill. Does he take you out on the town? Buy you nice dinners?"

Well, no, they'd stayed at Miranda's tiny house the entire time. "Mom—"

"Does he introduce you to his friends? Take you to his house?"

An uncomfortable feeling prickled through Miranda. She said nothing.

"Oh, baby," her mother said in a sad, sad voice. "Did you forget how he treated you all those years ago?"

A knot burned in her throat and she stood. "I haven't forgotten."

The conversation with her mother had been disturbing in its accuracy—and at the same time, inaccuracy. Her mind was full of questions that she had no answers for. Was Dane using her? But she'd approached him, she'd been the one to declare their relationship a secret. It had been her idea for them to use each other for sex. It had been Dane that had said he was going to break the news to Colt and Grant, let them know he and Miranda were together. They'd taken it surprisingly well, given that Dane had been sleeping with a client. There'd been no fallout at all.

That bothered her a little.

Her head was full of questions that she had no answers to,

and she needed to talk to someone. Instead of getting back in her car, she headed down the street to Beth Ann's salon.

As she entered, another woman was leaving—Mary Ellen Greenwood. She gave Miranda a dismissive look as she entered, clutching her purse more tightly under her arm, as if Miranda's presence might somehow contaminate her.

Miranda put a hand to the collar of her shirt and tugged it upward.

Beth Ann was sweeping hair in the main salon room and looked up as Miranda entered. "Hey, honey," she said, her voice uncertain.

"My mom is crying," she gestured down the street to the antiques store. "She thinks Dane's using me."

Beth Ann sighed and shook her head, continuing to sweep.

"Well?"

"Well what?" Beth Ann looked up, her expression grim. "Do you want me to tell you the truth, or do you want me to tell you what you want to hear?"

Ouch. Miranda stared at her. "I want you to tell me the truth, Beth Ann. You're my best friend. If I can't count on you, who can I count on?"

Beth Ann patted the barber's chair. "Sit. I'll tell you what I know."

As Miranda sat down, Beth Ann swept a hot pink leopard cape over Miranda's shoulders. "I went and visited Colt the other day . . ."

SIXTEEN

Her eyebrows waxed, nails manicured, and heart aching, Miranda got back into the car and stared out the windshield without seeing a thing.

Dane hadn't told the others he was dating her. He'd told her he would, and that everything was okay. Why was he keeping her a secret from his friends, unless he'd never planned to take things seriously between them at all?

Worst of all, everyone in town knew. She'd stopped by the hardware store and had heard the "Boobs of Bluebonnet" whispered again, and her heart sank. In a small town, it was impossible to keep a secret, but damn. If everyone already knew they were sleeping together, why hadn't he told his friends—the ones that counted?

It was just like before, except worse. Because she should have known better this time.

Her phone rang and Miranda jumped, digging her cell phone out of her purse. Was it Dane calling? Had his class been canceled and and he'd decided to swing by? She hated the little thrilling flip her heart had given at the thought. But that was silly—he didn't even have her number.

The caller ID showed a phone number she didn't recognize. "Hello?"

"Miranda Hill?" The chirpy voice said on the other end. "This is Kacee Youngblood with HGI Incorporated. I wanted to give you the details about your drug test. We'll need you to complete it before you begin work here at HGI."

"Oh, of course," she mumbled, and halfheartedly listened as the woman chirped instructions in her ear. She hung up after agreeing to head into Houston tomorrow to get the tests taken care of.

Her mind was still stuck on Dane, and her heart felt like it was shattering into a million pieces. When had this turnabout happened? When had she gone from user to the one being used? Was she truly that stupid? He'd promised her he'd tell them. Promised. And he'd been so sweet and charming about it. He'd been the one to suggest it, not her.

Someone was lying to her. Maybe Beth Ann had heard wrong. Maybe Colt was lying.

Instead of going home, she turned her car onto the highway, heading for the Daughtry Ranch, her heart aching with every mile. When she turned in, the parking lot had a scatter of cars. They had a class today. She stepped over the rope railing that served as a partition for the parking lot and began to stride through the grass, heading for one of the trails. This class would be students. He couldn't be taking them far—

"Can I help you?"

A man jogged up behind her, and Miranda wasn't thrilled to see it was Grant.

"Hey, Miranda," Grant said with an easy smile. "We didn't get a chance to talk the other day. It's nice to see you again—"

"I'm looking for Dane," she said, continuing to stomp forward.

"He's out in a class right now. He won't be back until tomorrow." Grant parked himself in front of her, effectively blocking the path. "Is there something that I can help you with?"

"I really need to talk to Dane, actually—"

Grant didn't budge, but he gave her a friendly smile and gestured back at the main cabin. "You want to come in and hang out for a bit since you're here? Colt's out with students, too, so it's just me and Brenna. We can catch up—I hear you've been here in Bluebonnet for the past nine years."

Oh, lovely. Like she wanted to talk about the town right now. "I just . . ."

Grant smiled at her. "This is perfect, actually. We were hoping you'd come back. We need your picture for the student hall of fame board."

She gestured at the woods. "But Dane—"

"He doesn't have to be involved for the picture," Grant said with an easy smile. "It's fine."

She stared at him for a long, long moment, not moving. Waiting for him to break character, to show her that he'd been teasing and he knew perfectly well that she was in a relationship with Dane. That he was just giving her a hard time.

But he said nothing, continued to patiently wait for her.

"Did you know I fucked Dane?"

He stiffened, his smiling expression growing dark. "Excuse me?"

"I was one of Dane's students," she pointed out, hurt by his shocked surprise and wanting to hurt back. "I approached him that first night and made a pass at him. Then we met in the woods and he fucked me. And then we fucked almost every night out there."

Grant's face grew stiff with anger, his mouth thinning. "Are you serious?"

"Yes, actually. He loves fucking me. In fact, we're still fucking," she said with a bitter laugh. "He disappears at my house every night and we fuck like bunnies until morning." Fury and hurt exploded through her. "He told me he was going to tell you and Colt that we're sleeping together, but it looks like that was a lie. I'm guessing that isn't the only thing he's lied about lately, huh?"

The words choked in her throat, and she whirled to go, stomping away on the gravel path back to the parking lot. She waited for him to try and stop her, but he didn't, and when she looked back, Grant was staring at the woods with a thoughtful expression.

Miranda slammed the car door and drove home.

Time to put the plan in action.

"Just remember that we do all kinds of survival classes—from school-age to adult, beginners to experts." Dane said as he shook hands and offered pamphlets. The class had gone well—it was their first school group, and he'd been a little nervous, but the kids had taken to the classes with enthusiasm. There'd been no problems on the overnight, and they'd all had a good time telling stories around the campfire and bunking out. The class should have wrapped earlier today, but the kids had been so enthusiastic that he'd dragged the lessons out for a bit longer and then treated them to a round of paintball, and they'd been more than happy to take him up on it. It had been fun. He liked kids. He wouldn't mind doing more classes with children, he decided, and made a mental note to ask Brenna to schedule more of them. Maybe they could do a summer survival camp for kids.

Brenna jogged up next to him. "Oh, good. You're back. Grant's been looking for you since yesterday."

He tried not to groan. Grant was not his favorite person to see at the end of a class. The micromanager in his friend wanted a complete detail of how the class had gone, from what tasks they'd performed to what each person had worn. Grant wanted to take all the details that he could and record them, and then study and analyze in the hopes of improving the client experience. Of course, Colt thought he did it just to keep himself occupied. Dane wasn't sure. Either way, a long, intensive, detailed narration was not what he had in mind right now. He missed Miranda and wanted to go home and curl up in bed with her. "Grant? What about?"

"Dunno," Brenna said, shrugging her shoulders and wrinkling her nose, as if the thought of Grant made her queasy. "He was upset about something. Insisted on talking to you as soon as you got back. If you want to run out, now's the time."

He grinned at Brenna. She was like a kid sister to him and Colt. To Grant, she was a messy, disorganized, lackadaisical nemesis. She didn't care for Grant's micromanagement either, and would have been fired a long time ago if it wasn't for Colt and Dane. "All right," he said, and squinted up at the setting sun. "It's getting late. I'm going to head into town for the night. If he's looking for me, tell him I'll be back tomorrow morning for the next class."

She winked at him, her green eyes laughing. "Got it. I will thoroughly enjoy telling him that."

"I imagine you will." Dane laughed.

Miranda's street was dark, but the lights were on in her bedroom, and he knocked at the front door softly. The wildflowers in his hand had seemed vibrant when he'd picked them back at the ranch, but they had wilted in the car on the drive over. Hopefully that wasn't a sign of how the evening would go.

"It's open," she called.

He stepped inside. The living room was dark and tidied—the boxes that had scattered the room were stacked neatly in the corner of the room. He couldn't tell where she'd unpacked more, however. Lights flickered in the bedroom, and he headed in that direction.

The room was lit with dozens of flickering candles, the bed stripped of everything but a sheet. Miranda lay on the bed, completely naked except for a pair of red fuck-me pumps and a slick of lip gloss. His cock went immediately hard at the sight.

"Welcome back," she said in a soft, throaty voice. "I missed you."

Damn, he'd missed her, too. He watched her sit up, dark brown hair spilling over her shoulder, and felt as if he was going to lose control right then and there. The sultry way she was eyeing him did crazy things to his mind.

"This is a nice surprise," he said, grinning, and presented the flowers. "Makes mine seem kind of pathetic in comparison."

"That's okay," she said lightly, getting up from the bed and taking the flowers out of his hands. "I'll make up for it."

Her hands were immediately on his shirt, tugging it over his head and then tossing it to the side. He leaned in to kiss her, but she gave him a teasing, coy smile. "My turn to lead tonight."

He raised an eyebrow. "Oh?" Dane sucked in a breath when her hand went to his cock and stroked it through the fabric of his jeans.

"Hard already," she purred. "Guess you did miss me."

"Like crazy," he said, leaning in to kiss her.

Again, she moved away, giving him a coquettish little frown. "My games tonight."

"You want to be in charge?" At her sexy little nod, he felt a thrill flow through his body. "All right."

She ran her hands over his skin as she undressed him, ripping his clothes away from his body.

It was an incredible turn-on, and yet . . . there was something about Miranda's single-mindedness that was bothering him. When she ripped his boxers away, he grasped her hands and pulled her naked body against his. "Slow down. We have all night."

She relaxed against him, her hands stroking over his skin. "Sorry," she said with a breathless smile. "I was getting carried away."

"Oh?"

"I have a surprise for you." There was a fierce glint in her eyes.

His hands slid down, cupped her beautiful ass and pulled her against him. "I'm all ears."

She wriggled out of his grasp and crossed the room to the side of the bed. Miranda reached into her nightstand and pulled out a pair of handcuffs.

And she gave him an expectant look.

Well, damn. His sweet little Miranda was taking control of her wilder side, and he liked it. Dane grinned. "Are those for me to use on you?"

"After I get to play with you," she said coyly. "Volunteers get a special treat."

"Then I'm definitely volunteering," he murmured huskily. With that, he extended a wrist out to her.

She linked the handcuffs over one wrist, and trembled. So turned on she was shivering? The thought made him even harder, and he groaned, nuzzling into her thick, silky hair. She shuddered at his touch and led him to the bed, then handcuffed one wrist to one of the wooden posts of her bed. He lay on his back, testing his left wrist, which she'd cuffed to the left post on her bed; his arm stretched over his head, though not uncomfortably so. To his surprise, she took out a second set of handcuffs and reached for his other wrist, her eyes hot as she gazed at him.

Did she expect him to flinch away? He offered her his wrist. "I'm all yours."

She gave him a wry smile and locked his other cuffed wrist to the opposite post on the bed, then crawled over him. The brushing of her ass and breasts against his body was driving him wild, and he groaned low in his throat, his balls tight with pleasure.

To his surprise, though, she continued off the bed and moved to the far side of the room. Another surprise? He strained against the cuffs as she rummaged in a drawer, trying to see what she'd pull out. A feather? Chocolate sauce? A dildo? Damn, he hoped not. He swung a lot of ways, but a chick using a dildo on him wasn't really his thing—

Suddenly, she turned and he was blinded by a flash. "What the—"

Click. Click click click.

He stared up at Miranda. She held a camera, and she was taking pictures of him. Naked. And turned on. Cuffed to her bed.

He jerked. He hadn't given permission for this, and this felt . . . invasive. "Miranda, what the fuck? Put the camera down."

"No." Her voice was hard and cold. *Click click.*

He stared at her. What the hell was her problem? "This isn't funny. Put the camera down."

"You're right, it's not funny." She took a few more snaps and then changed the settings on the camera, glancing through the photos she'd just taken. "And now you know how it feels, don't you?"

"What the fuck are you talking about?" He was starting to get mad now, jerking at the cuffs. Damn it, he'd trusted her to tie him up, and this was what she did? "Miranda, untie me—now. Now."

"You know what I'm talking about," she cried, setting the camera aside and shrugging on a sundress and panties.

Dread crawled through his stomach as he watched her dress. She . . . she wasn't leaving, was she? Why was she getting dressed? The uneasy feeling in his mind intensified. Even more upsetting was the look of anguish on her face. "Miranda—"

"I thought you were different! I thought you had changed, and then I find out *nothing* has changed."

"Miranda, I don't understand—"

"Why are the pictures still up? After all this time? Do you hate me? Is that it? Is that why you didn't tell your friends about me? Just having a laugh with slutty Miranda Hill, is that it?"

Pictures? What pictures? The ones she'd just taken? She wasn't making sense. She knew he hadn't said anything? And wait—Slutty? "No! I—What are you talking about?"

She straightened her dress and picked up the camera again, breasts heaving as if she couldn't get enough air. "You and I are through tonight, Dane Croft. Through once and for all. I was an idiot, because after we started talking again, I thought maybe you'd changed. You weren't the asshole that I thought you were, but I suppose it's my fault for being stupid enough to fall for a pretty face. Well, it's my fault no longer." She shook the camera. "I have these pictures of you, Dane. That's why I went on that camping trip. It wasn't to learn survival skills. It was to get compromising pictures of you and ruin your life the way you ruined mine. I got what I wanted, and you can expect these pictures to show up on the Internet in the next few days." She tapped her chin. "Or maybe I'll sell them to a tabloid. I haven't decided."

"Miranda!"

"Good-bye, Dane. You're never going to see me again." With that, she exited the room.

He stared at her in shock. What the fuck was all that? Why was she taking pictures of him—naked, for fuck's sake—and declaring that she was never going to see him again? He was in her goddamn house. She had to be coming back.

She *was* coming back, wasn't she?

Suddenly paranoid, he jerked at the cuffs, twisting his hands. Tight and unyielding. He couldn't slip his wrists through.

Damn. Maybe if he jerked hard, he could break the bed. He didn't know what the fuck was going on—or why Miranda had suddenly gone psycho—but he intended to find out.

Juuuuust as soon as he got free.

For the next few minutes, he strained hard, clenching his fists and jerking at the bedpost. It was no good—he couldn't get the right angle. Dammit.

He heard the door in the living room and stiffened. Had she called in someone else? Was she inviting her friends to come and gawk? They wouldn't have much to see—his cock had pretty much shriveled at this point.

But no—Miranda stumbled in a moment later, clutching the camera and crying as if her heart were breaking. It made his own gut give a miserable twist—God, why was she so very unhappy? His own anger at her disappeared at the sight of her misery.

"I can't do it," she sobbed. "I can't do it. I know what it's like, and I can't do it to another person. Especially not you."

"Do what?" he said, jerking at the cuffs again. He needed to get free. Then he could touch her, comfort her, figure out what in the hell was going on in her head. "Miranda, get me out of here—"

"No," she said, wiping her eyes. "I'm not going to do it. With the pictures. Put them on the Internet." Her eyes were wild and glassy. "Even a jerk like you doesn't deserve that."

"Deserve what? I don't even know what you're talking about."

"Yes you do," she yelled at him, and looked as if she wanted to throw the camera at his head. "Quit playing dumb, Dane. You already ruined my life once. I won't let you ruin it again because I was stupid enough to fall in love with you. And I won't ruin yours either." She flung the camera down at the end of the bed. "I'll call someone at the ranch to come get you in a half hour. And don't come looking for me or call me and try to explain, because I don't want to hear it. We're done, you and I. This time for good."

She wiped her cheeks and left.

He stared after her, but she didn't come back. Maybe she wouldn't this time. What had she been going on about? Something with pictures and him ruining her life. It made no sense—he hadn't seen her since he last left Bluebonnet right after high school, and she'd been the one to turn him away, not the other way around. He didn't understand, and Miranda had been incomprehensible.

She'd been totally heartbroken, too, and it clenched at his heart. What was so wrong that she wanted to hurt him to try and fix it?

She said she'd fallen in love with him. He'd fallen for her, too—hell, he'd been in love with her for the past nine years and was just too damn dumb to see it. Whatever she'd felt, she needed to destroy it, he thought, and kicked the camera. It shot against the wall and shattered into several pieces.

He wanted to go after her. Have her explain herself. Shake some sense into her. Hold her and stroke her hair until the tears went away, and fix her problems for her. He wasn't even mad anymore, just downright confused. Dane couldn't stay mad—not when she cried as if her heart was breaking. Hell, her sobs were breaking his heart. All he wanted was to comfort her.

But he couldn't do anything, because she'd chosen to cut him out of her life in this bizarre manner. He was stuck until someone came to rescue him. And so he sat, and waited, and seethed with worry for Miranda.

Someone knocked at the door a short time later. "Come in," he shouted, wishing he had something to cover up with. "I'm in the bedroom."

Footsteps, and then a tall, lean figure leaned in the doorway of the bedroom. Cool eyes narrowed at him, and Colt rubbed his head. "'Preciate the offer, bro, but you ain't my type."

"Very funny," Dane said, jerking at the handcuffs again. "Just get me down from here so I can find Miranda and paddle her ass until she tells me what's going on."

The keys had been left in the nightstand, and it took mere seconds for Dane to be freed. He rubbed his wrists and then dressed without a word. When he put his shoes back on, he went over to the camera, and stomped it to bits, taking out some of his aggression on it.

"Pics of your bad side?"

He turned and scowled at his friend. "You know anything about Miranda Hill and something that ruined her life?"

"Nope," Colt said. "You fuckin' her?"

He narrowed his eyes at Colt. "She's my girlfriend. Was my girlfriend."

Colt scowled. "Fucking a *client*?"

"It's not like that. And it's not fucking. Quit saying that or I'm going to punch it out of your mouth. Hear me?"

Colt scowled for a moment longer, then nodded. "Her prissy friend knows something 'bout this. She came by to yell at me a couple days ago."

"Then let's pay her a visit," Dane said grimly.

• • •

"Why am I not surprised it's a beauty parlor?" Colt said with disgust as they pulled up in front of the bright pink sign and shop window painted with garishly bright flowers. "Shoulda known."

Dane vaulted from the jeep as soon as it stopped, barely pausing to clear the curb. The sign in the window was off, but there was a light on inside. He banged on the door repeatedly. She had to be inside. Had to be.

After two minutes of straight banging, he heard someone inside and then the rest of the lights flicked on. A familiar blonde glared out at him from the other side of the window. "I'm closed. Come back tomorrow."

"I'm looking for Miranda," he shouted through the glass.

"Not here. And even if she was, I wouldn't let her talk to the likes of you." She gave him a cool look and flicked the light off again, clearly intending to leave him standing out there.

He banged on the door again, harder. After a moment, Beth Ann flicked the lights on again. "Don't make me call the cops."

"We just want to talk," Colt said gruffly at his side, his gaze hot on the blonde. "'Bout Miranda."

She scowled at both of them but hesitated. "I'm not leaving my salon open late if no one's getting their hair cut, understand?"

"Fine," said Colt, and gave a crisp nod.

Beth Ann opened the door and heaved an exasperated sigh. "Don't you two make me regret this."

Dane walked into the shop after Colt. It was cute and bright and covered in bottles of all kinds of girly stuff. It smelled faintly floral, and he recognized the scent—Miranda's shampoo. Just the scent sent a bolt of unhappiness through him. "Where's Miranda?"

"Probably halfway to Houston by now," Beth Ann said, and picked up the pink leopard cape. "Who am I cutting?"

Colt removed his hat and sat in the chair, and Beth Ann gave a delicate snort. Colt's hair was already cut razor short and close to his scalp. She must have been a sadist, because she put that ugly pink cape on Colt and pumped the foot bar on the chair to adjust the height.

Colt glared into the mirror.

"Houston?" Dane said, leaning against the wall and crossing his arms tight over his chest. "Why the hell is she going to Houston?"

Beth Ann started the clippers and began to run them over the back of Colt's neck. "Because she's moving there? You need to listen when a girl tells you something, Dane Croft. You're not God's gift to women."

Dane frowned at her. "What are you talking about? Why is Miranda moving? She just moved in."

In the chair, wearing the pink cape, Colt sat stone-faced, watching his reflection in the mirror. His eyes shifted a fraction, and Dane realized that it wasn't his reflection he was watching—it was the perfect blonde his gaze was focused on. Watching her like an eagle sights prey. He wondered if Beth Ann had any idea that Colt was watching her so carefully.

But he didn't have time for this shit, and Beth Ann wasn't volunteering information about Miranda, which was why he was here, not to see Colt staring at the blonde with possessive eyes. "Well? Why is Miranda moving if she just bought a house?"

"Oh, honey," Beth Ann said in a tone that was a little sorry and a lot mocking. "Bless your heart. She wasn't moving in, she was moving out. She couldn't wait to leave this darn town. Been waiting nine years to get out."

"Nine years? Why?"

"Because of those damn photos—" she snapped, then pursed her glossy lips. "Sorry. Language. But you know what I'm talking about."

"No," he gritted. "I don't."

She narrowed her blue eyes at him, then moved across the tiny salon to a laptop on a small desk. As she bent over, he watched Colt's expression narrow a bit more, as if his world had suddenly focused in on a soft pair of hips in a jean skirt.

"This," Beth Ann said, moving to the side and showing him the screen. "This is why she couldn't wait to leave."

He moved forward and stared. It was a horrible website, with an ugly background and noisy graphics on it. The URL read "Boobs of Bluebonnet" and he stared at a picture of Miranda's perky breasts, that beauty mark under her left one staring back at him. Some asshole had his hand down her pants and his other underneath her breasts, as if plumping them for the camera. Even worse, her head was tilted back in ecstasy.

"Who's the dick?" he growled, the urge to beat the shit out of someone rising. His fists clenched, hard.

Beth Ann frowned at him and scrolled the website down to the next photo. This one clearly showed the face of the man as Miranda knelt before him, with his hand twisted in her hair as if she were about to suck him off. "You are, you stupid fool. And you ruined her life."

• • •

When they left the salon, Dane sat in the car, numb. Colt drove, every once in a while scratching at his neck for phantom hairs left from the shave.

Dane didn't know what to think anymore.

Miranda thought he'd ruined her life. She thought he'd taken the photos. Thought he was getting some sort of psycho revenge on her when he'd left all those years ago. Beth Ann had spilled the whole story, though she'd clearly been reluctant to divulge her best friend's secrets. She was only telling him, she said, what anyone in town would tell him. How Miranda's mom had had a nervous breakdown and Miranda had had to run the store until she recovered. The rumors. The nickname.

The photos had followed her for the last nine years. And all this time he'd never known. No wonder her mom had freaked when he'd entered the store. No wonder Miranda had taken his picture and said she'd wanted to ruin his life.

Hell, he didn't blame her. He knew what it was like in small towns, and Bluebonnet was one of the smallest. You knew everyone, and everyone knew *everything* about you. And everyone knew Miranda's breasts intimately.

God, poor Miranda. She'd been so strong to quietly suffer all these years and put up with shit for her mother's sake. Beth Ann had explained that she'd gotten her master's from nearby Sam Houston State University and had applied for jobs, eventually landing a plush one at a big corporation in downtown Houston. Beth Ann wouldn't say where.

He didn't blame her . . . and at the same time, he wanted to shake the news out of her.

"Will she be back?" he'd asked, feeling like the world had just fallen out from under his feet.

"Don't know," said Beth Ann. "I have her number, but she's turned her phone off for the move. She said she'd call me in a few weeks, when she's settled. Wants to get a fresh start first." Her hurt was obvious, and she gave Dane an accusatory look. She'd been closed out of Miranda's life, too, and it was no thanks to him. Judging from the look on her face, Beth Ann wouldn't be forgetting that anytime soon.

He didn't care. All he could see was Miranda's tearful face, sobbing as she left the camera with him. Even though she'd wanted revenge . . . she hadn't been able to do it.

She'd said she'd fallen in love with him. It was like a knife twisting in his gut. He'd loved her all these years and she'd thought the worst of him.

He thought back—the pictures must have happened at the after-graduation party at Chad's house. He'd never known there was a camera in the closet—he'd been too caught up in the beautiful girl in his arms and the fact that he was finally, finally getting to touch her. He'd had a call that day from the NHL, and between that and Miranda, he just wasn't thinking about anything else. His head had been full of hockey hopes and dreams and he'd been cocky and arrogant.

And he hadn't realized.

Rage pulsed through him and he slammed his fist into the passenger side of the car. "Fuck!"

"Tryin' to deploy my air bag?" Colt asked casually.

"I want to punch the fuck out of that asshole who did this to her," Dane snarled. "I want to slam his face into the ground and make him realize how much he hurt her."

He'd hurt her . . . and Dane couldn't fix it. He wanted to fix it, and didn't know how.

Colt gave him a long look, and then turned the car back around.

"Where are we going?"

"To the bar. We're gonna ask some friends how our high school buddies are doing."

Dane nodded, rubbing his knuckles, contemplating another jab to the panel, or maybe putting his fist through the glass. Her pain ate away at him, gnawed in his belly and he couldn't do a damn thing about it. He'd somehow caused this. Some jackass had ruined her life, and he'd been completely clueless about the entire thing.

Colt glanced over. "Why didn't you say something? 'Bout you and Miranda?"

His jaw tensed. Dane stared out the window, his mood black. "I was going to tell Grant first. Get the bad shit over with. Then I was going to let you know."

There was a long moment of silence in the cab. Then Colt spoke again. "You know I don't care who you're fucking around with as long you keep it on the DL."

Unusually chatty for Colt. Dane knew his friend was pissed that he hadn't been looped in. When he got mad, he got talky. "Yeah, and as soon as Grant finds out I've been sleeping with a client, he'll blow his lid."

"He's concerned about the business, that's all. You planning on fucking all our clients?"

Dane scowled at his friend.

"Exactly my point. So this ain't a big deal. Just tell the man and be done with it."

He should have. Of course, now Miranda was gone, and it was too late.

Bluebonnet boasted exactly one place that served alcohol. It was a Tex-Mex restaurant in a converted house, but it had a bar, and that was good enough for most of the residents of Bluebonnet. After hours, the men in town showed up to drink a few beers, watch sports on the TV on the wall, or rack up a few balls in the town's only pool table.

Dane walked up to the bar, ordered a longneck. He chatted with the bartender for a few minutes. The man—who'd likely been tending the same bar since Dane was last in town nine years ago—was all too eager to hear stories of Dane's time in the NHL. He told a few stories, had the men at the bar smiling, and then eased into other topics.

"Seems like everyone still lives here in town."

"Yup. Seems like."

"Chad Mickleson still live around here?"

"Yup."

Dane nodded, took a sip of his beer, tried to act casual. He had a guess as to who had taken those pictures, and he wanted to talk to the guy. "You know how I can get ahold of him?"

"Sure do." He gave vague directions to a nearby car garage and Dane made a mental note to visit there in the morning.

"What about Miranda Hill?" He asked casually, almost afraid of what he'd hear. "You know anything about her?"

"Ol' boobs? Yeah, She's legendary around here," the man said, grinning. "Turned into a hot little librarian. Why? You planning on tapping that?"

"That's my girlfriend," he growled.

The conversation ceased.

"You know who took those pictures of her?"

"Well," the bartender said slowly. "Kinda thought you did."

Minutes passed like hours, and Dane tossed and turned in his bunk. His own house was a small cabin on the edge of the Daughtry Ranch, and he normally liked it just fine, but tonight it was too quiet. He missed Miranda, her warm breath tickling his chest as she slept, the soft curve of her body against his.

How quickly he'd gotten used to having her in his life. How hollow he felt right now since she'd run away from him. He was filled with the same helpless rage he always felt when thinking about it.

When the sun came up, he was in his jeep and heading to the garage, his mind full of grim determination and Miranda's sad hopelessness. The directions the bartender had given him were dead on, and he pulled in.

A mechanic came out to greet him, wiping his hands. "Need an oil change?"

"I'm looking for Chad Mickleson," Dane said. "He work here?"

"Yup, he's just inside," the man said, then broke into a wide grin. "Hey, aren't you—"

Shit. "Yes."

"I'll be damned," the man said, following him in. "Hey, Len! You'll never guess who just drove up! The local legend himself."

Dane ignored him, striding into the garage, looking for a face he only vaguely remembered. Sandy brown hair and big eyebrows—that was all he remembered of the guy.

One of the mechanics turned around and boom, there he was. Dane's hands instantly clenched to fists—if he'd have had his hockey gloves on, he'd have dropped them.

The other man's eyes lit up. "Holy shit. Dane Croft. How are you, man?"

Dane punched him square in the jaw. The man went down like a light and dropped to the floor of the garage. Someone yelled.

"You and I have a lot of talking to do," Dane said in a low, dangerous voice. "Now get up."

SEVENTEEN

One month later

Miranda stared at her Outlook calendar in dismay. She clicked on the meeting, then buzzed her secretary. "Shirley, could you come in please?"

The woman—easily three decades older than Miranda—hefted in and gave her a patient smile. "What can I help you with?"

Miranda pointed at her computer monitor. "Why do I have a three-hour conference call on Saturday?"

"Oh, that." Shirley picked a piece of lint from her black cardigan. "You have a meeting with the CFO of the fabrication division."

"On a Saturday?"

Shirley blinked. "Your Friday and your Monday are booked solid."

They were? Miranda clicked on the calendar again and swore

under her breath. Sure enough. They hadn't even left her enough time to run to the restroom or catch lunch. She'd seen a few women wear their headsets into the bathroom stalls and had thought they were absentminded.

Perhaps they'd simply had too many meetings.

"Thanks, Shirley," Miranda said, feeling a little bit sour. Life at HGI was definitely . . . fast-paced. They loved projects, and collaborations, and meetings. They *loved* meetings. She'd half joked with someone that they needed meetings just to determine if they needed meetings or not, but no one had laughed. Probably too close to the truth.

She stared out the window of her tiny corner office and down the busy streets of downtown Houston. It was just a big change, she told herself for the hundredth time. Once she settled in, she'd start to like her job. Maybe she'd even appreciate the constant stream of meetings.

Eventually.

With a sigh, she turned and swiveled in her ergonomic chair. A meeting invite flashed onto her screen and she ignored it, feeling the sudden urge to rebel. Loosening one of the buttons of her severe black-jacketed pantsuit, she stared at the only picture on her desk—of her and Beth Ann holding up beers while boating at the lake. She picked up the picture and stared at it for a good long minute. The setting sun on the water made her think of that week in the woods. And that week in the woods reminded her of Dane, and camping, and that last night at her campsite, where it had been just the two of them in her tiny lean-to. That evening had been so perfect; they'd had sex, laughed, cuddled, and they hadn't worried about others discovering them. It had been just the two of them in a small slice of paradise. She'd felt so at home, like she'd waited nine years for a missing part of her to come back.

Which was stupid, really. But a sudden pang of homesickness shot through her and she picked up the phone and began to dial.

"California Dreamin'," a cheerful voice answered. "This is Beth Ann."

"Hey," Miranda said softly. "It's me."

A pause, then a girlish squeal on the other end. "Oh my God! Miranda! Hang on, let me set Bessie Roberson under the dryer." The phone clanged against something on the other end of the line and Miranda heard a soft murmur of conversation, and then the buzz of the dryer in the background. The phone picked up again and Beth Ann returned. "Dang, girl! I've missed you. How are you?"

"I'm good."

"How's the new job? Your mom and I have been wondering how it's going over there."

"It's good," she said, then sighed. "Just really different."

"Uh-oh," Beth Ann said in a teasing voice. "Different as in good, or different as in 'Oh mercy, what have I gotten myself into?' "

"It's hard to say," Miranda confessed. "It's everything I thought it would be—corner office, amazing benefits, and everyone here is so driven . . ."

"But?"

"But they're driving me crazy," Miranda confessed. "I have four more meetings today. Seven tomorrow and one on Saturday. Then I start over again on Monday. I'm starting to see PowerPoint slides when I close my eyes at night."

Beth Ann laughed.

"I'd laugh, too, except it's too pathetic," Miranda said caustically. "It's just . . . I don't know. It's not what I expected on that point. I thought I'd do more stuff myself. Instead, I'm just advising everyone else and making sure projects stay on task, and then turning around and reporting to the big guys."

"You miss your library?"

"I do," Miranda said softly, thinking of the slightly dusty smell, the silence-but-not-silence, the rows and rows of books. "I didn't realize how much control over things I had there until I got this big fancy job . . . and now it feels like I have no control." After a minute, she blurted, "And, well, it's not the only thing I miss."

"You miss me, too, right?" Beth Ann said with a grin. "And your mom? We miss you like crazy, honey, but we're proud of you."

"I miss you guys," Miranda admitted. Then she added, "And—"

"You miss Dane, don'tcha?"

Miranda swallowed, the knot in her throat making it hard to speak. "You think I'm stupid, don't you?"

Beth Ann chuckled. "Let me tell you a little story, Miranda Jane. Seems I had a couple of visitors that night you left town."

"Oh?"

"Yep. One big pissed-off ex-hockey player and his buddy showed up, demanding to know where you went. And when I told him you'd gone and skipped out of town, well . . . you could have knocked him over with a feather."

Miranda smiled at the visual.

"He couldn't imagine why you'd lied to him, so I tried explaining to him that he'd ruined your life, and you know what he told me?"

Her throat ached, it was so tight. "What?"

"The boy didn't know what I was talking about," she said. "I had to pull up the pictures to show him because he didn't believe me. And when I did show him, he asked me who the guy was in the photos!"

A cold chill shivered over Miranda. "What do you mean? How did he not know?"

"I know! That's what I said. When I told him that it was him, I thought he was going to fall over in shock. And then he got real mad, Miranda. Real mad. I've never seen a man get so angry. He didn't put his fist in the wall or anything, but he looked like someone had just shot his dog or something."

Dane had been . . . angry? And confused? He'd seemed so confused at her anger the last time she'd seen him, too, when he'd been handcuffed to her bed and her heart had been breaking with every moment. She'd thought he'd been playing stupid to defuse her anger, but . . . what if he was telling the truth? It didn't make sense . . . did it?

"So you aren't going to believe what happens next, right? Tommi Jo told me that he went to Maya Loco asking how he could find Chad Mickleson. And when someone brought up your name and the boobs thing, he shut them down, real polite-like, and told them you were his girlfriend and not to be talking about you."

Her heart gave a funny tingle. "He . . . did?"

"Oh, it gets better, girl," Beth Ann said, pleasure in her voice. "So . . . the next morning, he shows up at the garage where Chad's working, walks up to the man, and punches him flat."

She gasped. "What?"

"It's true! Said they needed to have some kind of talk. I don't know what about, but I hear from Tommi Jo that Dane was plenty, plenty mad at Chad and had to be talked down a few times."

"Did someone call the cops?"

"Not from what I heard. Tommi Jo said that the guys talked for a long time, and then Dane came out and signed some autographs and gave some of the guys invites to a free class or two, and that was that."

So strange. "I don't understand."

"Me either," Beth Ann said sweetly. "But I do know your pictures aren't on the Internet anymore. I checked. It's gone."

"Gone?" Unbelievable. She grabbed her smart phone and punched in the URL. Sure enough, it didn't come up. Was it possible? Hope and joy surged in her chest. Dane had realized it was hurting her and had taken the pictures down? "They're not there anymore?"

"Nope. Tommi Jo thinks Dane was defending your reputation. She said your name came up a few times, though she couldn't hear everything that was said."

Damn Tommi Jo. Why hadn't she gotten more than just pieces of the conversation? Her curiosity burned in her chest. "I wonder what they were saying."

"Don't know. But I know what I do know. Someone mentioned that you had a big collection of teen books at your library that you'd bought out of your own pocket, because the city wouldn't give you the money for that vampire stuff, right? Well, Dane overheard that at your mom's store, and I heard he went down to the library the next day and donated ten thousand dollars of his own money. Isn't that something?"

It was dizzying. Why had he done that? Why was he so generous on a pet project of hers at an old job that she wouldn't be returning to? She thought of all the books that would buy. The teens in town would flock to the library for more than just the Internet. Oh, she'd love that. The big-city libraries carried so many books that she couldn't possibly compete, but with that . . . she could start a reading club, just for teens, maybe get a manga section . . .

"Wait," she said, something registering in her brain. "Did you say he heard that at my mom's store?" She cringed at the thought. "Mom hates Dane. Even the mention of his name will send her into hysterics."

"You should ask your mom about that," Beth Ann said slyly. "I hear Dane's been at her store almost every day lately."

They chatted for a few more minutes about inane things, and then promised to check in with each other again very soon. As soon as Miranda hung up the phone, Shirley was on the line, buzzing in.

"Miranda? They're waiting for you in the Indigo Conference Room."

"Be right there," Miranda said. Then she added, "And I need you to clear my Saturday. I'm going out of town."

"Out of town?" Shirley repeated disapprovingly. "But the meeting with—"

"Can wait," she said firmly. "I'm going back to Bluebonnet for some unfinished business."

When she drove into town, nothing looked different. She'd been away for a whole month and it was like she'd never left. Well, one thing had changed—there was a big banner on the gazebo in the town square for the upcoming Hill Country Spring Festival, but they trotted that thing out every year.

So why was it that when she looked at the too-small, overly intrusive, Podunk town she grew up in, it no longer filled her with helpless anger? Why did it fill her with nostalgia instead?

Surely she didn't miss Bluebonnet, of all places.

She drove down Main Street—her mom's shop had several cars in front of it, which meant she was busy. Miranda opted to head to her library instead, see how things were going.

Because Bluebonnet was a small town, the library was sandwiched into City Hall, squished between the Water Department and the police station. When she walked in, the smell of the place made her heart flutter with longing. The faint scent of dust and old paper made her senses tingle, and a possessive surge came over her. This was *her* library. She'd missed it. She moved to the new releases section and ran a hand over the spines, looking for new books purchased with Dane's donation. Nothing—they were all books she'd purchased. She glanced over at the checkout counter—it was stacked high with books waiting to be returned to the shelves. Perhaps old Mrs. Murellen, her replacement, was running a bit behind. Well, she had a little time to kill. Miranda picked up a few books and began to shelve them. As she did, she noticed that when she put them on the shelves, even more books seemed out of place, and she continued to put books in their proper homes, frowning as she did. She'd never let her library get so sloppy when it had been hers.

You didn't want it, though, did you? she reminded herself. *You wanted to be a corporate big shot, and now you are.*

Right. She shelved the last book and resisted the urge to dust and straighten. That was someone else's job now. She turned the corner and nearly ran into a student.

"Oh, I'm sorry," Miranda said with a smile, recognizing Trisha Ellis. "I didn't see you there."

The girl's face widened into a smile, and for a moment, Miranda thought she was going to hug her. "Ms. Hill—I am so glad to see you. I can't find the teen books!"

Inwardly, Miranda groaned. Not again. "Did you check in our normal hiding place under the nine hundreds?"

"They're not there, and the fake slipcovers you made are gone," she said, her expression crushed. "I think they took them off the shelves again."

It had been an ongoing battle with the city council, who thought the books that teenagers were reading were trash. They didn't seem to understand how wonderful it was that they were reading at all, so Miranda had purchased her own small library of popular teen novels and shelved them with fake jackets that a few of the students had helped her create. They were the most popular section in the library.

"I'll check with Mrs. Murellen," Miranda said, heading toward the counter. Trisha trotted on her heels close behind.

There was no one at the counter, books stacked everywhere, the return bin overflowing. Trisha immediately started to pick through the return bin, looking for missed favorites. Miranda slipped behind the counter and went to the back office, knocking softly. No response. She opened the door.

Mrs. Murellen sat behind her desk, chin propped on a hand, snoring.

"Mrs. Murellen," Miranda said, her voice sharp. "Wake up."

The older woman snorted awake, and peered at Miranda. "Oh my goodness. Did you come back for your job?"

"No—"

Mrs. Murellen looked sad. "Oh."

"Someone here is looking for the teen reading books. Where did you move them to?"

"I took them off the shelves," Mrs. Murellen said, adjusting her glasses as she stood up. "Did you know that they were about vampires? Sexy vampires? Terrible stuff."

"They're perfectly fine," Miranda explained, going through the shelf of books in the tiny office. Sure enough, it was crammed full of P. C. Cast, Richelle Mead, and Stephenie Meyer, as well as anything that had a teenager on the cover. She sighed and grabbed several of them off the shelf.

"Those are going to be removed from circulation—"

"No they're not," Miranda said firmly, and handed them to an excitedly waiting Trisha. "I think we should talk."

Miranda spent the next hour straightening up at the library, doing her best not to lecture Mrs. Murellen, and reshelving the teen literature. She couldn't be mad—it was obvious Mrs. Murellen didn't want to be Bluebonnet's only librarian; she'd offered Miranda her job back three times in a half hour. When that didn't work, she tried to get Miranda's advice on what to spend Dane's donation on—she had no idea what books to buy, and didn't know where to start.

Miranda came up with a list of bestsellers that she'd had her eye on and wrote Mrs. Murellen a lengthy shopping detail, as well as a to-do list of chores that she was neglecting. Miranda shouldn't have come back. Her mind was now filled with treacherous ideas. Ideas of returning and running things with a firmer hand. Ideas of how to spend the money Dane had donated.

Ideas of driving over to the Daughtry Ranch and throwing Dane down on the floor, apologizing, and then making love to him until the sun came up.

But she'd burned that bridge.

Across town, Beth Ann picked up her phone and dialed. "Wilderness Survival Expeditions," a gruff voice said.

Great, she'd gotten Colt. "This is Beth Ann. Let me talk to Dane."

"He's out." Short, abrupt. Why was she not surprised? The man acted like it was a crime to string more than two words together.

"Why is he out?" she persisted.

"Class."

"Yeah, well, you'd better go get him," she said irritably. The man crawled under her skin way too fast. "Because you'll never guess who just drove back into town. And I think he'll want to see her."

Colt found Dane surrounded by a group of students. They crouched in a clearing, Dane at the center of the group. Ignoring their surprised looks and Dane's puzzled one, he quickly told Dane the details of Beth Ann's phone call.

"She's here?" Dane stared at Colt, disbelieving. He dropped the fire-making implements in his hands. "You're sure?"

"No, I lied." Colt turned around to leave.

Dane lurched forward over the group and grabbed Colt by the shoulders. He turned and looked his buddy in the eyes. "Miranda's back?"

"That's what Beth Ann said," Colt drawled. "And that's why my ass is out here and not playing Xbox."

Dane ran a hand down his face and then looked over at Colt. He glanced at the waiting students, then back at Colt. "I'm gonna need your help."

"All ears, buddy." He couldn't resist the grin that crossed his face at Dane's hopeful expression.

He began to pace. Colt crossed his arms and leaned on a nearby tree, watching him.

"I need a way to say that I'm sorry."

"Didn't do anything wrong," Colt pointed out.

"No, I know. I'm not apologizing for me. I'm apologizing for the situation." He paused, put his hands on his hips and stared up at the sky, thoughtfully. "Needs to be a big gesture."

"She won't care if it's big or not," Colt felt he had to point out.

"Yeah, but I care," Dane said. He paced for a moment, then snapped his fingers and dashed off into the woods.

Colt looked back at the confused students, then at his retreating friend. "Class dismissed. Brenna will be out here in a bit to lead you guys home," he said, then dashed off after Dane with a grin. Whatever he had in mind, it ought to be interesting.

EIGHTEEN

Miranda walked into her mother's store, and for the second time since returning to Bluebonnet that day, she got that weird feeling of déjà vu. It was like she'd left and returned to a town that was the same . . . and yet not. Her mother's cluttered store, exactly the same for all twenty-seven years of Miranda's life, was different. Not much, but enough that it bothered her as she looked around. Miranda stared at the overflowing shelves and tried to figure out what it was. After a moment, it hit her.

None of the heavy shelves were leaning anymore. They had all been repaired, the warped wood of each slat replaced, the contents dusted. She glanced outside and sure enough, the crooked sign she'd been so used to seeing had been repaired as well.

Her mother finished ringing up some customers, and when they left, Miranda stepped forward.

Tanya Hill gasped with delight at her daughter and flung her arms open, and they hugged for a long, long minute.

"How's it going, Mom?" she asked with a smile. Her mother looked happy—healthy. Smiling. God, that was so good to see. She'd been so worried that her mother was going to have another one of her depressive episodes while Miranda was gone, and then she'd have to return to town.

A little sad part of her twinged at that. Surely it wasn't disappointment? That was so wrong of her. She immediately shut down the thought. Her mother didn't need her here, babysitting her in town, and she was finally free. Miranda should have been thrilled, and she'd hated that the first thing that came to mind was hurt. Didn't her mother miss her?

"I'm good, I'm good," her mother gushed. "I went to an estate sale and picked up all kinds of things for cheap, Miranda. You wouldn't believe the deals I got!" As her mother went on about the sale, showing her new items in the store, Miranda couldn't help but make a mental note of all the small changes.

"Did you hire a carpenter, Mama? I saw the sign was fixed."

Her mother beamed. "No. That nice Dane Croft came by and fixed it for me."

The world spun. She never thought she'd hear her mother say *nice* and *Dane* in the same sentence. "What?" she said weakly. "You hate him."

"I did hate him," her mother said proudly. "But that was before he got that horrible Chad Mickleson to take down those pictures of you."

"What?"

"Yes," her mother said solemnly. "He punched Chad right in the face in front of everyone, and then made him go home and take down those pictures while he watched."

"But . . . I thought . . ." She felt weak, and collapsed onto an antique wooden stool nearby. Beth Ann had told her that the pictures were down, but she hadn't realized that it was because Dane had threatened someone *else* and forced them to take it down. She thought he'd finally had a change of heart. "I thought Dane put those pictures up."

"So did I," her mother said with a sniff. "All this time it was that horrible Chad. You know I never liked him. Shifty eyes. Anyway, after Dane had the pictures taken down, he came over here and apologized to me. Said he'd been unfair when we'd talked on the phone all those years ago, and he wanted to make it up to me. And he offered to fix my sign."

Her head wouldn't stop spinning. Miranda pressed a hand to her forehead, unable to comprehend. "I'm sorry, what? What calls are you talking about?"

"Back when he left for the NHL," her mother said patiently. "He kept calling for you and I wouldn't let him talk to you. We got into a nasty argument. That was when I had my nervous breakdown."

"Dane called for me back then?" she said weakly, surprised. She'd never known. "Why didn't you tell me?"

"Why, darling, I didn't want to upset you. He was an awful boy back then, but he's turned into a nice man now."

Oh *God.* Not only had Dane been innocent of the picture-taking, but he'd called and asked for her after he'd left for the NHL? He wasn't the bastard she'd made him out to be? Miranda remembered his confusion that evening a month ago, as he'd stared up at her, handcuffed to her bed. Totally betrayed. He hadn't understood why she'd been so upset.

Because he'd *truly* had no idea.

God, she was going to throw up. She clutched her stomach, horrified.

Dane . . . hadn't been the one all those years? Her revenge? Her burning hatred? Directed at the wrong person?

And . . . oh God. Dane had really liked her?

Oh my *God*. And she'd ruined it. Acted like a crazy woman, screaming and crying at him. Handcuffed him to the bed and left him there. Taken naked pictures of him. Taken what they'd had and stomped it into the ground.

"Mom," she said softly.

"Are you all right, honey?"

"I think I'm going to be sick." She was going to pass out. She really was. She bent over and put her head between her knees, breathing hard. Horror swirled in her stomach, a hard knot that threatened to make her puke.

Her mother patted her back. "I'll get you some water, dear."

Miranda didn't move. Maybe she could curl up right here and die. She'd ruined one of the best things that had ever happened to her. For nine years she'd obsessed over Dane Croft, and when she'd gone and fallen in love with the man and he'd seemed to care for her back . . . she'd destroyed it all just to get revenge. And why? Just because he hadn't told his buddies about her? She'd told him *not* to when they'd gotten together.

Miranda buried her face in her hands and moaned. She'd been so stupid.

A horn honked outside. Once, twice, three times. She glanced up, but didn't see anything outside the cluttered shop windows. Her mother went to the window, and then covered her mouth, smothering a laugh. "You had better come see this," she declared.

"I don't care, Mama," she said weakly, lost in thought. God, how could she have been so cruel to him?

"I really think you should, Miranda Jane Hill."

Curious despite her nauseated misery, Miranda pulled herself from the chair and followed her mother over to the front door of the shop.

There, coming down the street, was a naked man. A very, very naked man. He wore nothing—even his feet were bare, and his body was corded with muscle. She could see tan lines on his arms and collarbone from a shirt, and she automatically looked south for more tan lines. His hands were in front of his privates, and he was holding something white and round there. She squinted, but the window was dirty and cluttered, and it was hard to see. Two people stood behind the man, and as he strode down the sidewalk, she noticed that cars were stopping to honk. The man was oblivious, striding forward with purpose in his step, ignoring the photographer that hovered a few feet away, rapidly taking pictures with an oversized camera and keeping just a few paces in front of the man as he walked.

What an idiot, she thought, her hand going to the high collar of her shirt even as she admired his body. Whatever this stupid gesture was for, he was never going to be able to live down the pictures. She knew that full well . . .

Then she recognized what the white thing in front of his privates was—a hockey helmet. She swallowed hard, and moved to the front door, scarcely able to breathe.

And she went out in the street and stared.

And *stared.*

From behind Dane, Beth Ann giggled. The man standing next to her didn't crack a smile, but it didn't matter—Miranda barely glanced at him. Her gaze went to the bronzed body of Dane Croft, completely naked and heading in her direction. Crowds of people had started to come out of the shops, flooding onto Main Street and whispering. A few women catcalled at his bare ass.

"Dane," Miranda hissed as he walked down the sidewalk and moved to stand in front of her. "What the hell are you doing?"

He grinned at her, her heart flipping at the sight of those flashing white teeth. The photographer clicked away, but Dane seemed oblivious. "I wanted to talk to you before you run away again, and I figured this might be the best way to do it."

She stared around nervously as even more people flooded into the street to watch. Even the cars nearby slowed down and parked to watch the show. And God, he was *really* naked. "Dane—"

"Let me speak, Miranda," he said softly. "I have a lot to say."

She swallowed the knot in her throat. "All right."

Dane's face grew serious and he stared down at her, his green eyes thoughtful. "Miranda, I came out here today, naked," he said, pausing to look at the audience, and then shifted on his feet and turned back to her, "to tell you that I was an idiot in high school."

"I don't—"

"I'm not done," he said with a grin. "Just getting started."

She raised a brow at him and crossed her arms over her chest, waiting.

"I," he repeated loudly, "was an idiot. When I got the offer to play for the NHL, I forgot about everything else. I'd trained for the past ten years to get there, driving back and forth to Houston every morning before dawn to get a few hours of practice in before school, and practice after school. I never imagined that when I was in high school, I'd meet a girl with pretty brown hair and smiling eyes who would make me think that there was anything in my life other than hockey. But when the NHL called, I went." He tilted his head at her. "And it never occurred to me until just now that I never said good-bye to that pretty girl. I just up and left."

She said nothing, stone-faced.

"I do remember that I tried calling her over and over again when the initial excitement of the NHL wore off and I missed her," Dane said slowly, his eyes on her. "But by then, her mama didn't like me much and I couldn't figure out why she wouldn't let her come to the phone. So I stopped calling and went on with my life. And, well, like I said, I was an idiot. I let myself get carried away with my own celebrity, because I was a legend in my own mind. I played hard, and partied hard, and didn't care about anything until I woke up one day and everything was gone." He gave a small shrug of his shoulders. "Just like that, I had nothing left, all because I didn't listen to anyone. But it was a good thing, because it made me strong. When I lost everything, I had to rebuild myself into a different person. One who could stand on his own. One who didn't have to have hockey or celebrity to have meaning in his life. And it brought me back here to the pretty girl with the long brown hair that I'd never stopped thinking about."

His green gaze grew tender and he looked as if he'd like to reach out and touch her, but stopped himself.

Her breath caught in her throat.

"And when I saw that girl again, I knew I had to have her. So when she flirted with me, I flirted back. And before I knew it, we were seeing a lot of each other, and I couldn't figure out why this lovely, gorgeous girl was keeping secrets. And then, one day, I found out. And we broke up."

Her cheeks flushed, remembering that ugly night. How she'd screamed at him and sobbed, while he'd stared up at her, betrayed and uncomprehending. It wasn't her proudest moment.

"And I didn't understand at first," he said softly, so low that only she could hear it. "How one thing that was so small could ruin someone's life. And when I did understand it, I thought to myself, how is this girl ever going to forgive me?"

"But it wasn't you, was it?" she said softly, hanging her head in shame. "I was wrong. I should have asked—"

"Hush. You're ruining my story," he said with a louder drawl. "So anyhow, I thought to myself, what do I want most in this world?"

She looked back up at him sharply.

"Is it a business with my friends, or hockey, or something else? And I realized it was something else." His gaze softened as he looked at her, a curve of a smile playing at his mouth. "A something else with pretty brown eyes and a killer pair of"—he coughed—"heels."

Behind him, the crowd laughed.

"And I had to figure out how to show this smart, funny, wonderful, strong woman that she's the most important thing in my life. So I quit my job and abandoned a bunch of clients back in the woods." His grin grew sheepish. "Pretty sure we're going to have a bunch of angry students asking for refunds once they find their way back to the ranch."

She gasped.

"And I took off all my clothes and went to the paper," he said, grinning. "And told them that I was going to march down the street naked so I could know what it felt like to be so exposed to everyone."

Tears pricked in her eyes. This stupid, beautiful man.

"And I'm pretty sure there's a cop somewhere back there, waiting to arrest my ass," Dane said wryly. "But I want to finish my apology first."

"What are you apologizing for? It wasn't you who took the photos—"

To her surprise, he handed her the helmet and dropped to his knee, stark naked, in the middle of the street. She blushed as she realized just how naked he was, and barely noticed that Beth Ann stepped forward and handed him something.

"Miss Miranda Jane Hill," he said loudly. "I am very sorry that I fell in love with you back when we were both eighteen years old and it took me nine years of being an idiot to figure it out. I still love you and want to be with you. Will you marry me?"

With that, he flipped open a ring box and showed her the diamond inside.

Her eyes widened and she stared down at it, half horrified, half shocked.

The entire street was deadly silent.

"Mommy, I can see that man's peepee," said a child nearby.

A strangled giggle erupted from Miranda's throat, and she smothered it with her free hand. He knelt there, staring earnestly up at her, so beautiful and serious.

He understood. He understood what it was like—of course he did. He'd been a tabloid mainstay back when he was famous. Why had she been too wrapped up in herself to realize that?

And now he knelt here naked, in front of her, in front of the whole town, to put them on an equal playing field. He couldn't make it right for her, but he could put himself in an equally embarrassing situation, just so she knew that he knew how it felt. A tear slid down her cheek.

Dane looked utterly crushed at the sight. "Damn, Miranda. I didn't mean to make you cry."

He began to get up, and she rushed forward, flinging her arms around his neck. "You're such an idiot," she sobbed.

"I know," he said, patting her hair.

"I'm an idiot, too."

"I know," he said, and she could hear the chuckle in his voice. "Is that a yes?"

"Yes," she said, and the town square erupted in cheers.

NINETEEN

In the spirit of things, the cops let Dane off with a warning, a towel was quickly located, and Beth Ann fussed over Miranda and Dane as Colt glowered at her.

Miranda's mother hugged them both, whispered into Miranda's ear that she and Dane needed some alone time, and took the opportunity to usher onlookers into her shop.

"My car's nearby," Miranda told Dane breathlessly, clutching his hand in hers. "Want to go somewhere private?"

He gave her a smoldering look. "Absolutely. But my car's nearby, too, and my clothes are in it. I can drive."

"Your car, then. We can't go to my place, though. My house is being rented out," she said with a grimace.

"We'll go to my place."

She looked at him in surprise. "At the ranch?" He'd never invited her back before. "Are you sure?"

"One hundred percent," he said and leaned in and gave her a hard, quick kiss. "I'm quitting anyhow. Grant is going to have a fit when he finds out I just abandoned a class in the woods to come here. If I can't be with you, I'm going to find something else to do. Maybe I'll teach hockey."

She stared at him in surprise. "You hate hockey now."

"It reminds me of a part of my life when I was too stupid and full of myself to think about anyone else. But it's something I need to face at some point."

They turned down the highway and sat in silence. Miranda twisted the ring on her finger. It felt so alien, but in a good way. She glanced over at Dane and wondered if he was regretting his impulsive proposal. He'd grown so silent. She chewed on her lip, thinking.

He glanced over at her and pulled in down a gravel path into the woods. "You still have boxes?"

Her brows furrowed. "I guess so. Why?"

"We'll need them if I'm moving to Houston to be with you."

Her jaw dropped as he got out of the car and then jogged around it to open her door. As she got out of the car, she stared up at him. "You want to move to be with me?"

He gave her an odd look. "Miranda, I just told you that I love you and I want to marry you. One of us is going to have to move, and I wouldn't ask you to give up your career."

A knot formed in her throat. "You wouldn't?"

"Of course not."

She gave him a weak smile. "What if I kind of hate my career?"

"What do you mean?" He grabbed her and swung her into his arms, and she clung to his neck. "Don't you like your job?"

She gave a wry laugh. "I think I like the concept of it more than the actual job. I bet you think that's stupid, right?"

His mouth tugged up on one side. "Actually, that sounds a lot like me back when I was in the NHL."

They approached his small cabin and she saw a note stuck to the door, pinned there by a hunting knife. She leaned forward in his arms and grabbed the note, tearing it down. " 'Dane,' " she read, " 'if you think you can quit on us, you're a bigger jackass than we thought. See you tomorrow.' It's signed by Grant."

He grunted, and then a slow smile spread over his face. "Guess I still have a job."

She was happy for him. He loved what he did, and he was good at it. Miranda stared at the paper, then back up at him, and smiled. "Mrs. Murellen asked me if I wanted my job back at the library."

His eyes burned into hers. "Miranda, I don't want you to give up anything—"

"It's what I want," she said, then brushed her fingers across his stubbled cheek. "Are we going to go inside or not? I'm afraid if we stand out here for much longer, we're going to be attacked by a rabid emu."

Heat flared in his eyes and he hastily opened the door, kicking it wide and staggering in. As soon as they were inside, he set her on her feet and whirled to shut the door.

She glanced around—a plain sofa sat in the corner of the room and there was a queen-sized bed, but no TV or electronics.

A stack of books lay next to the wood-burning stove. "Wow. You live pretty simply."

He shrugged and put his hands to the sides of her face, cupping her cheeks as he tilted her face toward his. His mouth licked at hers and she felt the shiver of delight all the way down to her toes. "God, Miranda, the last month has been hell," his voice was ragged with need, and he closed his eyes, pressing his forehead against hers. "I thought I'd lost you again just when I'd found you."

"I'm so sorry, Dane," she whispered. "You must think I'm crazy."

"I don't," he said vehemently. "I think you were hurt and you thought I caused it. I'm surprised you ever wanted to touch me again." He leaned down and kissed her nose, then her cheeks, kiss after kiss, so delicate and heartfelt that her own heart ached in her chest. "Was it for the revenge?"

"At first," she admitted, and hated when he flinched. "But then, after we slept together, it was for *me* and I just kept telling myself that it was for revenge."

He kissed her mouth again, slowly, sweetly. "I'm glad."

She was, too. So, so glad. Impulsively, her hand slid to the front of his pants and caressed his cock. He was hard and straining, the length of him making her pussy slick with anticipation. "Are you going to fuck me or are we going to stand here and talk all day?"

"You want to be fucked?" he said in a low, dangerous voice, his hand sliding to her skirt and pushing it up until his hand rested on the damp V of her pussy.

She whimpered and clutched his shirt. "We need to make it over to that bed, and fast."

He hauled her up against him and her legs went around his waist, her sex cradled against his cock. She moaned again as he carried her to the bed, his mouth slanting over hers in hard kiss after kiss.

"How important are those panties to you?" he growled against her mouth.

"Totally unimportant," she breathed and slicked her tongue into his mouth, darting and flicking.

"Good." He dropped her on the bed, then reached under her skirt again, pushing it up around her waist. He tugged her panties off and tossed them aside. One finger slid across her pussy, then delved deep into the well of her sex, and she gasped at the surge of pleasure. "I want to take you right now. Fast and hard until you're screaming my name."

"So do it," she breathed with excitement, and her pussy clenched against his finger. "What's stopping you?"

"Condoms," he said. "They're out in the jeep—"

"Fuck the condoms," she said and locked one leg around his back, trying to pull him forward. "I'm on the pill. Get those pants off and get inside me."

His groan was swallowed by a hard kiss, this time from her, and both sets of hands fumbled at his belt. Miranda ran her fingers over the length of him under the pants, so excited she could hardly stand it. She was so wet and needed him so badly.

His belt flew to the ground, then his pants, and he slid out of his boxers an instant later, and then his hot, warm length was probing at the aching core of her.

"You sure, Miranda?"

"God yes," she breathed. "Please. I need you."

He surged deep, and her moan caught in the back of her throat as a broken little gasp at the burn of him. It had been a month since they'd had sex, and she stretched and tensed around him, the sensation of being filled so tightly making her toes curl and her pussy throb.

"I can feel you all around me," he gritted out. "So fucking hot." His hands locked around her hips and he pulled out, then thrust deep again, causing her toes to curl once more. She dug her heels into his buttocks, urging him forward.

"Again," she breathed. "Please."

He surged deep again, and then again, the next thrust causing her to moan his name.

He groaned. "Not going to last."

"Then touch me," she said, her breath coming out in short, excited pants.

He began to thrust again, his hips rocking against hers. His hand moved between them and slid into the wet heat of her folds, seeking her clit. When he found it, her entire body tensed and she shrieked her pleasure. He began to stroke it in time with his thrusts, the rhythm hard and fast, the touches on her clit feather light.

She came mere seconds later, a scream building in her throat, her fingernails digging into his skin. "Dane!"

He growled low in his throat as she clenched around his hard cock, and then suddenly he was leaning on her hard, his thrusts coming so rapid and rough that she thought they'd fall off the edge of the bed where she perched. But he stared down at her with wild green eyes, thrusting deep. Their eyes connected and when he pumped into her, it was even more intense because they were connected.

"I love you," she whispered on his next thrust.

He came with a yell, and she felt him deep inside her, coming hard. He tensed and rocked against her a few moments more, still staring into her eyes with his beautiful green ones, and then he collapsed on top of her.

She hugged him close, and caught the glint of her ring in a beam of sunlight. A ring. She was engaged to Dane Croft. Holy shit. "Are you sure you want to do this?"

"At least twice a day for the next thirty years," he said in a husky voice, and she felt him kiss her collarbone.

She laughed. "No, dummy. The ring. Marriage."

He rolled over on the bed and dragged her over him until they'd switched places and she lay sprawled atop of him. Then he went very still, his eyes serious. "Don't you want to marry me?"

"Of course," she said with a smile. "But don't you think we're moving too fast?"

"I like fast women," he said, reaching down and playing with a lock of her hair. "I seem to recall someone who seduced me in the woods the very first night of class."

"Are you complaining?" she said with a grin.

He pulled her down for another kiss. "Never."